Memories of a
Mombasa Gigolo

Memories of a Mombasa Gigolo

Krishna Washburn

Order this book online at **www.trafford.com**
or email orders@trafford.com

Most Trafford titles are also available at major online book retailers.

Printed in the United States of America.

ISBN: 978-1-4269-7880-7 (sc)
ISBN: 978-1-4269-7879-1 (hc)
ISBN: 978-1-4269-7878-4 (e)

Library of Congress Control Number: 2011913069

Trafford rev. 08/02/2011

 www.trafford.com

North America & International
toll-free: 1 888 232 4444 (USA & Canada)
phone: 250 383 6864 ♦ fax: 812 355 4082

For Jonathan, my husband, my hero

"Never love anybody who treats you like you're ordinary."
— Oscar Wilde

Sunday, November 10, 1912 – New Notebook, M. Mudigonda, Solicitor

My testicles hurt. They hurt far too much for what they've actually experienced, or at least I think this is the case, so I wonder if there's something else wrong with me. I suppose they did get their fair share of attention this evening, but maybe I'm getting sick, maybe I've caught some rare disease, something for which the primary symptom is aching testes, accompanied by fatigue, malaise, and depression. Well, maybe it's not as bad as all that. She was a lovely woman, and I'd like to think I did everything I could do make her happy. I didn't even deserve the chance.

That's the way it is with women, I suppose. I love them, I think they're all marvelous, I don't deserve the attention of any of them, so when I receive some of this attention, I am ready to serve, which is the way it ought to be anyway.

Oh, that's why they hurt so badly. Note: fingernails feel fantastic in the right context, but are quite destructive to scrotum skin. On the upside: no diseases. Not yet, at least!

It's a funny thing. I never imagined myself in the position I am currently, and I don't know whether it's good fortune or bad fortune or just plain chance. No, I was never supposed to be a promiscuous lover. First of all, I am the ugliest man to have ever lived, and second of all, I really haven't the formal education for this sort of thing, in spite of everyone thinking the opposite. I have learned certain things, I have always had a student's mindset, but it's not as if I'm this magnificent storehouse of sexual knowledge. How does one even acquire something like that? Well, if I keep on using my imagination and working hard, when I'm sixty, maybe I shall be the sex expert that others think me to be, and by then, I'll be asthmatic, cirrhotic, and too fat to stand, thus rendering my knowledge moot. Or maybe not, I don't know. I don't even know why I'm thinking about this business, when I could be reminiscing about my latest adventure.

Note: too fat to stand status approaching rapidly. Time to use the digital cure again.

Ethel: Beautiful lady, husband a rich farmer at the interior of Kenya, don't know which city, friends with Hadleigh by virtue of having been at school in Kent with Hadleigh's sister, Louisa. Initially approached Hadleigh, as usual, but was redirected to me. She had heard some rumor about a man putting his tongue to a lady's delicate parts, but was certain that her husband would think she had been unfaithful to him if she asked for this kind treatment, and so went searching for an opportunity to actually be unfaithful in order to preserve the aura of fidelity. I believe it, sadly. It seems to me that most of the women I meet have really selfish, oafish, stupid husbands who never want to be nice to their wives and automatically assume adultery with the slightest change in routine. Why on earth is that? Don't these men realize that they are setting themselves up for what they fear the most? Unless, of course, what really turns them on, rather than trying new things and having a good time in bed, is being cuckolded. To be honest, I don't even think of myself as an affair. I think of myself as a servant, a devotee to the female temple, providing the services that these stupid men refuse to offer, and really, if I were to be a proper affair, I ought to be handsome, or at least pleasant to look upon. I am ugly, and the attendant attitude towards having a private rendezvous with me is typically as follows: "I simply must have this, darling Manik, and no man would ever suspect, what with your piebald skin imprinted with smallpox scars and bright red eye, that I would choose you for a lover." I am a safe choice. That does not bother me, actually. I like making women feel safe.

Back to beautiful Ethel. Lovely, lovely body! Medium height, at once both plump and slim, lovely, lovely bosoms! Perhaps the finest I have ever seen: larger than average, but no fold against the rib cage, just perfectly conical protuberances, bouncy, dense, small pink nipples. Some tiny dark hairs visible against her pale skin, very decorative. Very plump thighs, but tiny slim ankles, lovely smooth feet. Two delicious small rolls of flesh between bosom and belly, which is very, very soft, with a tiny, closed navel. Very thin arms, thin neck, soft pink cheeks, small chin, sleepy-looking greenish eyes. I didn't always like those weird greenish eyes that white people sometimes have, reminded me of fish, but Ethel's are lovely, just lovely, lovely. Thick hair, color of coffee, on her head and on her pubis. Why oh why would her stupid white farmer husband not want to do anything this beautiful woman requests? Really, really enjoyed treating her to a moment of worship; she was not difficult to undress, unlike so many of the cunnilingus girls who just want me to hide under their skirts. I explain: it's a mild quirk of mine. Nobody wears clothes in my bedroom. This is also a good way to deter any women who are on the fence as to whether they really want to practice their infidelities with me. If they cannot handle the sight of the world's ugliest man naked, then they shouldn't cheat on their husbands with me. I am always surprised at how many women happily subject themselves to my hideous nudity but then blanch at considering their own, in spite of being very beautiful women indeed. If I were a woman as lovely as the ones I have known, I should never, ever, wear any clothes at all and treat the world to my loveliness.

Ethel was so shocked by the touch of my tongue at first that she nearly levitated off the bed. I apologized, ready to retreat, as I have learned that sometimes the tongue, even when gently applied, hurts some very sensitive women. With this awareness, I try to be very careful, and insist that the lady be fully honest with me, that there is nothing she can say that would insult or emasculate me. She reassured me that it did not hurt, but that she didn't know it would be so soft and she was alarmed by the disconnect with her expectations. She told me to try again. I didn't go for the clitoris right away, but first gave gentle affection to her labia minora, of which the left was significantly longer than the right. Charming, charming! I tickled the little one first, and then took the longer one into my mouth and sucked on it, not too hard I think, but relished its soft, ruffled texture on my tongue. No nibbling, not for a first time, and not so much flicking the tongue at the clitoris as delicately polishing it. Everything I did, no matter how light, elicited an exaggerated reflexive response, which I will confess kept me completely on edge, terrified that I was doing something wrong. Up Ethel's back would arch, her breath would sharply expel itself from her lips, and I was constantly getting my head locked between her thighs, her lovely, lovely, soft, plump, dimpled thighs that didn't hurt at all in their softness, but prevented my escape, even for the quickest gasp of air. I persevered, and kept on in my careful, restrained attentions, but then decided to give a rapid series of licks to that depth just beneath the clitoris. Ethel sat up bolt straight at this action and screamed. She then fell upon me like a pouncing cat upon a mouse, wrapping her arms around my back, and began to beg me to kiss her.

"Oh, you might not like it," I warned.

"Please," she begged in half-whisper. I had to obey. I righted myself and went into her embrace slowly and carefully, partly to give her a chance to reconsider, and also because any task that requires the shifting of my abdominal weight takes a bit of time. I kissed her, first just soft open lips, then with my tongue, taking breaks to kiss her down her chin, down her neck, but always returning to her hot breath, as she chanted "my god my god my god," which I know has nothing to do with me, but everything to do with what white people say when they want to fuck. So I figured, what did I have to lose? I was ready to go, why not sneak on in and have a bloody good time in a well-primed vessel, already wet to dripping?

"Do you want me to make love to you?" I asked.

"Yes!" she replied, falling to her back. I was not really in the mood for top-position intercourse, but I honestly think that the white people don't know any other way. I crept on top of her, careful not to subject her to nineteen and a half stone of man (or twenty, let's be honest with ourselves) right out of the gate, and figured if I witnessed any discomfort, I could always pick her up and bounce her on my lap, which I ended up doing anyway. When I get inside, and everything is so nice and soft and moist and suctioned, I sometimes lose track of what I'm doing. I think I started off as a proper white man, but then that's when her naughty little hand got involved, sneaking itself around me, and latching itself cruelly and affectionately to my testicles. Those sharp little nails, how good they felt then, and how bad they feel now! I think I must have reacted by slipping my arms around her back and pulling her to my lap, and giving her the good upward thrust. It's amazing how light women always feel in this position, how easy to lift and bounce, no matter how plump or solidly built they seem to be. Ethel really seemed to enjoy this, and then actually assisted me in my continuation with the force of her beloved quadriceps. I must correct myself: it is not her bosom I like best, it is her thighs, without question, her thighs were even better than her bosom. Oh precious thighs, so dimpled and soft! The only problem with this position is extraction. I was trying to last as long as I could, but her blushing face and laughter brought me too far along to go back. My solution, not recommended for the future: lifting Ethel right over my shoulder and making an appalling mess of things, dripping down the sides, dripping onto the sheets. I decided to ignore it, it's not as if I haven't made acquaintance of my own semen before, and stood up on the bed, Ethel draped over my shoulder, squealing and kicking her feet, and as I myself was in quite a vulnerable state and rather wobbly, decided to lower myself again and, pulling her by the legs, arranged her back on the mattress, out of view of my emissions. I decided to play the loyal lapdog and put my head upon that magnificent bosom. Oh, I really can't choose now between bosom and thighs, what is wrong with me?

We had a bit of pillow talk as she recovered. She smoked a cigarette with me, and stroked my hair, which I should note: longest point has hit hip bone length. We talked about the taste of her vaginal juices, which we decided were most similar to camembert. I teased her a bit, because it made her laugh. "That husband of yours, a dairy farmer, he should long to taste camembert between your lovely, lovely thighs."

"Oh, if only, sweet darling Manik," she replied.

"You can stay as long as you want," I suggested, stroking the underside of her elegantly erect breast. "And you can have whatever you want from me. I don't ask for anything, and if you want to look away from me and never speak to me again the moment you leave this room, I understand. I only exist for your desires, to make you happy."

She kissed me on my forehead, and then once on each eyelid. "It's a shame you say things like that Manik. You're a wonderful man and a generous lover."

"I only say it because it's the truth."

"Oh, sweet Manik, sweet gentle Manik, I wish you were a happy man."

"How could I not be a happy man? Do you see where my pockmarked face is nestled?"

She laughed and pulled my hair off my neck, arranging it across the bed behind me. She did not stay much longer, and I helped her dress. I don't think she'll be back in my bed again, because the ones who say the nicest, friendliest things are always the ones I never see again. I think it's because they feel guilty for using me, but I like being used, I don't know how I can convince them of this. I think it's because we had a mostly sober go of it. Drunk women are far more likely to come back to me, because they don't feel as guilty, they don't start thinking of me as a person. To be honest, even I don't think of myself as a person much of the time.

My favorite regular visitor is Lila, an elegant woman of a certain age, who only shows up very, very late at night, usually unexpected, and is always kind enough to be tipsy, and to help me get a bit tipsy as well. I sometimes think that she actually likes me, but not so much as a lover, but more like a son, a son who she sits astride like a pony. She came by to see me just about a week ago; it's a pretty regular schedule now, about once a month, I should try to guess when she'll appear, so I won't always be so flustered and clumsy when she comes to the door. But then again, I think that's one of the things she likes about me. Oh, she fed me the best single malt scotch whiskey, and brought me an unnecessary amount of chocolate, what a lovely, lovely woman! I cannot understand how her husband could have grown weary of her because of a few gray hairs and a few creases on her face, because she is positively lovely in every way, the dear little woman with her dear tiny hands and her dear tiny waist, and she is just so much fun in bed, game for absolutely anything. I will worship at the altar of Lila for all eternity if given that opportunity.

Lila and I love to play games, silly, childish, drunken games. We play that she is the teacher and I am her recalcitrant student, and she plays that she is spanking me with a paddle; it doesn't hurt, it's just for fun. I don't think she'd care to actually hurt me, she isn't that sort of lady, although I have encountered many ladies whose primary agenda is to cause me physical pain. That's actually all right with me, it doesn't matter, whatever makes them happy is what I want to do, even if it means being bitten, being slapped, being punched or kicked or hit with blunt objects, or having more sensitive parts of my body subjected to the torture of pins or sharp fingernails. Lila just wants to play, she wants to laugh and to hear me laugh. The more I think about it, the more I think she actually likes me. She always stays until morning, and she'll ask me questions about the cases I've been handling at the office, asking me if I'm overworked or not feeling healthy. She asks me if Hadleigh's been giving me trouble with his incessant legal incompetence. That's really very nice, isn't it, even if it isn't sincere, but I actually think it is quite sincere indeed. She has a lot of pet names for me, I think because she hasn't really accepted the fact that I am Indian, rather than just a deformed Englishman: Dearest Magpie, Dearest Samson, Dearest Tum-Tum. I am actually quite fond of being called Dearest Tum-Tum, as it is typically accompanied by a lovely rub of the belly, which is so soothing after a hard day's binge. I have been bingeing so badly these last few weeks, I am always in some state of recovery, it's really not good at all, and I am getting very, very fat again. But being Lila's Dearest Tum-Tum, that is quite cheering, it makes being obscenely fat all the more bearable.

Wednesday, November 13, 1912

Lila came to call unexpectedly last night! Oh, just when I think of her, she comes to me; perhaps we have a psychic bond, perhaps she loves me, oh my foolish heart, to mistake such a thing! I do love her, I do love her passionately, I love waking up next to her in the morning, smelling her skin, touching its delicate softness. Do men not know that the skin of a woman well protected from the sun only grows softer and more fragile, more inviting with age? I am hung over. We got bloody well drunk last night after our games were done: nurse and patient, we played. It should be no surprise that my medicine were to be sucked from her sweet and tender breast, and then given as a suppository in the form of a tiny finger. And astride me, as she always perches herself so regally! Is there any sight so lovely as Lila seated on my hard penis, legs spread wide across my lap, her back so straight, her downcast eyes, of purest blue, looking down upon me like a mythical queen. What majesty she evokes! What regal beauty in her noble face, so refined and elegant! She tells me she is past the change; I don't have to fret about semen expulsion, which makes things ever so relaxed. Why on earth is the ideal the girl just finished childhood? Can she inspire the same worship as this queen among women, Lila, Queen of Mombasa?

And so nice to me she is, kissing me in the morning, running her fingers through my tangled curls. No Dearest Tum-Tum, sadly, I had been looking forward to that. Maybe I've just gotten too fat to merit such an adorable moniker, but I did earn a Dearest Samson! That's nearly as good. She mentioned to me a lady of her acquaintance who might need my services. I always play the fool with Lila, she likes to correct me:

"Oh, does she need a criminal appeal done, my lady?"

"Lawyering is not what Hazel needs, Dearest Samson. It is a job best done undressed, my silly boy, my darling one."

"Undressed? Does she wish to run my bath for me?"

"I'll run the bath for you, Dearest Samson! But you'll have to be as kind and as sensitive as you can be, no mischief. She is a lady in a state of disability."

"Whatever it is that she needs, my lady, I will provide."

And with that, gone with the wind, vanished into the seaside mist. I wonder where she lives, I wonder how she gets here, and how she gets home. I would buy her a motorcar if she needed one. But now, I have a new lady to nurture and love. I will tell Hadleigh, I suppose, just so he won't throw a fit that I've got him out of the loop. Hazel. That is a beautiful name. It makes me think of dewdrops. I wonder what disability dare inflict her? If Lila cares for her, she must be lovely.

Monday, November 18, 1912

Hazel has posted me a letter. I can't say I receive letters very often from the ladies I admire and tend, so it was a welcome surprise. I have told Hadleigh about Hazel, simply as a friend of Lila, and he was frustrated to not have heard of her. He is hunting for information and gossip in town, I just know it, the lousy busybody. I wish he didn't have to involve himself, but it seems utterly against his nature, he must stick his nose into everything I do. I am keeping this letter a secret from him, I am keeping it close to me forever.

Lovely Hazel has only been in Kenya for a few months, but was born in Rhodesia. Her husband has relocated the family to Mombasa to help her forget about her deep, tragic sadness, the death of her youngest son in a riding accident. She apologizes for her sadness, explaining that she is owed no more mourning, now two years since losing her beloved Kurt, a boy of eleven and full of all the life and vigor that makes a mother happy. What a cruel world it is that tells lovely, lovely Hazel that she can no longer cry for her innocent son, taken too soon, just because two measly years have passed. Twenty years have passed since my childhood bride Madhulika's death, ten years since my sweet Mai's, but I cry still! I should cry right now, for Mai, for Madhulika, for Hazel, for Kurt, and, lastly, even though I don't deserve it, for poor pathetic me, still grieving and pathetic after all these years, still ugly, still red-eyed, still bingeing and fat. Note: attempt to purge last night went badly; two fingers no longer enough?

Hazel, forced from her bereavement, transplanted from her home where her son lies buried, has begun to pull out her own hair. She confesses to wearing a wig, to drawing on her eyebrows with a pencil.

Her husband will not touch her. But I will, I will touch her. I will share in her sadness. I will remind her that she is a woman, a mother, a wife, and deserving of all the love in the world.

We are having a little chat first, a quiet spot on the beach. The waves on the Indian Ocean are so warm, but also loud these days, that being outdoors is more private than indoors, a human voice only able to travel a few inches to the receptacle of the ear. I will be kind to her. I hope I do not frighten her too much. I shall hope that she doesn't really need me.

Thursday, November 21, 1912

My precious Hazel.

You have left behind a garden of mementoes, a lacy field of pubic hairs on my bed that you pulled out in your sleep. A good Brahmin would have his servant throw them away, burn the sheets, scorn the woman who polluted his space, but I shall collect each and every hair, put it in an envelope, and remember you, each hair representing a tear that you shed in my presence. You do not need to say a word: you are beautiful, with hair or without.

Hazel was not meant to spend the night, but who am I to turn away a lady's sudden change of heart? She buried her face in my neck and wrapped her arm around my chest and told me that she didn't want to leave. I asked her the requisite question: "Will your husband expect you home?"

"Most certainly," was the reply.

"Will he know how to find you?"

"No."

"What will happen to you if you don't go home?"

"I don't care."

"Truly? Don't think of me. Think of yourself. If you get the rod for thoughts of pleasing me, I'll let you know straight away that it doesn't please me in the slightest." I don't know why women think that letting themselves be beaten would ever make me happy. I refuse to comprehend the mysteries of female submission; maybe my own prejudices are showing, maybe I should analyze them, but I won't. I won't, because then I may have to examine the origins of my own submissive tendencies, and that, I'm afraid, will ruin everything for me. It's better I don't know myself too well.

This is a serious problem: self-knowledge. Hazel appears to know me, possibly as much as I know myself, and it made matters difficult for myself. First of all, that piercing gaze while we sat on the beach together: fearless, utterly fearless. That's all I have! Those first five minutes of enervation, that's all I have to protect myself, and she just bypassed them, as if I had merely been Hadleigh after staying up all night, without a shave, with gin splashed on his tuxedo shirtfront. Benign, not in the least intimidating. It must be Hadleigh after a hard night – Hadleigh at his best is probably twice as terrifying as I could ever be, red eye and all, but tired, damp, stubbled Hadleigh, there never existed a more harmless potted fern, with the eyelids low over those horrible, clever eyes of his, drunk, giggling like a little girl at whatever stupid thing that I might say. That's how Hazel looked at me, like how I look at exhausted, inebriated Hadleigh. She saw me for what I truly am: a quivering jelly, simultaneously apprehensive and desirous of being consumed, swallowed, digested. What is that stupid children's story that Hadleigh likes, that he quotes, Eat Me, Drink Me, as if I cared, but for the fact that those labels should be hanging around my neck.

And yet! The cracking in her throat as she speaks to me about her emotions! It is not me that she fears, but herself. And so, we two, fearing nothing more than the faces that stare at us in the mirror, were meant to be in sacred union. She began to cry almost immediately. Her hand was so cold when I held it. She saturated her handkerchief, and then saturated mine. I offered her the ends of Shiva's locks; I would expect a laugh, not the earnest and grateful eye-wiping that I witnessed. Hungry for hair. We made a date for last night. She came alone, a full hour earlier than I expected, which I actually appreciate. I spend the whole evening panicked anyway waiting, I cannot work, all I can do is smoke, smoke, smoke, scratch my scalp, smoke some more, call downstairs for tea and biscuits every twenty minutes, knowing full well I should just have them send up everything they have all at once. So, catching me off guard is the best, most compassionate thing one could do for me. She came inside slowly, in a stately way, and, without thinking, I laid down my rule: no clothes in my bed. Instead of grasping anxiously for corset or stocking, Hazel's little hand went to her wig. I decided to give her one last chance to back away from me, to obey her fear.

"Only if you take it off, sweet Manik." Quick to adopt my given name, so desperate to please me. Don't try to please me, Hazel, I felt myself saying inside my head. I agreed, but decided to undress myself first, in order to instill that sort of horror, at least. Then, when I approached her, I started from the top down, without warning. But still, no fear of me, only of herself. She clenched her eyes shut tightly.

Hazel is not completely bald. She has an uneven pattern of dark hair on her pale scalp. The hairline is completely undisturbed, with long, lonely hairs framing her face, in some areas as wide as an inch, in others only as wide as a single hair. There are large patches on either side of her head, over her ears, with only vellus down. No real rhyme or reason, I am describing it poorly, for it is not nearly as even or symmetrical as I have just made it sound. A better metaphor: as confounding as patching pattern on right quadricep. No islets, but completely uneven, variegated frontiers = right quadricep. Islets, speckles, and spots = left quadricep. Oh, how clear it is to me now, my memory crystallized. Really, when generals plan their battles, they should use my thighs as descriptive terminologies for locations of the enemy. "I am aware, sergeant major, that the Zulu are concentrated in discreet cells across the territory. It is like Manik Mudigonda's left quadricep out there." I am stupid and self-indulgent. The things I do to amuse myself, it's shameful.

Complex pattern of baldness included, Hazel is exceptionally beautiful. Light corseting, no bruising, thank goodness. Sweet little handfuls of breast, but the ribcage still well covered. Appendectomy scar, oh, no more beautiful sight than an appendectomy scar. I wish everyone had an appendectomy scar. You can't die from acute appendicitis if it's already gone. I wish my sweet Mai had had an appendectomy scar. Her teeth are extraordinary! There must be good water in Rhodesia, the blinding white of her smile. I did get her to smile, I did. There are times when being a clumsy oaf is something I actually like about myself. A cigarette situation, naturally. I was excited already, so I spit it on the floor, and then, realizing how grotesque myself to be, threw both hands to my face in shame. I heard her laugh, so I peeked: a smile, prettiest smile perhaps I have ever seen.

She wanted to cozy herself on the bed for a while before getting down to business. Made her laugh as I fell over myself to help her along as she opened herself with an index finger. Then, looked at me in sudden surprise.

"I hadn't noticed just how fat you are! You are really quite fat, sweet Manik." Not said anxiously, but perhaps out of concern. I am at that degree of fatness that merits concern, now, I suppose.

Undeterred, as I am when it comes to these matters, I inserted my tongue just under the clitoral hood and earned a little squeak of approval. Then, removing it, I affirmed her observation. "I am extraordinarily fat. I have been fatter, but I was once thin, I was. You would have liked me better then, beautiful Hazel."

"And you would have liked me better with all my hair, sweet Manik." The choke of sadness in her voice revealed itself again.

"I should say not. Because with all your hair, beautiful Hazel, I would not find myself with my head between your graceful legs."

"Oh, I wouldn't say that."

"But I would, because it is the truth. And the reason why I exist. To make you happy when you need it most. I only exist to make you happy." And that pleased her.

"I have never made love with a fat man before. Perhaps I should enjoy it."

"I always enjoy it." And that was that, that was the right thing to say. It was time to put my tongue right deep inside, and then replace it with my penis, as quickly as possible. Sideways insertion, interlacing legs. I wanted to do interlacing legs with Hazel: I wanted to continue to enjoy them as much as possible. Nice, steady rhythm right at the beginning, teen tal speed, and I wrapped my arms around her, just tightly enough. She relaxed in my embrace and let me do all the work, just tilting her head back and sighing. She did a lot of pillow talk. I don't think she does pillow talk with her husband, because this was transgressive pillow talk, the pillow talk of a woman enjoying a well-deserved affair with a man to whom she owed no obedience. I was a bad and dirty boy who loved a good fuck, a bad and naughty boy who couldn't control himself, a bad and dirty wog looking for a good fuck from a white woman, a bad and filthy ugly Hindu with a big, filthy bickie, a sweet and greedy boy with a bad little sweet tooth, a sweet and naughty fat boy with no self control. I can tolerate most of that, just not wog, that I don't really like, but pillow talk isn't real talk, I know. Hazel would never go talking about me to a neighbor as some dirty wog. Part of me wishes, though, that she would call me a sweet and naughty fat boy in public. For some perverse reason, that would feel quite erotic to me. When it was my time, we were deep in conversation.

"I've got to pull out."

"Don't you dare."

"I've got to pull out, I'll come in you."

"Come in me, come in me."

"I've got to pull out!"

"I want to suckle a wog baby. Come in me."

"I'm pulling out!"

"No, come in me!"

So I did. It wasn't really up to me at that point, as time was up, and she had clamped a hand on each of my buttocks, firmly adhering us together. Wog baby indeed; Hazel was no fool and quickly sat herself up, discretely letting the fluids drip down her velvet passage onto my bed sheets as she guided my lips to her soft little bosom. I was her wog baby. How she stroked my cheeks, my hair, my belly, like a good, kind mother would. I could sense the misplaced maternal feelings emitting from her fingertips, but she could tell that I appreciated them. And then, she began to cry again, her grief emerging fresh from her eyes, and we just cried together for a while, kissing away each other's tears. I told her that I was sorry. She told me that she was sorry as well. This tenderness is what led to her desire to stay, I think, the safe space where she could cry for her lost son. So, when she told me that she would not be hit, only scolded, I pressed my hand gently around her back.

"You are safe with me," I whispered to her. "You are safe with your fat, ugly boy."

"Sweet Manik, why didn't I die with him?"

"Maybe the world could not stand to lose so much beauty at one time."

"I'll never be beautiful again."

"If you think that a few missing hairs makes you any less beautiful, precious, beautiful Hazel, you are wrong, for you know that if your boy Kurt were here with you, he would grin and laugh for the love of his beautiful mother."

And she wept into my neck, softly, rubbing my chest to soothe herself, for a little while, and peacefully fell asleep, comforted, fulfilled, in my bed beside me. She awoke calmly and quickly stole away in the morning before I could rouse myself, but her dreams had been fitful, her hands working obsessively on her pudendum, and so, my collection of Hazel's hairs.

Monday, November 25, 1912

Flirting with my cleaning woman! Oh, I like her very much, I always have. I will start to use an ashtray just to please her. What bright and impish eyes she has. No chance, but I suspect that she knows what I do outside the law office. I wish I knew her real name. I don't like calling her Constance. Insulting to both of us. I may as well call myself Oliver. I will ask her, I will put her at ease, she has known me for quite a few years, she is accustomed to me. I have no chance, but I will find out her real name, I am determined.

Tuesday, November 26, 1912

Hadleigh has sent me a new friend: a newlywed with a problem related to deflowering. I think it's odd, that the first thought would be to call on me, as I think that there are physicians better suited to the task, but I don't know, I won't refuse. Probably it has to do with the maintenance of the fragile male ego; most certainly he'd rather not a physician involved, that would imply that there is something deficient about him. I am easier to obscure than a doctor, and I'm free of charge. But a newlywed! She will reject me for certain. Young girls don't want me, they like knights in shining armor. I am a bit intimidated by young girls, anyway. They are rather prejudiced. I blame plays and poetry.

Wednesday, November 27, 1912

Kaweria! No more of that Constance business. Kaweria, now that is a lovely name, proper name for a Taita lady. I will chant it to myself as I fall asleep tonight, so that I can dream of her. I have been rather civilized as of late: no cigarettes on the floor! Not one. And she noticed! She must know that I'm doing it for her.

Thursday, November 28, 1912

A sigh of relief: a virgin, but not a teenager as I feared. Hadleigh reminded me of who she is: I met her at my last birthday party, apparently, and I had a lovely, tipsy chat with her. Hadleigh thinks she sat on the arm of my chair to speak with me. It was my birthday, after all. I wonder if I tried to kiss her, no doubt I did. I think I remember her, I do think I remember her: blonde. Blonde is hard to forget. Sort of a wallflower type, plain little face. Well, not what I would call plain, as I don't think that her type of face is plain at all, but fashion today says that a flat, round face is plain. I think it's more to do with her desire to look a little plain, out of shyness, anxiety with men and our evil ways. And there she was, working so hard to be plain, trying to be nice to me on my birthday, and I spoil everything, not finding her plain in the least. Unfashionably plump. Has everyone forgotten that not even ten years ago, we were all quite enamored with plump? And now, it is completely out of style, now it is a lean, trim girl. Bah, foolishness. Neither one is better. Why can't fashion concern itself with cuts and colors and leave the things that ladies cannot change to nature? White people and fashion, the stupidest marriage ever. I suppose being white, you need to make some problems for yourself in order to keep life interesting. Perhaps I should regard myself as lucky, for I shall never be in fashion.

Let's look at Hadleigh's note: Viola Simpkins. Simpkins! Ugh! Hideous name. Doubtlessly hideous man attached to it, cannot even deflower his wife. Viola is pretty, though, which is fortunate. Oh, I remember her quite clearly now! Viola Simpkins, nee Belvoir, pronounced Beaver. Hilarious to say, but quite aesthetic on paper. Viola Belvoir, a certain balance with the repeated letters. Poor thing, just to rid herself of Beaver and ending up with Simpkins instead. Is it an improvement? I cannot say. I do remember her telling me about how she was "finally" engaged to be married. A full twenty-six years of age, "finally" engaged. Is that really very old? I hope ages mean different things for men than for women, because I must be an antique at thirty-one. Actually, that's a rather nice match of ages: twenty-six and thirty-one. Looks nicer than twenty-five and thirty, for some reason. She seemed very excited to get married to this Simpkins, who was a big, handsome, English dolt if I recall correctly, but she suspected that he was primarily interested in her father's title, English stupidity as usual. Because surely he finds her plain, because of a flat cheekbone and a wide hip that are really not in the least inferior to a jutting cheekbone and a narrow hip. And it wouldn't shock me in the least if Simpkins the dolt has mistaken these utterly neutral physical features for the reason as to why he can't break open the vase. Stupid, stupid, stupid.

Neutral, what I am a talking about? Stop thinking about what white people think! Stop it! Viola's appearance is not neutral! It is nothing but exceptionally appealing, for any man with half a brain (which excludes most white men, come to think of it). A young, charming blonde woman! What on earth could there be to complain about? Sweet little cherub's face, like a Raphaelite putti, with pink cheeks and a little round chin, what could be prettier? And I know myself, I know that my tastes are quite democratic, and I do like mostly every woman, but I do know one thing about myself, and that is that I absolutely relish a plump woman! Just think about those big, gorgeous bosoms! That big, delicious bottom balanced on the arm of a chair, and to think! It won't even be my birthday!

Friday, November 29, 1912

Kaweria teased me today! Teased me about the state of my sink, about the hair clogging the drain. She knows I'm not losing my hair, so it's completely fine to tease me. I explained that each individual hair is so big and troublemaking that it doesn't take much to stop up the sink, and then! She came right to me and asked to look!

"Oh, examine it, Miss Kaweria, you'll see I'm being quite honest," I said, providing a lock of the white and unruly.

She took it in her fingers as if it were something valuable. "Mr. Mudi, this is some hair," she said, laughing. "What will I do with your drain?"

"I would shave it all off if it meant it made your day easier, Miss Kaweria."

"No, no! Not hair like that, Mr. Mudi. Hair like that break the razor for certain. No, it's my job, I'll clean it up for you, maybe use a fish hook, lift it all out at once."

"I don't deserve you, Miss Kaweria."

"Not for me to say, Mr. Mudi." And off she saunters. "Smoking neatly these days, Mr. Mudi, though. Thank you very much."

"I shall smoke as neatly as you please, Miss Kaweria."

No chance, no chance, don't forget it, no chance at all, none.

Sunday, December 1, 1912

Dear George Simpkins: I am running away with your wife, I am kidnapping her, binding and gagging her, and running away with her to Uganda. You shall never find us. I will send out trained killers to rid the world of you, you pox, you blight on humanity.

Dear George Simpkins: Viola and I are running away together. Don't look in Uganda, we're not going there. We are going to have lots and lots of sexual relations, because we find it completely uncomplicated and extremely enjoyable. You stupid twat.

Dear George Simpkins: I have primed the vessel for you. It was absurdly simple and incredibly fun, and I cannot understand what was going wrong for you, unless you are utterly and completely impotent, you drooling idiot.

Dear George Simpkins: I have broken Viola's hymen for you. Have at it. Please realize that having sex with your wife is a very, very good time to be had.

What is wrong with you, George Simpkins? A weak, homosexual constitution? It took nothing, nothing at all to deflower your beautiful, precious Viola. Let me tell you, George Simpkins, that as your lovely Viola disrobed in my bedroom, she was not fretting over any non-existent plainness, or over the clear and foreboding hideousness present in front of her, but rather worrying her poor head about you, and your frustrations with her, how you castigate her, a virgin girl, for not knowing how best to help you along. Selfish brute: these things are learned, not inborn! That I know to be utterly and completely true. Viola wanted to know all sorts of things, things that surely you should have told her, but no, you would rather scold her. Who do I hate more than you, George Simpkins? At the moment, nobody.

Did you know, George Simpkins, that your wife did not even know what testicles are? That she has been avoiding them out of confusion? You blither, George Simpkins.

Ah, but who cares about George Simpkins? Not I! No, I have not a care for George Simpkins. I care only for his adorable wife, Viola, for it is Viola who, upon the removal of her outer garments, resembles nothing more than Rubens' Venus at her mirror. She was so glad to be ending her suffering, she really looked at the upcoming activity as a panacea, a procedure if you will, a solution to her husband's problem. She got right on the bed, cocked up her lovely pink knees and looked me helplessly in my red eye.

"You do think you can fix it for me, Manik?" she asks.

"Don't tell George this, but I don't think it's you that needs fixing," I reply.

"He's so unhappy."

"Let's first make you happy, Viola, and then we'll worry about George. What about that?"

"Making George happy will make me happy, Manik."

How depressing. Now, I am no expert in virginity. I have dealt in matters of female virginity only three times before, and once with my own virginity, to whom I owe my education to the beautiful and painful Consuelo, how I would have married her, what a fool I was. But Viola's virginity was no obstacle at all! I was really prepared for the worst, that was why I agreed to take the superior position. I sat on my mismatched haunches and slowly, slowly, ticklingly, checked Viola's fresh, pink external surfaces with just my glans, foreskin unretracted. Dry, dry, totally dry. I made some play with a fingertip around the edges, I made headway rather easily, a fingertip fluttering on either side until moisture began to appear. "Tell George he has to let you wet up first," I told her. "Tell him he has to be nice to you."

This made her laugh, and she flushed. She was ready. I smiled at her like a slave to love. "I'm sorry to do this to you, precious Viola, but to relieve you of your burden, I'm going to have to be a bit of a burden to you. Is that all right?"

She looked at me with genuine confusion. For someone who knows nothing, euphemism simply doesn't work, I suppose. "I'm going to put myself inside you, very slowly, very gently, I promise, and if anything doesn't feel right, you must tell me and I will fix it, but in order to do that, I don't know if you've noticed, but there is something in the way." I put a hand to the old solar plexus in all of its unrelenting volume. Oh, how she laughed! So heartening.

"So, where shall you put it, then, Manik?" she giggled. Sweet, sweet giggling, like a naughty little girl. How could I not love her?

"Well, there's only one place it can go, and that is where it always is: directly in front of me. And, precious Viola, that is right about here." I put my hand now to her own, sweetly round and plush belly, maybe tickled her a little bit. Adorable giggling! "So, let me know if I'm too much for you."

"I'm a big girl myself, Manik!" Bless, how the ladies like to argue that useless point. I am inevitably more than twice their size, but they love to claim gargantuan proportions, how silly. But at least I had permission to be somewhat less than elegant, to lift up my belly and flop it directly on top of her own. And then I proceeded, both of us as ready as we would ever be. I was so nervous, the sweat already coming up on my face, but with one cautious thrust, and one tiny pop, and not a single drop of blood, it was done! Now, I was unsure as to whether it was expected that I should stop as soon as this goal was reached, but Viola squealed and arched her back, her hand to her lovely, soft, pink breasts. There was no going back for me! I latched my arms around those pretty pink knees and got to work, the best kind of work! And how helpful and receptive she is, precious, precious Viola! Bouncing right along with me, laughing away. We joined hands at one point, straight arms and locked elbows, and she leaned back on the tension, her head bobbing up and down. I swear, I have not had so much fun since my birthday. So easy and unserious, this serious matter of virginity removal, that was how Viola made it for me. I loved every second of it! Ejaculation also awkward and silly, but awfully fun, and a good education for precious Viola.

What we learned: first of all, semen is white, not at all watery, and makes a mess on the bed. Semen is made in the testicles, which are certainly not off limits, and every man has them and every man likes a lady's attention there. Semen tastes like itself. Ejaculation makes a man very, very tired indeed, especially ones that smoke and drink and eat themselves into oblivion, who have bad knees and who have finally succeeded in forcing themselves to vomit at least once a day. But, tired though I might have been, certainly not too tired to give a short lesson in gynecological anatomy involving a mirror and a delicate touch. We learned about our clitoris, our labia, our vagina, our cervix, our perineum, and we learned that urination has nothing to do with any of them.

"So, do we like relations, now, precious Viola?" I asked, winded and happy, now dragging myself up to Viola's side, lighting myself a cigarette, wrapping my arm around her soft and lovely shoulders.

"I should say!" English girl, I love you!

"And you'll teach George everything he needs to know?"

"Oh, I shall try. I had no idea it would be so painless! How George has rubbed me raw, so awful, Manik. But now I'm all ready for him, he'll be so happy. Thank you so much, Manik, what a friend you are." I am a friend! What better gift!

"How could he not be happy, when he has a wife like you, precious Viola! Do you know what you are, dear and beautiful lady? You are a natural, a stellar, tops lover. If George gives you any trouble, just tell him that you're a tops lover, that it's his job to live up to you, now."

"And what happens afterwards?" she asks.

"Well, you could always try putting your head on his chest, running your fingers through the hair, that sort of thing." I urged Viola's golden-locked head to the spot above my heart, where she shall always be, until the end of time.

"Shame he hasn't any."

"Hasn't any at all? How old is George, by the way?"

"He is thirty-one."

"I'm thirty-one, you know. He ought to have hair on his chest by now. No wonder the poor devil can't figure out how to make you happy. He does have hair in his crotch, though, right, precious Viola?"

"Assuredly."

"Thank goodness for that."

"What's it for?"

"What's it for? Oh, sweet mystery of life!"

And she laughed again, her wonderful, adorable laugh! "You'll be my teacher, then? If I have questions that I need answered, can I ask you?"

"I should be so lucky! Anything you want to know, anything you want to try, need demonstrated, anything. I would be your specialist tutor for all you could possibly want to know."

"Good! What a relief!" And she luxuriated on my chest for a few minutes more, thinking, running her fingers through the hair, and let me admire the way her beautiful, fair, pink flesh folds off her frame. That is what I love about a plump woman: so much to touch and to admire, so much interest, so many places for my wandering fingers to visit. I let those fingers of mine do a bit of light tracing, it was not appropriate, but I just could not resist. I got what I deserved: a pretty little pink fingertip tracing the borders of my patches. Fitting punishment. That, and also letting her go home, all dressed and pretty, back home to that bastard, George Simpkins. I should have made a move at my birthday party, I should have put a stop to things then. It's clear that we do get along, and that she does like me, does trust me, and she likes me in bed. I should have told her that George Simpkins, while handsome, will be a lousy lover and a terrible husband, and that she should run away with me to Uganda or Ethiopia or Somalia and we should have a happy life together, fucking and loving and having incredible fun. I make so much more money than George Simpkins does, I would take better care of her. And I would have inherited a lordship, how funny! We would have been such a natural pair together, I would have been such a good husband, the right age and everything. The ways I comfort myself. I am pathetic. Beautiful, blonde, plump, cheerful Viola married to me, the worst and ugliest member of the species. An Indian can't inherit a lordship, anyway, I fantasize too much. But if she came running to me in the middle of the night, begging me to run away with her to Uganda...

Monday, December 2, 1912

Heating up with Kaweria! She does know, she does know what I do for recreation, I knew she did.

"Some girls don't know anything, do they, Mr. Mudi?" she asked, pulling off the bedclothes. "Young girls. Don't know anything, do they?"

"Not a thing, lovely Miss Kaweria." I lit a cigarette, tried to look as endearing as possible.

"Why do you play around with young girls, Mr. Mudi? You ought to be looking for a real woman for yourself."

"If only, Miss Kaweria, a real woman were looking for me."

"Maybe, Mr. Mudi. Maybe."

"I doubt it, Miss Kaweria. You know of any real woman interested in a man with a red eye and pockmarks?"

"Somebody for everybody, Mr. Mudi. Somebody for everybody."

I don't know what that means, but at least I know she wants to be nice to me. How nice? I don't know. Wait! Yes I do. I have no chance, no chance, no chance at all. None.

Friday, December 6, 1912

Is there in this world a man who hates himself as I hate myself? Truly, if only I could live in a different body, one even just slightly better functioning than this one. Maybe even just a body without a red eye. Sometimes small changes can work wonders. Oh, but truly, if I could make myself a new body to inhabit, I'm sure that my brain would be ever so much happier. I would be so well-behaved, I would go to bed on time, I would only smoke ten cigarettes a day, I would eat three reasonable meals and elegantly refuse sweets, I would marry a sensible woman who wanted a sensible husband, be a reasonable father of a reasonable number of children, perhaps four, make a law practice on my own in Mombasa and let Hadleigh fend for himself, so that way I'd be home at half-past seven every night. Features of new body: no red eyes, no pockmarks, fully functional knees, heart, and lungs, fully trim and graceful proportions, a whole new mouth of Rhodesia teeth that I would not spoil from complex adventures in initiating the gag reflex. Let's say, white? No, no, I don't hate myself that much. Not white, although it would be fully more useful than being any other color, easier to find that sensible wife in need of a sensible husband. Sticking with brown. But not a Brahmin, no, absolutely not. What a rotten lot that has been for me. I think, maybe Muslim. Yes, that would absolutely lead me in the right direction. No drinking at all, no, not at all. A lean, handsome, teetotalling Muslim husband, that's what I'd like to be. Muslims, they can have four wives, I heard something like that once. A lean, handsome, teetotalling, polygamist Muslim husband. I could do well like that. But only in this hypothetical new body. Oh, science, work on that for me!

I can't believe my bad luck. Well, it's not really that bad of luck, if I look at it in the right way, because I could have no beautiful women knocking on my door during the wee small hours of the morning. But it is very bad luck if I look at it in terms of the fact that I doubt I will ever see Lila again. Please, let this not be true. I miss her already. I just want to cry. Maybe I'll stay home from the office today, I'll just stay in bed and indulge myself.

It must have been just before two this morning when she arrived. I didn't expect anything, of course, so I had been in the throngs of bingeing for most of the preceding three hours. What a struggle it had been, I just could not stop myself. Really bad, sugar binge, the worst kind, making myself completely sick. Sugar binge is so painful, because even when my stomach is aching in the absolute worst way, the hunger just rages and rages, there is just no resolution to the problem, and when alcohol gets itself involved, there is just nothing good about it. I couldn't have been leaning back on my bed for more than fifteen minutes when Lila knocked on the door. I was fighting some acid in my throat and some really horrible heartburn, I could hardly drag myself to answer. And there was Lila, beautiful, already drunk, a fallen star from the sky in her bright loveliness, and there was I, disheveled, mostly undressed already. I played that she had just woken me and kissed her in a sweet and sleepy way and apologized for my appearance.

"Oh, hair everywhere, that is how I like you best, Dearest Samson!" she teased, putting her fingers right into the roots. Lila, please do not forsake me for my weaknesses! I can be just the paramour you want, I promise!

I brought her inside: presents for me! Sweet sherry and chocolate, oh, how excellent the night would have been if only she'd appeared sooner. But who was I to refuse her? I opened the bottle, poured for us both, and she commenced to feeding me chocolate as we chatted about our game. I should have insisted that she save the chocolate for later, but it just tastes so sweet coming from Lila's beautiful little fingers. What would we play? We agreed upon nanny and bad little charge. I went right to work carelessly smearing said chocolate across my face and lifting up the sides of Lila's dress, making her screech at me, and threaten me with spankings. Grabbed me right by the hair at one point in order to wipe off my face, scolding me all the while as she complained that she couldn't find a hanky, and would have to use her tongue instead. I admit to breaking character to kiss those clever lips, to getting very, very involved in kissing indeed. Things would be going quickly, it was obvious, and that was really all my own fault, what an idiot I am, and seeing that things would be going quickly, I stupidly tore myself away from Lila's loving embrace and got it into my head that I ought to go make myself vomit to lighten the load, make coitus all the better. I should have stuck it out full-bellied, that was arguably the stupidest decision I have ever made.

First, to the basin: one finger, pointless to try. Two fingers, no progress. Hurting my uvula. Three fingers, starting to gag. Lila calling for me, I'm replying while choking on three fingers in my throat. Deciding to just bite the bullet and put all four fingers down there, and it all started coming up, with all the agony and bile that I deserved. Why, oh why, do I always think that vomiting is going to be a quick, painless ordeal? I find myself retching and spitting and I find Lila standing over me, in just pantalettes, an expression of concern on her face. Oh, concern. How I hate concern. I should be able to enjoy Lila pulling my hair into a queue, I should be able to enjoy her running a bath for me and helping me in, joining me, stroking me, curling up in my lap in the fragranced water, but the specter of concern ruins it for me. Well, not completely. I am a Brahmin boy after all, I like being looked after. I also appreciated how quiet Lila was, not really saying much at all to me, mostly just rubbing my poor stomach, wiping water over my face and neck. Just the occasional "Poor sweet Dearest Magpie" or "Poor sweet Dearest Tum-Tum." But then, she must have been sobering up, tragedy of all tragedies, and whispers, her head on my chest as the bathwater cooled, "My sweetest Dearest Tum-Tum, maybe you should take better care of yourself." Oh, the humiliation. How can I insist on more drinking and playing about after that sort of admonishment? Fortune only smiled upon me when I regained some certain blood flow and Lila climbed upon me. My mood was distinctly improved, as was, I suspect hers. Note: if I ever find myself in the situation where I feel like a ton of lead, relations in a full bathtub are the best solution to that problem. Lifted me right up! Even with my stomach aching with sharp pains, exhausted, I really gave Lila a good ride, especially fun, rewarding.

I'm so glad it went well, because I don't think she shall ever return. I think Lila has had her fill of me. I am repulsive. To think, I thought she could maintain some long-term affection for me! Not Lila, Queen of Mombasa. If she wants to find a generous younger man who will want to play games and let her straddle his hips, truly, she should not have any difficulty. I am the worst she could do. There are hundreds of unattached men in Kenya who would be so fortunate as to have Lila as their unexpected nocturnal visitor, handsome, healthy, strong young men. I am none of those things. None of them.

Wednesday, December 11, 1912

Suicidal today. I'd do it if I could write a decent note. I am terrible at letters. If not for Mr. Wangai, I'd never a proper letter out for the courts, I swear.

Dear

To whom does one address a suicide note if nobody loves you?

Dear stranger finding this note and my huge, bloated, rotting carcass,

Why does it need to be addressed to anyone at all? Why not just make it a simple explanation?

I have killed myself today because I am suicidal.

Well, now, that's stupid. Redundant.

For anyone curious as to why I have chosen to end my pointless life, just be good enough and look at me. That should be reason enough. Nobody wants me, nobody loves me, and that's completely understandable. The world would be such a better place without me. I have suffered endless pain and unhappiness, and surely have done nothing but spread those cancerous diseases to everyone I have ever encountered. Thank me for this, my sole intelligent act.

And then, how to kill myself, that's always the question. I shouldn't do it at home, I don't want Kaweria to have to clean me up. I'll kill myself in the office, let Hadleigh deal with me. Hang myself. Stout rope, a very strong beam. No, I'll end up caving in the whole ceiling. Poison shouldn't work, I don't even know how to get any poison that's guaranteed to work. Knife to the inside arms, that's the only solution. Just cut right down the veins. I can do it, I know I can. I wonder how difficult it will be to break the skin.

Thursday, December 12, 1912

Postponing suicide. Kaweria pinched me on the chin today. Reason to live! Just chatting as she cleared the room this morning, I was still not totally dressed, trying to force my last unaltered waistcoat to button at least partially, and she was in such a playful mood! "What would you do without someone to clean up after you, Mr. Mudi?"

"Drown in my own squalor, surely, Miss Kaweria."

"And after having been so tidy for so long, it's as if you just can't help yourself. There's a word for people like you, Mr. Mudi."

"Anal expulsive?"

"No, no! I wouldn't say it!" And how she grinned at me, with teeth from Rhodesia, surely, those sparkling eyes, always teasing me. "Well, at least in your flat, I earn my money, Mr. Mudi."

"I will have them in the offices downstairs raise your pay."

And she pinched me right on the chin! Oh, happy day. Suicide staved off for now.

Friday, December 13, 1912

I do not need to kill myself. Hadleigh will kill me. Or I will kill him. One or the other. Fight to the death is in order. I think I should surely win, though, I have the fire in the loins for it. Wrench his head off like a wine bottle cork. How I hate him, ruined my week totally for mistakes. How can one man make so many errors in a single document? How? I'm no divorce specialist, but Hadleigh's mistakes should be plain to a layman. I'll kill him, I'll kill him one day, I know I will. At least I'll know how to defend myself. Hadleigh had better never get married, because he'll never manage to divorce himself. He'll end up throwing title and fortune into a sinkhole of taxation. Maybe I'd like to witness that, that's a reason to live.

I wish I hated him this much all of the time. It would make my life so much easier. Because I know that in a few hours time, I will be back to loving him as if he were my brother, in fact, quite a bit more than the brother that this world has brought me. I must try to train myself to hate him all of the time, and then I won't be stuck working in the office all weekend long on his cases while he goes out and has fun with the white people. Why do I let him do this to me? Because I'm lonely, because I rely on him to fix that for me. So I'll waste a whole weekend on his errors, and then, next weekend, maybe I'll be rewarded with some company.

I need some company.

Monday, December 16, 1912

Sick and lonely.

Tuesday, December 17, 1912

Note: Don't self-abuse while wearing a glove. It doesn't feel like somebody else, it just makes too much friction.

Wednesday, December 18, 1912

Note: Three suits ready at tailor's in a week, before the end-of-year celebrations. Thank goodness for that. No room to breathe in these damn trousers.

Thursday, December 19, 1912

Note: Hadleigh going on long weekend in Nairobi. Steal his liquor and his cigarettes before he locks up.

Monday, December 23, 1912

Note: Must find new rape barrister; Lord Etheridge retiring. What a job description: rape barrister. That makes me a rape solicitor. That sounds absolutely terrible. Rape solicitor! Sounds as if I go around begging to be raped. Well, that's not too far from how I'm feeling these days. Hello madam, I am a rape solicitor, may I solicit you for a rape?

Thursday, December 26, 1912

Who knew that line would work! Lucky thing, being drunk and silly. If Hadleigh finds out that his cook and I had relations in his top-floor bedroom while he entertained his guests in the ballroom, he shall surely die. Dead, utterly and completely, I have no doubt. I'll save that information for a time when he really deserves it. Not now, he did, after all, throw that lovely Christmas party, and I did get plenty of attention from the charming Miss Njeri. Miss Njeri is a Luo lady, and those ladies are extremely beautiful, intelligent, and obliging to a man of a certain girth and a certain state of non-circumcision. I have fancied Miss Njeri ever since Hadleigh took her on, she is just lovely! She has always appreciated my admiration of her cooking, and especially appreciated my excited consumption of such, used as she is to Hadleigh's guests whose idea of a meal is three olives in a glass of gin. It was bound to happen eventually, wasn't it? I was bound to get bored stiff of Hadleigh's party, as I always do, and find my way to Miss Njeri's side, let her feed me so that I can compliment her. She stuffed me up with kuku paka, which I told her reminded me of being fed by my mother at home. Really, so much similarity, the powdered spices and all. I think it's only white people who don't know about giving food any flavor. She invited me to take off my jacket, to make myself at home. It must have been three in the morning, cooking for a drunk and tired Indian man who misses his mother, what a sweet lady, Miss Njeri. I was really thinking that was as good as it was going to get, but it did get better. First, some foolish banter about business, needing a new rape barrister, being a rape solicitor. "Maybe that could be arranged!" she said, and with one deft little hand, opened up my collar. I don't even know how she did it, the sides went winging right out, I could have fainted dead away.

And so, the quest began, stumbling up the staircases, looking for an unoccupied room. Knocking on doors, it was like a game. "Who is it?" "Mudigonda." "Go away." I got a lot of that, and fortune favoring the inebriated, found it actually quite funny. Up to the topmost floor, into Hadleigh's neglected little nursery, and onto the lovely soft mattress. Njeri was so obliging, helping me undress when I hardly knew up or down, such comments and teasing she made!

"Where all your good color gone to? Wearing these suits rub it away?" she teased, tapping her fingertips to my patches.

"I only had so much good color when I was born, lovely, lovely, Njeri. But you're right, I should be in dhoti kurta, not in serge, as you should be in beads."

"Or perhaps we're both best in nothing?"

"That could be true, that could be true."

"I always like you, Bwom-Bwom." That is her pet name for me, she says it means something on the lines of big fellow. "I don't like any Indian but you."

"Aren't I lucky!"

"You act like you were born here, like an African man, like you belong. You look outside, you see everything, not just the money in your wallet. You could be Luo. You are not handsome, but very, very nice."

"You are too kind, Njeri. I wish I were Luo. I wish I were your husband!"

And how she laughed. The ladies always find me the most amusing when I'm drunk and naked, why is that? "You do wish you were my husband! He would not let you buy me from him, no! Who cooks for him, then? Who gives him good loving?"

"Show me the good loving that he would miss so much."

"Oh no. Not for you, Bwom-Bwom. The rape solicitor needs a rape. I'll be a bit rough with you."

"Be a bit rough. I'll like it."

And she was really only a bit rough, actually very gentle. Just a few little bites on my bottom lip, under my chin, a little bit of tugging on my hair. I liked it very, very much, very playful. If Njeri thinks that that sort of lovely teasing is aggressive, I wonder how soft she is with her husband! And Njeri is so soft, so, so soft. She has eight children, eight beautiful, happy children, isn't that wonderful? A lovely, soft, gentle mother with soft, tender flesh for me to caress, and the most extraordinary soft bosoms, having fed eight lucky children and one big husband at home, now feeding me. We experimented with some different positions, but settled on her sitting on my lap, so I could cup each lovely breast in one of my lucky, lucky hands, and run my tongue up and down her beautiful, long neck, bounce her on my thighs. I wish I could have eight children with Njeri, Njeri with her soft, soft lips and her soft, soft bosoms. I love the way she styles her hair, I cannot even comprehend the beauty of her short, slim braids, I buried my nose in them as I kept her bouncing in my lap. It is unique; most Luo women prefer a simple crop, but Njeri, she is aware of her exceptional beauty, she has every right to be vain. Her lips are shaped like the petals of the rarest, most beautiful orchid, her ears, tiny shells, so perfect to explore with the tip of my tongue. Oh, beautiful Njeri. You nourish me.

I hope with every ounce of my being that her husband never finds out. I shall never tell Hadleigh, never. I will protect Njeri, I will protect her until my dying day.

Monday, December 30, 1912

Kaweria laughed at my tedious joke this morning – I don't even remember how it went, I'd stolen it from Hadleigh, which means that it was certainly not funny, but she laughed anyway. Also, fixed the handkerchief in my top pocket for me. My adoration of her is becoming unbearable, truly unbearable. I sob at night when I think of her.

What is it about her? Why does she invade my mental space in this way? I think it is her femininity. She is so feminine, perhaps the most feminine lady I have ever encountered. She has such a lovely, feminine voice, so light and soft, like a warm breeze coming in over the Indian Ocean. Everything she does seems touched by femininity, walking, talking, even scrubbing. It takes a very special lady to look like a princess while scrubbing away my hair and its accompanying emollients in the sink. Her hands are so long and graceful and don't look at all suited for cleaning up my flat. I wish she didn't have to clean when she came by in the morning, I wish she could just have tea with me instead. But I do need cleaning, don't I? I'll hire someone else to clean while Kaweria has tea. Someone uninteresting. A man. Make Hadleigh do it. Then hire someone to clean up after Hadleigh.

Thursday, January 2, 1913

I got such special treat for my New Year's Eve, totally unplanned, and truly exceptional. Do we not remember our most precious friend, the soft and gentle Gladys, who has been our most treasured company for the last five years, nearly six? It is true, a sighting of Gladys is rare, once or twice a year at the very most, but it always ends the same way, with a tender hour of worship. But this time, this time was entirely more special than any other time. Beautiful Gladys has finally been blessed with fertility, and she is now expecting her first child, an event much longed-for during all these years that I have known her, and she saw it fit, once reunited in Hadleigh's drawing room, to celebrate with me! I do not know how I have been so lucky, other than the fact that our acquaintance is so occasional, to have maintained such a long lasting, precious bond, that I might be permitted to interrupt her days of confinement. For this, I cannot be angry at Hadleigh, to have orchestrated such a wonderful reunion, and under such happy circumstances, in such a natural, unforced setting as one of his tedious gambling parties. Gladys flattered me, saying that she most likely would not have attended, if not for my own presence there. If only this were true.

Gladys, always the paragon of gentle womanhood, has attained her twenty-ninth year a few weeks ago, but I do not attribute her overwhelming increase in beauty to the significance of this year, although twenty-nine is a year that I hope Gladys enjoys. Rather, I attribute her radiance to her expectant quality, truly and fully. It is only a month until the blessed event! Oh, if I could die now and be born as Gladys's child, to be held in those soft, gentle arms, to be lulled to sleep by her singing, to be nursed from her breast! And not just once a year, but every day!

I should continue researching suicide. There is no question that I find her extremely beautiful in her condition. Her chestnut curls but brighter and thicker, her cheeks yet more like rosy red apples, her smile quicker, her laughter more frequent, how happiness beautifies a lady. And more than happiness, the form of such exquisite beauty reclining on my bed! Those breasts, always plump and buoyant, now doubly so! What could be better? And the centerpiece, her precious belly, that I could worship as an avid disciple for just a day!

This day was, perhaps, the best of my life. When I walked into that much-dreaded drawing room, expecting another evening of drunken tedium, I heard a squeal of delight! A squeal of delight! For me! I know, impossible! And then, rushing like a carefree young girl to my side, lovely Gladys, clad all in soft pink and white. I grinned and took her elbow with her husband's permission; he thinks of me as totally benign, some hideous, neutered Oriental lapdog with which he may entertain his wife. I am fortunate to be thought of in such a demeaning way by so many men, for it enables for me so many liberties, and protects the ladies from explosive tempers. And so, off to a dark corner we went, to enjoy one another's company.

"Oh, Manik, I have missed you!" she breathlessly intoned, the gaslight sparkling against her most beautiful hair. "And, like always, you have grown!" When put in that sort of context, in the context of some sort of reliable amusement, my face need not heat up too much when Gladys puts her little hand so sweetly on my chronically engorged stomach. "But this time, my friend, so have I!" And then, sweet Gladys guides my foolish hand to that most blessed vessel, so perfect in its form, and right at that very moment, a tiny stirring inside! To say that joy spread across my face would be an understatement, for joy infused my every cell. I, still sober as the day I was born, burst out laughing. I threw all caution to the wind and took Gladys into a very, very inappropriate embrace, kissing her lovely small forehead and stammering out all sorts of congratulations. It was during our first meeting, surely, that she confessed that she wanted nothing more in this world than a baby of her own, and to see that wish finally fulfilled, I was extremely heartened. I had no illusions of being so fortunate as to experience Gladys in an intimate way, but I was compelled to sit her on one of Hadleigh's soft, well-appointed guest beds, and demand a tray of sweetmeats, that I might give offerings to this living goddess. However, once our privacy was secured, it was Gladys who made me an unrefusable offer. As I said, perhaps the very best day of my entire life.

"Manik, wouldn't you like to see how I've changed?" she asked, her voice so innocent, as if mentioning nothing more than showing me a new bracelet.

"I should want nothing more! The suggestions of your beautiful dress are more than I can bear."

"Then, help me with it. I am helpless these days without constant attention."

I was then sent to her back, my clumsy fingers trembling with anticipation as I undid her buttons, each button positively straining with the abundance of her flesh. It was so exciting, it's a wonder that I did not faint dead away. Then, at last, beautiful Gladys, doubtlessly a beautiful baby inside her, reclined on the soft cushions ahead of me, appearing like nothing more than the beauteous union between a pink rose in full bloom and a sweet, plump, exotic fruit, bursting with juices. I felt a powerfully magnetic draw to her belly, I could not tear my hands away, but she welcomed my caresses with the most beatific of smiles.

What is it, I wonder, that makes the belly of a pregnant woman so beautiful, and my own so detestable? It is not an issue of volume, clearly, as I will state that, proportionally, taking into consideration height and overall build, Gladys and I were well matched, something that did, of course, cheer me very much, but less for myself than for Gladys's happiness about the situation. It might be her happiness and my misery that emphasizes our contrast, but it is something more. Could it be that pregnancy is, in its very nature, a state of uncommon health and vibrancy, and my body is the product of incurable disease? It may simply have to do with the fact that Gladys is a woman, and women are, fundamentally, beautiful and wonderful and adorable, which makes their every feature lovelier. I will place my bets on the loveliness of all the parts together, the rosy thigh, the immeasurably fuller, more sensitive bosom, the beauty of her skin, her face, her delicate fingers happily tracing the gorgeous, soft curve of her abdomen. Perhaps it's something also to do with pretty women and their pretty, soft curves. It is the natural state of nearly every pretty woman, isn't it, to have at least a slight, soft arch at the middle, and with pregnancy, all that happens is that the overall shape of that soft arch is maintained, only that its ratio increases, doing nothing to impede the overall harmony of the lady's tender form. Well, whatever it is, it inspires in me such worship. I not only was compelled to caress Gladys's beautiful belly, but play her servant, and feed her from my unworthy fingertips. What playful coquettish greediness! I never witnessed such an enticing display! It was not three bites in that I was forced by heated passion to undress myself as well and curl up yet closer to beautiful Gladys. What a pleasant game it was!

"So, which shall be next, Princess Gladys? The little chocolate mousse tart?"

"Yes, please!" What a spoiled and adorable voice she put on for me! Could I have been luckier? And then, licking my fingertips with her rosebud lips, moans of happiness, gleeful laughter and belly stroking. How endearing and sensual! And every fourth delicate morsel or so, she would express some disdain and say, "That one is for you, sweet Manik." How thoughtful! Did I ever have so much fun? The answer is no. Never in my life. I think I am well suited for this sort of task, the feeding and pampering of pregnant women. Yes, yes I am. I should advertise. I wonder what sort of response I would get? I don't expect much. I would assume that most men would relish this sort of activity, being rewarding in so many ways. There are endless rewards to feeding a beautiful pregnant woman little delicacies. First of all, pregnancy is tiring, the creation of new life, and the expectant mother needs all the energy she can get. Secondly, one is doing at least one of the following: building the health and strength of a child, building the health and strength of his mother, and making that child's accommodations softer, more comforting and luxurious. Thirdly, one can take the lady's castoffs as his own. Fourthly, watching a beautiful woman be exceptionally happy never becomes tiresome, especially as she smiles at you and bounces and jiggles and touches herself in alluring ways. Fifthly, she may reward you with some other sort of activity. Such was my own good luck! I reiterate once again, the best day of my life.

"Oh, look at that, all our sweeties gone," I teased, lightly brushing my eyelash against Gladys's red cheek.

"All gone? What a shame." And she pouted that naughty little bottom lip at me and balanced both pretty hands on that beautiful belly. I am glad to be getting older, for not three years ago, I would have had to focus my every cell not to expel myself right on the bed sheets instantly. Especially when she parted her beautiful lips again in smiling and announced cheerfully: "We could always play our other game."

"You would be up to it, in your delicate condition?" That is Manik Mudigonda forcing himself to appear polite.

"I only came to dreadful old Hadleigh's dreadful old party in order to enjoy time with you, Manik, and I think I enjoy you best when you are making use of that ruffle-edged mace of yours."

"It is a bit ruffly, isn't it?" I pulled whatever foreskin that had not been stretched into my erection over my glans to make a little chrysanthemum bud for Gladys's delight. What a funny thing about Gladys, with so many exotic features to fixate upon, she has not placed her interest in red eye or white hair or patches or pockmarks, but on my long foreskin. Funny, funny girl! She always says, "Oh, I only know about Roundheads, I never knew any Cavaliers." I have absolutely no idea what that means, but it never ceases to charm me.

"Let me unwrap my present and then, let's find a way that makes us happy." Gladys spent a good few seconds rolling my foreskin up and down before letting me get to business. She isn't squeamish, she'll be such a good mother. I decided that the only position that would be accommodating to both of our physiques would be from behind. In order to protect her, I lifted and balanced Gladys on all edges with pillows so that she could remain on her knees and her belly would be gently cushioned. She laughed with pleasure at my thoughtfulness. That's why she likes me, I think, because I always think these things through. I think she finds me careful, trustworthy. And, in order that every precaution be made for Gladys's comfort and safety, I also wrapped both of my arms around her hips, just under the bottom curve of her belly so that with each thrust, I would be slightly lifting her rather than pushing her down. Oh, the weight and softness of her belly pressed against my arms, they had never been happier. My own central heft was blessed to have Gladys's voluminous bottom upon which to rest, and she swore to me how the light friction there tickled her. And then! Yet another surprise! I was warning her that I was not long for this world, and she announces to me, "Come in the other one, Manik!" So I did! When do I have permission to encroach upon a lady's derriere? And without shrieking or anything? Without question, if I have had better days, I cannot remember them now!

And of course, recovery was just as nice. We curled up in Hadleigh's fancy Egyptian cotton sheets together and talked about such lovely things. Gladys and I played at baby names together; so soon before the little one's emergence, and still undecided, that is Gladys!

"I know it's customary, but I don't want William. Everyone is William, it's so plain! Not saying that my William is plain, of course, my sweet Manik, but it can't be William."

"Any baby of yours cannot be plain, beautiful Gladys. So, what do you really want?"

"I was thinking something lively, bright, energetic! Maybe Henry."

"Gladys, how is Henry that much better than William? Be honest with me, you know that I like everything you say and do."

"Well all right. I was really thinking of Cyprian! But it will be William at worst and Henry at best, you know my Bill won't go for anything fun. That's why I need you in my life, Manik, that's all you are, just sweet, darling fun."

"I think of you the same way, Gladys." Truer words I have never said. "But what if a girl? A girl running around with a name like Henry, that is very imaginative."

"I haven't any good ideas for a girl at all, Manik! It had better end up a boy, because I just don't know any good girls' names."

"Well, let's think. What's your favorite letter?"

"Favorite letter? I haven't any favorite letter! What's your favorite letter, Manik?"

"I should think it should be obvious!"

"Well, clearly, that would be M."

"Naturally."

"Oh, there's no good girls' names starting with M! Mary, that's the plainest, dullest name ever. And Margaret is a name for a girl who scolds her friends and has a sour face. Martha is dull and bossy, and Mildred is just so horrid. That's all I know. What M names do you know?"

"English names? I don't know any English names at all! I'm lucky to know yours!"

"Well, Indian names, then."

"You'd give your daughter an Indian name? When you fear that Bill will find Henry too exciting for a boy?"

"He won't care! He'd just be reeling from shock if it weren't a boy, he wouldn't notice anything odd until she's four years old. Come on, give me some ideas, Manik, just a few!"

"Well, let's see. There's Mohini, that's for a sexy girl like you. Or Mukta, that's a little pretty pearl like you. Or Malti, that's a pretty little flower like you..."

"What pretty names and pretty meanings! Tell me some more."

I was actually running out of names in my own memory banks at that time, so I began to think of names that I shouldn't say aloud. "There's

Madhulika, that's the sweetest flower's nectar. And there's Mira, the prayerful one, who worships a romantic god."

"What's that last one again?"

"Mira?"

"That's very pretty. And I think it could pass for English, don't you?"

"I hadn't thought, really."

"And what romantic god? I like that, tell me about that."

"Oh, Lord Krishna, he's, well, the playboy god. He's blue and handsome and lives in the country and all the pretty cowherd girls dance with him."

"He's blue!"

"Or black. But these days, usually blue. Dark blue, like the night sky. But very sexy, dances, plays the flute, lithe physique, you know, like mine." Making Gladys laugh is all too easy!

"That does it, Manik. Mira it shall be! What would I do without you? The blue playboy god, I like that as well. Blue, black, brown, white, red, and spotted ... Indians do come in just every color, it seems."

"Oh, Gladys, let me disabuse you of the misapprehension that the patterned variety is at all common – I am entirely unique."

"Manik, let's get dressed and try to talk Bill into taking me to India once the baby is born." And so we rejoined Hadleigh's dreadful party, Gladys tight on my elbow. That bastard Bill Hendricks always gives me this stupid, toothy grin, like I've done him some great favor, and kisses his wife when the clock strikes midnight. Sometimes I wish he knew. He always makes some horrid remark on the lines of Gladys's cheerful enthusiasm being so exhausting to him. Last night was no different, but I was already a sheet to the wind by the time he made it, and so have forgotten it, thank goodness. It is one of the many things I like about life in Mombasa, that the society is casual enough that the rules of confinement are largely ignored. Having to drink myself silly without Gladys sitting beside me, just because of her delicate condition, that would have been ever so depressing. I love Mombasa, nearly as much as I love Cape Town, I think, but as I grow older, Mombasa suits me very well. I am writing Gladys as soon as she leaves for Nairobi, I must hear word from her about her baby. I am desperately hoping for a girl, named after my sweet Mai or not: the world needs more ladies like Gladys. I would wait until she grew up and I would marry her, unlucky as I was only to meet Gladys after she'd married Bill Hendricks. But then again,

I never even would have met Gladys if not for Bill Hendricks, and she would have wasted her charms on England. Also, and I have put thought into this, in regards to Gladys, and to many other ladies for whom I care very much, it is likely that it is their married status that gives women the courage to even engage me in conversation. Otherwise, I would terrify them, I know it. So, really, I should be, in a way, thankful to Bill Hendricks and his ilk, for providing the proper environment for their wives to have affairs with me. But I am not really thankful, no, not really. I hate them all. And really, if I look at things institutionally, it's their fault that I am not married yet. I would be absolutely the best husband that has ever lived, I absolutely would, because I understand what it's like to be a woman, to be restricted and controlled because of the rules that men make. I wouldn't be some stupid, rod-wielding enforcer if I were married, because I wouldn't want my wife falling into the arms of some other man, who I would grin at stupidly at parties after he'd just ejaculated inside her rectum. I would just strive to be a good fucker, the best I could possibly be, just as I do now, seriously, as a vocation. More men should make that their true vocation, I think, it would be a better world.

Friday, January 17, 1913

Note: Must take a break from vomiting. If it means gaining a half a stone in a week, then so be it. Not even a matter of gag reflex right now, but there are so many holes in my teeth right now, the acid has given me some sort of abscess on the bottom left and that has to go away first before I can return to any sort of reduction or maintenance regimen. So much bloody agony. So glad I saw Gladys for New Year's rather than the upcoming weekend.

Wednesday, January 29, 1913

Note: How is it possible that I am this fat? How? I can barely chew, it's obscene. Abscess or none, I am going back to vomiting.

Saturday, February 1, 1913

Note: Maybe too hasty with my return to vomiting. Teeth exceptionally painful now. No solution whatsoever but suck on clove oil until this all passes.

Monday, February 3, 1913

Oh, beautiful Kaweria, I love you so much, I love you more than life itself. It's a real shame that I have no chance whatsoever with Kaweria, because she is just so wonderful. She noticed me suffering with horrendous toothache agony, with a swollen jaw and all that humiliation, and she got salted ice for me as a surprise this morning! Is that not the most thoughtful thing anyone has ever done? And, not to mention, working wonders. I wish I had the courage to ask Kaweria about her family, but I am so shy and immature around her, she is so beautiful and feminine, with just the gentlest, softest hands in the world. If she isn't married, I will ask her to marry me. No I won't, because I am a coward. A big, fat, hideous coward with a toothache.

Wednesday, February 5, 1913

News from Gladys! The telegram says she is now mother to a baby boy, born on the first of this month, seven pounds and four ounces, named William Hendricks the fourth. A shame. I will tell her to call him Henry when Bill is not around. I shall call him Henry, should I ever meet this golden child. No, I shall call him Cyprian. If it were my son, I would have let Gladys name him Cyprian, just to see her beautiful, happy face. Gladys will be the prettiest, tenderest, most cheerful little mother any boy could ever want. I wish Gladys would adopt me as her absurdly old little boy. I want to send Gladys a present of congratulations, but I don't know what's appropriate. I would actually want to give her a big cash sum, so she could spend it on dresses and pretty things for herself, but that's an odd gift. I can't see Bill Hendricks finding it at all acceptable. And jewelry is out of the question, that suggests too much. Oh, I am hopeless. I refuse to send a pram!

Friday, February 7, 1913

Have I begun to hallucinate in my dull, lonely condition, now over a month without any company whatsoever? Did I see Lila walking along the shoreline today, about a mile ahead of myself? I should have tried to catch up with her, but I was afraid. I want to see Lila so badly, but after our last time together, I feel so much shame, so much discomfort. This is the longest I have gone without seeing her since we first met. I feel as if I have lost one of the best friends I have ever had, and I am suffering her loss extremely. I brought this upon myself. It is my own ugly weakness that has driven her away. Oh, Lila, I miss you. I think I'll stay home and cry tonight, I won't follow Hadleigh to whatever pointless event he's attending tonight. I want my Lila. I think I love her most of anyone in the world, and I've lost her. I hate myself. I hate myself. I hate myself.

Saturday, February 8, 1913

Went wandering the shorefront all day, trying to find the spot where I thought I saw Lila yesterday. Of course, she was not there. I am just going to have to accept that my relationship with Lila is over. Our relationship was based on my willingness to play games with her and to make her feel happy. That was all I had to do. It should have been so easy! But no, no, I had to ruin it. I could have had Lila in my life until my dying day, but now, I will just have to mourn her loss. I hate myself.

Monday, February 10, 1913

Hazel came by for tea today! I was so happy to see her, and not only because I love her, but because I was hoping for word about Lila. Hazel told me that she has not heard from Lila at all for just as long as I have, that she was hoping that I had some word. I have many conflicting emotions about this situation, because if Lila has gone traveling without telling anyone, and she really doesn't hate me, and she may come back some day and give me a spanking, well, nothing in the world should make me happier. But then again, if Lila has disappeared without telling either Hazel or myself, something could be very wrong, and that upsets me greatly. As much as I hate to do so, I am going to have to go to my last resort: I must send Hadleigh into the rumor mill to find out news about Lila. He'll find out the truth. And I don't care if she's gone away because she hates me and is disgusted by me, if she is happy and safe, that will be enough for me. I love her enough for that to be my only goal: to know that somewhere, anywhere, Lila Gorringe and her crystal blue eyes are gazing happily at a beautiful world that loves her.

Hazel is coming by in three nights' time. I will try to make the flat comfortable. I think Kaweria would like Hazel. If Hazel is lonely without Lila, perhaps I should introduce them to one another. I might do that, Hazel should not feel abandoned. And perhaps it would endear Kaweria to me to come to understand my deep love and affection for ladies, regardless of age.

Wednesday, February 12, 1913

Extremely hung over today. I let Hadleigh bring me to bed last night, I think. I know I ought to be looking forward to my evening with Hazel, but I am depressed, very depressed. I thought I could work late and just focus on writing the Sibunya appeal, and while I managed to do that, I do not know how, as I've just finished reading what I wrote and somehow it all makes sense, I should have just gone to bed. Why don't I ever want to go to sleep? And then, why do I never want to wake up again? I drink too much. I drink much too much. I smoke too much also, but that's manageable, and it doesn't disable me. I drink to disability, and I am ashamed about that. I never thought I would end up this way, I was such a religious boy, but now? I think I am a drunk. Hadleigh easily drinks as much as I do, but I don't think of him as a drunk. He keeps control over himself and I don't. It should be a motivation to me not to get drunk in the office because I don't want Hadleigh putting me to bed, not because he holds it over my head, because he doesn't, but because I just don't like it. It's not the care that I don't like, because I'll take what I can get, and I like being looked after, but I don't want him to think I like it. I never want to encourage Hadleigh; I may owe him in some ways, but I have to figure out a way to differentiate myself from him, to separate myself.

If Lila came back to me, I would ask her to run away with me.

Friday, February 14, 1913

I think that today is Valentine's Day, either today or tomorrow, I am not sure, but I am feeling love in my heart, regardless.

I think I have made a good decision in introducing Hazel and Kaweria to one another. Hazel was a little bit embarrassed to be seen in the early morning in my bedroom, although she was nothing but elegantly dressed. I think I may have embarrassed Kaweria as well, but I kept to my plan and I made no insinuations of any kind other than that since I consider both ladies as my friends, they should be friends to one another. I told Kaweria to take my tea, and when she refused, I offered to clean the flat myself. I think I gave both ladies plenty of amusement as I clumsily swept dust off the floor and right into my eyes. To say that there was not some intentionality in the sacrifice of my vision would be a lie: the sound of beautiful women laughing is the best sound to me in all the world. Also, in discovering their mutual amusement in the form of a big, bumbling, piebald Indian solicitor making a mess of his flat, they could find some instant conversation, which they did. By the time I had upset my floor lamp, they were calling for me back at the divan.

"Mr. Mudi, you should stick to lawyering. Housemaid is not the job for you!" Kaweria teased, pinching my chin in that charming way that she does. "What do you think, Mrs. Kroes?"

"I don't know, Mrs. Idim, I might pay good money to watch him clean my drapes!"

But how did this lovely morning of teasing and budding friendship come about? It did not begin with so much happiness. Rather, it began with some really awful sadness and some of the worst news I have heard in years. Hazel came to me, early once again, with news of Lila, who has resurfaced. My Lila is sick, with some unknown cancer, and she is ashamed of her illness. In fact, dearest Hazel was sworn not to tell me, specifically, but I am glad that she disobeyed Lila's request. I am bereft. It has been so long now, and Hadleigh came up with nothing in the rumor mill. Lila has truly crawled inside her den. I have tried to understand why she has chosen to refuse attention and comfort, and I think I can sympathize. It's the faces I would not be able to bear, the faces of helpless concern. Does Lila think that I would be wearing that kind of face if she came to me frail and unwell? That saddens me. The only thing that saddens me more is thinking of Lila, sick at home with a harsh, judgmental husband, stoically averting his eyes from her suffering.

With this sort of news, my mood went very dark, but I tried my best to hide it, as my vocation is not to consume my own sympathy but to give it to poor, lovely Hazel. Poor, lovely Hazel has an entirely different pattern of plucked and growing hairs than when I saw her last; there is a funny little maze now snaking from a hole in her no-longer impenetrable hairline right in the center. I should not know this. We did not set out with the intention of undressing, let alone making love, but both happened anyway, which is what happens when I hold a woman of delicate emotions against my chest for too long, I suppose. It was a way for us to cope with our feelings, to spread warmth and comfort. The mood was not the same as the first time we'd made love, it was quite different. Hazel's pillow talk was entirely different, and went from mild insults to instructions: hold me closer, hold me tighter, go in slower, go in deeper, kiss me, kiss me again, pull me closer, closer, closer. Once again she refused to let me pull out; she is just begging for an unacceptably dusky baby. Then, she took hold of my queue, loosened the ribbon, and draped my hair over her face and bosom. She sighed, hiding inside my white canopy of curls, and her tensions melted away. I did not bother to ask; I knew that she was staying the night. Keeping Hazel in my bed while the stars are bright seems to be easy, but when the sun begins to threaten our safety, she becomes uneasy. It took some real convincing to get her to stay until nine o' clock, when Kaweria arrives, and at least twenty minutes of cunnilingus. I also demanded that Hazel let me dress her myself, which also let me keep my own pace. But it was the right decision. Hazel and Kaweria have now found one another.

Tuesday, February 18, 1913

Kaweria is a goddess, she is all good and holy things. To think, for all these months that I was wondering where Lila lives, Kaweria has been cleaning her house, which is less than a quarter mile away. She and Hazel discovered their shared connection with Lila, and it has cemented their bond, and Kaweria, in all her wisdom, has told me where I can find Lila, and also, when to find Lila. Lila's husband is going to Nairobi on Thursday and won't return until Saturday morning. It is time for me to take a risk. Cowardice, be gone of me. I have something important to do.

Saturday, February 22, 1913

I am childish, foolish, immature in every way, and I have no right to ever complain of any misfortune that comes to me. I hate myself. I hate myself. I hate myself. All of those times that I suffered, drunkenly, grieving for my own lost love, it was so stupid and selfish. I feel so stupid and selfish now, especially.

I spent a full day at Lila's farmhouse. I walked behind Kaweria as she went to her evening job, quiet, anxious, but stupidly thrilled to be walking outside with Kaweria, fool that I am. Part of the way she even allowed me to offer my elbow to her, for the road was quite congested. Sweet, feminine Kaweria introduced me as a surprise gift and called for me to pop my head through the doorway to Lila's bedroom, a sheepish smile on my ugly face. The expression of shock and the hand clutching her bosom made me think for a moment that I had overstepped my bounds, something that I really try not to do with women who do not really belong to me, as none of them do, but I could not help myself. I have been crying for days, I could not pass up this chance to spend time with Lila, I would have regretted it until the day I died. But then, her expression softened; I do not think she has ever seen me not through the haze of alcoholic romance, and I think she realized just how unimpressive I am in my ugliness. I am not a demon, I am a toadstool. Kaweria gave me a knowing look and left us alone: there is no way that she does not know exactly what I do now, I wonder what she thinks of me, I wonder why she does not mind any association. Kaweria is a forgiving goddess.

I came creeping slowly, quietly, but still awkwardly, to Lila's bedside, watching a very beautiful, sad smile slowly bloom on her delicate face, but when I got close enough to see how, in spite of her skin going very translucent and gray and her limbs going very, very thin indeed, her blue eyes still sparkled like aquamarines set in silver, I sat myself beside her on the bed and pulled her into my arms. I held her very close to me so that she wouldn't be able to see my face, wouldn't be able to see how wet my cheeks had become with my tears. I waited until I could show some composure to let her go, and then I just looked into her blue eyes, just stared, and appreciated her, until she spoke at last.

"Oh, sweet Dearest Magpie, make yourself comfortable, for goodness sake! Come up here next to me and let me enjoy your visit. And for all that's good and holy, take off that collar and that waistcoat, you are cutting off your circulation."

Who was I to fight such gentle demands? Collar and waistcoat were thrust aside, and soon was everything else, as Lila invited me under her bedclothes. She wanted to touch me. I don't know what it was, perhaps that she is so ill and full of thoughts, that she said some very strange things to me. She kept pressing her hands into my arms, my back, and talked to me.

"Are you really a grown man, Dearest Magpie?"

"I have been for many, many years."

"Because you strike me as so young. You strike me as very fresh and very young, seventeen or eighteen at the very most."

"Why do you think me so young, beautiful Lila?"

"You're a very big lad, but your flesh is so resilient, so fresh and strong, it springs back when I press into it. You feel young. You smell young as well, like fancy, dandy boys' cigarettes and dandy boys' pomades. Your face is so mysterious to me, but it could not be the face of anything but some sweet and silly boy. Everything about you seems so young, so full of life. You make me feel young, Dearest Magpie, Dearest Samson, my most charming Dearest Tum-Tum."

I felt so strange and sad at these words, especially since I think of myself as wearing my age in a very obvious way, heavy and weary and aching, but who am I to shatter Lila's fantasy, of what she wishes me to be, of what she needs me to be? She made no mention of my infirmity during our last encounter, and in fact, seemed to have kindly and judiciously forgotten it. She seemed to want to bury herself inside me, and kept pressing her face into my chest, tucking her hands into my armpits. I did not make any advances upon her, and her only touches and caresses were those of exploration, affection, not of erotica. I just let her run her hands over me for a few hours, let them trace over ears and lips, poke into small creases and rolls, massage shoulders and elbows, and travel slowly over my largest expanses.

It was an odd experience, now that I am reliving it through my memory. She was served her meals in bed and calmly requested that meals be prepared for me as well, as if the presence of a fat, particolored stranger laying naked in her bed were only the most normal and natural of circumstances. What loyalty in her serving ladies she must inspire, as they truly did not give me much attention at all, other than to feed me and to bring me ashtrays. I spent a whole day and a whole night in Lila's bed, never more than a finger-joint's length away from her. I liked it. It felt good to me.

It was not until the next morning that Lila made some confessions to me about the gravity of her situation. I, of course, was not blind to how wan and thin she has become, but she told me that a cancer has taken hold of her womb, that she is in such blinding pain all of the time. Blinding pain, but still so tender and sweet, her personality unchanged! She bleeds from this cancer constantly, a never-ending menstruation in a post-menstrual body. She confessed that this constant stream of blood she feared would pollute my Brahmin flesh, which was truly a strange phrase to come from a very English lady who has never even acknowledged my Indian origin, let alone my religious heritage, I suspected out of some discomfort with these facts. Apparently, discomfort or none, these thoughts do indeed occupy her consciousness. I assured her that I am a bad Brahmin and that I can't be polluted, that I consider myself undefilable. She laughed at me, that lovely, lovely laugh.

"I was born in India, did you know that, Dearest Tum-Tum?"

"You were? Where were you born, beautiful Lila?"

"I was born in Calcutta."

"I went to college there. I was valedictorian of University of Calcutta for 1903."

"Bright boy."

"So you must know all about Calcutta, then, beautiful Lila?"

"Hardly."

"I could say the same."

"I fell in love with this very handsome young priest whose temple I would pass while in the carriage with Mater and Pater every weekend. I would look at him, and he would look at me, and then one day, I snuck out to go and talk to him. I couldn't have been older than thirteen, I was a wily maiden, and I don't think he was out of his teenage years either.

His English was poor, and I didn't know his language, but I just wanted to flirt with him. That's all I've ever wanted to do, is flirt with boys that I shouldn't. It's a wonder I married Stephen, he has no interest in flirting at all. You love flirting, don't you, Dearest Tum-Tum?"

"It's what I live for."

"I think that's why I've always liked to have you around."

And so we commenced to flirting. I didn't dare hurt Lila, but I wanted to give some relief to her in her situation, so I kissed with her, kissed her entire body, and petted her softly, and although I suspected that a full-blown oral relation would not be welcome, I softly pressed my lips into her precious blossom and licked away the blood. She grinned broadly and rested her head on my chest for a while to rest afterwards.

It was hard to leave, but I did. I didn't want Lila's husband's suspicions to be too aroused, and I wanted to give Kaweria the chance to change Lila's bedclothes for her, wash away any stray white hairs or drops of precious blood. I hope he travels again soon, especially if Lila's condition does not improve. I will devote as much time to her as is possible. I do not know for certain, but one gets a sense about these sorts of things. I don't want yesterday to have been my last farewell kiss to Lila.

Friday, February 28, 1913

What a funny world it is. Am I a good man or a bad one? If I am a good man, then karma must be rewarding me. If I am a bad man, then I have proven that life is by its very nature unfair. I have been upset every day about Lila, as it would only be normal to be, and Hadleigh is constantly abusing me about my bleak mood.

"Why do you get so damned attached to every woman who jumps into bed with you, Manikji? It's not as if Lila hasn't lived a long, interesting life. And there's no saying that she won't get well, right old fellow? I can't bear you being morbid all day."

"Who else can I be attached to if not Lila, Hadleigh?"

"I don't understand why you need to be attached to anybody, Manikji. Most any other man with your sex life would be happy all of the time. But you, you have things just so, and yet you still manage to brood all of the time. Have supper with me tonight at the cottage, help me plan a do."

"You mean, listen to you plan a do."

"I'm trying to be nice to you, Manik! You are my most treasured friend, it hurts me to see you so beside yourself. Just come home with me and you can eat and drink and smoke and do all the things you like, but do cheer up. Misery may suit you, but it doesn't suit me!"

So I joined Hadleigh at his thirty-room cottage and listened to him gossip and prattle for the evening. I tried to pay attention, I really did, but it's almost impossible to listen to Hadleigh with both of my ears. Njeri spotted me as she served us our fine repast and gave me this spectacularly electric smile. I felt twenty times better in an instant! How seductively she walked out of the informal dining room, I know she was swaying those hips to delight me. That would have been enough of a reason to listen to Hadleigh talk, to see Njeri walk by, but she had some plans for me. As the evening wore on, late of course, because we both got to drinking in front of the fireplace, I kept thinking about Njeri and her smile, and an amazing thing happened: I let Hadleigh drink more than myself. In fact, I let Hadleigh pass out with his knees thrown over the arm of his massive leather wingback chair with a fag burning down to his knuckles. I fought gravity and pulled myself to a wobbly stagger with the intent of heading back to the Cecil, and Njeri spotted me, lost in the vast maze of Hadleigh's gargantuan house, a beautiful young woman by her side.

"Hello, my Bwom-Bwom," she grinned, taking my hands in a friendly gesture of greeting.

"Good evening to you, lovely Miss Njeri," I replied, feeling really not so much more than tipsy.

"I want to introduce to you my daughter, Akinyi."

"I should have known that this beautiful young lady would be your daughter, Miss Njeri, as she resembles you in all your resplendence." I decided to play at being Indian and gave Akinyi the pressed palms and a bow and an awkward facial expression. She was confused and did the same thing. How adorable!

"I told you, Akinyi, that Mr. Mudi, he is a very nice man, always has something nice to say. I tell her all about how good you are, Bwom-Bwom."

"That mustn't have taken very long, Miss Njeri."

Lovely Njeri brought our fortunate little group down to the servant's level, my favorite part of Hadleigh's abode, and sat us down to speak privately. I lit myself a cigarette and listened to Njeri's story. "She needs to learn, Bwom-Bwom, about the two kinds of beauty. There is young, perfect beauty, but then there is the other kind of beauty, the kind that keeps grown people together, the kind that can't be seen. My daughter, she has heard bad news about her husband, Otieno, who has been away in the army. My husband and I, we tried to give our daughter the best match for her, someone brave and who works hard, but she falls in love with his face! So she hears that he has gotten injury to that beautiful face, and what does she do? She comes running to mother, afraid. She says she can't be wife to an ugly man. I thought maybe you would know what to say to a girl like this, my Bwom-Bwom. Maybe you would know the right thing to say."

I looked at Akinyi, who was looking down at her lap, clearly ashamed of her mother's honesty, and I pitied her. She was so very young, how on earth could she be expected to understand the point her mother was trying to make? And marriages like ours, that happen before we reach our intellectual maturity, we are bound to be confused. I thought for too long, perhaps, for something helpful to say, because Njeri interrupted my chain of thought.

"I will tell you what I think this girl need. I think this girl need to learn how good an ugly man can be, and then, when Otieno comes home, she will be able to understand him, appreciate him, be a good wife, not run away to mother. That is what I think Akinyi needs, Bwom-Bwom. Would you talk to her for me, just for a while? Teach her, please."

I don't think I actually voiced any real agreement to this gracious request, but I found myself alone in the back garden with Akinyi, seated on the veranda in Hadleigh's new wicker benches, watching the moths fly into his line of oil torches that rival the brightness of Mombasa's glorious starry sky. I lit myself another cigarette and looked over at Akinyi, who seemed on the verge of tears. I felt so awful for her.

"I am so sorry about your husband's injury, beautiful Miss Akinyi. Life is cruel, it isn't right that a young and beautiful wife should have to suffer so," I babbled, uncomfortable in the awkward silence. She looked up at me with a dry face, but one in the grip of suffering so keen, it sharpened the corners of her beautiful dark eyes. I felt my chest tighten up and I started to puff a bit harder.

"Sir," she said, the first word I ever heard her say, "Sir, have you committed some impropriety with my mother?"

I was not prepared. I coughed. I fell back on lawyering's language to protect myself. "Well, I can't really answer that question with any degree of accuracy, as the definitions of propriety are so variant and flexible, you understand, Miss Akinyi..."

"It does not matter," she interrupted me in a plain way, keeping her gaze directly in my direction. "Whatever it is, you have made her very happy, Mr. Mudi. She cares for you very much."

"Your mother is an exceptionally lovely woman, and I do not deserve any affection that she might have for me, but appreciate it greatly and reciprocate in equal or greater measure, Miss Akinyi."

"She is a good mother and kind, but Mr. Mudi," the young woman took a deep breath and paused, lifting her eyes to the constellations for a moment, "Mr. Mudi, she cannot understand me. I cannot go back to Otieno, I cannot. It will kill me. I am not like other women, I am strange, she cannot understand me, Mr. Mudi."

"Miss Akinyi," I leaned in a few inches closer, only so that I could speak softly, "If you don't love your husband and can't bear to be with him again, then you are not strange at all. If he is unkind to you, or if you love another, or if you are just not a good match, you know that Lord Greenwich and I, we mediate divorces. It should be no shame to you, if it is what you need, then I can help you. This need not be discussed with your mother or anyone if you don't wish it, and I would protect you personally."

"But to get a divorce, Mr. Mudi, there has to be some reason, some reason said aloud for all to hear. I cannot say my reason."

"You could say it to me. I am a vault of secrets. I am not like anybody else, it is completely safe to tell me anything you want to say."

"You will think that I am sick!" Akinyi choked, now clearly fighting with all of her might against crying, but refusing to give in. What a strong constitution, so clearly her mother's daughter, utterly courageous.

"No, I most certainly will not, Miss Akinyi. I look at myself in the mirror every day, it is very difficult to shock me." I gave the young angel a flash of the old red eye and a self-deprecating smile, and she coughed a sad little laugh.

"I don't really want to divorce my husband, Mr. Mudi," she said now in a calmer voice. "I do love him, he understands me. I don't think many other men would understand me as Otieno has. He is a good husband. But his face, Mr. Mudi, it was all that mattered to me."

"It is only his face injured, Miss Akinyi?"

"Yes, sir."

"Well, that is not such a bad thing," I began to rationalize, taking into consideration that Akinyi said that she did love her husband. "There is more to a man than just his face. He can still be a good husband to you, surely. Consider for a moment my own face. It is really quite appallingly horrible, and yet I manage to gain the trust and affection of your most lovely and good mother."

"Oh, Mr. Mudi, your face is not so bad," Akinyi crooned with tilted head.

"Don't go trying to comfort me, Miss Akinyi! It is my job to comfort you, you are the one in pain."

"Your skin is ugly, yes, but your face has a good shape, Mr. Mudi. You have a good nose."

"How on earth did a girl so young learn to flatter like that, Miss Akinyi, when it is your beautiful nose that should inspire a thousand songs and dances?"

"No, Mr. Mudi, you do have a good nose. It is the perfect size, not too large or too small, and it has a good, even shape. I want to look at your nose, Mr. Mudi."

Silly and awkward would be good words to express my emotional state at that moment, but I made a space on my bench and welcomed Akinyi to sit beside me. First, she just sort of stared, thoughtfully at my pockmarked proboscis, and gave an approving hum. Then, she lifted a soft hand and waited for some cue from me to let her touch my face. Carefully, almost scientifically, she used her fingers to gently measure and assess my nose. It was absolutely a strange experience, but who am I to judge anyone's interests? I see nothing particularly appealing about my nose, but clearly Akinyi did. "That's what I like, Mr. Mudi, noses. That is all I like, all I care about. Your nose is very good."

"Thank you, Miss Akinyi."

"Crushed Otieno's nose."

"Crushed?"

"I cannot go back to him. My happiness gone."

"Because of his nose?"

"It sounds horrible, I am so sorry. It is more than what it seems, I swear to you, Mr. Mudi..." she began to needlessly apologize and shake her head, looking back down to her lap again. I interrupted her.

"No, no, Miss Akinyi, it must be more, I can understand, please explain it to me, there is nothing you could say that would make me think ill of you."

"Truly, sir?"

"Truly."

"Mr. Mudi," she started again, mustering her every ounce of strength, "I am different."

"I think I am coming to understand that."

"Other women, they want fucking, they care about that, big arms, big penis, big chest. I do that only to make Otieno happy. I don't care about it, not at all. Only one thing excites me, only one thing makes me happy." She tapped a delicate fingertip to my nose.

"His nose?"

"Yes. And now... without it, I can never be happy again!"

"Show me what you mean."

Out of pure confusion and curiosity, I took Akinyi's hand and rested her index and middle fingers on my nose. I really wasn't expecting much of a response, but Akinyi positively shuddered with nervous anticipation, her hand, now trembling as it caressed my right nostril.

"Your bridge... starts so high..." she stammered. "Do you use snuff?"

"Not regularly, I'm more of a cigarette man." How stupid I must have sounded.

"I have snuff. I keep it here." She reached between her firm, young breasts and pulled out a tiny pouch. I marveled at how dexterous her hands were, even as they shook, one stroking my septum and the other procuring a very, very liberal pinch of snuff in the other. I stayed very still, and really quite calm considering, and she all but jammed the snuff halfway up my sinuses with her finger. Thus graciously and strangely violated, I instantly started sneezing. I naturally moved to turn my face away and procure my handkerchief, but Akinyi uttered a sharp, "No!" and held my chin firmly in place. I wanted to protest, as I could feel fluid ready to run down my philtrum, but Akinyi then pressed her soft, beautiful, copper-rose lips to my nostrils, covering them completely. Then she sucked hard, pulling down the mucous into her mouth and swallowed.

What was I to do? She seemed so happy! I wrapped my arms around her and let her continue her activities, sucking my nasal secretions, dodging her tongue up my nostrils, tastebuds massaged by cilia. It wasn't bad at all, really. It was really very intimate, very affectionate, and I could understand why this was the act that Akinyi found erotic. Why not noses indeed?

It took a long time for Akinyi to be satisfied with her exploration of my nose, a solid half hour I would guess. When she finished, she throbbed out a sigh of satisfaction and fell backward onto the quilting covering the back of the bench, her hand at her bosom.

"I am sorry," she apologized in her convalescence.

"Don't be sorry. That was really wonderful. It pleased you?"

"That is the only thing that pleases me."

And it became entirely clear to me Akinyi's situation. It would be like Lila or Gladys's husband coming home with no genitalia, Otieno returning without the nose that his wife requires. It was pure tragedy. "You need a nose to make you happy Miss Akinyi. If you want a divorce, I will help figure out a way to protect you. If you don't want a divorce, then my nose is at your disposal, whenever you need it. And not a word to your mother, I promise you."

"Thank you, Mr. Mudi."

"Manik is better."

"I will call you Umba, Umba my nose."

"I will always, always be your nose if you want me to be."

I returned Akinyi to her mother, who smiled at me in her teasing way. "I knew he would help you, girl," she said, collecting her beautiful daughter in her arms. "She will be all right now, Bwom Bwom?"

"I will be all right, Mama," Akinyi replied sweetly, lowering her beautiful pointed chin and pursing her beautiful, sucking lips. And away they went.

Maybe Kaweria is right. Somebody for everybody, something for each person. We all need something different, and that's what makes us human. Akinyi's tastes may be less conventional than mine, but I am by my very existence an unconventional man. And while I can't say that nasal intercourse is really the thing for me, it made me happy to have made Akinyi happy.

If I catch a cold, I should be certain to let her know.

Saturday, March 1, 1913

Further thoughts on my encounter with Akinyi: I am starting to think that I really enjoyed it, strange though it was. I think I liked it because it reduced me to a single part; I was nothing but my nose. No skin, no eye, no belly to think about, just a nose, and I should say, and this is probably Akinyi's influence, my nose is arguably among my least offensive features. I suppose other men might find it reductionist, dehumanizing to be seen as nothing but a single part, but I don't. I have decided that I find it entirely freeing. I should like nothing more than to be just a nose and nothing else. Or maybe just a nose and just a penis. I can see this line of thought going in a bad direction.

Tuesday, March 4, 1913

Sibunya appeal successful! Done at last, done at last, the man is free, his charges erased. Who committed the crime, then? To tell the truth, I could care less. It is a far, far worse thing to punish an innocent man than it is to let a criminal roam free. If I ever free myself from the tyranny of Hadleigh's mediocrity and start my own private practice, I should do nothing but criminal appeals. I think it's the most important function I could possibly perform, and it's something nobody else wants to do. I was born to do the things that nobody else wants to do. Wait, now, was I really? It makes me sound like a Dalit. Well, so be it: I'll be the Dalit of the legal profession.

Friday, March 7, 1913

I had a very odd day today, capping off a very odd few weeks. First of all, I decided to leaf through this notebook and realized that, the prior entry an exception, I really never write about work, which is how I spend almost all of my time. I never put in fewer than ten hours on a weekday, and I rarely take more than one weekend a month away from the office. One would think that I might have more to say about what occupies the majority of my time, and yet I am rarely driven in fits of passion to write about it in my notebook. What do I write about? Eating, drinking, smoking, vomiting, and fucking. It makes me seem entirely base and uncerebral, which is an entirely inaccurate picture of who I am and the way I live. Weeks go by and the only conversation I have with anyone that isn't related to my ongoing cases is fifteen minutes of flirting in the morning with Kaweria. It isn't that I am cold or unsentimental, because I am a warm, blobby, congealed pudding oozing over the edge of the plate with unrestrained sentimentality. It is my focused industriousness that helps keep me from becoming an utterly and completely feeble-brained depressive. I have tried, and failed of course, to explain this crucial element of my personality to Hadleigh and he sees it as entirely paradoxical and impossible, and, since he is a lord, he has decided that I've just made it all up, that I'm actually a spectacular legal automaton who, when he runs out of drafts to proofread, suddenly becomes a mess of emotion. He cannot comprehend having two strains of thought at the same time: at once, fully focused on professional matters and also a fully emotional person. I don't have the same allowance of error that he has been granted due to his station in the world; everything I do must be perfect, and so it is. How lovely it must be to blame every stupid mistake or exhibition of elaborate laziness on one's current emotional state and receive no criticism whatsoever. Hadleigh can be entirely incompetent and all he needs is the shallowest of excuses, and the man hardly has any real feelings anyway! It's all artificial, I know that everything he does and says is theatre, and yet his emotions are so much realer than mine are. Honestly, it makes me feel as if I am nothing but a dream.

Or a nightmare.

Well, anyway, I am a bit messy right now, I am exhausted but cannot sleep. I am resisting the urge to go vomit up the contents of my stomach and have smoked ten cigarettes in the last hour. I am not drinking, not drinking at all, I am not going to drink anymore I don't think, I don't want to drink anymore. I was not just three sheets to the wind a few hours ago, but the whole clothesline, and I should not drink anything else. I am not sure if I am feeling frightened or depressed.

It all started out innocuously enough. Kaweria was inquiring as to my plans for the day at the office in her lovely, charming way.

"Not a long day, I don't think, Miss Kaweria. Home before midnight for certain."

"I worry that you are working yourself into an early grave, Mr. Mudi! You need some evenings away from your books, my friend."

"If only I didn't have to spend my evenings alone, Miss Kaweria, I would be motivated to take time off."

"Do you know, Mr. Mudi, who wants to spend the evening with you?"

And of course my heart began to squeeze itself up in the middle of my chest, because I knew that whatever it was that Kaweria was about to say, I would be at risk of cardiac arrest for excitement and joy. "Please don't say Lord Greenwich, Miss Kaweria."

"Mrs. Gorringe would like you to come to call this evening."

"Mrs. Gorringe! At her farmhouse? I shall drop everything and attend to her Miss Kaweria!"

"Yes, sir, her farmhouse. And I was given express orders to tell you to dress nicely, Mr. Mudi."

"Dress nicely? Miss Kaweria, you know that I have no such ability. I am presuming that my current dress is positively horrible."

"I am only the messenger, Mr. Mudi. I'm sure you'll clean up right well."

"Miss Kaweria, I'm afraid that this is as cleaned up as I can get."

Kaweria gave me her beautiful, chime-like laugh, like the most perfect embodiment of feminine loveliness, brushed some cigarette ash off my lapel and gave a good tug on the bottom of my waistcoat, just to see it ride up again. "If we smoked more carefully, perhaps, Mr. Mudi?"

"It's beyond my abilities, Miss Kaweria, you have said so yourself!"

"Don't arrive too late, Mr. Mudi. Mrs. Gorringe will be waiting for you."

And so, with these special instructions, I left the office with only a silent wag of recognition to Mr. Wangai and not a word to Hadleigh at a respectable five o' clock, headed back to the Cecil, and played at dress-up in the mirror for twenty minutes before going to Lila's farmhouse. I simply cannot dress myself! Why do my clothes never, ever fit properly? Even after holding steady at an even twenty stone for a full week, of which I am inordinately proud, although I absolutely should not be, because I'm still a full stone up since my birthday and probably the fattest man in Mombasa, I just can't get anything to lie nicely. I spend a small fortune on tailoring every month, and yet, never anything to show for it at all. Even things like sleeves, which should not be changeable things, pull up far too high above my cuffs. I always look terrible. Hadleigh would say that Western dress just doesn't suit me, which is probably true, but I refuse to give in! One day I will get a suit that fits me. So, I went with my least offensive option, the pure white linen that I can at least fasten, in spite of buckling at every seam, and also in spite of the glossy red enamel buttons that Hadleigh demanded I add for additional cost, saying that it set off my coloring. I argued that I do not want to emphasize and repeat the color of my red eye, but I submit to him, I always submit to him.

I was greeted by the same collection of servants that waited on me as I spent a day in Lila's bed not long ago, and was guided into Lila's well-appointed parlor, where she was elegantly propped up on a beautiful shantung divan. She was not really dressed, only just delicately wrapped in a Japanese Kimono, but this, of course, mattered nothing to me at all: Lila is always beautiful. When I arrived, I all but cracked my cheeks for smiles and Lila breathlessly called for me, her slender arms outstretched.

"My dearest Magpie!"

I rushed to those most precious, dainty hands and, taking them one in each of my own, stooped over and began kissing them. Ready for an evening together, I thought nothing of it at all, especially since all of

Lila's servants have seen me laying naked in her bed. But then, Lila spoke again, somewhere into the ether behind my head.

"Oh, hello, Stephen dear. This is my friend I've been telling you about, the Honorable Brahmin Manik Mudigonda, Lord Greenwich's law partner in downtown Mombasa. Manik, let me introduce you to my husband, Sir Stephen Gorringe."

Sir Stephen Gorringe! Right there in the room with me! I had been imagining Lila's husband for so long, and he had been, perhaps, the man I hated the most of any in the entire world, George Simpkins, Bill Hendricks, and Pier Kroes included. I had been loathing Sir Stephen Gorringe since my first encounter with Lila, to think, that he would be unkind to her, unkind to this absolute angel of a woman, just the thought of Sir Stephen Gorringe was enough to make me cough up enough venom to poison an elephant. I would fantasize about giving Sir Stephen Gorringe a real dressing down, really tell him what a rat and a monstrous beast he is, and then I'd give him a whollop right in his face and knee him in the groin, and Lila would be so impressed with me, she would just sigh in admiration of my defense of her, and here I was, my sworn enemy not three feet away.

And what did this blight of humanity do? He gave me the nicest, sincerest smile I had ever seen, and put out his hand for me to shake it. "Brahmin Mudigonda, it is a pleasure!" he said.

I must have looked an absolute ass, stooped over his ailing wife, her blue-veined hands pressed against my mottled lips. It was all I could do to force myself not to cry out, "I have fucked your wife many, many times!" I would not have said it as either an apology or a boast, but rather an uncontrollable reflex. Lila must have sensed my confusion, because she gave my hands a squeeze and winked her eye. Up I stood, and put my palm to Sir Stephen's. "A pleasure, Sir Stephen."

I looked at him, I saw him all at once, his visage burned itself into my memory instantly. I don't know what I had been expecting, some hulking, moss-furred beast with claws, perhaps, but he looked so small, just an ordinary elderly Englishman with gray hair and a well-maintained set of muttonchop sideburns, and truly, one of the most benevolent faces I have ever seen. It was his size that struck me the most, because he seemed positively tiny. Looking back on that moment now, I realize that it was not so much that Sir Stephen is small, but that I always forget that I am fully six feet in height. Sir Stephen is most likely an average-sized man. I am actually quite tall, I always forget that. It probably comes from growing up with a father fully six feet and an inch and a brother of fully seven feet at the barest minimum. That and the fact that the only other man who I see standing up with any regularity is Hadleigh, and we are the same height. Hadleigh seems such a natural six-footer, he is always so graceful. And yet, it is I who has been tall his entire life, and Hadleigh who showed no particular gift for height until his middle teens. I suppose I should be happy to be tall. If I ever made a classified advertisement for a wife I could include that. I would write: Extremely high caste Brahmin solicitor, 31, with excellent salary, six feet tall, no signs of balding, and not badly proportioned nose seeks wife that he does not need to share with another husband. Valedictorian University of Calcutta 1903. I wish I had studied fraud more carefully back in Cape Town, but I'm rather certain that an advertisement like that would fall under the definition of misrepresentation.

And so I'm standing there, my grin still in place, having my hand shaken, and Sir Stephen starts overflowing with complimentary speech. "I am so pleased to finally meet you, Brahmin Mudigonda, my wife has spoken about you in such glowing terms, particularly about your kindness to her during her recent illness, and I said to her, 'Lila, I simply must meet this lovely man, you must have him over to our home so that I might repay him for his generosity!' You see, Brahmin Mudigonda, anyone who is as good to my wife as you are should be considered among my dearest friends. She is, and has always been, the light of my life, my greatest joy, and the center of my world since we married thirty years ago this coming December!"

This was Sir Stephen Gorringe, the cruel, insulting, negligent husband? What a sweet and gentle man he is! How hurt he would be if ever he discovered the indiscretions I have had with Lila, it would kill him instantly. He spent the better part of the next hour telling me about his courtship with Lila, how he had never loved any other woman, how his love for her has only grown, especially now, as Lila's illness has brought them yet closer together. He sat beside her on the shantung divan, caressing her hand, and Lila's clear blue eyes fixed on him like a young girl in the first flush of love's passion. "I felt terrible having to leave Lila for business while she was so ill, but she told me how you left your cases to sit beside her for a whole day and keep her company until my return, how you have spoken about India together, your shared experiences in that land that I have never seen. It heartened me, Brahmin Mudigonda, that Lila needn't suffer alone. Your presence in her life has done wonders, and I thank you."

We had a wonderful evening. We talked about the Empire and its diverse lands, we spoke of the joys of traveling in Africa, and, primarily, we shared our love for Lila. It's an odd thing, I do not feel as if Lila has deceived me at all in her characterization of her husband. Even the most kind and loving people can be unkind, and the injury caused by one with whom such deep and lasting love is shared is surely the sharpest and the slowest to heal. In fact, I am, in many ways, very happy. It does make me happy that Lila does not live with some horrible, cruel man, that she is treasured and caressed by a man who truly appreciates her, because, first and foremost, Lila deserves all of the love and happiness in this world. It is for this reason that I also do not regret my affairs with Lila, not in the least, in fact, I feel incredibly privileged to have been welcomed into Lila and Sir Stephen's beautiful world, to have benefitted from their great love.

But it's the fucking that is the problem, isn't it? How I wish I could not only rhapsodize to Sir Stephen about Lila's marvelous sense of humor, but also how well it transfers into the erotic realm, how I wish I could share that happiness with him, tell him all of the real stories of how kind and wonderful Lila has been to me, even to the extent that she soothed and nursed me after I made myself sick. In a different world, he would be proud of his wife, proud of her beauty, her cleverness, and her generosity. But, since it's fucking, it would ruin that poor man's life. Does fucking really need to ruin everything? It's only the greatest thing in life, isn't it? I have never felt so grateful for my red eye and pockmarks, for my piebaldness, for my badly fitting suit and twenty stone physique, how it protected that dear, wonderful man as he walked into his drawing room to find his wife's hands against my lips. I never wish him a moment's unhappiness.

We were served the evening meal at half past nine in a relaxed, casual way, so as not to require Lila to move from her spot on the divan. Afterwards, I was treated to some very old, expensive ports and brandies, and in the spirit of reciprocity, I introduced Sir Stephen to my tobacco formulation, which he, like everyone else, finds is far better than whatever Egyptian dreck they've been smoking. I did not leave to go home until nearly midnight, and as I prepared to go, Sir Stephen spoke softly into my ear: "Brahmin Mudigonda, as you are probably aware, Lord Greenwich has arranged for our estates. Would it be too much to ask if you would not examine the documents for us and make certain that everything is in order? Lila, bless her heart, is a wonderful, brave little soldier, but the doctors are running out of ideas. I would just feel so much better, it would put my mind at ease knowing that you've arranged for everything for us."

"Sir Stephen, it would be nothing but an honor."

"And your fee...?"

"I have no fee for friends. Say not another word."

Sir Stephen did not say another word, but forced a bottle of the much-appreciated brandy into the crook of my left elbow, and, a brave expression on his face, sent me out into the starry Mombasa night. As I made my way back to the Cecil, I drank the lot, took a binge that I can hardly remember, and propped myself up on the mattress to digest the night's events.

I think I'm mostly just sad. Yes, mostly just sad. A bit happy, a bit afraid, but mostly just sad. Lila may belong, truly and fully, to Sir Stephen, but she is, and will always be, my Lila. Oh god, let those doctors get some more ideas.

Wednesday, March 12, 1913

I have decided to make regular visits to Lila's farmhouse, at least once every third day, even if it is only for an hour, even if it means going straight back to the office afterwards. I think that it's what I should do. I wish I knew how to contact Hazel, I would love to bring her along and we three could spend time together. And I wish I could bring Kaweria as well. I would really like that, I would feel almost like a normal person with a normal network of friends.

It's amazing, really, how little perception and reality have to do with one another. I think that anyone who makes my acquaintance, either socially or, more likely, professionally, would be able to ascertain my station in Mombasa society with relative ease. I am obviously Hadleigh's best friend, and, by extension, a key player in the party circuit, and yes, my birthday is something of a local holiday, but this has less to do with any real social power that I wield and more to do with the enormous social power that Hadleigh wields. And while it's true that I have made certain social connections through Hadleigh's celebratory machinations, most of them are little more than acquaintances. For every Gladys, there are a hundred people who know my face but would never consider me a friend. And, among these acquaintances, I would estimate that the vast majority are distinctly prejudiced against me, whether for racial or religious reasons, or just because of my appearance. To be perfectly honest, I dislike, no, hate nearly all of them. The men, I'm talking about the men, really. I like women very much. And still, among all of the women I have known, I serve only two purposes: one that I enjoy and one that I do not. I enjoy being an undetectable sexual outlet. I do not enjoy being an exotic grotesque about which myths hang like garlands of marigolds over a wedding tent so that stereotypes can be enforced and perpetuated. I do also understand how these two purposes are inextricably linked. In order to be the local easy fuck, I must also be the local wog.

So that is what is not real. What is real? Who, if pressed, if I were ever allowed to be honest with the world, would I count among my real friends? Not Hadleigh. I don't actually like him most of the time, and I doubt he has ever had my best interests at heart. That would rule him out as my real friend. Lila, I would say that Lila is my real friend. Hazel. Kaweria. That's about it. Lila, Hazel, Kaweria. Three people who I really care for, who I suspect actually care for me as well. Lila, Lila most of all. Lila is my best friend. That is the true reality of the situation. Lila is my best friend. My best friend is dying.

Friday, March 14, 1913

Five to six thirty spent at Lila's farmhouse today. How is she always in such good spirits? She is in chronic pain, I know she is, I can tell from the way she breathes, the way the air pauses between inhalations and exhalations, how she can only breathe laterally, the ribcage only tipping upwards after each painful breath. In spite of her husband being at home and greeting me, I sat on the edge of her mattress in the bedroom and kissed her hands and face profusely, and let her play with my waistcoat buttons. She pointed out to me that I can sit on my hair now. I can't believe I had not noticed this fact, as it must have been evident for quite a while. If I do not make an effort to sweep the length of my hair to the side, I will find myself seated on at least four inches of hair. "Never in my life had I even imagined a man with hair like yours, Dearest Magpie," she teased. "It looks and feels like industrial-strength silk fishing line and your queue is easily half-a-foot around for thickness."

"Oh Lila," I replied, "There is no special skill in growing hair other than negligence."

"I'm glad you wear it long. Most men, even if blessed with this sort of hair, would not. Why did you choose to grow it?"

"I think it started out as the desire to hide my red eye, but then... well, I don't know really. I just don't care for haircuts. They feel like punishment to me."

"Oh, they are punishment, Dearest Magpie, I agree. They always start out with the best of intentions and end up with disappointment."

"I appreciate that characterization, beautiful Lila. You, my most precious friend, are the opposite of a haircut."

This made her laugh, but her laugh is changed in her pain, shallower, breathier. I knew fair well that I made absolutely no sense at all, but my only goal is to be charming, to let Lila know how much I love her.

Monday, March 17, 1913

I have stayed home from the office today. I feel distinctly unwell and my joints have introduced me to an entirely new kind of pain. I am normally so good with hangovers, but today I am entirely disabled. Kaweria was so sweet to me this morning, finding me still in bed, face buried in my pillow. She crept over so softly, picked up my hair which was dragging on the floor and rested it beside me on my mattress.

"Lord Greenwich's party go well, Mr. Mudi?" she whispered.

"Spectacularly well," I replied, my voice well awake but the rest of me asleep.

"Should I be quiet this morning with the housekeeping?"

"Oh no, I'm fine. Make all the noise that pleases you. I'm sure I'll get up eventually and get out of your way."

"No hurry, Mr. Mudi! Here." She went to my writing desk and brought over my ashtray and my silver cigarette set to my nightstand. "That's how you can help me, Mr. Mudi. That and keeping your hair off the floor. But you stay in bed now, it does not bother me in the least."

"I can sit on my hair now, Miss Kaweria."

"Hush."

And with that imperative, I fell back asleep for probably another three hours. I will probably fall back asleep again after I've examined the events of Hadleigh's "do." I really think I hate Hadleigh, I think I hate him the most of anyone in the whole world. And yet, I do also love him, I do, in a masochistic sort of way, as my polar opposite, much as oppositely charged magnets draw in upon one another.

Well, I don't know what Hadleigh was thinking when he sent that little girl over to talk to me. No, I do know exactly what he was thinking:

Go have a fuck, Manik. It will make you feel better. And yes, that's true, a fuck does make me feel better, but that little girl was pure cruelty.

I shouldn't call her a little girl. She swore that she is twenty-one years of age, but Akinyi is only nineteen and looks like a young woman in full bloom. Akinyi is also twice as beautiful, but that's a silly comparison to make, because Akinyi is probably one of the most beautiful human beings to have ever existed on this earth. It is not as if Eleanor is without her charms, because she is very pretty, but there is something about her that just speaks too much of childishness and bullying. I know that beggars can't be choosers, but really? This was what Hadleigh had in store to cheer me up?

I was seated in my preferred corner, close to the bar, away from the English people, and up bounds this little sprite, a glint of mischief in her green eyes, and addresses me without any reference to decorum or manners. That part does not bother me, no, I like familiarity, this was not the problem.

"You're Manik Mudigonda, aren't you?"

I immediately got to my feet, made a stupid bow and took Eleanor's hand, sure that if anyone were watching me, I would look nothing but a proper gentleman with a piebald face and a red eye. "I am indeed, dear lady. A pleasure to make your acquaintance."

"I came to your birthday party. I didn't know it was for you, though. I just thought it was a party."

"Well, with so many guests, I doubt you were the only one in attendance under any similar misapprehension, dear lady. I'm glad to meet you, Miss...?"

"I'm Eleanor Chiswick, I'm Admiral Chiswick's daughter, he's frightfully important in His Majesty's Royal Navy." She gave a toss to her loose curls, the color of which resembled bleached almonds, or dark wheat, or some other, beautiful, dark golden shade. Hadleigh says the proper term is "blondette," but that means nothing to me. "Horace says that if a girl tells you to do something, you have to do it, is that true?"

"Oh, Mr. Hadleigh said that, did he?"

"Well, is it true or not?"

"Strictly speaking?" I started to feel uncomfortable. I fumbled for a cigarette in order to stall for time. "I wouldn't say that I *have* to obey orders made by a lady, but that I do like making ladies happy, and am inclined to do those things that would bring them pleasure."

"So, yes, then. If I told you to do something, you'd do it, that's what you're saying."

I started puffing away like a chimney, pulling the cigarette to my lips at rapid speed. I felt so awkward at that moment, my face started to heat up. I just couldn't respond. I decided to take a closer look at Eleanor, which was difficult as she stood over a foot below me, a positively tiny young woman. Probably not smaller than my mother was, but she seemed very, very little to me. She pursed her tiny pink lips and sucked her teeth. "Oh, don't worry, I won't tell you do anything stupid, like steal something or break into someone's house."

"I didn't think..."

"I just want to have some fun with you."

"Oh... oh! Oh, grand. Excellent. So, Mr. Hadleigh..."

"Yes, he told me all about you."

"Oh, he did. Fine. Well, that's very nice of him, very nice of you, really, er, Miss Eleanor..."

"So, let's go, then, Manik Mudigonda."

I'm sure I continued to sputter and mumble as Eleanor linked her elbow with mine and, unsmilingly, escorted me upstairs to Hadleigh's own bedroom. Hadleigh has the most absurd bedroom; it is nearly as large as his ballroom, with a huge, ugly lion skin rug on the floor, and a Louis XIV gilded canopy bed, which, in spite of looking quite regal, is just about the most uncomfortable sleeping surface upon which I have ever had the poor fortune to spend the night. It seems soft and luxurious at first glance, purple and gold silk feather comforters layered one on top of one another, but they are so soft that I of the exceptionally heavy body sink right through them and end up with a plank lodged in the middle of my back. Hadleigh and his favors: affairs in the most unpleasant room of his house. Once ensconced in this unsatisfactory chamber, I began to slowly undress, undoing cufflinks, collar, removing jacket and cravat, and I was about to give my little lecture about enforced nudity, when Eleanor interrupted.

"What do you think you're doing? You thoughtless oaf, you're supposed to help me undress first before tending to yourself. Don't you know that? Horace told me that you know how to conduct an affair. Clearly, you do not. Now, come over here and undo the back of my dress."

She seated herself impatiently on the edge of Hadleigh's miserable bed and I quickly attended to her side, my fingers carefully undoing buttons, and slowly sliding yellow satin off Eleanor's tiny shoulders. I then went to work on her corselet, which was, thank goodness, a modern lace-once-and-buckle model with attached garters. Undressed, Eleanor seemed nothing more than a slip of a girl, just barely pubescent, and it bothered me. Her hips were unexpanded and her legs like slender reeds, her breasts were but little soft buds, scooped at the top and pointing upwards, and while her belly was charmingly round, it was not so much due to any natural feminine plumpness, which I positively adore and worship, but from a lack of muscle tone, which correlated with her swayback unaccompanied by any impressive achievement in gluteal development. A child, in so many words. Now, Hadleigh knows fair well that I far prefer the mature ladies, we've been through this a thousand times, and yet, somewhere in the back of his mind, he thinks I yearn for a replacement for my long lost child bride. And perhaps I do, but I remind him that I am thirty-one years old now, and Madhulika, if she had lived, would be twenty-nine. Twenty-nine, that is a suitable age for a woman in my embrace. I still miss her so much, I miss not only her nine year old self, but the twenty-nine year old self that I am deprived of knowing. Her soft, straight hair. Her hare lip. Her voice, her voice I miss the most of all. Her happiness always sounded so wild, so unrestrained. She loved me, sometimes she was rough with me, but she loved me and that made it all right. I would give it all up, everything I have, everything I've ever worked for, just to have her back.

My head is aching me, I have grown morbid.

I haven't eaten yet today. Good. I want to be hungry. I don't want to eat at all today. I just want to smoke today. Lay in bed and smoke and ache and be hungry.

Well, she swore that she was twenty-one. She swore that she had a fiance who was in His Majesty's Royal Navy and who was stationed in Somalia, fighting the territory battles with Hassan's military, the Germans, and the Ottoman Turks. "We shall be married next June when he has a scheduled leave. In England, of course, a real wedding. But I've already had relations several times, too bad for him."

"Too bad indeed," I muttered, convinced that, even if Eleanor was not really twenty-one, she was certainly too old for her youthful appearance. It isn't that she isn't pretty, because she is quite lovely indeed. That little doll's face, those pink lips and delicate, animated cheeks, the mysteriously lovely "blondette" colored hair, her porcelain skin. If only a bit plumper, just a bit plumper, that would be all required to help make her seem a bit more like her age, if her limbs were just a bit fuller, her hips, and she could be positively beautiful, especially with that lovely soft belly, if it were formed from flesh and not from weakness. If I were that young sailor, I would either coax her to eat or give her a baby right away. Well, maybe not a baby right away, she doesn't seem fit and strong enough for childbirth yet, it would be unwise. I would wait until she'd filled out first.

I can't say that I like Eleanor, but I would marry her. That might be something to occupy my time when I am not with Lila, trying to convince Eleanor to marry me instead of her fiancé. That would be diverting, and, of course, a complete waste of time.

While Eleanor told me about her fiancé, whose name has blissfully erased itself from my memory banks, I undressed myself. When I was done, Eleanor sat herself up quite straight, and, midway through a sentence about His Majesty's Royal Navy, she announced, "Just look at that codling! I thought fat men were supposed to have small ones. It's as thick as my wrist."

"Thank you?"

"Well, maybe this will be worthwhile after all and Horace isn't such a stupid boast. It's the least I deserve, what for putting up with a big fat wog with white patches and pockmarks all over himself and a bloody red eye." She sensed some wincing from me at that turn of phrase, and, sensing my weakness, began to crawl across Hadleigh's bed, looking up at me with a cruel expression. "What, did I hurt your feelings?"

I blustered out some vague denials. "You shouldn't care. I like you, you're polite." She then took a handful of my flesh and carefully examined its texture, squeezing me. "You're very big and cushiony, you're like a sofa. I want to sit on you. Get down on all fours, I want to see how good you are for a sofa. Do it. It will make me happy."

And, as if under a spell, I did as I was told and Eleanor sat upon me. She weighed nearly nothing, that was not the problem, but my knees are always problematic, always sore and weak. "Oh, you are a very good sofa. I'd sit on you every day."

And I know I meant to say thank you, but I just couldn't make myself. I felt a little bit faint, to tell the truth, probably the blood wasn't going to my head properly. "Now, bring me over to the mirror, I want to look at myself sitting on you. Come now, man, get a move on." I was definitely feeling dizzy at this point and it took me a few seconds to realize that Eleanor meant for me to crawl on my hands and knees over to Hadleigh's superfluous floor-to-ceiling mirror. This mirror is another feature of Hadleigh's bedroom that irks me, not so much that a floor-to-ceiling mirror is inherently a bad thing, but that only a man as physically attractive as Hadleigh would have one installed so prominently in the room where he has to see himself woken up first thing in the morning. I imagine that he gets out of bed, swipes his fingers through his hair and leaps up, perfect and unrumpled, looks in the mirror and smiles, knowing that today, like all days, was going to be a good day.

And so, I crawled like an obedient servant to the mirror and let Eleanor admire herself seated upon my back. She tried out different poses: drawing her legs up to the side, reclined on her side with one knee cocked up, lying face down with her feet up in the air, the ankles crossed, and then straddling me. It was in this pose that Eleanor discovered my hair. "Look at all your curls! Does it hurt if I pull them?"

"Oh, you can pull them, I don't mind," I replied, and normally, yes, I like a bit of a playful tug, it's just about the best thing about having long hair, having women play with it. But Eleanor must have had my agony in mind, for, instead of taking the lot, or a thick bundle of locks, she began to pull on tiny bunches right at the nape of my neck, and with extreme force, so as to stun me into silent, tooth-grinding agony. She must have sensed my painful response because she began to laugh, a laugh like mean child teasing a bird in a cage.

"You're a sweet boy," she cackled, tangling her fingers in my hair and resting her chest on my trapezius. "I think I do like you after all." She then proceeded to dismount. "Get up, now, boy, stand up. Come on, faster." When she heard both of my knees pop like shotguns she began to laugh again and took me by the wrist, pulling me to Hadleigh's bed. "I'm going to take away your strength, lie down, lie down on your back. Don't say anything, just do it."

I lay down on the bed as I was told, already acutely aware of the bed boards under my spine, and Eleanor slithered on top of me. As anxious as I was, I was enthralled at her touch, that is, until she dug a spindly knee into each of my shoulders in just such a location as to completely impede the movement of my arms. It was fascinating in a way; I think that Eleanor must know about some central nerve that can be pinched up there, I wonder how she learned about that. As my arms went numb, she went to work doing some macramé to my hair, I was unsure exactly what, but she must not have realized that she had positioned her navel directly in front of my mouth. My tongue cannot resist a navel. It made her squeal and leap backwards.

"You did not have permission to do that!" she shouted at me. She had jumped off my chest, so I thought I might try to sit up to apologize when I realized that she had tied my hair to Hadleigh's headboard. "Don't struggle. Stay still. Don't say anything, be quiet." Eleanor then got searching around the room and pulled the two handkerchiefs out of my jacket top pocket. "I don't want you making a sound." Back onto my chest she did climb, putting a knee on either side of my throat, and tied one handkerchief tightly to cover my mouth, and then another around my eyes. I tried not to panic, I stayed still, and I tried not to move my face, tried not to move my arms, and tried to force myself to relax, but I grew curious and my hands began to creep up to the headboard. Immediately, I felt my wrists being bound as well, tied up behind my head. I had, up until this point, been slightly drunk, but just when one needs to be drunk, one is no longer, why is that?

Truth be told, I was terrified. She seemed to vanish for a moment, I could hear nothing, feel no heat from her small body, and I was almost certain that she had left me, naked, gagged and blindfolded with my hair and wrists tied to the headboard, for Hadleigh's cleaning lady to discover in the morning. I waited, I began to sweat, and then to shiver. Tears were threatening to fill my pressed-shut eyes. It seemed like such a long time had passed, she was surely gone. My arms began to spasm. I began to reason with myself: I am a very large person, I have a certain degree of physical strength, there was no way that a little strip of cloth could restrain my arms indefinitely. I could focus all of my strength on those bonds and rip right through, I was sure of it. First, I would force myself to relax, and then I would tear myself free. I took a deep breath, and then another, I felt my legs go limp, my neck, when suddenly I felt Eleanor's lips softly clamp down over the head of my penis. I suddenly lost all interest in freedom.

Oh, Eleanor, cruel mistress, I miss your tongue. First, the lips running tightly down the shaft, and then the tongue, flickering, and then prodding itself under my foreskin, slowly, seductively rolling it down as I quickly became as hard as I could possibly be. This was singularly wonderful, the tight suction, the soft texture of her mouth. "God, you're big, I'll never get the whole thing in," Eleanor muttered, shoving me between her cheek and her gums momentarily. She gave it a try; I could hear her gag a little bit and then laugh. "No, I just can't do it." I could feel her arms creep up my sides, and I could feel her trying to insert me. It took a few tries, and then she gave a huge exhalation, her shins pressed tightly against my hips: I was in. She pinched a nipple between each thumb and forefinger and shuddered. Well, that was it. I gave Eleanor the ride of her life. I had her bouncing so hard, she shrieked with every landing. I may have been her slave for the evening, but I wasn't going to let her think that she had robbed me of all of my strength, all of my power. She started to wail like a siren, and I could feel multiple flushes of fluid running down her passageways, the droplets snaking themselves into my pubic hair, but I was not going to release myself, no, absolutely not, I was going to push myself past the point of ejaculative necessity, because, not only did Eleanor deserve it, but also because there was no way I was releasing my sperm into a seven stone child without any hips. I kept on, harder, yet harder, fighting the urge as best I could, until I felt Eleanor suddenly tighten and dry up. "Oh my God, that is enough!" I stopped immediately. The second my glans hit air I spilled over.

I could hear Eleanor's heavy breathing, I felt her small body throw itself onto the bed, so I stayed relatively calm. Then, a little head propped itself on my stomach and, even in my situation, I could feel nothing but happiness. "You're mad," she said softly. "I didn't want to like you, because you're really incredibly fat and ugly, but I like you very much. You're grand for a fucker. And you're much more comfortable than Hadleigh's bed, this mattress is awful."

I gave my bound head a nod in agreement, and Eleanor burst out laughing. "Oh, you don't have to stay tied up any more, you're a good boy, you've done your job." With that, I could feel Eleanor release the handkerchief around my eyes, and then get to work on my hair, my wrists, saving my mouth for last. Finally free, I stayed still, sticky drops of semen drying and irritating my entire genital region, and gave Eleanor an ingratiating smile. She rewarded me with one of the same, at last. "So what do you want?" she asked me.

"A smoke?"

"All right, you can have a smoke. Then, clean yourself up, you nasty bugger, and I'll let you dress me." My back and neck intensely stiff and sore, Eleanor graciously placed cigarette case and lighter in my right hand. I had earned special privileges, it was apparent. And in that way, being subjected to her trials was extremely worthwhile. Just a bit of abuse and fear, that's all it was. I got my penis sucked and I had a bloody good fuck! Success! And a cigarette afterward.

We returned to the party looking none the worse for wear, except I think my hair looked a bit out of sorts, but that happens from time to time anyway so I doubt anyone noticed anything different. I spent the rest of the night waiting on Eleanor's whimsies: punch, seats, opening purses, putting on and removing wraps. I felt positively useful.

That does it. I am not making the same mistake twice. I let Viola slip through my fingers and let her bind herself to George Simpkins, I am going to give it all I've got to make Eleanor my own. I acknowledge that failure is not only an option, but also a likelihood, but I refuse to give in to regret. I am going to try to marry Eleanor Chiswick and that's that! But first, I'm going to get rid of this hangover and try to get my knees and elbows to bend again.

Tuesday, March 18, 1913

In spite of still feeling very poorly, I made certain to get to the edge of Lila's bed by five o' clock this evening. I am proud of myself that I'm keeping my promises, I want to be a good friend to Lila. There I sat beside her, one leg extended for soreness and the other dangling over the edge, holding her hand, stroking it. I always try to ask her about her health, but she always deflects my questions back to me so that I am forced to talk about myself.

"So, Dearest Magpie, how went Lord Greenwich's party? Hedonistic and expensive, I should guess."

"They're always the same, Lila, you know how it is. I show up late, drink too much, and miss everything."

"Because you're not in the ballroom, I know." I looked down at her beautiful, delicate hand, how perfect, how slender her fingers are. Even as ill as she is, Lila is so beautiful, she is what all slender women ought to look like, the length of her arms, her graceful neck, the elegant mark of her waist. I was a little bit embarrassed, but I trust Lila, I do trust her. "So, did you enjoy yourself?"

"I think I'll try to marry her," I whispered.

"Oh, is that so, my Dearest Tum-Tum!" Lila replied in a soft, cheerful voice, rubbing my belly and smiling at me. I felt so shy. "What is her name? Perhaps I know of her."

"Eleanor Chiswick, Admiral Chiswick's daughter."

"I have met the Admiral, yes, but I don't know his daughter at all. And she hasn't any husband yet?"

"Only a fiancé in His Majesty's Royal Navy, fighting some wars in Somalia. So, I thought I might give it a try."

"I think that's wonderful, Dearest Tum-Tum, it isn't good for you, always being on your own. Do you love her?"

"Of course I love her."

"Well, tell me about her, what is she like?"

"Oh, I don't know..."

"Don't be shy. Come out with the truth, you know it doesn't bother me."

"Well, she's a bit too young for me, really, I wish she were a little older."

"How old, then?"

"Twenty-one, she says."

"I don't think twenty-one is too young for you, Dearest Tum-Tum. You're a very young man yourself, still a boy, really. Probably a younger bride would suit you better."

"Oh, no, her age isn't really the problem... it's..."

"Come now, you can say it."

"Well, Lila, she's a bit too thin... she hasn't... she hasn't any hips."

"Oh dear," Lila replied, her smile only growing, her voice teasing. "Are you sure you want to marry her, Dearest Tum-Tum?"

"I do! I do want to marry her."

"Be honest with me, now. It's not just a lack of hips, is it?"

"She is, she is rather mean to me. But Lila, she, she sucked on me, and I didn't ask for it or anything!"

"Oh, I see! Well, then obviously you have to marry her, don't you, Dearest Tum-Tum? But tell me, how is she mean to you? I'm not sure if I can approve."

"She bullies me. It's not anything I'm unaccustomed to, of course. She's rather rough with me."

"And that will account for your poor knees, wouldn't it, Dearest Magpie?"

"She insults me. She calls me names."

"What sort of names?"

"It's not important."

"Yes, it's very important."

"She called me a wog."

"My sweetest, most precious Dearest Tum-Tum, who I love so much," she began, undoing a few more buttons on my waistcoat and slipping her little hand inside. "I know that you're a very intelligent young man, and you can make decisions perfectly well on your own, but I'd like to think that I know certain things about you. You are such a joy, such a sweet, playful darling, who loves games and frolics and teasing, and you're such a wonderful, adorable flirt. A little play spanking is not the same as sending you home with purple bruises on your wrists, barely able to bend your legs, that isn't really what you like. But even if it were, I would tell you to walk the other way. That girl has no respect for you, Dearest Tum-Tum. You should know better than to let anyone speak to you that way. And it hurts you, I know it does, I see it in that big red eye of yours. Why on earth would you want to marry a girl who would say that to you?"

I felt tears welling up immediately, but I fought them. I really sucked them back down my throat, I fought them like my life depended on it. "I want to get married. I want somebody to love me."

"Then you shouldn't marry that girl, my sweetest, Dearest Tum-Tum," Lila said in the softest, gentlest voice anyone could ever imagine.

"I'm not a good catch. I shouldn't really expect anybody to love me, I should just try to get married so I won't be alone forever."

"I love you."

"I know you do." I could feel my resolve failing, but I decided not to fight anymore. I just let myself choke up, and I just started sobbing like an utter fool. Lila bid me to recline fully beside her and just let the tears saturate her pillow. I just didn't care, I let it all go, and Lila didn't seem to care too much about it, either, she just hushed me and stroked me. I don't know how long I cried but by the time I composed myself enough to head back to the office, seven o' clock was threatening to chime. I shook hands and bid adieu to Sir Stephen as I headed for the front door, and he must have noticed my face, because he nodded his head and said, "I feel the same way very often these days, Brahmin Mudigonda."

Thursday, March 20, 1913

I made the error of trying to talk to Hadleigh about serious emotional topics today, and I feel nothing but regret for this choice. He asked me what I thought of Eleanor, and if I wouldn't mind seeing her again.

"You know I don't turn down seeing any ladies, Hadleigh, that's just against my nature," I explained, acting as if I were out of cigarettes and helping myself to Hadleigh's collection.

"You're right, I don't know why I bother to ask, old boy. It's just that I think she could be persuaded, if you know what I mean. Something having to do with your magic wand no doubt."

"Hadleigh," I started, knowing already that I was making a mistake, "Hadleigh, have you ever wanted to get married?"

"Oh God no. Absolutely not, Manikji, I wouldn't even consider such a thing," he scoffed, tossing his head back as if I'd made some great joke.

"I'd like some advice anyway, I think."

"Advice! Oh, do ask away, Manikji, to think that you consider me expert in some arena."

"All right, now, say you wanted to get married, which I know that you don't, but for the sake of argument, imagine that you wanted to get married, but most of the women you know are either already married or don't like you. And let's just say, in this scenario, that you encountered a woman who wasn't married and that you think does like you. You'd try to marry her, wouldn't you?"

"Hang on a moment, old chap, I can't possibly imagine this sort of setup as myself, I think I'll have to do it as you. Excuse me, I need to get into character." Hadleigh lit himself a cigarette, started to puff on it in the corner of his mouth while scowling, sat in my visitor's chair, unbuttoned half of his waistcoat buttons, and, leaning on his elbow, propped up his head with his fist. Then, he pantomimed sweeping some long hair over his shoulder with his free arm.

"Hadleigh, stop making fun of me, I don't find it humorous in the least."

"Well, I don't find anything humorous, everything is miserable and depressing and I hate myself," he grumbled out, lowering his voice an octave or two. That bastard! I don't know why I put up with him.

"You're not helping me at all. Just try to answer my question, won't you?"

"Oh, all right," Hadleigh conceded, straightening himself up again. "I was just having so much fun being you for a minute."

"It isn't fun being me!"

"Excellent! I should remember that line for the next time I impersonate you, that is a real corker, 'It isn't fun being me,' I'll send the boys at the embassy into fits of laughter with that one. Now, about your question... I've forgotten it."

"My question, Hadleigh, is if you wanted to get married, but no ladies were either eligible or interested but one, would you try to marry her?"

"I suppose I would, yes."

"Even if she weren't terribly nice to you?"

"I don't know. Is she beautiful?"

"In a way."

"Are we talking about Eleanor?"

"In all likelihood."

At that very moment, Hadleigh just burst out laughing so hard that his face went fully red and he started to cough. "You can't marry Eleanor! She and her father hate Indians!"

"But she said that she liked me, and that I was a sweet boy... and you said that she might want to see me again. I'm confused."

"Oh, she likes you perfectly well enough for sexual purposes, and why shouldn't she? But that doesn't mean she refuses to subscribe fully to the belief in the complete superiority of the white race. I like that she said you're a sweet boy, because you are, but don't think you can change her, Manikji. It isn't meant to be. So, what do you say? Do you want to try for this weekend? It is Easter after all, time for celebrating and all that, and I've not planned any party this year, I'm going to Murchison Falls with some old school friends to shoot at some bee-eaters."

"I suppose." There are times when I really wish I could say no.

Saturday, March 22, 1913

Spent an hour with Lila this evening, as tomorrow is Easter Sunday, which neither of us care about very much. Her health is declining, in just these few days her health has declined severely. Her breathing is very impeded, it is obvious. She won't say so, although I have asked in many ways, but I suspect that her cancer is spread. And yet, still so sweet, still so interested in whatever foolishness I have to say, so worried about me. I am a distraction, I know. I have always been Lila's distraction. I did not mention to her that I am seeing Eleanor again, and she did not mention our previous conversation either. She wanted to talk about other things.

"You've put on a bit of weight, Dearest Tum-Tum."

"I always do."

"Have you ever tried fletcherizing?"

"Don't talk to me about fletcherizing, Lila! Do you have any idea what happened to me last year when I tried fletcherizing? Do you remember when I put on two stone in a month right before my thirtieth birthday? My jaw ached and I hadn't a thing to wear."

"Luckily, it was before your birthday! You're one of those people, Dearest Magpie, who looks far better undressed than clothed."

I laughed. I'm so glad Lila still has the strength to flirt with me. It is such a comforting thing, being able to talk to someone who knows the reality of my life so well and who has no prejudices against it. "I'm going to have to disagree with you there, Lila, my beautiful Lila. The less of this skin visible, the better. Yours, on the other hand, I could never see enough of yours."

"What was it like growing up with your coloration, Dearest Magpie?"

"Horrible! No, there was absolutely nothing good about it. Other boys are horrid. And my family was always distressed about it, my father especially. With very few exceptions, I was treated uniformly poorly."

"That's very sad to hear, Dearest Magpie. But tell me, who were the exceptions?"

"My mother, as I grew up, came to love me very much."

"Mother's boy, I should have guessed," Lila teased, stroking the side of my cheek. "I'm sure you were such a good son."

"Not any better than any other son, I wouldn't think. But I did well in school."

"Who else was kind to you? Did you have a girlfriend?"

"I had a wife!"

"You didn't!"

"I most certainly did. For just less than a year. When I was ten, eleven years old." I always get anxiety when I tell a white person about my brief, early marriage. They hardly ever understand the circumstances, and they never understand the emotional bond that I formed with Madhulika. And yet, propped up on the side of Lila's bed with her hand up my waistcoat as it always is, stroking my binge-sore belly, I just felt so secure, so calm. "But you know how it goes, you marry two deformed children to one another, resentment builds up, fear of more deformed children, and they take your wife away from you and she gets burned. I was destroyed, Lila, I was broken in a thousand pieces, and I've never found the glue to put myself back together again."

Lila didn't say a word, but coaxed me to bring my face to hers, and she kissed me on the lips. I could tell that she understood. I wanted to stay longer, but I had to go. I have a new emergency appeal on the hot plate and I can't waste any time. The statute of limitations is almost up, and execution day is even sooner. Time to save a criminal's life! But I hate leaving Lila, I hate it.

Sunday, March 23, 1913

The worst has happened.

I can't go to the funeral, I can't go, I can't. I want to die. I hate myself. Knife down the veins of my wrists, I can do it, I know that I can.

Shiva, Shivaya, I spend my entire life devoted to you, worshipping your powers of destruction, and what do you do to me? You destroy only the people I love. You are cruel, you are heartless, you are no longer god to me, no longer god but demon. I take away your agency, I am going to destroy myself, you can't destroy me, I'll do it myself.

Saturday, March 29, 1913

I'll go the memorial. I should have gone to the funeral, but I just couldn't drag myself. I'll go. I'll try to dress nicely. I'll go, I'll give my sympathy to Sir Stephen. Hazel will be there, I'll see Hazel, Hazel will give me strength. Kaweria may be there as well. Kaweria has been very gentle to me every day this past week.

Sunday, March 30, 1913

Oh, I'm glad to have gone to Lila's memorial, not that it makes me really feel much better, but everyone seemed to have been expecting me. I should have showed up at two o' clock, but I couldn't get myself to arrive on time, it was just impossible. Even Hadleigh was there ahead of me. Sir Stephen approached me and held tight onto my hand, and talked to me for a long time. But I can't think about it now, I'll think about it later.

Thursday, April 3, 1913

Eleanor coming over Sunday afternoon at 3 o' clock. Why am I doing this again?

Friday, April 4, 1913

I think I'm ready to think about Lila's memorial. I ought to at least try. It's either that or binge and drink myself into oblivion every night. I have done nothing but binge for a week and a half. I start out the morning immediately in the binge mindset, I take my first opportunity, whatever it is, and start gorging myself until I'm completely sick, but I'm tending to eat past that point, eat past the nausea, and believe it or not, it does go away, I can break through that wall. I'm only limited by the elasticity of my internal organs. I binged practically the entire day yesterday while I was working at the office and topped it off with another heavy binge, a race that had me breaking a sweat, after I got home, and then, which was the fun part, drank a fifth and a half of gin. I was so drunk and exhausted, but I couldn't sleep because of the aching of my stomach. Since I haven't given myself a break, I am just rock hard distended all of the time, I can't breathe in very much, and my clothes feel like torture devices. I have not had either the inclination or the courage to measure how much weight I've put on, but I think I'm staring three hundred dead in the eye. Maybe I'm not, maybe it just seems that way because I'm so bloated and irritated, if I gave my body a rest, let my stomach empty itself, I might not have changed so much. Not until then can I really know for sure. But I do know that I'm poisoning myself, truly I am, but it's slowly. It's not at all a useful substitute for suicide. So if I don't commit suicide, I shouldn't try to kill myself slowly.

Sir Stephen is a wonderful man. We spoke at length together as soon as I arrived. He held onto my hand, strong, masculine tears glinting in his eyes. That's the way I wish I could be, I wish I could be bereaved in such an understated, elegant, manly way. He asked me about how I had known

Lila, why we had become friends. I made up something innocuous on the spot, some imaginary train ride to Kisumu, a train ride I have never taken, but have been planning to take since the railway's opening. He was fully deceived, I am certain of it, because he then told me, with the greatest sincerity, that he reckoned that he had never seen Lila care so much for someone as much as she cared for me. I hardly knew what to say, but I thanked him, I told him that he was mistaken, for there was only one locus mundi in Lila's heart, which of course belonged to her husband.

The good man introduced me to Lila's daughter, Florence, who had with her a young son in her left hand and another child in her belly. The small boy quickly hid himself behind his mother's dress as soon as I appeared, poor little fellow. To Florence I also told a combination of truths and lies. The truths were that I loved her mother and that I was so sorry for her death. The lies were more preponderant. I told her that Lila often spoke of her daughter, with great love and pride. This was not true. Lila had only ever mentioned Florence to me in passing, and had, in that brief mention, called her a snob and a materialist. I also told her that her mother's great beauty had bestowed itself upon her. This is only half a lie, because Florence is quite a beautiful lady, but clearly only resembles Sir Stephen, and still cannot even hold a candle to Lila's crystal eyes and delicate bearing. Florence acted quite surprised at all I said, but surprised with pleasure. Her greatest surprise was my existence, the fact that her father had introduced me as her late mother's closest friend. "Mother did love India," she fluttered, trying to tie up the loose ends of her mother's life in a neat bow.

Hazel I found in quite a terrible state of unhappiness, she was fighting against the urge to cry and losing terribly. I met her two eldest daughters as well, Elsa and Rosa, pretty young hoydens of fourteen and sixteen, uncertain of how to comfort their mother's sorrow. Although wary of me, they quickly appreciated my desire to intervene, to take my seat beside Hazel, to wrap my arm around her back and to press my forehead against hers. I pulled my hair over both of our faces so that she could cry in private. I told her in a whispering voice to come and find me whenever she needed me, at the office or at home, that I was always available at a moment's notice to help her. I stroked her arm and hushed her until she calmed herself and could let air into her lungs again. "I cannot bear losing anyone else," she confessed to me.

"Nor can I," I replied, in such a way that it comforted Hazel. Not without a certain level of anxiety and discomfort, she introduced me to her daughters properly as her solicitor and her friend. They were disinclined to speak with me, but smiled at me graciously. They did not remain for much longer, as Hazel needed to rest and Elsa, the older girl, thought it was best that she not exhaust herself. Elsa is an understanding daughter, I can see that. She has seen her mother suffer before, she knows the best thing to do.

I considered leaving as well after Hazel departed, because I, too, was feeling some awful strain, but Hadleigh insisted that I stay for a while, so that we could leave together. He kept his arm around my shoulders for the duration of our stay. He spoke with nearly everyone there, mostly people that I did not know better than acquaintances, but I, for the most part, stayed relatively quiet. I smoked, had a few drinks, and listened absently to Hadleigh talk, not really paying attention, but soothed by the familiar sound of his voice. He allowed me to give a final farewell to Sir Stephen, and then we were on our way. As we walked, I realized that he was actually guiding me back the Cecil, which I thought was surprisingly thoughtful. When we had reached our destination, he took both of my hands and looked me in the eyes. "I'm sorry for what I said about Lila. I'm very sorry for you, Manikji. If you need anything at all, you know that you should call for me immediately, don't you? And if you want to stay with me at the cottage, my doors are always open, you do know that, Manikji?"

If I'd had an ounce of strength, I would have told Hadleigh that there was nowhere I'd rather not be than his big bloody cottage, but I thanked him, which was the right thing to do. He had done what he could do to look after me. He let go of my left hand but kept the right, and kissed it. That was very sweet of him. I can't really hate that man, he isn't all bad. He is taking me to his tailor's tomorrow as well, so that I can try and try in vain as always to have a suit made that will fit me. I will ask if I couldn't get some rush tailoring done on the white linen. I need to look my best on Sunday when Eleanor comes to call.

Sunday, April 6, 1913

So, here I am, sitting, smoking, being nervous on Sunday morning after having barely a night of sleep on Saturday night. I don't know why I'm doing this, this is incontrovertibly a terrible idea. I am bereaved, I need to be treated gently. Lila would treat me gently.

What would Lila think of me if she saw me right now? She would smile at me, perhaps, in her wonderful, flirtatious way. She would notice my hair, she would notice my suit, perhaps. I have taken special pains to make myself look and smell the best that I can. If I'm going to be fat, I must at least be fragrant, with good hair, and a suit that buttons. After a morning spent soaking in Yeardley Lavender, I spent over an hour oiling and combing and styling my hair; it is positively gleaming. Every good whore has to have a gimmick. Let's check the mirror again. Face: ugly, pockmarked, and puffy. Eyes: the brown eye is bloodshot; the red eye is also bloodshot. Ears: I'm wearing my gold hoops today, Hadleigh told me that I must. They are growing on me, I think. Teeth: horrifying. Beard: neck completely covered in razor burn, but cheeks are fine. Collar: brand new and white. Cravat: poorly tied, but also brand new and white. Do I try to tie it again? No, I'll just make it worse, surely. And what of the state of my belly? Filled to the brim and aching. Waistcoat, although newly let-out, is already too small. I saw a very handsome fat man the other day by the seaside, his body seemed so well shaped and firm and natural. I was so jealous of him. I just seem to go from over-swollen and taut to soft and squashy. If I must be fat, I'd not be fat like this.

I love cigarettes, cigarettes are marvelous things.

I don't want to see Eleanor, I'm making a mistake. I want my Lila. I just want my Lila, I don't want to be bullied today. I don't want her to hurt me. But I don't want to be by myself.

Sunday, April 6, 1913, continued

Feeling strange, happy and depressed at the same time. I know I haven't been expurgating lately, I've been trying to break the habit, or maybe, if I'm to be honest with myself, I just haven't had the dedication, I've been so unhappy. I ought to take it up again. No particular reason I can think of, as I'm growing resigned to being as fat as I am, but because I think I need the refractory period. I need pain, I need distractions.

Eleanor was quite a distraction. I was so afraid of her arrival, my hands were trembling when I answered the door. She has been gone for about two hours now, but it feels like I've been in this room alone for an age. But my fear, it was so overwhelming, I couldn't think of anything else, it just erased my other concerns, and while fear is awful, it doesn't compare with grief, grief is the absolute worst feeling of them all.

Eleanor can be very lovely when she is dressed up. Olive green georgette, ruffles at the bosom, her hair dressed so elegantly with a positively enormous peridot on a hairpin, revealing the delicate beauty of the nape of her neck. It was not really a Sunday afternoon sort of costume, it was more a dress for seduction. I tried to act no differently than if she had been any other lady, if she had been just an Ethel or a Viola. I greeted her with a kiss and a bow and guided her to my tea table, where I had set up a lovely little spread, hoping to tempt her. Naturally, I had been tempting myself for the previous twenty minutes as I waited for her, and had no self control, but I had been clever enough to order up as much as I did, it looked positively elegant and normal when she arrived. I was pleased with myself, I thought I made a good impression, my confidence started to build and I started to think of marriage once again, as foolish as that sort of thought is. I thought she might be interested in conversation, so I poured us tea, lit myself a cigarette, and gave the lady an expression of subservient admiration.

"You're a very odd duck," she announced, knitting her brow and watching me smoke and take my lumps. "It's as if you thought you were having me over for tea."

I opened my mouth to give an answer, but I had none. Eleanor is so skilled at silencing me. I took a drag and looked into her cruel, green eyes, hoping to find some answer there.

"You've gone about it entirely wrong. I don't want you doing anything I haven't told you to do. I don't like you taking so much liberty. It's bad enough you cancelled for Easter weekend, but Horace said you had a good excuse, that your friend had died of cancer, but you should not have cancelled, that was very bad form. You are supposed to do what I say, you understand? No serving tea. Did I tell you to serve tea?"

"No."

"Then why are you doing it?"

"I thought you might want tea?"

"Come here. Now, boy, come here."

I got up and followed Eleanor's hand gestures until I found myself crouched a few inches from Eleanor's face. She took a sip of tea and sprayed it in my face. That was really enough for me, I had had it. I didn't care if I was going to upset her or not, I was going to state my case.

"That was uncalled for," I replied, keeping as calm as I could, wiping tea from my eyelashes, and I took off my suit jacket, throwing it on the floor like I really didn't give a damn. "I should have cancelled this engagement permanently. I am currently bereaved and I don't have the strength for this sort of thing, this game that you like so much. If you want me to fuck you, I'll be more than happy to oblige, but I'm not going to be your coolie and play along in your mean, childish tussles."

"Oh, you don't want to do what I say, is that what you're saying?" Eleanor replied, an even sharper tone in her voice.

"No, I don't want to do what you say." I felt a huge lump rise up in my throat and my heart began to race and tighten up, I could hardly breathe. I nearly fainted. I watched her slowly get to her feet and stare up at me with this viperish expression.

"You're going to cry, aren't you?"

"Why do you say that?"

"Because you're crying. You're crying, you big fat coward."

"I'm not crying."

"Yes you are, you're crying." And she took off her little black net glove and wiped a tear off my cheek, showing me the little droplet of saltwater as it hung from her fingertip. I was speechless once again. She smiled broadly at me, as if she were truly pleased.

"I like you very much, you're just the right amount of challenge," she said proudly, shaking the tear away. "Undress me, boy."

I got to work, only stopping to wipe my eyes and sniffle occasionally, undoing the hooks at the back of Eleanor's dress. "And I don't like being called boy. I'm ten years your senior, and I don't think you say it in a very nice way," I complained.

"What should I call you, then? Dog? Slave?"

"Manik is my name, I prefer being called Manik."

"What about scum, I could call you scum."

"Manik is fine."

"No, I don't like Manik, I won't call you that."

"You could call me Magpie, you could call me Dearest Magpie. I wouldn't mind that. Or Dearest Samson. Or Dearest Tum-Tum, I like that especially."

"Did you come up with those names on your own?" Eleanor snapped, turning around and prying herself out of her corselet with both arms. I took a step backwards.

"No. Another lover gave them to me," I said as strongly as I could.

"Another lover?"

"Yes."

"Who is she?"

"I won't say."

"Who is she? Tell me at once!" Eleanor, her stockings falling slowly down her thin legs, tapped the center of my chest with one of her little hands. "Who is it?"

"I won't say!" I fought, every cell of my body in refusal.

"It's the dead woman, isn't it? It is! It's the dead woman, the one you're crying about, she gave you those names. Oh, how nice," she hissed, cruelty oozing from her every pore. "I bet you loved it, all those darling little pet names she had for you. I bet it made you feel very special. Well, let me tell you right now that she didn't love you, she just wanted that big club in your trousers. That's how she manipulated you, by making you feel wanted. It's all a lie. It was all about getting what she wanted from you. Aw, poor beastie, makes you cry, doesn't it? Because there's only one reason why any woman would ever want you around, and it's your great big hammer. Magpie, that's the funniest one of all, that she would give you a sweet little name after your horrifying, scaly, speckled skin? Her husband must have been a limp rag."

I tried to look angry, and I was, but I was primarily terrified. I don't know why! I don't know why I would ever be so afraid of somebody whose throat I could crush with one hand, but I can't do that sort of thing anyway, so maybe that's why I was so afraid. I knew my fear was ridiculous, I could see this tiny little girl glaring at me, naked but for some drooping stockings and a peridot hairpin, I should have laughed at her, but I was so frightened, I'm so ashamed of it, but it's the truth, that's how I felt. I had wasted my courage, because now was the time when I should have told her that she didn't know Lila, she didn't know my relationship with Lila, or her relationship with Sir Stephen, that it was none of her business, that she would never know the tenderness, the kindness, the true and genuine caring that Lila possessed as long as she lived. Instead, I broke down crying again, stumbled to my bed, and threw myself upon it face first. I didn't hear Eleanor follow me, but I could feel her hop up onto the bed as well and put her fingers in my hair.

"You can let yourself out," I sobbed, hardly understanding why I was crying.

"You're all upset now, aren't you?" she asked in almost a whisper.

"Yes I am."

"Well, that's silly. What are you so upset about? You're too sensitive. A big bloke like you, you need to toughen up. Come on, give us a kiss."

I cupped my hands around my eyes and wiped my face a few times, and then managed to look up at Eleanor. My eyes were about level with that pretty little spot where the thigh creases against the abdomen, two tiny folds drawing the eye down to the lightly befurred mons veneris, how beautiful it seemed to me at that moment. What a pretty little belly she has, the prettiest thing about her. She picked up my chin in her hand and slowly lifted me to seated. And I kissed her, I kissed her like my life depended on it, I dug my hands into her hair and let my tongue explore all of the curves of her lips. When I paused, she smiled at me, and I felt as if I had earned something.

"Get undressed," she told me.

So I did. I watched Eleanor's eyes and hands and followed her directions, first stripping down, then returning to the bed, then kissing her down her throat, her tiny breasts, and then burying my face between her thighs, the top of my head pressed against her soft belly, my tongue reaching down for her sharp little clitoris. She whispered, "Fuck me on top," but I shook my head no. "You'll suffocate," I replied.

"Don't fight me, do what I say," she whispered again.

"No, I don't think I will!" And I didn't! I picked Eleanor up and placed her like Vlad the Impaler would put an enemy's head on a spike and jostled her on my lap for a good while. Then, I laid down, and, wrapping my arms around her rib cage, pulled her down with me, and cocked up my legs to maintain the connection. I had not done this position in years, but I think I will do it more often, the woman laying on top of my chest on her back, it's like a rear-entry but upside-down, marvelous, marvelous fun, and when I had to come, I just pulled her up a few inches and let myself spurt straight upwards. It felt so transgressive, just pulling her around the way I wanted her, and an awful little part of my mind was telling me that she was so angry at me for being so disobedient, and it drove me crazy, it felt so erotic, so extremely erotic. I was enthralled.

She was angry at me. I loosened my grip on her and just splayed my limbs, laying flat on my back, and she rolled around to face me. She smacked me on the cheek. "You see why I ought to keep you tied up? I can't trust you to obey me until I have you under control."

But I was post-orgasmic, I was hyperventilating and happy, so I just sort of grinned at her and said, "It's great like that, isn't it? I never do it that way, I like it a lot."

"Well, next time, I'll tie you up and you'll have to do what I say."

"All right. But it was great, wasn't it?" She frowned at me and sat herself cross-legged on my stomach and tried to impart some furious gaze upon me, but I could tell that she liked it, she just didn't like that she liked it. I liked somewhat knowing that for all the control she has over me, all of the fear that she inspired in my heart, that in a way I was still the winner. Ugh, I can't believe I just wrote that, as if lovemaking should be a competition of some kind, that's an awful thought. I shouldn't see Eleanor again anytime soon, it's not good for me. She started pinching me very hard all over my body until I arose to clean her with a sponge and dress her. While running the damp sponge over her fragile arms and her sharp, cutting shoulder blades, I don't know why, but I started feeling scared again. I just don't understand myself at all. I started cringing and my heart started going a mile a minute, but I dressed Eleanor quietly, obediently, down to her little black net gloves and her miniscule black satin slippers. She sat in judgment at the tea table and watched me tend to myself, making remarks about how I do everything wrong.

Things that I do wrong: I should wear hosiery and I don't; I should get a new pair of shoes because mine look as if they are one hundred years old; I shouldn't serve cucumber sandwiches with butter, they're only properly served with mayonnaise and dill; I shouldn't use a bristle-brush on my hair because it makes it stand up off my head too much; I shouldn't wear my trousers so low down at my hips because that's why my waistcoat always rides up. I should have explained to Eleanor that I don't mean to wear my trousers so low down at my hips, but when waist measurements are in a constant state of increase, sometimes there's just nowhere else for them to go. I know that tailor's wisdom says that trousers belong at navel-level, but that is also the most uncomfortable place for them to be, especially when one is in the possession of a chronic stomachache.

Eleanor had me walk her to her chauffer which had been stationed two streets away. I was to hold her hand up at her shoulder as if I were doing some odd, 18th-century European court dance. White people never cease to amuse and fascinate me. How I hate them. Then, I head back home to sit utterly and completely still and smoke for two hours before I could manage a single thought in my head. That's what makes it worthwhile to me: the empty, thoughtless head. How comforting that feeling. Just the wind rattling around in there. I should bite the bullet and let Hadleigh dose me with opium some time, but I'm so wary of it. They say it binds up your intestines, and that is the last problem I need. I do a good enough job of that on my own. I would like to vanish from this world and be a thoughtless vapor, though, that I would like. No thoughts, no feelings, just a machine, just do what I'm told to do, be obedient, be in control of my actions but absent, gone. I would be a better person that way, I think.

I wonder what Eleanor would think of me if I were just an obedient shell. Perhaps she would like that. Perhaps she wouldn't like it at all, I don't know. I'm afraid of her. But she says she'll want to see me again, how about that. Isn't that interesting?

Tuesday, April 8, 1913

Starting to feel a bit better, I think. Pulling myself together. Found an excellent precedent for the Mota rape appeal, that cheered me, I thought I was hopeless for that one. Rape cases are so bloody difficult, the law is so confusing and contradictory and every case practically stands alone. Everybody knows that the courts end up deciding these things based on gut feelings and morals and he-said-she-said, honestly, that's the big lie about rape law. It's not murder, in murder we're more than happy to suspend emotion and judgment until every fact has been enumerated, every piece of evidence uncovered, every expert consulted, and there must be real proof to convict. With rape it's not like that, it's either that the man is a monster or the woman is an adulteress. I do miss working with Lord Etheridge on these sorts of cases, he was a rare person, he could keep his head about these sorts of things. But even so, I don't think that there are many people who choose to look at a rape case in the same way that I do, I think that my viewpoint mustn't be shared by many. There are so many things to consider when reading a rape. Of course, there's always the very obvious situations where a woman is horrifyingly brutalized, those are clearly not worth the effort, but you do what you can to lighten the sentence. But there are cases when the rape reads like a breach of trust. And, of course, those rapes that could have become, if not for the psychological weakness of the perpetrator, intensely beautiful romances. Those are the men I try my best to protect. A sudden surge of madness and he ruins his life and the life of the woman he loves. Some men are born that way, I think. It's a very sad thing. I wasn't born that way, I am certain of it, but that doesn't mean that I couldn't understand someone that was. I think that it's like a disease lying dormant within, and then, at the worst possible time, emerges, like herpes blisters on the wedding night. I hope I never get herpes, oh, that would be the end of me.

No, I'm not like that. I like it when women are happy and safe, I like being their big, ugly down coverlet. I know that I don't like feeling afraid. Why would a woman want to feel afraid? I don't understand it when other people make that rationale, "Oh, women like it, they like being afraid." Being afraid is awful.

I miss Lila. She always made me feel so secure.

Saturday, April 12, 1913

Hazel is coming by tomorrow night, oh, I'm so, so glad. I had not seen her since Lila's memorial and I have been worried sick over her. I was starting to worry that her daughters had said something about me to their father, that he had grown suspicious and hurt her, I was really starting to panic. She has just been at home, grieving much like myself, and decided that she would call for me at the office today. I'm so glad to spend some time with her, I shall try my best to make her happy.

Monday, April 14, 1913

I really am feeling much better now, so much better. I think I'll be a good boy and work like mad today, I'll work all night long, and I won't drink, and I'll manage to vomit at least twice. Today will be a good day. Lila would want me to have good days.

Hazel is the perfect antidote to that cruel little girl, she is just so sweet and lovely. Of all the ladies that I've had the pleasure to please, I think that our personalities are the most similar. We both get a bit wrapped up in sadness, it's hard for us to brighten up again. Well, she has done precisely that for me, without a doubt.

It was quite late when she arrived, but I'd not been home more than half an hour anyway at eleven o' clock, and I'd been rushing up room service, trying to shave, smoking and panicking like I always do, up until she arrived. A vision in blue, my Hazel, that very light, pale, crystal blue that will be Lila's eyes to me forever. The first thing she did was fall into my chest and hold me, the laughter of relief escaping gratefully from her lips and from mine. "Oh, thank you so much, dear sweet Manik, I so needed a night to recover," she sighed.

"Why are you thanking me? I'm the one who should be thanking you for the company!" I replied, no more honest words had I ever spoken. It felt so lovely to just say what I wanted to say. I decided to tease her, to make a farce of the evening, and began fiddling with a hook at the back of her gown. "You know, I was recently informed that I don't know how to conduct an affair properly, because I'm always in a rush to take off my clothes, that I'm supposed to undress the lady first, what do you think about that, beautiful Hazel?"

"Oh, poppycock," she laughed, sitting herself on the bed to let me do precisely what she had insulted. "Silliness, rules about affairs. I thought that the whole point of affairs is that rules can be broken."

"Hazel, you read my mind and I love you for it."

"But tell me," she asked, in a soft voice, turning her head over her shoulder slightly as I opened the back of her dress, "what's this I hear about you trying to get married? I've heard some rumors that you're chasing after some young slip of a thing with a fiancé in His Majesty's Royal Navy."

"Just rumors, beautiful Hazel, just rumors. She doesn't like me enough."

"But there was some girl you were considering, then, that's true."

"You know me, Hazel, I'm such a romantic. I gave it a try, I failed, I'll try again at the very next opportunity."

"So you're trying to get married, sweet Manik?" she asked, a more serious tone creeping into her voice.

"Of course I am!" I joked, seating myself in front of Hazel to gently pull off her gloves, roll them down her beautiful long arms. "Don't you think I'd be a good husband?"

"I think you'd be too good of a husband, sweet Manik," she replied, a very, very tender expression on her regal face. "I'm just being selfish, I know."

"What do you mean?"

"If you had a wife I couldn't come running to you in the middle of the night."

"I think in your case, beautiful Hazel, exceptions would have to be made." With that I finished the job and had Hazel before me in all of her unclothed resplendence, and I think she must have liked what I said because she kissed me on the cheek. There was no better time to remove the wig and discover that matters had gotten thoroughly worse, with larger empty patches and the longest hairs knotted against one another. I said nothing but kissed her back. "All right, proper affair, now I get to undress myself, isn't it?"

"What a gentleman you are, sweet Manik."

As I rended at my clothes, I continued my banter; anything to bring that enchanting smile to Hazel's lips. "I was also told recently that I dress exceedingly poorly and that I wear my trousers too low, but truthfully, I knew this already and was hardly insulted at all."

But then, I heard a wince of pain come from Hazel's direction and I halted, anxious to find out its cause. She got up, an expression of sharp agony on her face, and slowly, gingerly, placed a hand on some new stretch marks at the lower edge of my belly. "Oh, Manik, you poor dear."

Concern. I hate concern. "No, they don't hurt, Hazel, it doesn't matter."

"But you've put on so much weight..."

"No, not really, I haven't, my skin just tears easily."

"It can't be comfortable for you..."

"I'm fine. I'm well accustomed to being fat, I'm afraid."

"Are you all right, dear? Is it just Lila?"

And I hung my head ashamed and crossed my arms over my chest for a moment before beginning to stroke Hazel's hand as she sadly examined my red stripes. "Of course it's Lila. I have feelings, you understand."

"Of course I do. I have feelings myself. Oh!" Hazel gasped and put a hand to her mouth, bringing me to seated on the bed beside her. "Oh, I've made you feel badly, I'm so sorry."

"No, don't apologize!" I insisted, shaking my head. "No, you haven't done any such thing. It's actually quite a wonderful thing, to know that you would care so much about me as to be... concerned."

"You say that word, Manik, like it were poison," she said sweetly, smiling in a sad and beautiful way.

"You exaggerate, surely," I chuffed, looking away for a second, only to lift my head to see Hazel's hand twisting and pulling at some of her longer hairs just over the ear. "Hazel."

She looked at me startled, not only shocked that I had noticed that she was about to pull out a hair, but shocked that she was actually doing it. Her face went fully flushed immediately, and it was I who regretted for a moment my expression of concern, but I thought to myself that perhaps I had the tact and the love for this darling, precious woman to do something about her problem in a way that she could never do about mine. I put my hand to Hazel's darling little head, not caring whether it landed on hair or not.

"Hazel, my beautiful Hazel," I started, trying to make my words soft and harmless. "Why do you pull your hair?"

"Because I'm upset," she replied, lowering her eyes.

"Well, I know, of course. But how do you choose a hair to pull?"

"Manik, you don't really want to know about that, do you?" she asked, looking me right in the eyes for a moment. I flashed my red iris at her. "You do really want to know, don't you, well, I suppose if I were to tell anyone, I should tell someone who wants to know."

I smiled at her in my stupid way and plopped my head on her long, lean, elegant thigh like a puppy. She rubbed my chest and began to arrange my hair across her lap, like a blanket. "Just look at all your lovely hair. You'd never want to pull out these beautiful curls, would you?" I just grinned stupidly and shrugged. "Well, this is what my fingers want to do. They go creeping along the edges of where I've just pulled and I feel for a hair that feels harder than the rest, a hard, long hair and it feels wrong, it feels out of place, so first I try to pull it towards hair more like itself, but then it starts to take on an odd texture, a bad texture, so I pull it out. And then, suddenly, a hair beside it, which had been, up until that very second, completely inoffensive, starts to feel hard and bad as well, and I just have to rid myself of that one as well."

"Thank you, Hazel," I purred, nuzzling my head. "That was hard for you, but I'm glad to know."

"No, it wasn't terribly hard for me, no, actually. You make it so easy, Manik. You help me feel safe, my sweet, fat, ugly boy." And I just started to beam with happiness, I just felt rays of sunshine pouring out of my ears, pink clouds of joy covering my eyes. That's what I love to hear, that's my absolute favorite thing in the whole world. Hazel can call me a boy, she can call me a fat, ugly boy and it's wonderful, it means something different, it's said in a loving way, in a sexual way. I love it. I rolled my head to a side and kissed Hazel on the inside of her knee, wrapping my arms around her hips. Oh, hips again, hips at last, how I've missed hips! Nice, big, gorgeous hips with long, slim, beautiful legs attached, Hazel's beautiful legs. And I started to think, love spurred me on to logic, for it never goes in the other direction:

"Hazel, do you think that if all of your hair were the same texture and the same length, you would not want to pull on it?"

She thought about it, she thought very seriously, I could tell by the expression on her face, and she looked down at me and nodded. "Yes, I think that if that were the case, I wouldn't want to pull my hair, it wouldn't give me the same compulsion."

"Well, I have a crazy idea. You already know that I'm a madman and I'm mad, mad for you, but I was just thinking: what if we shaved it all off and let it grow in at the same rate, and you wouldn't pull on it as it grew because it would all feel the same. You'd get your hair back, you'd feel better."

"I couldn't shave off my hair, Manik, you are mad!" she squealed, all but dissolving into laughter, tickling me under the chin.

"And why not? Nobody would ever know, your head is always covered anyway."

"Well, my husband! What would he think?"

"He'd think you were trying to get control of your problem, so that you could be close again." I whispered, opening my eyes wide and stroking Hazel's back.

"Do you really think?"

"Yes I do really think."

"Oh Manik," she intoned, breath coming fast from her lips.

"I know that's what you want."

"You are so good, so kind. Manik, my sweet Manik, you are too good to be any woman's husband."

"With me, beautiful Hazel, flattery gets you everywhere."

It was not ten minutes later that I found myself standing behind Hazel as she sat nervously at my sink, ready to initiate herself into complete baldness. I began mixing my shaving soap and I was singing a little bit, putting on a show, putting a new blade into my razor. She giggled with nerves, but I was rather certain that she was ready. I began to gently cover her dear little head in foam, continuing to sing, until I'd made a darling little white cap for her.

"How it does suit Madam!" I teased, making Hazel's lovely little face burst into apprehensive glee.

"Do you think so? I do, I think I might just walk around with shaving foam all of the time, Manik. And, sweet Manik my dear, has anyone told you that you have quite a lovely voice hidden away in those smoky lungs of yours?"

"I gave singing lessons to some boys in Cape Town when I was in law school there. I'm actually a terrible ham, I love to sing."

"Afrikaner boys?"

"Naturally."

"They must have loved you."

"The moment of truth!" I exclaimed, singing like a Brahmin presiding over a live sacrifice, "The razor is readied, your barber is readied, is my lady readied?"

"I am." Hazel pronounced, tightening her lips and sharpening her gaze.

In less than ten minutes, all of Hazel's remaining hair was clogging up my drain for Kaweria to fish out later. I rinsed away the last shreds, the last split ends, and gently rubbed my hand over the pale, bare scalp. We looked in the mirror together. Hazel was clearly acting in courage, in hopes of bringing her husband close to her once again, but when I saw her new appearance, I was overwhelmed.

"Hazel!" I all but shouted. "Hazel, you are beautiful!"

"What are you talking about, Manik?"

"Hazel, you should never have any hair at all, look right in that mirror at how impossibly beautiful you are. You look like an ethereal super-human goddess of beauty. Oh, Hazel, Hazel, I must kiss you, forgive me, but I can restrain myself no longer."

"Oh, you sweet, wonderful madman," Hazel laughed, and then laughed and cried at the same time as I began to kiss her, and then swept her up in my arms, carrying her like the most beautiful, fragile, porcelain doll, her long, beautiful legs draped over my forearm. I carried her to the bed as if she were my own bride, and how I wished that she was.

"Hazel, Hazel, my darling, the center of my universe," I gushed, unable to think of anything else in the world. "You will not need to wait for your hair to grow back to recapture your husband's heart, because the moment he sees you like this, he will melt, I tell you, melt into a sweet, sticky pool of passion for you, because you are easily the most beautiful thing in all creation. And you can trust me that I know what I'm talking about, as only the ugliest thing in all creation could recognize his polar opposite."

And so we fell deeply into one another's embrace, arms holding one another close at the sides, and Hazel stroked me down the leg with her slender ankle, opening her most beautiful dewy orchid of worship for me, and I made love like I had not made love since Hazel was last in my bed. One does not fuck Hazel Kroes, one worships Hazel Kroes, one makes deep, emotional love to Hazel Kroes. And once again! Her pillow talk! Just thinking about the way Hazel's voice sounds when she pillow talks at me, it is electrifying.

"Tell me that I'm beautiful, Manik."

"You are so beautiful."

"Tell me again."

"You are so beautiful."

"Do you love me?"

"I love you!"

"Say you love me again."

"I love you!"

"Say it again, Manik!"

"I love you!"

"Tell me that I'm beautiful and that you love me."

"You're beautiful and I love you!"

"Don't come yet, don't come yet. Keep at it, Manik. Do you still think I'm beautiful?"

"You're beautiful! And I'm going to come."

"Don't come yet, I want to come, don't come yet."

"I'm trying!"

"Don't come yet!"

"I'm trying!"

And she let out a scream! A blood-curdling, spectacular scream that I swear totally scared away all of the gnats at my window, it was amazing. If I weren't able to see her face, I would have thought her dying. She wrapped one fist around the bed sheets and one around a hank of my hair and absolutely rattled the bed with vibration. And then I came. Inside her again, damn, but I know that she likes it that way. I loved every damn second of it. And the cuddling afterwards, the kissing, all of it, Hazel's beautiful arms and legs all over me, her beautiful, beautiful, gleaming, perfect, flawless bald head, I could not count how many times I kissed it, caressed it. I love her. Stupid me, I love her so much. Part of me wishes I did make her pregnant, I would take her for my own, I would love her daughters and her eldest son like they were my own children, and we would forget all about those twenty years of Pier Kroes as if they were just a mistake, just a dream. A beautiful wife, four children in one fell swoop! My every wish granted in a moment of ecstasy, one simultaneous orgasm of incomparable perfection. Oh, Hazel, I will take you back to Rhodesia. I will treasure you for all eternity. But I know I didn't, I know I didn't make her pregnant, Hazel knows better than that. She wants Pier to love her again, I know, that's what this was all about. So, perhaps, I've given her something better than my eternal love and companionship. I've given her back her marriage. And for that I should be happy. I was a good person last night, curled up next to that beautiful woman, fast asleep in my arms, the moonlight reflecting luminescent white off her scalp. Off she went in the morning, so happy she was, and so was I.

Monday, April 14, 1913, continued

I cannot concentrate, I just need to have my curiosity satisfied, just this once! It's not fair! Not fair at all. Ugh, I am such a stupid, over-sexed waste of space.

I honestly thought it had to be a rat, or at least a very impressive insect that made Kaweria screech like that this morning, I was probably more afraid than she was. So, I asked her if she was all right, and what is my answer?

"Mr. Mudi, there are *black hairs* in your drain!"

And I just burst out laughing. "Miss Kaweria, I think I'm just getting old and my hair is going black, that's all."

"Look at this!" she announced, an expression of utter shock and horror on her face, a fish hook hung with both black and white hairs tangled together. She was not amused. I decided to tell her the truth, she is the light of my life.

"I cut someone's hair for her the other day, there's nothing to get concerned about, Miss Kaweria, I'm sorry to have startled you," I apologized, embarrassedly lighting myself a cigarette.

"You're not satisfied just being a solicitor then, Mr. Mudi, you want to be a barber as well? I can't help but worry about you, my friend," she teased breathlessly, calming herself down.

"Do you want to know the truth, Miss Kaweria?"

"It is easier than playing detective, Mr. Mudi."

"I cut Mrs. Kroes hair for her."

"Mrs. Kroes?" Her voice became interested, tender and sweet, and, putting the fish hook into the bin, she came closer to me and started fiddling with my cravat. "You did cut Mrs. Kroes' hair?"

"More specifically, I helped her shave it off so that way it can all grow back at the same length and she won't want to pull it out anymore." I knew that I was taking a risk by confessing Hazel's problem aloud to Kaweria, but I am pretty certain that the two ladies have grown to be very good friends since Lila became ill, and I made an assumption. I could tell from the expression on Kaweria's face that I had assumed correctly.

"She let you take care of that for her, Mr. Mudi? She must trust you very much," she sweetly intoned, trying to affix my cravat in place with a ruby stud which had been a birthday gift from Hadleigh a few years ago. "I'm so glad she's finally done it, I have been telling her that it's the only way."

"Did you really, Miss Kaweria?" Now it was my turn to be surprised and intrigued. "Yes, it is the only way for her, isn't it?"

"I'll bet she looks much better as well, Mr. Mudi." What a sweet and flirtatious way Kaweria has in saying such innocent, simple things, I love her so.

"To tell the truth, Miss Kaweria, she looks very beautiful."

"I knew that she would! Some people look better with a bare head. She has a long neck and a good chin, you know, like mine. That's why I keep my hair shaved. Then, there are people like you, Mr. Mudi, who are best suited for long hair. Everyone is different, different faces, different bones, but we all try to be beautiful, don't we, Mr. Mudi?"

And with that, Kaweria took my red satin ribbon from my bureau top and, wrapping her arms around my neck, tied a perfect bow around my queue without even having to look at it, and pinched me on the chin like she does. What a positively marvelous lady she is, I love her so much, I could not believe how candidly she spoke with me, how kindly, how unnecessarily flattering, jokes about being beautiful, she is just wonderful. I know that I just stood there smiling and idiotic, smoking like a chimney, in awe of her. I was in such awe of her that it took me a few seconds to realize that since Kaweria always wears a very stylish red or green wrap around her head, that I did not know that she kept her head shaved as well. Now I am desperately intrigued and I want so see so badly! Oh, I want to see how beautiful she is, my desire is overpowering. But I can't just ask, it's not the sort of thing I could do, even now all of this time we've known one another, all of the strange closeness that we've developed, that I don't know where she lives, I don't know if she is married, I don't know if she has any children, and, to be perfectly honest, I've only known her real name for a few months. How could I ask to see her without her wrap? I simply can't, it would be a terrible violation.

How I wish I could do the things that she can do, by virtue of being a lady. She can fix my cravat for me, tie up my hair for me. I wish I could do things like that for her.

I know that Kaweria is miles too good for me, and hasn't any interest in me beyond that of some sort of odd friendship, but why do I have so little courage to ask her more about herself? What is it that makes me so anxious? What's holding me back? For women I care for far less I have stripped off all of my clothes and demanded detailed accounts of their everyday lives. Why should Kaweria be so different for me? But she is, she is different. She is different because she is perfect. Kaweria is perfect, she is everything any woman would ever want to be: beautiful, intelligent, compassionate, tolerant, industrious, clever, flirtatious, understanding, patient. Hazel is depressive, Eleanor is mean, Njeri is condescending, Gladys is frivolous, Viola is fussy, Akinyi is a truly odd young lady, and even Lila was proud. Kaweria is perfect. She is perfect and I want to see her perfectly shorn head.

Thursday, April 17, 1913

I had a very clear and distinct sense memory today. I had just left the Cecil for my brief constitutional to the office, and I was having a smoke and clearing my head as always, nothing out of the ordinary. Kaweria and I had exchanged some very lovely pleasantries, helped me when my earring fell behind my bed stand, and I was just ruminating on how fortunate I am to have her close to me, especially as I am coping with Lila's death, and as if I were living it all again, I was ten years old, at home in Varanasi, on some early morning. This was back when Madhulika was my wife, back when I was at my most happy. She almost always arose before me, and would sometimes shake me awake, as hard as she could, so we could play together. That was what we did, we played together. We were too young for anything else, I doubt she knew anything, and I knew absolutely nothing at all, I had been kept as innocent as is possible to keep a ten year old Brahmin husband who already shares a bed with his wife. I was a natural sound sleeper in those days, my head loved the pillow, and I would be so groggy, but Madhulika would do anything in her power to wake me up so I could get dressed, do puja, and then go out into the oleander trees and play games with her all day. Sometimes I was really reluctant to arise, but sometimes I would make it a game as well. She would shake my shoulders, "Manik, Manik, wake up, hurry! It's morning, wake up!" And she'd get me all the way seated just to watch me fall flat back onto the mattress in refusal. "No! Don't go back to sleep, wake up!" This one morning, I must have really given her the impression that I was absolutely not going to get up on my own, because she started to dress me, she pulled the kurta over my head, she began putting the rings on my fingers, and started frantically rubbing orange oil into my hair. I could not stay asleep through that rough treatment, it was impossible, so I decided to give in and open my eyes, and there she was, seated beside me, using both of her little henna-patterned hands to thread the earring through my left ear. Her expression was so intent, and her face so close to me, but her gaze was at my ear, not into my eyes, and for some reason, it made me so happy. I watched her for a few seconds until she felt the heat coming from my red eye and she saw that I was awake, smiling at her, and she stopped her rush and smiled back at me. Madhulika's smile was like nothing else in the world. She had the most beautiful cleft lip that has ever existed. And I think it was at that moment that I realized that not only were we husband and wife, and not only were we friends and playmates, but that there was something else there, something that we would know one day when we were older, another kind of love.

I would have loved her forever. I would have been a good husband, I would have loved and protected her, I would have been faithful to her, I would always have stayed close by her side. I was robbed of that, it was stolen from me. But I can remember that morning, watching Madhulika lace in my earring, I can remember her black eyelashes hooded deeply over her eyes as she concentrated, the sound of her breath, the careful touch of her hands, the smell of the orange oil. Why do I remember this now, and why so clearly? I don't know. I don't understand myself.

Wednesday, April 23, 1913

I may have to re-think my disdain for personal shopping. I have always disliked buying things for myself, it always seems like such an unpleasant task, so intimate, so uncomfortable. Part of that may come from some inborn Brahmin prejudice against doing absolutely anything for oneself, and always having someone else do things for me, I do prefer that very strongly. It's one of the Cecil's great perks, I just leave my list in an envelope around the door handle and lo and behold, no matter what time of night I come home, everything I want will be right there, waiting for me, wrapped in plain white paper. Specifically, there are three shopping tasks that I cannot bear to do myself: the tobacconist, the off-license, and the candy shop. Well, actually, I don't mind going to the tobacconist, and, in fact, I rather like it, it's quite genteel, elegant, and discreet. It's a gentleman's place. The only problem is that the tobacconist in downtown Mombasa is adjacent to the off-license and the candy store, and I cannot walk past those stores without getting into trouble, or, at least, feeling awkward and terrible. When I find myself in Nairobi or in Malindi, I go the tobacconist myself without reservations, but not when I am at home. It's one thing to come home to a beautiful white paper parcel containing three kilos of chocolate and two bottles of scotch whiskey and it's another thing to ask a shop keeper to give them to you. A tobacconist is not going to think much of a purchase of fifty pre-rolled cigarettes, even if I were to go in and buy them every single day. A shop keeper in an off-license or a candy shop will absolutely think quite a lot about someone who looks like me coming in and making similar high-volume purchases on a daily basis. When I was in law school, Hadleigh was my candy shop liaison, he never minded, and surely, nobody thought anything of it at all, because he is so flawless in his appearance, and when he goes into an off-license, well, everyone knows that he is constantly entertaining and is incredibly popular and also doesn't think a thing of it. I prefer not having to make human contact when obtaining these sensitive items.

But perhaps, given today's events, I should revise my feelings. Today, while starting in an awful way, ended quite nicely. The awful beginning: in spite of having had relatively good control of myself for the last few days, I was just hit with depression not long into the workday. Lila. Lila and Madhulika. I was writing, working on another new rape with Mr. Faraday, he has been a poor replacement for Lord Etheridge, and I just broke down, I was inconsolable. Normally, this would not be a problem, my office door is shut and nobody bothers me for the most part, except, of course, for Hadleigh, who burst in at that very moment, saw me in a state, and ordered me to go out into the sunshine, have a smoke, take a walk, and not come back until I'd pulled myself together. I wasn't going to argue. My first inclination was to go to the seashore, which is, of course, my favorite place. The only coastline more beautiful than Mombasa's is the Cape of Good Hope, that is probably the most beautiful place in the entire world, and I should have gone, that probably would have done me an absolute world of good, but I noticed that my cigarette case was half empty and I'd lost track of how many I'd smoked that day, and it was only about eleven o' clock, so I figured I would just pop into the tobacconist on the way to the seashore and not get into any trouble at all. Tobacconist: no trouble. Candy shop next to tobacconist: trouble. But I figured, I'm a grown man, I can go into a candy shop and not make a scene, and in I went, putting on some very false confidence because I knew that today was going to be a bad decision and poor control sort of a day, and, naturally, made a scene. A twenty-one stone piebald Indian man in a suit that is splitting at the seams enters a candy shop. He buys, almost accidentally, about a quarter of the shop's inventory, including some varieties of candy (horehound drops), that he does not even like (ate them anyway), and this is an act of considerable restraint on his part. A scene. And there was this very pretty older Luo lady watching me behind the counter, I was thinking that she must have been the mother of the girl at the register, just staring at me, wide-eyed, fascinated practically, and I am humiliated. But, I make it out alive and decide that, well, since I did so well at the candy shop, there can't be any harm in going next door to the off-license and making an ass of myself in there as well. It is not five minutes later that, cradled in my arms are two bottles of Bols gin and a bottle of old sherry to counteract the fact that I'd just purchased two bottles of Bols gin, which is foul and obscene, and I turn around to exit in shame and haste and there is that beautiful Luo lady again, at the doorway, looking right at me. I think sweat must have started to rain down my face, I just couldn't believe it. I didn't know what to do. Pretend that I didn't recognize her? Pretend that she wasn't there at all? Will myself to have a heart attack and die? Will myself to become suddenly invisible?

She smiled at me. I approached the doorway, hoping for the best. "I thought that I might recognize you, sir," she said in somewhat heavily accented English. "You work in town?"

Cigarette well-adhered to my bottom lip, I decided to act as if I were fine, as if there could be nothing out of the ordinary going on, nothing upsetting me at all. "Yes, I do, dear lady. I am one of the solicitors at the edge of the road to the seashore. Surely you've seen our sign."

"Yes," she replied thoughtfully, lowering her eyelids slightly and looking at me with just a bit too much discernment. "Lord Greenwich and..."

"I'm the and. Manik Mudigonda at your service, madam." I had no free hand, so, balancing cigarette, bottles, and bags, gave her a good, woggy bow.

"Walk with me sir," she requested, some shy suspicion in her voice. "I may have some need for you."

"Oh, do you, madam?" I asked, at once immediately relieved. "Yes, of course, we shall depart." The lady took hold of my elbow and I began to talk about the practice. "We do practically everything, Lord Greenwich and I, but we have our specialties. Lord Greenwich's strengths lie in family law, in divorce and inheritance, wills and trusts and those sorts of matters. My inclination leans more towards criminal cases, but I'm mostly an appeals man, nobody knows me but for the name at the top of the document in court. But we can do just about anything, lawsuits, malpractice, negligence, anything. What did you have in mind, dear lady?"

"My daughter, she is betrothed, but I want to break the contract for her, Mr, er..."

"Mudigonda. You can call me Mr. Mudi, everybody does."

"Solicitors can break contracts for marriage, can't they, Mr. Mudi?"

"Well, it depends. That's more Lord Greenwich's expertise, you could always consult with him, I'm sure he'd think up some remedy for you and your daughter."

"Oh no, Mr. Mudi, I think I would only want you." And she looked at me in an odd way, as if she were surveying a plot of land for purchase. "Where do you come from, sir?"

"Me? South Africa of course!"

"South Africa? No, sir, where do you really come from?" I love playing coy, it never fails to bring a smile.

"India, dear lady. India. Perhaps you've heard of Benares, the city of funeral pyres?"

"Yes, sir, I have heard of it," she replied, that suspicious tone re-emerging once again. I had no idea where she was leading me, I felt as if we were wandering with no direction at all in town, a very odd thing. "I thought you might be an Indian, but I..."

"I know, most Indians don't come in this color pattern, I understand, dear lady."

"And most Indians aren't so nice and big like you are, either, Mr. Mudi." The Luo appreciation for a large physique is something that never ceases to cheer me, even on the worst days. "You are easily twice the size of my daughter's man."

"Is that so, Miss...?"

"Dede Aboyo, Miss Dede."

"Miss Dede."

"He is no good, that young man. A bad temper, no grace, not good with people. I want better for my daughter, you see."

"Naturally, of course, you would want the best match for your daughter, I understand completely, Miss Dede."

"Your wife is a lucky woman, Mr. Mudi."

I laughed bit, hiding the sadness in my heart with a smile. "If only that I had a wife, Miss Dede."

"No wife, Mr. Mudi? Perhaps you should marry my daughter!"

"That pretty young girl behind the register?"

"Yes, that is my daughter, that is my Subira. You find her pretty?"

"How old is she, Miss Dede?"

"She is nearly fourteen, sir, and a smart girl, a hard worker."

"Fourteen? No, no, no! I am much, much too old for her, no, it can't be done, not at all, Miss Dede. Thank you for the flattery, that is very kind, I'll half the bill for you."

"Oh, no young girl for you, Mr. Mudi?" Miss Dede said softly, in an almost teasing way.

"No young girl for me, Miss Dede. She wouldn't like me anyway. Young girls, they like handsome husbands with beautiful clear faces, strong arms, you know, they don't like men that look like me, you know how it is, Miss Dede. She'd be running back home to you in half a day."

She took a look at my face carefully again, and suddenly took notice of my red eye, which gave her a start, of course. "You are probably right, Mr. Mudi. For Subira, you are probably not to her liking."

"And I've had smallpox, bad match all around, Miss Dede."

"It is so hard to find a good match for a good daughter," she sighed.

"I could only imagine, Miss Dede."

At this point, we had drifted out of Mombasa proper into Kuze and we were passing by a relatively well-known house of ill-repute. From said house, a familiar voice was heard calling out to me: "Oh, Mr. Mudi! Hello Mr. Mudi! Give us a cigarette, Mr. Mudi!"

It was my friend, Nia, whom I have had the pleasure not to see for nearly a full year. Miss Dede gave me quite the expression to see a Swahili prostitute calling out to me with such affection and familiarity. "Do you spend much time in such company, Mr. Mudi?"

"Not at all!" I broke out laughing, this being, of course, the truth. "I handle their legal matters only, Miss Dede. Solicitors are not only for the upstanding, but for everyone, you see. And anyway, truth be told, Miss Dede, even if I were to spend much time in such company, it would be a complicated matter. We would not know who should pay whom."

"That is very interesting Mr. Mudi you should say," Miss Dede replied, once again deep in thought; the woman must be a philosopher, thought is constantly evident in her eyes.

"You wouldn't mind, actually, Miss Dede? I have to go light a cigarette for a friend."

"Please, Mr. Mudi. I will come to your office another day, I did not mean to interrupt your plans." And the lady quickly but gently released my elbow and started backing away from me. "I will come to your office another day, Mr. Mudi. It was very nice to meet you!" And in half a second, she vanished. Nia, had, of course, not ceased her calling out to me, the waving of her hands, and I was most certainly obliged to go provide her with a smoke. As I finally made my approach, she began clapping her hands and ululating for me. I cannot count how many times I have gotten Nia and her sisters out of trouble, but I have a deep, lasting affection for the young lady and her consistently ebullient personality.

Carefully putting down my parcels, I produced a cigarette for the lady and she took it with an expression of extreme happiness. What a stupid show I put on with my lighter, I am such a fool for women.

"I miss you, my friend, Mr. Mudi!" she laughed, taking her dainty puffs and grinning at me. "How is business! I never see you!"

"Business is booming, Miss Nia!" I cheerfully replied, so glad that this was true, I have not a single debt and I am very proud of my savings. "In one way I am glad not to see you, Miss Nia, because I know that means things are going well for you, but seeing you always makes the day much better."

"Sit! Sit down with me, talk to me, my friend!" She pulled up the wicker rocking chair for me and fluffed the cushions for me, sweet lady. "So, business is good for you? Law business?"

"Law business, yes, of course."

"Married yet, Mr. Mudi?"

"No, not yet, Miss Nia."

"That lady not your wife?"

"That lady who was with me? No, no, I don't even know that lady, Miss Nia! She just wanted to talk about business, she wants me to break a contract for her, law business, law business only."

"Oh, she looked like your wife! You look married, Mr. Mudi. Something different about you, you look married."

"No, no, Miss Nia, you are confusing looking married with looking fatter."

"That's what it is, yes!" Nia laughed, clapping her hands again. "She likes you, though, Mr. Mudi, I can tell. Law business going well, love business must also be going well, one would guess from the looks of your long hair."

"Love business is better than ever, Miss Nia."

"That is what I like best about you, Mr. Mudi. You really understand what it's like for the ladies like myself. So understanding and good. No need for any wife if the love business is doing well, Mr. Mudi, I would think."

"I wish I could feel that way, Miss Nia. You know how I am, romantic."

"I am romantic, too! One day a prince will discover me, don't you think, Mr. Mudi?"

"I keep telling you, Miss Nia, I am that prince! In India I was a prince."

"I know you are a true prince, Mr. Mudi, but I don't mean like that sort of prince! I mean a prince with a palace and a life of leisure."

"I had a palace! I lived in a palace for most of my life."

"But Mr. Mudi..."

"I know, I know, a handsome prince. And yes, I do think that handsome prince will discover you one day, Miss Nia, in fact, I have no doubt in my mind."

Miss Nia continued to tell me some stories about her recent adventures, all excellent stories, all instantly forgotten as soon as I left her side. She made me a julep and chatted at me while we smoked in the midday sunlight for at least an hour, when a young sailor appeared, clearly in need of some attention. I bid my adieus and headed back to the office at last, with cigarettes, candy, and alcohol in tow. I started to panic that I had, perhaps, been gone too long and that trouble would be waiting for me, but Mr. Wangai seemed perfectly calm and Hadleigh was not even there himself, so everything seems to be fine for now.

I really ought to, if not go buy my huge quantities of vice-related necessities by myself, go into town more often, socialize without Hadleigh around. I go through these extroverted phases sometimes, and I'll go looking for a chat in town, but they are few and far between. I should make myself go on casual wanders more often. Ladies, I like talking to ladies. That's it, mostly. I should go talk to ladies with far greater frequency. It's just about the only thing that really does make me happy. I will let someone else go to the tobacconist, the candy shop, and the off-license for me, though, I can't handle that sort of stress on regular basis.

Thursday, April 24, 1913

Hadleigh is acting strangely. That is an odd sentence to write, especially since Hadleigh is invariably strange all of the time, but he is acting strangely in a new and different way, in a way that betrays some sort of anxiety or worry. I won't ask him about it, no, I shouldn't want to know anyway, but I will keep an eye on him. He ingratiates himself too willingly to some of the settlers here, and he gets himself into awkward positions sometimes, promises that can't be kept, those sorts of circumstances. I do not want to involve myself in those sorts of things.

Friday, April 25, 1913

Mr. Wangai's daughter is suddenly overwhelmingly beautiful! I remember Wakesho when she was just a little girl, oh, incredible how time flies. I'm glad that Mr. Wangai is in no rush to marry her away, she is his youngest child, that last little surprise child that helps remind everyone of how old they are, and, at the same time, makes them feel young. If I had a daughter like Wakesho, I would want to keep her at home as long as she could bear it, protect her, teach her about life so that she would not have to learn it on her own, thrown into the water of adulthood to drown alone. And no love matches, absolutely not. I know how awful men are, I would vet every suitor myself, I would research them and subject them to every possible test and trial.

Good question for daughter's suitors: Would you consider yourself a patient man or a man of action? This is a good question because it seems to have two perfectly good answers and the young imbecile would fall into a sense of false security and tell the truth. Of course, there is only one good answer, which is to be patient. I would not marry my daughter to any man who would not be willing to wait for her for five years, ten years, twenty years if necessary. And nobody who considers himself romantic, that is just code for depressive. No bad tempers, no angry men. No dangerous professions, no surgeons or soldiers.

If I had a daughter I would tell her the truth about everything, I would never, ever lie to her, even about myself. If I had a son, though, I might be inclined to obscure a few certain truths. My speculation doesn't matter anyway, I haven't any children and doubt I ever shall, unless I've accidentally impregnated Hazel, which is unlikely.

Wednesday, April 30, 1913

Miss Dede came to the office today, that was a surprise. I wasn't really expecting her to come at all, not after being witness to Nia's show of affection, but I suppose she does need that contract broken. I strongly dislike the betrothal contracts that the English have imposed on the Kenyan people in the spirit of compromise; they do not make any cultural sense and end up making more problems than solving them. They are supposed to take into account the differences in marital traditions between the various groups, but Luo marriage has nothing to do with Kikuyu marriage has nothing to do with Muslim marriage, nothing at all! And the Maasai want nothing to do with any of it, who could blame them, and yet the English insist that they, too, are included under this system, which I am certain they could only state with such confidence in the case of a cheerful ignorance of reality. In the end, what you have is a useless document which is simultaneously too vague and too inflexible. Bizarre and irritating. This is why I am normally more than happy to throw these matters to Hadleigh, he loves pulling strings and making deals with the higher-ups, getting around the rules rather than conforming to them. Give me a murderer or a rapist any day, leave those damn betrothals and divorces to Hadleigh.

I think I like Miss Dede herself very much, though. She has a very thoughtful way of speaking, she always takes her time before she says anything, weighing every word so carefully. I wish I were more like that. I either can't think of anything to say at all or I just babble incoherently. I suspect a superlative intellect, keen perceptive abilities. It is indeed better that I handle her contract for her rather than Hadleigh, she wouldn't like all of his smoke and mirrors and shallow polish. She'd see right through him, she'd take her business elsewhere. At least I have a certain facility with logic and maths, Hadleigh wouldn't know a legally equivalent contrapositive if it up and bit him on the bum.

I like that she is being careful about who her daughter marries, and told her to that effect. "Miss Dede, it pleases me extraordinarily the care you have for your daughter's fate and future. It seems to me that you are not only wise but also compassionate, the only problem that you cannot solve is that truly, no man alive could ever suffice as your son-in-law, all and any would find themselves insufficient."

We had, up until that moment, been quite serious and focused on the matter at hand, and I think that Miss Dede was rather surprised by my seemingly sudden explosion of compliments. It is just the way I am: white lies and laudations, they grow in my bone marrow and circulate through my veins. She looked away from me immediately, down at her long, elegant hands resting in her lap. I waited for a reply, it felt like a century would pass, I lit myself a cigarette and fidgeted as I waited.

"The way you put words together, Mr. Mudi. It is a shame you did not become a barrister," was her reply, completely not what I had expected. "Or a poet."

"Oh, no, Miss Dede, I have no ear for poetry or literature at all, I'm afraid, and I haven't the dramatic personality required to be a good barrister. A solicitor me for certain." I should not have responded to her in that way, it was self-indulgent and grotesque, turning the conversation to myself like that, ugh, how I hate myself, I need to learn how to think before I speak. I should have just thanked her and returned to our discussion of the contract. That's what I should have done. Instead, I relied on Miss Dede to actually drive our conversation back to where it should have been, that was awful of me.

"How long will all of this take, Mr. Mudi? When will the contract legally be broken?"

"Oh! Well, I suspect that it will take ten to twelve weeks in all. I know that sounds like a long time, but your situation is quite simple, it should be one of the quickest matters that the magistrates will officiate of this kind. I hope that timetable doesn't disappoint you terribly."

"No, Mr. Mudi, I understand that things take time."

"Anything involving English courts takes a very long time indeed. But I can assure you that I will make certain that your introductory petition is filed first thing tomorrow morning so we can begin the long slog as soon as possible." I got up at that time, trying not to move too quickly or too awkwardly, unused as I am still to the new stone that is making itself very much at home on my body, and opened the office door, too lazy and uncouth I am to actually go to Hadleigh's office, I just yelled out to him: "Oh, Lord Greenwich! Notarizing!"

Hadleigh replied, "Be there in just a moment, my dear Honorable Brahmin Mudigonda!"

When shall I ever tire of using formal address with Hadleigh in front of clients? The answer is never, never ever. Hadleigh appears, readies his pen, and, for some reason, notices that this is a betrothal-related document and gives me quite a dirty look. "Tomorrow I shall have you notarize a death row appeal, Manikji," he whispered to me, not a bit irritated I could tell. I don't care. I passed the petition on to Mr. Wangai and escorted Miss Dede to the door. Then, out of the blue, probably still annoyed with me for commencing a family law matter without even so much as consulting him, he gives me a jolly big punch on the arm.

"For all that's good and holy, Hadleigh! It's just one little contract nullification, I'm not trying to render you obsolete or anything!"

"Just don't get any ideas!" he snarled, walking back to his office. "I saw that look in your eyes, and I'm telling you, it's a very bad idea, it makes it very difficult for me to look after you."

What on earth is he talking about? Does he think he's looking after me when I'm the one constantly fixing his errors and solving his dilemmas? What an utter arse. And then, before he left to go to his club, he asks me when I'm going to be seeing Eleanor again, that she'd be more than happy to see me. I do not want to see Eleanor anymore, and I've told him as much, but he is really pushing the envelope with me, reminding me cruelly that it's rare that I get such a good thing and I should appreciate it rather than toss it away, that I'm ungrateful for all of his largesse. Well, yes, I am ungrateful for your largesse most of the time, Hadleigh, and honestly, who could blame me? But I wasn't going to ruffle his feathers any more than I had already, he was in such an awful snit, I didn't want to listen to any more of his piss and vinegar. Anyway, my birthday isn't that far away and I'm hoping for a good birthday party with lots of drinks and ladies, it's not worthwhile to antagonize the great pillock. Lots of drinks and ladies!

Friday, May 2, 1913

Maybe I should see Eleanor again. Nobody else is looking for me, that's for certain. She wants to come over on Thursday at midday. At worst, I will get back on Hadleigh's good side. Birthday party! Thirty-two years old and nothing but trouble, that's what I'm going to be.

Friday, May 2, 1913, continued

Referring to previous entry, I am not yet thirty-two years old, but I am already nothing but trouble, nothing but trouble, that's what I am. I shouldn't have done it, but it was too easy. I understand what Hadleigh was talking about now. Well, he can go jump off a cliff.

In fact, I don't even care if he finds out, I don't care what he thinks. It's not about him, not everything is about bloody Hadleigh. I still shouldn't have done it, though, it was probably a mistake, but I feel all right about it, really, even though I shouldn't. Actually, I feel quite wonderful.

The betrothal was broken as far as I was concerned, I just needed to finalize a few things with Dede. She came to the office at the end of the day, Hadleigh was already gone and Mr. Wangai was on his way out when she arrived. I cut the fee absurdly, but Hadleigh doesn't need to know, he never checks the ledgers and even if he did, he wouldn't know what he was looking at, ants crawling across the page. I was in no rush, and I sensed that neither was she. I decided to lean back, have a smoke, and just talk to her, just talk to her about herself. She is brilliant, an amazing political mind. Her take on the Somalian question was so comprehensive and well thought out, I felt completely out of the loop, which I am. I should pay better attention to current affairs. It's one thing, reading science research and keeping up to date in mechanics and chemistry, and it's another thing to understand the causes of war, political allegiances, the interconnectedness of policies that often seem so remote to me. I think I just sat there with the cigarette on my bottom lip and listened to her speak, overjoyed to actually have an intelligent conversation for once.

"Would you come by my office and enlighten me once a week, Miss Dede? I need you to teach me how the world works," I told her. "I don't think I've cared so much about Europe in my entire life."

And the eyes went down again, down to her lap just like they did before, and I had to wait again, wait for her to process an unwanted compliment. Finally, she looked up at me again. "Mr. Mudi, I want to ask you a question about our first encounter, when we walked together into Kuze and you told me how you helped the prostitutes with the law. I recall that you said that you did not frequent them, because if you did, you would not know who would pay whom. I thought at first that was a strange thing to say, but they do pay you for the work you do for them. Is that what you meant?"

Truth be told, that was not at all what I meant, and I couldn't believe how vivid Dede's memory of my words were, and how much thought she had put into them. Obviously, her interpretation was flawless, but I was really thinking that since both Nia and I are whores, what would one whore charge the other. "Yes, yes that's what I meant, Miss Dede."

"I thought as much, but part of me thought it might mean something else."

"What did you think it might mean, Miss Dede?"

"It isn't important," the lady stood up and started organizing her documents to bring home, so I stood up as well. She stopped suddenly and looked me right in my eyes. Her bottom lip seemed to tremble. "Mr. Mudi, I am sorry."

"Sorry for what, Miss Dede? I'm afraid I don't understand."

"You confuse my mind... my heart."

"Your heart, Miss Dede?"

"I cannot say without being quite frank, Mr. Mudi."

"Be frank then, it will not bother me, there is nothing that you could say that would bother me."

"You must know... your face..."

"I know my face very well indeed."

"With..." Dede pointed to my red eye. "And..." Dede began to move her hand as if it were tracing the outline of the white skin surrounding my red eye on the left. "And all..." Dede gestured to the more severe pockmarks on my forehead and my neck.

"I'm quite ugly, aren't I, Miss Dede?" I said softly, giving a self-deprecating smile.

"I should think that you are, Mr. Mudi. And yet... I find you quite lovely. You listen to me and talk to me and you seem quite lovely, a wonderful big man with wonderful hair like nothing I've ever seen, a sweet voice, kind."

I was so intensely moved, listening to Dede's earnest phrases, spoken just above a whisper, her eyes moist. I walked closer to her and we looked carefully at one another. I had been trying so hard to ignore how beautiful Dede is, I had been trying so hard to be professional, but oh, it was like a dream, like the most wonderful dream I've ever had, suddenly coming true. And I don't normally do things like this, I don't, but I took Dede's hand in mine and I kissed it, not like a gentleman, but as if I would have inhaled it. I shouldn't have done that, it was overstepping a boundary. I sometimes worry that I have ruined myself, that I can no longer separate my life as a sexual object from my life as a professional man, I think that this is evidence of the decompartmentalization of my psyche, it isn't good.

Sunday, May 4, 1913

Resolution: It is now seven weeks until my birthday. I will endeavor a simple task, borne of reason and mathematical possibility. I am at twenty-one stone three. I will attempt to attain twenty stone ten by my birthday. That is a pound a week, that is modest, reasonable, and entirely possible without either starving myself or the use of chemical emetics, and absolutely necessary, this has gone on long enough and an end must come. I want to be fuck ready for my birthday, damn it! Ideally, I'd be back at nineteen stone like I was last birthday, which I thought was a horror and a shame at the moment, but now seems to me so much better than where I am. Since 1903 I have been nineteen stone five separate times. I have been twenty stone four times. I have been twenty-one stone twice, but this is the only time I've broken twenty-one stone. Three pounds to three hundred, damn, where I swore I'd never be again. And I know myself, once three hundred comes around, four hundred seems far too attainable, and I am not a teenager anymore, I can't carry myself around at four hundred pounds.

I'd kill a man to be eleven stone. If I were to lose a pound a week, I would get to eleven stone in two years and nine months. That's an awfully long time. All right, new goal: I am at twenty-one stone three. In seven weeks if I lose three pounds a week, I can get to nineteen stone ten by my birthday and eleven stone in under a year. Ipecac, old friend, we are on a mission.

Thursday, May 8, 1913

Eleanor will be by soon, so I am nervous. Oh dread. The things I endure in order to ensure a good birthday, abuse and starvation only two of them. Things I want for my birthday: unlimited alcohol, unlimited cigarettes, and a minimum of three orgasms. And to be thin. And married to a beautiful woman that loves me. And to be rich beyond my wildest dreams with unlimited freedom. Come to think of it, I rarely dream about uncountable wealth. I usually just dream about the beautiful woman. But maybe the uncountable wealth would help me obtain and keep the beautiful woman.

I am a little bit lightheaded. I have vomited absolutely every single thing I've consumed for two whole days, which is good, but I haven't adjusted yet. But I think it must be working, because this morning after I'd oiled and fashioned my hair, Kaweria told me that I looked very nice today.

"Just wait, Miss Kaweria, in less than a year, I'll be eleven stone. I'll look very nice then."

"I would not recognize you, Mr. Mudi! Be careful with yourself," she teased, smoothing out my lapels and pinning a lovely little red orchid to my buttonhole. What a charming surprise, how thoughtful she is, knowing not at all my plans for the day. I wonder where she got the orchid; it's quite remarkably pretty and is yet to show even the slightest wilting. I like it very much. I also like that she has pinned it to the right lapel and not the left, given its color.

Shakti protect me, I see Eleanor coming up the walkway.

Thursday, May 8, 1913, continued

Well, today was interesting, to say the least. I'm achy and tired and so hungry I could eat a bag of sand. Dash it all, I should eat something if I'm going to be drinking, I'll throw it up later when my knees start to work again. It was really among the best days I've ever had, spent the way I like to spend my days: fucking. This whiskey is foul, serves me right for not examining carefully what I nick from Hadleigh.

Ad venture the first: Eleanor comes to call. I had no tea set up, as I was not told to have tea set up, the first words out of her mouth are: "Oh, you haven't any tea?"

"Should I call down for tea, Eleanor, do you want it?" I asked nervously, afraid that this might be a trick. "Tell me exactly what you want."

"Have them bring up tea and some proper luncheon. Beef and salads."

"They won't bring me beef, Eleanor, they know I can't eat it." I instantly started to regret making this admission, fear crawling up my back as to what implications it might have in Eleanor's cruel brain, what activity she might have in mind, but fortunately, her impatience overrode her desire to punish me.

"Then tell them to bring up bloody anything, just do it, do it now!" she shouted, already in a tantrum. She began pacing around my flat, a hard scowl on her little face, her thin arms crossed tightly over her chest. For a moment, as I caught a glimpse of her while I called down to the kitchen, I thought she was actually rather adorable, the angry little sprite, and couldn't possibly be taken so seriously. So charmed I was as I hung up the telephone that I approached her and scooped her up in my arms, seating her easily on my right forearm, my left arm supporting her back.

"Luncheon coming up soon, my little princess, my little Elly Belly darling," I sang, planting a kiss on her forehead.

"Put me down this instant!" she demanded, pounding little, ineffectual fists to my chest.

"Do you know, I don't actually have to put you down if I don't care to, and there really isn't much you can do about it, is there?" I continued to sing, bouncing Eleanor up and down on my arm. "I like you up here, it's so easy to give you little kisses." And so, powdering her upturned nose with kisses, happiness began to swell my heart, that is, until I could feel a sharp tug on my earring.

"I'll pull it through if you don't put me down," she hissed, sounding like nothing more than a spitting cobra. She tugged again, so sharp, so quick, so painfully, so clearly marked with just enough restraint as to make it clear that one's earlobe is in clear and present danger of splitting in half. All of my courage disappeared, I remembered that it was not any sweet little Elly Belly I had cradled in my arms but a woman who never failed to hurt me. I slowly and carefully lowered her to the bed's edge, dipping my head as well, Eleanor refusing to give up her grip until both of my hands were behind my back. At that moment, I heard the room service waiters bringing in luncheon, so I quickly and embarrassedly ran off to tip the gentlemen before they departed. Eleanor came to the tea table and waited for me to both seat her and serve her, which was an exercise in anxiety, that sort of anxiety that makes doing even the simplest activities all but impossible: pouring a cup of tea, lighting a cigarette.

"That's disgusting," she said.

"What is?"

"You smoke and eat at the same time, that's disgusting."

"Why is it disgusting?"

"You are repellent." She gave me a glare and I was compelled, heart beating, to stub out my cigarette on my tea saucer even though it was not even a third burned away and I had really wanted it. "You are truly one of the most disgusting people I have ever met. In addition to being incomprehensibly ugly, you are slovenly, you smoke without any manners, you are an habitual drunkard, you eat like a wild animal, and I've heard that you put your hand down your own throat and make yourself vomit, is that true?"

"No, it isn't true in the least, who told you that?"

"Everybody knows, everybody talks about it."

"Well, it isn't true, it's just rumors."

"I don't think it's rumors, I think it's true. Just look at your face, you're sweating like a criminal on the stand. You nasty, disgusting, filthy beast."

I was getting very upset at this point, so I decided that, birthday party be damned, this time I was definitely going to stand up for myself and give Eleanor what she deserved. I lit myself another cigarette and, taking a good drag on it, took a firm bite of cress sandwich and began to extrapolate my argument with my mouth full. "I think you're the really odd one because, in spite of thinking me repulsive, just this horrible, filthy, disgusting savage, you come over to my home on scheduled dates and scold me if I cancel. Anybody can be a sloven, it takes a truly twisted mind to want to associate with someone so offensive. I might be disgusting, but at least I'm sane. Go on, why do you keep looking at me if it turns you off so badly? Turn your head! Go home, see if I care."

Eleanor was incensed. She leapt to her feet and, latching on tightly to my earring once again, pulled me from the tea table and dragged me to the basin on the floor under the sink, pushing my head to it.

"Do it, make yourself sick. I want to see how you do it."

"What are you talking about?" I replied, my voice cracking in an obvious way. I was losing my ground.

"Go on, put your hand in it, make yourself sick. Show me how it's done."

"No, I won't do it. I can't."

"You can't? Why not?" She tangled her fingers tightly in my hair and put a knee to the back of my head, pushing it down. "Just do it, I want to see you do it."

"I can't because I haven't..." and I stopped myself. I was starting to feel like I might faint, or that my neck might snap.

"You haven't what? What do you need to make yourself sick? Admit it, admit it! You do make yourself vomit, don't you? You have a ritual, a little routine, a little magic spell that makes it all so harmless, don't you? Don't you? So, what is it? What do you do?"

I stopped resisting Eleanor's knee and just folded in on myself. I was broken. I started to cry, but quietly, into my hands. She climbed upon my shoulders and, hiking up the hem of her dress, pressed her knees on either side of my throat very, very hard, her hands still laced tightly into my hair, her entire weight hanging off my scalp. I didn't move, I stayed completely still, trying to stop myself crying. "Tell me what it is," she hissed, over and over again, spitting as she tormented me, the blood rushing to my face, I felt so helpless that I just gave in.

"I'll tell you," I whispered at last.

"You will?" she snarled.

"I'll tell you."

"Tell me."

"My stomach isn't full enough. And I have to be drunk."

"How drunk do you have to be?"

"Just a bit," I sobbed.

"Just a bit drunk. All right, then that's what we'll do. Up you go, sport."

My word. I was actually feeling quite all right about my time with Eleanor, but now, I'm feeling not well at all about it. It's an odd thing, my feelings waver back and forth. At the time, it's horrible, it's like the absolute worst kind of torture, but then for a while afterwards, it seems like all in good fun, only to switch back to being very bad memories indeed, memories that I am quick to forget. I am bloody well upset now, and bloody well hungry also. Oh, I ought to buck up, it wasn't really all that bad, it was just some awful little girl and a good solid fuck. Focus on the positive, that's what Hadleigh always tells me I ought to do. As much as I like this mushroom pie, it won't be easy disposing of it, I ought to ease up. Bugger all, I've had a day, I'll eat the lot and take care of it later.

So what happened then? Undressed Eleanor, undressed myself, and, docile as a goat to slaughter, allowed my hands to be tied behind my back and my ankles bound together in front of me. She asked if I could handle the blindfold, bless. I said no, and she gave me that kindness. Actually, tied up as I was, she was uncharacteristically gentle with me, which, now that I think of it, may have come more from a sense of scientific curiosity than any care she might have for me. She did not want to spoil her experiment: preparing a big fat glutton for a forced vomit. And truly, she let me orchestrate the show. We sat beside one another on the bed, very close and cozy, and, with no sense of rush or urgency, she fed me, tiny bite by tiny bite, from her own miniature fingertips. Lovely, really. I'd tenderly beg for a bit of pudding or biscuit or tart, or a sip of gin, or a puff on the cigarette resting in the tea saucer, and she would provide, her face as calm and focused as an anarchist building a highly explosive bomb. At even intervals she would ask me how I was doing. "Are you ready yet?" she'd inquire. It was so soothing, I think I'd actually forgotten how awful I'd felt just moments before, being bullied into admitting my worst and most shameful secret. "Not quite," I'd say softly, "but I'm doing well." Finally, I knew I was just about ready, but I started to think, reason suddenly popped up in my brain.

"Now, if you see me do what I'm about to do, you aren't going to be telling anybody about it, are you?" I asked, my tone absolutely pleading and desperate.

"Of course I'll tell everybody! It shall be the utter talk."

"Oh, you wouldn't really, would you? You wouldn't, you'd have no audience for that sort of thing, truly."

"It's the entire point of this exercise!"

"Is it then," I sighed. I don't know what helplessness has seeped itself through my bloodstream, but it is pervasive. "My birthday's coming up on June the twenty-second, you couldn't wait until it's passed if you absolutely must report your findings? You wouldn't spoil my birthday for me, would you?"

"That's weeks away!"

"You know, I could just decide not to do it, I've held far more in my stomach than this, it's not an absolute necessity, it's not as if I can't function without it. You're rather privileged, you know, I don't vomit on command for just anyone. If you wait until my birthday's passed, I'll do what you say and you won't hear another word of it, I promise. I beseech you, please, please, oh, please wait until my birthday's passed."

She thought about it, tiny pink lips pursed as tightly as a conch shell. She patted me on the face and nodded her head. I heaved a sigh of relief and she began to untie my hands and feet. "To the basin, boy. Go make yourself sick, you great awful gorger."

And so off I staggered, properly overfull and just a bit drunk. Eleanor followed close behind, crouching close for a ring-side view. One might have suspected some sort of performance anxiety, but I was able to behave more or less as I would if I'd been on my own. Testing fingers, failing with fingers, swig of gin, swig of ipecac, and three fingers behind the uvula. Up it all comes, those magnificent three minutes of agonizing relief, the horrible, blissful retching, spitting, sweating and shivering, kicking in the gut, and exhausted, useless panting afterwards, the blood having drained away from my head and extremities in its entirety. Perhaps not three minutes, perhaps more like eight or ten. I wish it were three, it would be so much more discreet at three.

"Dear God, that was the most repulsive thing I'd ever seen," Eleanor proclaimed, sounding almost elated in her excitement.

"Thank you, my dear," I replied, trembling over to the pitcher to rinse my mouth and get myself a cigarette to clear my throat. "Enjoy the show?"

"Completely and utterly awful in every way."

"I'll take that as a yes."

"I'm getting away from all that horror there. Meet you in bed, you ventripotent swine."

"All right, darling, I'll be along. Might have a shit to do, would you like an encore?"

"You revolting dog, for God's sake."

"It's an awful thing, being nauseous and constipated at once, you know, I wouldn't recommend it."

An awful groan resonated through the flat, but then, for I doubt she realizes the deft facility of my ears, I would swear in a court of law that I heard giggling of the most cheerful and impish kind as I've ever heard it. All worthwhile, really, all very worthwhile. Finished my smoke, had a few sips of gin, and walked into the bedroom with a macaroon in my teeth and a drink in my hand. I knew that Eleanor was fighting to keep her scowl, so I started to laugh myself. "Go on!" I teased her. "Go on, it is quite terrible and funny, isn't it?"

She turned herself away from me on the bed and hid her face under a pillow. I got down next to her. "You think I'm marvelous entertainment, don't you? I'm a splendid laugh, aren't I? If I didn't know better, I'd say you thought I was charming to the core. And you'd be right, because I absolutely am, I'm absolutely charming, even when I'm spitting up sultanas, and I think you're a bit in love with me. Which is excellent, actually, because I'm head over heels for you, to be quite honest." I knew that all of that was bollocks, but I felt like saying it anyway, because I was still just drunk enough to be saucy and not drunk enough to be sullen.

This quickly dissolved into a great wonderful fuck from the rear, ejaculate spluttering all over my bedclothes, absolutely excellent fun, accompanied by Eleanor's hateful screams of penetration as she twisted her feet furiously behind the backs of my knees. I let her pinch me quite sharply in a number of places and let her spit on me a few times as I dressed her again. It's a truly horrible relationship we've developed, and I should never, ever see her again, she upsets me terribly. But my birthday is coming up, and I'll do what I have to do, by hook or by crook.

When she marries that bastard in His Majesty's Royal Navy, I wonder if she'll think on me fondly, her lovely, fat, ugly wog who let himself be abused in a multitude of ways. She'll sigh in a romantic fashion, and look over to that man among men that she's married and regret that she'd get the rod if ever she tried to make him vomit into a basin for her own personal enjoyment and to provide her with some juicy gossip. Maybe she'll wish she'd thrown off conventions and appearances and married me instead.

But that was only adventure the first. Adventure the second: it was not even half past two when I returned to the office, light on my feet and in an excellent mood. Wrote an absolutely flawless appeal to the court for the Mweke murder, so flawless that as I re-read it, I deemed it as not needing a second draft, which pleased Mr. Wangai immensely. I decided that I would work late into the night, as excellent as I was feeling and bid the other two gentlemen good evening as I set myself up with my casebooks and my cases, Kaweria's red orchid still bright and fresh in my buttonhole.

At about seven o' clock, when I'd been working on my own for less than an hour, I heard a soft knock on my office door. I will admit to a certain level of paranoia from time to time, for although my work with criminal minds is quite indirect for the most part, every once in a while I wonder who it is who might come to call after hours when I am by myself. My fears were instantly allayed when I heard a soft, beautifully accented voice calling for me: "Mr. Mudi? You are still there?"

I opened the door, and standing before me, looking more lovely than I had remembered her, was Dede, looking up at me with such a gentle expression, a small, shy smile on her lips, her dark eyes wide like a child's. "How wonderful to see you, Miss Dede!" I choked, surprised and extremely happy at once.

"I know that you work late on your cases, Mr. Mudi, I don't want to interrupt you if you are busy," she said sweetly.

"You are never an interruption for me, Miss Dede. Please come in."

She came in. There was no mistaking that this was a social visit only, which was a balm to the both of us. Thus began our conversation about the latest policy discussions on land tenure and legislation in British West Africa, how glad we were to be on the coast of the Indian Ocean rather than the Atlantic, given how poorly things were going in the west. We made a few jokes at the expense of the British, that was quite healthy and relaxing, perhaps a bit too relaxing as I soon found myself seated on the same side of my desk as Dede. Of course, British legal discussions so easily degrade into a critique of British cuisine and its tragic failures. Dede was surprised and amused at the number of English dishes I have tasted and disliked.

"You look like you would be a man of discerning tastes, Mr. Mudi," she said in such a lovely, beautiful way.

"Oh no, I am the absolute opposite. In fact, in spite of having disliked so many of the delicacies featured in my diatribe, if you were to present me with one of them, it would be guaranteed that I would scoff it down in a minute's time." And how I made her laugh! She put her hand on my knee and laughed, how wonderful it was. "It wasn't particularity that made me so big, Miss Dede."

"I like you much too much, Mr. Mudi," she sighed, catching her breath.

"I feel the very same way about you, Miss Dede," I admitted, quite honestly. We held hands and looked each other in the eyes. Dede's eyes are singularly beautiful. They are shaped like almonds, they curl upwards in the corners, with curled eyelashes fringing around them, and they are just beautiful reflective black pools. Her cheeks are like plums, her lips like cherries.

"I have been married for twenty-eight years, Mr. Mudi."

"What a lucky man your husband must be."

"He is like you, a big man."

"He is an intelligent man to have found a woman like yourself."

"You remind me of him in many ways, Mr. Mudi, you remind me of him when he was young, and yet, there is something so different, so completely different about you. I think that is why I want to be close to you." At these words, Dede looked down, as is her fashion, and almost seemed ashamed of what she had just said. I began to softly stroke the side of her beautiful hand with my thumb, and she looked back up at me. It was magnetic. We leaned into one another and kissed, just about the best kiss I'd ever had in my entire life, it was so soft, so lingering, so intensely forbidden. We slowly got up from our seats and, keeping our lips together, wrapped our arms around one another, kissing and swaying from side to side like a bride and groom at the wedding. I pulled my chin away for a moment to catch my breath, but Dede took me by the cravat, effectively undoing it as she tugged, and pulled me back immediately. I gave an imperative moan, expressing need for communication.

"Wait, wait, I have something to show you, a place for us," I gasped, my heart beating like a thousand drums. I took her to our Texts Sources Records room where Hadleigh, in all of his foresight, installed an enormous velvet divan when we first moved to Mombasa. I don't even remember how many times I have made use of that magnificent item of furniture, it is just a brilliant, brilliant thing and never, ever stains. Who knew that semen was so easy to clean out of black velvet? When she saw it, Dede's jaw dropped and she looked at me with such an expression! She gave me a little tap on the bottom and laughed.

"Do all solicitors...?" she asked.

"No, no, no, no, just me, Dede my angel, just me. Because, like the prostitutes I defend... we're the same, you understand."

"I do understand. I understood it the first time you said it, I just couldn't believe it."

"It's very comfortable, you know," I teased, going over to the divan and slowly laying back, taking the weight off my feet, kicking off my shoes forcibly, putting one arm behind my head and the other out to welcome Dede. She came and lay down beside me, rubbing my chest with her lovely hand. I was already feeling extremely guilty and bad about the whole thing, but this was just too good to be true, I couldn't turn it down. I can't ever turn it down, I just can't. Hadleigh would have had me turn it down because he is severely opposed to my involvement with African women, he thinks that it lowers my cache as a supplicant of European women, but I think that's completely unfair and absurd, that I'm supposed to be perfectly happy to let Eleanor treat me really badly but turn down some real love making from Dede? No, no, I am not that much of a lapdog. I am a romantic, not a racist.

But Eleanor has taught me a few things, how to be a better affair. First of all, undress the lady before I undress myself, it's only polite. Never in my life have I seen bosoms like Dede's! Each one as big as my head! I was overwhelmed by them, I started to hyperventilate instantaneously, I was almost afraid to touch them, but then, I could not help but touch them, I could have died right then, a huge tit in either hand, a very, very happy man. And yet, she is perfectly proportionate, even with those spectacular bosoms, her hips broad, her waist marked so small, truly a goddess in every sense of the word, I was going absolutely mad. Dede helped to undress me, I did need the help because my fingertips were starting to sweat and my buttons were feeling fiddly. It was something I'd never witnessed before, the same gasps of amazement and admiration that had passed through my lips were now passing through Dede's lips. She took each of my arms in both of her hands and stroked them from top to bottom, one at a time, and then put a beautiful hand on either side of my belly, gazing with a certain kind of awe and fascination. At first I felt intense shame, I felt so impossibly hideous at that moment, so embarrassed of myself, naked in the presence of one of the world's most beautiful women, but then I realized that it was not unlike my encounter with Akinyi: I was just being objectified, fetishized, and it comforted me, I felt more at ease. It isn't so much being considered, and wrongly, beautiful, but rather, being an item of primal sexual desire, and with that I can cope. I began to kiss her again, on her lips, down her chin, on her breasts, and she caressed me, explored me with her hands, her lips. She turned her back to me and we lay like two spoons in a drawer on the black velvet divan. She kept her head tilted to mine so that we could continue to kiss, and I held her, one arm across her bust, one arm around her waist. Slowly, ever so slowly, she separated her thighs to make a space for me. I soon realized that she had been circumcised, like some Luo ladies are, all of her labia removed and her clitoris excised. I have only been with a few circumcised ladies, and I understand that the pleasure of lovemaking is oftentimes erased for them, so I knew that I needed to take extreme care with Dede. I would insert myself, but I would not thrust so much as try to caress what remaining nerve endings she maintained, keeping my focus on kisses and soft touches. Slow, careful, gentle, and I still came to the peak after a goodly long time, she enflamed my passions so. I tried to keep control and not rush to remove myself, keeping everything as beautiful and lovely as possible, and tried to catch as much seed as I could in my palm. Dede put her own hand underneath my own and caught the rest. What a tender, thoughtful lady.

We had a nice, long refractory period, kissing, holding one another. I told her to call me Manik, I told her that I loved her. I did, I did say that, even if I shouldn't have. I said, "Dede, I love you." She kissed me on my third eye and smiled. I asked her if I had been gentle enough with her. She told me that I was an angel. She did, she did say that. She said, "Manik, you are an angel."

I helped her dress again in her beautiful kitenge and forced myself back into my shirt and trousers, and guided her carefully to the door, kissing her a thousand times. I do not know if I will ever see her again, but oh, I want to see her again, I want to marry her.

So, here I am at midnight, drinking possibly poisonous whiskey and stuffing my face full of pie, exhausted from law business and love business. A very, very, very good day indeed. Not too many days like this, other than my birthday, that is. I really love Dede. I think that she is the angel, not me. I think that she could grow to truly love me. I could learn so much from her, and I could talk to her about anything, from politics to law to low humor. I wouldn't need to be thin. Damn her husband, damn her husband of twenty-eight years. Damn him.

Sunday, May 18, 1913

Results from the coffee scales: I am twenty stone eleven! Huzzah! Also: on the verge of fainting, nauseous, starving, with teeth that feel increasingly the texture of chalk. Or not even chalk, perhaps I should say toffee. And yet, for all that I am pleased to be on schedule to hit nineteen stone ten by my birthday, I am impossibly morose, just severely depressed, always on the verge of crying. At first I thought it the accompanying syndrome to being drunk on an empty stomach, Miserable Gut I call it, but it's a bit worse than merely that, I think. Bleak. Why should I feel so bleak when I can fasten one more waistcoat button?

Thursday, May 22, 1913

Thought about Lila and cried for an hour for no real reason at all today. Twenty stone nine. I am doing such a good job keeping up with vomiting, not wasting any time at all, in and out that's how it goes. Thinking constantly of death. I am starting to fear my own body, fear my own hands, what they might do to me. Last night I had a dream in which they just fell off, and instead of being horrified, I felt incredible relief. I'm keeping up appearances, though, nobody knows how poorly I'm doing, I think, except for Kaweria perhaps, my flat is in a terrible state every single day. Every morning she has gotten into the habit of putting in my cufflinks for me and telling me not to work too late. "Don't work too late tonight, Mr. Mudi," she says. "And don't go in too early, either. Don't run yourself down." I am running myself down.

Tuesday, May 27, 1913

Yet another thing has happened to send me hurtling into the caverns of despair, something that really ought to make me feel a good deal better, but it doesn't. In fact, it gives me such terrible distress and anxiety that my chest has been in an utter knot all day and I can hardly breathe. Twenty stone six. Hadleigh is extremely cross with me and I just cannot cope with it, that and the rejection. He stormed into my office with his arms crossed and a scowl on his face, which he never has, as he fears it will give him a crease between his eyebrows, so I knew that there was something the matter.

"What have you done, Manik? What have you done?"

"I haven't the slightest idea of what you could mean, Hadleigh," I replied, lighting myself a cigarette. No sooner had I started my first inhale that Hadleigh pulled it off my lip and threw it on the floor.

"Why doesn't Eleanor want to see you anymore? She says she's through with you. What have you done?"

"What does it matter to you, Hadleigh? And I can't imagine why, other than that she's through with me, they all end up through with me eventually, you know. And she is getting married at the end of June, that could be the reason." I tried to sound calm, but I was not. I strongly dislike Hadleigh when he is in a fit of temper, I never know what to do about it.

Hadleigh gave a quick exhale and pursed his lips together, looking away from me in his state of pique. "You couldn't have kept her interest just a little while longer?"

"I'm afraid that's not really up to me, is it?"

"I'm in quite a spot now, Manik. Quite a spot. I wish you kept me better informed about these sorts of things, I could give you some suggestions. First you say you're planning to marry her, and now she's lost interest in you. That isn't the trajectory I'd been hoping for."

"Well, I'm very sorry to hear that, Hadleigh, and if I can help you..."

"No, no. You've helped enough." And out he went. Now I'm terrified to leave the office, I'm just holed up permanently now, I suppose. Why doesn't Eleanor want to see me anymore? It upsets me, it really does, although it shouldn't. I was recalcitrant, but I don't think it was that which bothered her so much. I think she actually enjoyed my ugliness and repulsiveness for what they are worth. It must be one of two things, or perhaps both. It's either because I told her that I love her, or because I said that I thought she loved me. If it is the latter, then either I was fully incorrect, or I guessed so correctly that it frightened her away. What a painful world this is, that hate could have kept her in my bed and love could have driven her from it. I ruined it, I did ruin it, Hadleigh is right. I don't care so much that I've ruined it for him, I suppose, but I've turned her away from me. I will miss her horribly, I will miss her angry little face and her naughty little laugh and her sweet little porcelain belly. I would have let her torment me forever. I feel terrible about the whole ordeal, I cannot handle rejection like this.

Tuesday, May 27, 1913, continued

I couldn't bear the emotion. I wandered like a lost child into Hadleigh's office and, standing foolishly in the doorway with a cigarette on my lip, started to weep in my sickeningly messy way, with my nose dripping and all of it. If only I weren't really very upset indeed, it would have been a keen manipulative move on my part to get Hadleigh to forget my errors, but as usual, my tears were real. I am used to crying in front of Hadleigh, I do it all of the time. He sees it as an integral part of my personality, I reckon, a part that he actually likes very much for whatever strange reason. He doesn't want me to be too mature or too masculine, he wants to feel as if I need him, he likes to believe that he looks after me. He tutted me briefly and got up, wrapping an arm around my back as if he were my brave and generous older brother.

"Manikji," he said, tilting his head towards me.

"It was my fault. I'm an ass and I'm sorry. I... I told her that I love her. I'm sorry, I should have spoken with you, it was poor form and if I've put you in an awkward position..."

"You told her that you love her?"

"Because I do, Hadleigh, I do, I love her so very, very, very much," I choked, the tears being wiped as they fell by Hadleigh's handkerchief.

"Oh, Manikji," he sighed. "What do I always tell you about falling in love?"

"You tell me not to do it."

"And why do I tell you not to fall in love?"

"Because it always ends with me crying?"

"Well that, yes, but because love is poisonous, and women are bad, cruel creatures, and you are just too sensitive to handle one of your own.

You're a very sweet man, Manikji, a very sweet man with a big, lovely heart, and I admire you for it, but love is very bad for you. Just stick to fucking, my friend, and stay away from love."

"I know that I should, you're so right."

"And I don't want you to worry for even a moment about any problems I might have, because I've already come up with a solution, there's nothing for you to feel guilty about. Now, I know you've got a mountain of cases that you want to finish, but you should go on home and take the rest of the day off. There's always tomorrow. That's a good man, go on home, go have yourself a good drink and curl up with the latest Illustrated Science in your bed, you'll be all right."

"You're sure?"

"Of course I'm sure. Go on, leave your desk as it is, go rest your mind. And do have a proper, normal supper tonight, you're not looking well."

So I went home, sick and crying, but at least reassured that Hadleigh was no longer angry with me and would not cancel my birthday plans. I do everything Hadleigh tells me to do: here I am, in bed with a bottle of port and Illustrated Science. Proper, normal supper, though, no, I shan't manage that, I'm doing too well to give in to that.

Thursday, June 5, 1913

Oh, I do not feel well, I am cracking. I am always bleary, my throat hurts, my stomach hurts, my teeth hurt, I always have a headache, I'm always tired and on the verge of an emotional breakdown. The only comfort I seem to get is within the first few seconds after I finish a cigarette. Twenty stone one. I can't handle speaking on the telephone, I am burdening Mr. Wangai far too much, I am treating him very unfairly. I almost wish I could forget about it for today and be the dedicated, facile solicitor that I want to be, just be fat, happy, clear-headed Manik who can think and concentrate and write well and read for more than three minutes at a time. Just one solid meal, with rice and dhal and bread doused with butter and fruit and chocolate. Bread doused with butter, oh it makes me want to kill myself. And I know it wouldn't really do me any harm at all, but I just don't feel like I can, it feels impossible.

When I was a young boy, a young husband, I used to love to eat. My mother would cook for me, and it made me so happy, it was just perfect, unexamined pleasure. I never thought a thing about it. I was never sick, I was cheerful every day, and perhaps I was chubby but in the most harmless way. Harmless, that is the best word to describe myself as a child. I was taken straight from the breast to the lesson book, and then at ten they tied the thread on me, and moments later married me off to Madhulika. I was such a good little Brahmin husband. I was so naturally inclined to religion, to both study and ritual, and I loved it. I prayed and meditated every day, I wanted to do it, not like my brother who saw it as a dull burden of his birth. The pundit and everyone called me the Devi's Consort, and truly, they must have really thought that I was, the soft-cheeked boy who devoted himself to Shakti's worship, the red-eyed betrothed of Kali. If Madhulika had lived, if we had been allowed to grow up together, harmless I would have remained. A very minor Brahmin with one temple, but perhaps I would do well in government, for languages always came so easily to me in my youth. A very simple, quiet, harmless life, a wife who loved me, children of my own, I would be lenient, indulgent, patient and kind. I would never have tasted alcohol. I would never sleep by myself, Madhulika and I would always be together, safe in each other's embrace. Every day I would pray, pray in a fruitful, peaceful, productive manner, I would pray and I would eat without a single negative thought, and be at the very worst a bit chubby in a very harmless way.

It's only a red eye, it's only some white patches on my skin. I didn't need to be doomed to live this way. I could have been happy. I don't think I have any chance at happiness anymore. I should learn how to pray again, but I wouldn't know how to start. I can still recite every Upanishad from memory, but that doesn't really count.

Manik Mudigonda, aged 31, resides in the ancestral home of Mudigonda in the ancient city of Varanasi with his wife, Madhulika, aged 29, and his four children: his son Sahastrabahu, aged 13, his son Vaninath, aged 10, his daughter Shivapriya, aged 7, and his daughter, Bhagavati, aged 4. Both of their parents having passed away some time ago, Manik Mudigonda shares the ancestral home with his elder brother, Nilesh Mudigonda, aged 35, and his wife and children, as well as his uncle, Ganesh Mudigonda, aged 44, and his wife and children. Coming from one of the most ancient and exalted Brahmin lineages, Manik Mudigonda's primary occupation is the administration and dedication of the Temple Katha Kali, which has direct access to the river Ma Ganga, but he also works as a legal mediator between British colonial authorities and the traditional Indian representatives, protecting the rights and dignity of the residents of Uttar Pradesh state. A deeply religious man, he is beloved by everyone in his community, but anyone who knows him well would be able to say with conviction that his heart belongs only to his wife, Madhulika, who has been the center of his universe since they married in 1891. Perhaps the finest scholar that Varanasi has ever produced in all fields religious, scientific, mathematical, and rhetorical, Valedictorian University of Calcutta 1903, Manik Mudigonda is the most saught-after guru in the region for the education of young Brahmin men. A distinctly recognizable man, when asked about his unusual physical appearance, Manik Mudigonda explains that his red eye and uneven depigmentation are evidence of his special relationship with the Goddess, as Her Consort, which endows him with intense spiritual insight and the ability to grant powerful blessings upon all those who seek him. In order to celebrate his upcoming 32nd birthday on June the 22nd, a highly auspicious date, Manik Mudigonda is performing a religious sacrifice in his temple to which any and all devotees are welcome, irrespective of caste or cult.

Sunday, June 8, 1913

Reading that over, it makes me laugh. I'm actually quite funny, aren't I? Twenty stone even.

Friday, June 13, 1913

Tonight I must attend an intimate dinner party at Hadleigh's cottage. I do owe it to him, I know that I do, and Dorothy will be there, so it won't be completely awful, but I just don't know if I can cope with eating in front of other people at the moment, and tried to imply such to Hadleigh when he begged me my attendance.

"I'm having the Hopkinses for dinner tonight, and I need you to be there, Manikji," he said, a tone of desperation hazing over his words in bright blue.

"Anyone else? Just the Hopkinses? You know that I can't abide small parties, I always feel out of place and I'm never really welcome."

"I know that you don't like it, but I really do need you, as it's entirely likely that they will bring Dorothy along and you know I don't know what to do with her, it's always so awkward and it makes me terribly uncomfortable. And you like her, don't you, Manikji?"

"I have just as much affection for Dorothy Hopkins as you have discomfort."

"That isn't fair at all, Manikji. I'm in quite a spot, and it's much to do with you and your failures with Eleanor. This dinner has the potential to help solve my problem, you see. I just need Charles Hopkins on his own for forty-five minutes to an hour, I must speak with him, and I can't be staring at Dorothy out of the corner of my eye, distracting me. I know you think me shallow, but it's a cruel trick of nature, the creation of that sort of invalid. It's unpleasant for all parties involved."

"I should pray that I never lose the use of my legs Hadleigh, that it should disturb you so greatly."

Hadleigh frowned at me in such a bothered way, I felt rather bad for him at that moment. Poor, sad, lucky little Lord Greenwich. "What if I also said that I'm rather nervous about speaking with Mr. Hopkins and your just being there will soothe me immensely?"

"That's very kind, Hadleigh. You knew I would come anyway, but that is very kind."

"I haven't seen enough of you lately, you're tucked away in your little office, or in your little flat, so quiet and busy. And you're looking poorly, are you ill?"

"Just a bit ill I think, nothing to be concerned about."

"You wouldn't be eating properly, would you, Manik?"

"I don't know what your definition entails, Hadleigh."

"At least tonight I know that you shall, Miss Njeri just loves to cook for you specifically, you know, Manikji. You've got an awful greyish look to you, you need a bit of looking after. Do try to dress, and come a bit early if you could, not later than eight if at all possible. Thank you, my friend. At times like this the fact that I can rely upon you is truly my only comfort. And let me assure you, my plans for your upcoming birthday are quite exciting and extravagant, so you've that to look forward to as well. I know that's all you've been thinking about for over two months, old boy, and I won't play coy with you any longer."

"Oh, were you planning something for my birthday? I hadn't the foggiest," I teased, a big, silly grin on my face. Hadleigh was pleased and ruffled up my hair. I don't know how I'm going to face seven courses of food without getting drunk or vomiting or both.

Saturday, June 14, 1913

Hadleigh's little party was not nearly as bad as I thought it would be. I'm very glad that I attended. The Hopkinses as a family are fine, plain English people, farmers, individuals well-suited to the life of an East African settler. Mr. Hopkins and his wife are soft-spoken and pragmatic, and the two young men seem very wholesome. Indeed, they represent the very best kind of adolescent: comfortable engaging with their seniors, but not too old for their ages. I wish I had been like that when I was seventeen. But my conversation with these people was limited, which was fine by me; I am well assured of their prejudice by their daughter, Dorothy, for whom I care very much. She is a perfect example of how, in genetics, two similar parents may produce an offspring that resembles neither one. From two, simple, stalwart individuals with little inclination towards esoteric pursuits comes this incredibly witty and brilliant mind, a sharp, penetrative eye for truth. Hadleigh tuts about her, frets awfully, and when I point out to him the sparkling quality of conversation that Dorothy and I enjoy, he will usually reply with something about it all being an awful shame, just too bad that she is a cripple and therefore nothing but a drain on social circumstances. For some reason, although it is in a way quite a shame that Dorothy's physical limitations keep her from being able to do certain things that she might want to do, I do not see her that way at all. I find her quite lovely, just as she is.

Her condition is called cerebral palsy, and although some scientists say that it is caused by injuries during birth, I am more of the newer school which believes that it is an essential condition, not unlike my own. Hypertonia is the most marked symptom, tension that limits or prohibits voluntary movements to varying degrees, and so, oftentimes, as she tries to turn her head or extend her arm, she trembles. It is the trembling that Hadleigh cannot bear. I, on the other hand, actually find it quite captivating, it suits her brittle, clever sense of humor. Also captivating about Dorothy: hair the color of saffron, lips the color of capsicum, and cheeks at once so pale and so flushed. Her beauty is fragile, true, but not of the cold variety. Dorothy is warmth, she is heat.

I arrived early, just as Hadleigh had insisted that I do, in the pearl gray that only just barely fits me but looks very expensive, which is all that Hadleigh cares about, and as soon as I saw Dorothy arrive, pushed in by her younger brother, I chivalrously offered to relieve him. I found a place for us together for that endless interval of dull, awful conversation before Hadleigh allows food to be served. As soon as we were tucked away, I took the young lady's clenched and lovely hand and kissed it as is my fashion.

"Oh, I'm glad that you're here, Bacchus," she sighed. "I had hoped you would be, for I cannot bear Lord Greenwich's condescension without a friend by my side."

"You have taken the words straight from my mouth, Dorothy my dear," I laughed. "How do you find yourself these days?"

"I find myself in Malindi, primarily, staring out at the farm, bored senseless. I have been studying Italian, reading Dante's *Inferno*, do you know about Dante?"

"The name is familiar, but you know that literature is not my strong suit."

"You would like it, I think, you have that appreciation for darkness and death."

"Growing up watching rows of burning corpses will do that for you, I suppose, dearest Dorothy."

"Ah, well, it's all about the torments of Hell, where all those who have sinned go for their punishments after death. Do you know what punishment awaits panderers and flatterers? It is to be up to one's eyes in human excrement."

"To tell the truth, I think our mutual friend Lord Greenwich would not know the difference, so I think that a rather mild punishment indeed for the likes of him."

"Oh, Bacchus!" Dorothy exclaimed in her delicate way. "I always forget how much I enjoy spending time with you."

I was overtaken with emotion, and so, in my poor, ailing state, went directly to being a fool. "If you do like spending time with me, perhaps you would marry me?"

A burst of laughter, a quick reddening of the cheek, a wavering hand trying to make itself to the bosom. "Goodness no! I may be an invalid, but I do have my standards, Bacchus dear. I'd sooner a spinster stay than marry you!" I think she may have sensed my embarrassment and disappointment, and so continued on in order to brighten my mood again. "But I don't want you to think that it's the reason you normally hear. I have never found your mottled countenance anything but darling, and I think the weight you've put on really suits you, it is a rare man who can carry so much weight without looking off-balanced."

"Then it must be the other reason, then, is it not, dearest Dorothy?"

"No, it most certainly is not. Just because my immediate relations subscribe to those sorts of beliefs does not mean that I do. In fact, no subject inflames me more than the arguments in favor of subjugating races on the basis on some non-existent superiority, which is a sentiment rarely heard by a settler's daughter, I am certain."

"Then why not, my darling? Don't you think I would be a good husband?" I wheedled, trying to seem as if I were nothing but a cheerful playmate in our eternal game of flirtation.

"To be perfectly honest, Bacchus my dear, it is not your potential as a husband that I would question, but the fact that you seem to be willing to be any and every woman's husband. Any woman willing to talk to you for half an hour is bound to be assaulted by a proposal of marriage. Of course, it is one of your most wonderful characteristics, but I would not want to marry a man like that, so perpetually over-eager. You are, to adapt a turn of phrase, a man of loose morals and easy virtue."

"Oh, Dorothy, you would say such a thing to me?" I implored.

"Do not misunderstand me, Bacchus, for I would not change you and I admire your availability and generosity of spirit. I find you quite wonderful as you are, and surely there is a woman of intensely romantic spirit who might find you more than suitable, but for me, sweet Bacchus, I don't think you would be the right match. A romantic belongs with a romantic, and a sardonic belongs with a sardonic, it is the simple science of personality."

"Well, Dorothy my dear, in the science of magnetism, opposites attract, you know."

"Incorrigible!" she laughed, her eyes shut in happiness.

"No, no, you are right, Dorothy, you are absolutely right," I admitted, lighting myself a cigarette and pulling myself yet closer to the young lady.

"But you said yourself that you would not change me, and if I did not ask you to marry me, I would not be my poor, romantic, immoral self."

"Listen to you wheeze, Bacchus, you are getting a smoker's laugh, did you know that? You should cut back on cigarettes," she scolded, her little tight fist closing in by my chest.

"Do you not like it?" I asked, taking another deep inhale, pulling the gray vapors up from my bottom lip to my nostrils.

"I'm afraid I like it all too much. It suits you."

"Then I shall certainly not cut back on cigarettes, Dorothy my dear."

"No concern for your health, sweet Bacchus?"

"Bah. Health is greatly overrated I suspect."

"Cavalier, romantic, and nothing but trouble."

"That's me! Nothing but trouble! Manik Mudigonda, Brahmin, solicitor, and nothing but trouble. How did you know that I was nothing but trouble?" I enthused, overjoyed at having my mind and psyche probed so well.

"I think it's either to do with your lovely gold earrings, your terrible suit, or your endless lengths of hair. May I touch those silken curls? I am drawn to them like a moth to a flame, they are absolutely incredible. How on earth did you grow your hair like this, Bacchus?"

"I'm thinking of patenting the method, Dorothy my lovely," I joked, throwing a goodly long lock over the lady's wrists for her to examine. "I shall call it the Mudigonda Method and I will make a fortune."

"Oh, do tell me your secret! I won't tell a soul!"

"Are you certain that you won't go contacting the patent office in Nairobi the moment that this dreadful party ends? Do you swear?"

"I do swear, oh, please tell me!"

"It's a daily regimen. First you wake up in the morning, you look at your hair in the mirror, notice that it's very long, and, here's the difficult part, you don't cut it."

"That's all?"

"That's all."

"Nothing but trouble! Oh, Bacchus!" Dorothy laughed, tilting her head back in that beautiful, flower-like way. "Oh, do you think it will be a long time until they serve dinner? I should like a moment unnoticed with you."

"Unfortunately, from the looks of things, I think that Hadleigh is actually going to call for service now." I was correct in my assessment, as both Njeri and Akinyi and two other young ladies from the kitchen began to process into the dining room with trays and bottles. Njeri spotted me quickly and, subtly, gave me a wink and a smile, which I did in return. After she passed, Dorothy tutted me so I grinned at her like a loon. Not a minute later, Akinyi passed my way and fluttered her eyelashes at me, which I mirrored as well. Dorothy began to laugh again.

"The worst, most indiscriminate Casanova I have ever known, sweet Bacchus. Is there a woman left in Mombasa that you have not loved?"

"I hope so! My birthday is coming soon. Will you be coming?"

"Ah, Mudigondamas, of course. I know all about this year's plans."

"Do you? Do you really? Oh, please tell me! Who told you? How many people know? Is it the talk of the town? I want to know so badly, it's driving me mad, completely mad."

"I have been sworn to secrecy, Bacchus, I'm sorry. I will but tell you a single word if you would bring me to the table."

"Of course, of course," I hurried, excited about what that word might be, getting quickly behind Dorothy's chair.

"One thousand," was all the lady said.

"One thousand? Is that the word? One thousand what?"

"That's all you're getting for now, Bacchus my dear."

"Damn!"

"Swearing in front of ladies! This must interest you particularly, does it?"

I rolled my eyes a bit and smiled. "All solicitors swear continuously, it's required of the profession." I took my seat beside Dorothy at the dining table, and, reassuring her mother, took it upon myself to feed her. Dorothy cannot move her arms with sufficient dexterity or chew hard foods and so requires a bit of tender assistance in eating. I do not mind, rather I find it a real pleasure, particularly the prolonged eye contact, which is just rife for opportunities to flirt in a discreet, socially acceptable way: a slow blink, a half of a wink, a quick, teasing glance upwards, a little flash of my red eye, it's great, great fun. I hardly need words if I can have eye contact, and even if Dorothy's eyes cannot always appear as if they are focused, I know that she sees me clearly. Assisting Dorothy and enjoying my time with her far lessened the psychic burden of my own dining, a la Russe, course by miserable course, my own dishes served separately from the rest, prepared with perfect, vegetarian, Brahmin cleanliness by lovely Njeri herself. I think that Dorothy said something about making it seem as if I were a prince, but I was not going to point out the obvious, which is that I am actually a prince. I think that it spoils people's mental picture of what princes are like. If a prince could be a fat, piebald, red-eyed solicitor whose suits never fit, then any old bastard on the street could call himself a prince as well, I suppose.

After dessert and liqueurs, I all but received permission to abscond with Dorothy into some dark corner of his house so that Hadleigh could work his magic with the rest of the Hopkinses. As soon as we found ourselves alone, I carefully scooped Dorothy into my arms and silently carried her upstairs to the back-facing guest bed with the most tolerable mattress, which is essential for the support of her fragile back. Once alone, we commenced immediately to kissing, to slow, unhurried removal of silk dress, of linen suit. As soon as I laid beside her, naked, brushing my lips against her face, her hands unclenched and splayed outward, ready to take me in her embrace. I love Dorothy, she is wonderful. I twirled the very tips of my hair around her fingers, and, in as showy a display as can be done with this sort of thing, I flipped myself the other way around, putting my mouth in just the proper place, the hair remaining laced around her thumb, which she found very amusing indeed. I buried my face deep into her soft pelvis and let my tongue get to work right in the cleft, bordered on both sides by bright vermillion moss. I could tell that she was edging me closer, so I inched into her, the curves of our bodies fitting perfectly, until I could feel her returning the favor. I am a lucky, lucky, lucky man, and Dorothy is lovely, lovely, lovely in every possible way. We played at this for a very, very long time, and I refused to ejaculate, (there are some places that my well-traveled semen just shouldn't go) so I held up like a tree in the forest. This sort of fooling around lasted until we were both exhausted beyond all comprehension. Although we were gone for the better part of an hour, nobody seemed to have noticed that we were gone at all. Dorothy's hot, cerise lips, oh, how I love them, and her matching nipples and her utterly sultry chrysanthemum. Why won't she marry me? I'm not a Lothario, I'm merely a poor, helpless clinging vine. I will be happy to see her again on my birthday. What on earth could one thousand mean? One thousand, that is going to keep me awake all night long. If I went and took a vomit like a good boy, I'd probably forget all about it, but I don't know if I can really push myself into one tonight, my body almost feels good and I am enjoying it. It is that magical combination of mutual oral coitus, food cooked for me by Njeri, alcohol in moderation, and knowing that Dorothy would not change me, even if she would not marry me. Why does that comfort me so? Actually I am quite comforted, I might just fall asleep.

Tuesday, June 17, 1913

Bittersweet is the only way I can describe today's events. I think the fact that there is anything at all cutting the sadness in my bloodstream, however, only goes to show that I really am what I think I am: I am an acolyte to femininity, a willing servant, asking for very little in return for the chance to worship is its own reward. I'm really not such a bad man. I just pray in a different way now than the way I once did.

Today was my last morning waking up next to Hazel. I am sure of it, and it is for a good reason. She came to my flat unexpectedly last night, which she has never done before, but I am almost certain that she did it because I told her that it was Lila's signature: the moonlight surprise, a goddess bearing gifts. Her face was gleaming with joy, her cheeks as pink as a warm night's sunset, a color I had never before seen on Hazel's lovely face, and so captivating that I forgot myself and automatically began sharing her happiness without even knowing its source. She had caught me during a vomiter's recuperation, which is usually Manik Mudigonda at his absolute worst, his most morose, least energetic, and least eloquent, but these things did not matter once Hazel Kroes flings herself into my embrace, mashing her lips to mine so tightly that I'm certain she could taste the cigarette I'd just smoked. I hope she liked it.

Shakti incarnate, she began to back me into the flat, leading me right to the bed where I fell backwards, most certainly a stupid, stupid, cheerful smile on my face. She started to unbutton my shirt, to fight with my clothes as if they were serpents; I would have returned the favor if I could have slipped an arm through the frenzy around me, but I had to wait until her work was done, and even then, I was contending with hands grasping my shoulders and teeth biting onto my chest hair and tugging on it. I started to laugh at the wonderful madness of my circumstances, but, ceasing her delirium momentarily, Hazel put a finger to my lips and hushed me. With this arm occupied, she gymnastically snaked her other arm free from her dress and hushed me again. I tried to stop laughing, but the best I could do was continue to grin in my idiotic way.

"You," she moaned. "You, you wonderful, wonderful man, Manik Mudigonda, I love you!"

I opened my mouth to easily let that same three-word incantation slide from my tongue, but she still hushed me. If it was my job to keep quiet and make love to Hazel, I suppose I could handle that!

Once in her natural state, I quickly discovered that Hazel's hair had begun to grow, dark and soft and even, giving her beautiful, delicate face just the slightest hint of a young Brahmin boy a few weeks out from his Upanayana, when his relationship with the Devi should be the closest it will ever be. If it didn't suit her perfectly. As she continued to nip and claw at my flesh, I ran my hands over her velvety pate, only to notice that Hazel's eyebrows were now real rather than ersatz, and that eyelashes had begun to line her eyes once again. I was not to say anything, but I know what I would have said, if given the opportunity at that moment: you are yourself again, Hazel, and I love the healing you just as much as the broken you.

I felt last night that she wanted to devour me, like an overripe mango. Yes, I felt distinctly of a mango, the bites and the sucking of my juices. A necklace of bruises drapes over my chest like a chain of office, I will mourn them when they fade. I just laid back and let her consume me, I was happy to be the prasad on the altar. As she crept up my body, leading her lips to align with mine, I began to angle myself and was gleefully welcomed with a total saturation of moisture. Our arms wrapped tightly around one another, we both went into wild pulsations, not always in perfect sync, but I didn't care and I doubt that Hazel cared either. We started a little waltz: a few moments of dancing with the lady in superior and then a fast and forceful roll to place myself on top. We did this many times, it began to acquire a rhythm, not a simple, duple meter but more like the complex polyrhythms of the Chuka, dancing at the base of Mount Kenya.

The evolution of Hazel's pillow talk could be the pleasant subject of marvel and analysis for me for years to come. It was so intensely encouraging, I almost entered a trance. Manik, Manik, Manik I love you, Manik I love you, I love you, I love you, you god among men, you sexy sexy man I love you, I love you, I love you Manik, I love you, you beautiful, beautiful man, I love you, I love you, I love you Manik, I love you, you big, beautiful, wonderful, sexy man! At the climax it became a battle between our voices to see which would rise the highest: Hazel! Hazel I love you! Manik! Manik I love you! Hazel! Manik! It was as if we were, in our rolling and pulsating, becoming fused, a singular being, melted together in sweat and sexual juices and saliva, some embryonic conjoined creation ready to spring from the womb. And I came in her again, but I knew better than to fight it, I know that it's what she wants, but decided to see if I could push through the initial sensitivity to continue on, and did not do badly at all, did quite well indeed. When we finally collapsed in a hot, wet heap of humanity, Hazel's face buried in my neck, we both sort of sighed in that self-satisfied way.

"Well, hello there," I laughed, panting, reaching for a cigarette for each of us.

"Oh, Manik, my sweet Manik, you are the greatest friend that I have ever had, do you know that?" she said, the heart-shaped red rash of passion throbbing on her bosom.

"Am I really? I am honored!"

"Do you want to know what happened just the night before last, before Pier left for the mainland?"

"Tell me."

"Pier and I made love for the first time in nearly three years, Manik, my sweetness, and I've you to thank."

"Really? Is it true? Oh, Hazel! What beautiful news!" I gasped, taking liberty with my kisses on Hazel's short hair. She laughed and, lifting her face to meet mine, I could swear that her eyes sparkled at me like stars in the sky.

"When I first showed him my head shaved, he did not like it, he put me down and belittled me. But as the days went by, and I wasn't pulling, I wasn't obsessing with my hair in my fingers, he began to take notice of me again. By the time he could see the new growth, why, I'd say he was proud of me, Manik. First, he smiled at me, and then he started to help me more often at home with tasks, lighting the oven pilot light for me, things like that, things he would never stoop so low as to do in our entire marriage. And it started with just a kiss, just a little kiss, and I could swear he felt the imprint of your lips on me, how sweet and tender they have become, and he wanted to make love with me. And it was so lovely, Manik, so lovely. I mean, Pier, Pier is not the marathoner that you are, Manik, and how could he be without the practice, but it felt so wonderful, that my husband loved me again. Pier loves me again, Manik. Pier loves me!"

"Hazel, Hazel my queen, Pier has always loved you, and will always love you. And, let it be said, that the same is the case for me. I will always love you, Hazel."

"Oh Manik," she said in a beautiful, wistful exhale, the smoke from her lips mingling with the smoke from my own. "Oh, sweet Manik."

"You don't have to say it. I know it already."

"I don't want to say it."

"It isn't necessary. It was the goal of our journey together, wasn't it?"

"Was it? I don't remember anymore. I only remember you, and your sweet lips and warm body, your passion and your tenderness."

"Good. That's how it should be. When suffering ends, it should just vanish from your memory, that's how it ought to be. That way you can just go ahead and live life in a better, happier way. And it doesn't mean that you've forgotten what you've gone through, but it means that you're finished with the pain. It's the best thing, it means that you're well and normal."

And so she sighed and cozied her head on my chest, a hand sweetly and absently brushing over my belly, lifting the hair at the root. "You're an adorable, hairy fellow, aren't you?" she murmured, a slight giggle in her voice.

"My hair should be a natural resource. I could have territory battles over my head and chest, with the Italians crowding onto the backs of my hands."

"Oh! I thought you were going to say your back!" Hazel laughed.

"I have not got hair on my back!" I protested, most offended at this suggestion.

"No, you don't do you, sweet Manik. I think I was just confusing you with Pier for a moment."

"Is that so? Now, that's more than I ever needed to know about Pier Kroes. I was going to be so horrified, hair on my back indeed! Now, bottom, that's a whole other story."

"You and your big, hairy, spectacular bottom! You know that Lord Greenwich uses it as a selling point when talking about you to ladies, did you know that?"

"Unfortunately I do. He is quite the salesman, isn't he? Oh, and speaking of Lord Greenwich, it is my birthday party coming up shortly,

June twenty-second, that's my birthday, I'll be a full thirty-two years of age and nothing but trouble."

"Thirty-two? You're really that old, Manik? I never placed you at any older than twenty-five."

"Fat people don't wrinkle up so much I suppose," I teased. "So, will you be coming to my birthday party?"

"No, I'm afraid not, sweet Manik."

And I didn't say a word, just smiled, because this is exactly what I'd wanted to do, I wanted to make Hazel feel better again, and I suppose I have. This was what I needed to do, and truly, last night's affection was not required, but she gave it to me anyway. I didn't deserve it. How thoughtful that was, to spend one last night in my arms, kissing my neck while half asleep. Without question one of the best lovers I have ever had. How lucky I have been to even exist in the same room as Hazel, let alone be her lover, be her servant, gigolo. The luckiest gigolo in Mombasa.

Friday, June 20, 1913

Two days before my thirty-second birthday, I started the day off distraught: twenty stone seven. How is it that even when being somewhat diligent about expurgation and really giving a good attempt at limiting alcohol and sugar that I gain weight? It seems that the only way I can lose weight is by such severity as to make any other sort of simultaneous activity almost impossible. I must be constantly vomiting, constantly starving, constantly drunk or else I just swell up. My hopes for nineteen stone ten dashed away, and, the fool that I am, I start thinking longingly for twenty stone again! Or nineteen stone, for goodness sakes. And then I remember those fleeting, dizzy minutes in 1904 when I was eleven stone, I didn't appreciate them, I was so unhappy then, I should have been kicking up my heels while I could. At least I am not thirty stone like I was in 1899, which, for some reason, I did not despair nearly as much as I could have. All in all, I think that, when size is eliminated from the equation, I think I have had one rather happy year, which was age ten, and the rest of them have been pretty awful, but with minor improvements each year since age twenty-three. I don't fear getting older. I like it, I learn more every year, I get better at the things that interest me. The loss of my virginity certainly opened a new, better world to me, which has only been improving, really. Here is to thirty-two, to thirty-three, to thirty-four, and to lots and lots of romance. Maybe this year I will romance someone so well that I will be able to whisk her away to be my wife. That is always the goal. I thought it might be thirty-one, and before that, thirty, but thirty-two might be the year, it just might.

So, no, I am not completely miserable, although I might have been, and part of that derives itself from an early, serendipitous gift from

Hadleigh. He came in to the office late and kept poking his head in at me, saying nothing and smiling in an overly-excited, suspicious way. I could not tolerate it for long, so I gave in.

"There is absolutely something you want to say, Hadleigh, is there not? Go on, go ahead."

"Oh, please don't encourage me!" he cried out dramatically. "You know how impatient I can be, you should tell me to take my time and to wait until at least tomorrow."

"Hadleigh, I can't concentrate with you bubbling over like a fresh bottle of champagne. Get it over with, it will be better for both you and me."

"Do you insist?"

"I do absolutely insist."

"Well, since you insist!" And away he rushes. It is for moments like this that I renew my appreciation for Hadleigh, and remember why he is my best and closest friend. He returns with a massive box wrapped in decorated paper, green ribbons and white lace and hurls it on top of my desk, sending documents flying both left and right. "For your birthday, Manikji."

"You really shouldn't have, truly, the birthday party is more than a gift enough."

"Come on, now, Manikji, I know that you like a gift in your hands. Look at you, ruby tie pin, silver cigarette case and lighter, you love it when I give you birthday presents, you don't need to pretend."

"I can only admit this to you, you know. Don't go telling everyone in Mombasa that I'm a spoiled brat who loves being given things. And you know fair well that the only reason that I can admit it to you is because you, sir, are equally spoiled and you live to flaunt your Christmas haul every year."

"The two mad princes of Cape Town, Manikji."

"Two mad princes indeed. All right then, shall I stop trying to analyze the situation and open it?"

"Open it, man, open it!"

"Shall I make a show and preserve this beauteous wrapping, or just tear in?"

"For God's sake, Manik, just tear in! The suspense is killing me."

"Just as much me as you, my friend." And so, letter opener in hand, severed the ribbons and tore off the paper in a single swipe, to reveal the name of Hadleigh's tailor on the top of the box. "Oh, you didn't buy me clothes did you?" I said, disappointment clear in my voice. "Hadleigh, it won't fit me, you know how I've been these past few months. One moment fat and the next moment fatter."

"Just open the box, Manikji, just open it."

"I'd much have rather jewelry, Hadleigh."

"It is jewelry, it is. Open it!"

And inside that box was a gold silk sherwani embroidered in real gold threads, with genuine faceted citrine beads encrusting the collar, a gold satin sash and cuffs buttoned with such studs, surely no less than twenty-two karat gold. I knew instantly that I didn't want it. "Oh, no, Hadleigh, oh, no, this is terrible."

"I know, Manik, I knew you'd react like this."

"It must have cost you a fortune, Hadleigh. The expense..."

"A thousand pounds. I'll tell you right now. A thousand pounds."

"One thousand?" my ears perked up, remembering what Dorothy had told me, but I then quickly doubted the connection, as one thousand had to do with the party, not the gift. Then, after making this quick analysis, began to cough. "One thousand pounds! That's more than you pay Mr. Wangai for a year! And Hadleigh, Hadleigh my friend, I don't even want it, I don't want it. I'll look terrible in it, you'll see. We've had this discussion before, for goodness sake: I only wear Western dress, Hadleigh, I look so silly and obvious in things like this. And that's not to say that it isn't beautiful, because it is, and a stunning example of superior craftsmanship, but you know me, Hadleigh. You know I'm a plain linen and serge sort of man, I don't want to stand out in a crowd any more than I already do, and in this, Hadleigh, I will be visible from Uganda."

"Now, Manik, I knew you'd make all of these arguments, but hear me out for a moment."

"But, Hadleigh..."

"I've let you state your case, it's my turn, it's only fair."

"Fine then, state your case."

"I know perfectly well that you are, as you say, a 'plain linen and serge sort of man.' And in case you haven't noticed, you have a massive wardrobe at home of plain linen and serge that fit you badly and that look absolutely awful on you. You look positively dreadful every single day, and I know that you can't refute me because you know that I'm right. Confirm what I've just said, Manik."

"I confirm it. But it's because I'm ugly and piebald and pockmarked and as fat as a hippopotamus."

"No, it most certainly is not because of any of those things, because you're a very handsome man, those things aside. You've the most expressive face I have ever seen."

"My face does not wear clothes."

"But you know what does wear clothes? Your big, broad shoulders wear clothes. Before we continue this argument, just try it on, just see what you think. Please, I have gone to quite a lot of trouble and expense."

"This is true." I frowned and sighed and pulled out the sherwani, blinding in its gold glory. I threw my serge blazer with the brass buttons on my chair and stood up to put on this extremely expensive garment. I had a hard scowl on my face, but as I pulled on the sleeves and did up the buttons and frogs and tied the sash, an amazing thought entered my head. "Impossible, Hadleigh, impossible."

"What is it that's impossible, Manikji?"

"Hadleigh... how did you do this? What measurements did you use? What witch doctor did you consult?"

"Now, why would you be asking me that sort of thing, Manikji?" Hadleigh grinned, his voice and expression revealing some really detestable but deserved smugness.

"It fits me. It really does fit me, really! It's not hanging on me, it's not ready to burst at a single seam, it's not buckling, it's not riding up, the sleeves hit me at just the perfect spot, my neck isn't being strangled. I don't think I've worn anything that fits me in years, Hadleigh, and it fits me perfectly, just as I am at this very moment."

"Come on now, come to my office, I want you to see yourself in the mirror." After letting Hadleigh pull my hair together neatly and smooth out my shoulders, I obliged, and while, yes, I would never have chosen to dress in blazing gold sherwani, I looked in the mirror and I felt as if I were seeing someone else. Some elegant aristocrat whose garments skimmed his body with grace and perfection, someone very sure of himself, someone important, someone very mature and wise. A thirty-two year old Brahmin prince. I broke into tears instantly. Hadleigh immediately moved to comfort me. "What's the matter?"

"It isn't me, Hadleigh."

"What do you mean?"

"I know who I am. And that's not me."

"Of course it's you."

"No it isn't. Because I know who I am, I'm a fat, ugly, harried solicitor who works long hours and drinks too much, and I'm fine with that, really I am. But I have no idea who that person there is, no bloody idea."

"Well, here's a question for you, then. Do you like him?"

"I think he's magnificent."

"In that case, why don't you enjoy playing at being that magnificent man in the mirror for your birthday?"

"All right. All right. You know, when you put it that way... when you put it that way, Hadleigh, it seems really quite lovely. Yes, I'll be whoever he is for my birthday, what a wonderful gift you've given me, Hadleigh. You've given me exactly what I've always wanted."

"And what's that you've always wanted?"

"Not to be myself."

"Oh, Manik," Hadleigh smiled, his eyes to the ceiling like they do travel whenever I tell the truth. "So, tell me a bit about this magnificent fellow that you'll be impersonating. Does he fancy ladies?"

"I should say so! He's obviously married."

"Well, let's say he weren't married, or let's say he and his wife have an understanding, even better. Would he fancy the attention of some interested beautiful ladies at his upcoming birthday?"

"I think he would oblige, yes, I think so."

"Then he's in luck, because in addition to whatever ladies he fancies at any given moment, he is guaranteed engagements with the following four lovely damsels." And with that, Hadleigh produced me a small slip of paper with four names written on, none of which I recognized: Mary Delaney, Edna Johnson, Ruth Spencer, Clara de Vos.

"Really, Hadleigh?"

"Absolutely."

"Because I'm guaranteed at least also Gladys and Dorothy as well, aren't I? And probably more than that." I kept both Njeri and Akinyi in my head, for as good a friend as Hadleigh is, I still can't tell him everything.

"It's a good thing the party is four days long, then, isn't it?"

"Good thing indeed. I'll need just as many to recover. Oh Hadleigh," I opined. "Hadleigh, I shall always be your friend. You are so good to me."

"I always knew how wisely I chose when I decided to link my chain to you, Manikji, and if I can make you happy once a year, then my life is worthwhile. Anyway, you know perfectly well that in all things we are a team, brothers, you know? The more and more discerningly you womanize, the better things are for me."

"I never understand that logic, Hadleigh, but I will believe you if you say it's so. Just look at that man there, that great, oversexed prince. I will enjoy his harem for him. Mercy, do you realize that he has to stay this precise weight for two whole days until the party?"

"Weight fluctuations are not healthy, it's better he stays the same anyway, that's the advice I would give him."

"He wouldn't give a damn anyway, just look at him, he has greater concerns."

"Greater and more pleasant concerns."

"Indeed."

So, I'm really looking forward to Mudigondamas. It will be great fun, being this magnificent, wise, mature, and I dare say sensual thirty-two year old Brahmin prince. I will enjoy it very much. It will be a shame to have to go back to being myself again afterwards, but as they say, it's better to have loved and lost than never loved at all, and it's better to have been a real proper prince temporarily than to have never been one. Maybe Nia will come. Maybe then she'll believe me, and she'll let me sweep her off her feet and marry her, but the joke's on her, because when the party ends, she'll wake up to see this ugly, bookish solicitor puttering around, oiling his hair and smoking a cigarette as he tries to drag himself to the office in the morning.

Sunday, June 22, 1913

Oh, it's my birthday! It's my birthday today! I am so excited, so nervous, I have no idea of what to expect, other than it's going to be exciting and I am going to be one very lucky promiscuous man. I don't have to head out until sunset, so I tried to conserve energy by staying in bed in my dressing gown, but when Kaweria came by this morning, I just had to show her my new sherwani, I could not resist, I am such a child. She drowned me in compliments and told me that I looked like a crown prince on his wedding day. And she even teased me a little bit, how wonderful is that? She was telling me to have a good time for my birthday, "But I want you coming back home with all the parts you had when you left, Mr. Mudi."

"All of them?" I was really misbehaving, but it is my birthday, I'm entitled to misbehave.

"Yes, all of them! I want every hair on your head intact."

"I shall try."

I had champagne with breakfast. I am such a spoiled brat, spoiled, spoiled, spoiled. I need a spanking in my thousand pound sherwani. A thousand pounds! And I hardly care! A thousand pounds spent on one absurdly impractical sherwani for me? Why of course, please do go ahead. Give me ten of them, give me the Taj Mahal. I might thank you and give my blessings to you. It's an absolute shame, really, an absolute shame that my father and brother didn't see me fit to live a Brahmin's life, because I'd be the best, most disdainful, ungrateful Brahmin that has ever lived. Give me things, oh ye who has nothing! It is your privilege and my burden! Oh, I jest, I know, but it is my birthday and I'm allowed to be happy once a year.

Thursday, June 26, 1913

What exquisite agony. Oh my head. My head my head my head.
My head hurts so much I wish I could knock it against a rock and split
it open like a coconut. I never want to see sunlight again, never. I am
never going to drink again, that is it for me, I have learned my lesson. My
relationship with drink is officially over. I never want to see champagne
or cognac or gin or whiskey or hock or port or any of it ever again and I
mean it this time. Because, if I can divert my attention away from my
head, oh no I think I might still be a bit drunk, room spinning...

Friday, June 27, 1913

So this is the science experiment of the hour: it is an in-depth analysis to determine what part of my body hurts the most. Of course, the head is still a distinct front runner, the head is probably still the winner, but in addition to head, I must do a careful comparison that includes the following body parts: stomach, genitals, knees, and teeth. Since this is science, I must use a control, which is a part of my body that does not hurt, for which I nominate my left thumb which is still in reasonably good stead. All right now, state of control, left thumb: not hurting as far as I can tell. State of head: pounding alternating with throbbing, with searing knife pricks to the temples, and feels as if it has trebled in size. State of stomach: mercy, my poor belly, intensely queasy, burning, with a steady dull ache, trebled in size. State of genitals: terrifyingly sore, vibrant red, trebled in size. State of knees: they neither bend nor flex and if I tried to step on them I would collapse to the floor and remain there for the rest of my life. State of teeth: I have decided that I don't want teeth anymore, that they exist only to torture me, and I cannot even describe the almost electric pain that shocks me every time I am stupid enough to bite down. Excellent, so the results of my scientific inquiry are as such: the most painful part of my body is still my head.

Saturday, June 28, 1913

Back at the scene of the crime, hangover gone, feeling absolutely excellent in every way. I wish I felt this way every day. It's my skin, my skin feels better, and for some reason, my skin feeling better makes all of me feel better. There are many reasons to love the big, beautiful Mombasa seashore, but the air here does something to my skin that is so fascinating. My skin is paradoxical in many ways, especially since the smallpox in 1899. The smallpox scarring makes my skin look the texture of granite or brick, it looks as if it would be hard and rough and tough, when in reality the opposite is true. My skin is impossibly delicate and soft and thin, and constantly a bit damp, and most of the time it feels like it would easily just slough off my face in thick, gray rolls until the blood vessels were exposed. It makes me disinclined to touch the worst areas of my scarring, and for years I shaved my neck an inch at a time in fear of disturbing the unstable attachment between skin and throat. But, sit me on the seashore for a few days and the skin just solidifies, it becomes stronger, tighter to my body. It feels better, it feels more secure. It looks worse, though, because the pigmented parts get darker and the unpigmented parts stay white, except for this incongruous spray of temporary freckles that spread democratically over my nose, ignoring white and brown boundaries, that appear around my birthday and disappear a month later. My face is maddening, just maddening, but I feel quite well, I feel well-constructed and fit.

What a great party. I had the best time of my life, I had never had so much fun, in fact I did not know that fun like that could even exist. Fuck tally time: On Sunday I fucked Edna and I fucked Gladys. On Monday I fucked Mary and I fucked Katie and I fucked Ruth. On Tuesday I fucked

Njeri and I fucked Dorothy and Akinyi sucked on my nose. On Wednesday I fucked Clara and I fucked, now hang on, who was the last person I fucked? The Maasai lady, what was her name? What was her name, damn, I must remember. Think, Manik, think! This is very important. I have kept detailed records of every woman I have ever fucked in my entire fucking career, I can't ruin my record now! Short name, short name beginning with R. Resson, her name was Resson. She was my last birthday fuck, and she was beautiful. Fuck tally for thirty-second birthday: ten fucks in all! It's positively heroic. And of the new ladies, perhaps I will derive a new, long-term affair, I would like that. Perhaps a permanent affair. I would never explicitly ask for a permanent affair, or even suggest it, but I would like it. It would not be a real replacement to having a wife of my own, but perhaps I could be happy as just a permanent lover. Every Monday night or something to that effect, and I would have certain rights, like the right to insist on games and positions that I like particularly. I could protect myself from mistreatment.

So this is what panned out for me, my Mudigondamas celebration! The sun started to lower in the sky at about half past eight, and, donning my gold sherwani and gilt-edged dhoti (also a gift from Hadleigh; the silly man had the fabric starched and ironed into a big, Bengali fan on the bottom but I had Kaweria wash the pleats out for me – it was not worthwhile to explain to Hadleigh that while it is true that I am from the eastern half of the Indian subcontinent, I did not grow up that far east, and I am, in some ways, just a typical Bhojpuri boy who wouldn't be caught dead in dandy great fan pleats), strolled proudly out to Hadleigh's Benz, which was already outfitted with an exceptionally attractive young English couple, Mr. and Mrs. William Johnson, who have taken up residence in Kampala not but one year ago. While Hadleigh drove, he introduced us to one another, and, which was to be expected, Mr. Johnson is a great noisy windbag (a diplomat), all sound and fury signifying nothing, and his wife Edna is pretty and soft-spoken and twice as intelligent as her husband, with half as many things to say. She was clearly intimidated by my appearance, but was so well-mannered as to try her best not to let it show; I appreciate those efforts, I really do. I also liked how, in spite of her husband's name being William, and therefore "Bill," she calls him "Bob." A woman with her own agenda, a woman scheduled to have an affair with me.

After our brief sojourn, I discovered the meaning of one thousand: one thousand meters of Mombasa beachfront had been tied off to host the event, which had no fewer than one thousand guests and one thousand local musicians and dancers. The beach was covered with huge, Egyptian-style tents of every color, mine marked obviously in red for the ruby-eyed prince of Mudigonda. I say prince with such nonchalance for, upon my arrival to the party's campsite, I was loaded onto a gold-painted litter held up by six exceptionally strong Maasai warriors and a huge choir of Maasai singers clad in red and blue plaids gave me a spectacular concert as the sky behind them turned orange. I love Maasai singing, the complex polyphonies, there is so much to absorb, it helps me to forget myself. At the end of the formal concert, I was placed down on the ground again, given a fascinating, confusing cocktail with mysterious ingredients, and led to my own tent where Edna and I could get to know one another better. The choir continued to sing and improvise, and their beautiful voices carried through the soft, salty air, putting me very much in a good mood. Edna is delightful, a plump little peach with beautiful brown curls in her hair, and we took to flirting very easily. I told her the history of Mudigondamas, how my birthday became such a significant annual party, how it all originated with Hadleigh's desire to thank me for all I do for him every year and also to distract everyone in the ex-pat community from the fact that he, too, also has a birthday, whenever that may be, and, like everyone else in the world, he gets older. "Hadleigh would sooner live as a beggar than reveal how old he really is," I teased, lighting myself a cigarette. Edna laughed in a very natural way, and then leaned into me, allowing me to wrap my arm around her.

"He's a bit dishonest, old Hadleigh, isn't he?" she asked, as if the honesty of a solicitor were only the most obvious thing to question.

"Perhaps it would comfort you, dear Edna, to know that he is also proficient in lying to himself," was my reply.

"He was not at all forthcoming as to your true nature, Manik," she said tenderly, my name coming off her lips in such a kind way.

"Did he tell you that I was radiantly handsome? Are you disappointed? Because he should not have done that and I apologize."

"Oh, no, quite the contrary. I suppose I could divulge how it is that I find myself in this tent with you." The lady paused, but not in a bad way, in a thoughtful way. "I have had, for quite some time, a fantasy of being taken by a frightening stranger. I confessed this fantasy to a lady friend of mine, who surely is also a friend of yours, and suggested that I talk to Hadleigh about you. He wrote me a long description of you, that you were a big, terrifying hulk of a man with a red eye and patterned skin and long, wild, white hair, that you were a sullen Oriental with a resentful nature, and that you would play the part of the frightening stranger better than any other man. I got excited and agreed, but as today's date grew closer, I started to regret my decision, I started to really fear you, and then you appear in Hadleigh's Benz, and oh, you are a very imposing figure indeed, Manik. You took my breath away and my heart started to race."

"From the sound of it, Edna, Hadleigh was completely honest with you, I am all that he describes, and I did give you a fright, didn't I?"

"But you aren't, Manik, you aren't how I thought you would be at all. You have such a sweet voice, and such a gentle way about you. You've nearly no accent at all, a lovely way of speaking. Even the way you smoke, so calming and peaceful. I do not find you frightening in the least. In fact, I find you very comforting. It is not an hour I know you, and yet I feel safe with you, Manik."

"Oh dear. I feel badly about that now, I wish that I had known your fantasy so that I could have given it you properly. I am very sorry, Edna my darling."

"No, no!" the lady protested, putting a hand to the center of my citrine-bejeweled chest. "As the date approached, I did realize that it was not the frightening part of the fantasy that I wanted at all, in fact I had started to dread it. It was just the stranger. Someone different, someone," she whispered, carefully caressing a lock of my white hair, "very different indeed. And what a wonderful relief it is to find out that you are such a kind and charming man, even to apologize for not being frightful enough, that was so very dear. And Bob... Bob would never..."

"He'd never suspect. I know." I decided to move things along slowly and pressed my lips softly to Edna's cheek. "I like that you call him Bob rather than Bill."

"I shouldn't have married him. I don't even like his name." Edna looked down bashfully to her gloved hands.

"Well, Edna my darling, you need not waste another thought on him, at least for an hour or two. This is your time with the not-at-all frightening, terribly strange stranger, is it not? Tell me your desires and I will answer their call."

"My desires are simple," Edna purred, nuzzling her head beneath my chin. "Just be the opposite of my husband."

"And how can I do that?"

"The simple fact that you exist in the form that you do, and that you've any interest at all in my desires is a good start."

"Poor misguided Bob," I laughed, kissing Edna on the top of her head. "I suppose he's under that misapprehension that ladies haven't any desires at all. Have you ever insinuated as such?"

"I constantly insinuate, and oftentimes more than insinuate, but, in spite of the doctor saying that he isn't at all deaf, he never seems to hear me."

"I have excellent hearing. That's different, isn't it?"

"It must be those earrings."

And so I listened, attentive and interested. Things that Edna likes: kisses on her ears, little peck kisses in general, simultaneous undressing, face-to-face lovemaking, whispering while making love, being reassured that I can hear her, long, slow, deep thrusting, the taste of a smoker's semen, the overall design of my equipment, including its color pattern, eating sugared fruit with me, telling me jokes. A joke from Edna: A Viking longboat gets caught in a terrible storm, and all of the rowing slaves begin to cry in fear. The Viking king reassures them: "You have no reason to cry, as I've freed you all in my will!" What an awful joke! I laughed anyway. It's the delivery that matters most, I told her. Edna is so very sweet and pretty, everything about her is so small and plump and well-proportioned, especially her pretty red cheeks. If I have any hope of a permanent affair, I should hope for Edna! It was nearly midnight when she scampered away, giggling and still in a poorly secured state of undress. Concerned for her modesty, I emerged from the tent as well, my sherwani completely open, only to discover that nearly everyone around me was in a certain degree of undress as well. Only the first night as well! I suppose there was no resisting it, the air was so balmy, and a gigantic bonfire right at shore's edge demanded a certain degree of impropriety. The Maasai were still singing, but now joined by a group of Luo musicians with their nyatiti lyres and drums, playing off one another and, in a way that only music can do, bringing their two cultures together in harmony. I noticed that some of the men, all of the English ones naturally, were in a battle to throw one another into the ocean, and that, in spite of some exceptional efforts on the gang, they were failing to get Hadleigh in their grasp to give him the old heave-ho. I saw that my services were needed, and so, walking directly behind the foolish aristocrat, hurled him over my shoulder with one arm and, running like a rhinoceros in heat, chucked him into the waves like a javelin as he screamed and cursed at me. A round of applause broke out, but I lifted my arms to silence it.

"No need to thank me," I said. "It was my pleasure."

I heard Hadleigh shouting and spitting and running toward me, but he was caught by the crowd and pushed back in again. I knew that he would not be held for long, and my punishments were soon to come, but I was rescued by the lovely, cheerful, giggling voice of my Gladys, oh, my Gladys! After seeing that her husband was well-occupied with the drowning of my best friend, I scooped her up in my arms like an ape and kissed her, which made her squeal with delight and kick her dainty bare feet. She had me bring her to her little tent, where I met Gladys's two new favorite people. I was enthralled.

"Is this my nephew? Just look at this beautiful, radiant young prince!" I gushed as Gladys put the perfect, cheerful baby boy in my arms. "Well, hello, Cyprian!"

"Oh, Manik, you remembered!" Gladys opined, both hands to her heart, and then both arms around my back. "I do call him that when my Bill isn't around, although I shouldn't because it might confuse him, don't you think?"

"If you were my mother, Gladys, I shouldn't be confused about anything in the whole world. He is just a wonder, and so brave! Not a peep from him, being held by some big, scary man with a red eye, absolutely courageous. You have a proper hero here, Gladys, Arjun on the battlefield."

"He's up and happy because he knows what time it is, sweet Manik. Hand him here, it's time for his midnight feeding."

"Oh, I am always cheerful in time for my midnight feeding as well!" I replied, carefully handing the next Lord Downpatrick back to his eternally radiant mother. I had thought it impossible that Gladys post-partum would be even lovlier than Gladys in late pregnancy, but I had thought wrongly. While some women become old and haggard and tired-looking as new mothers, Gladys has only bloomed, her face ever lovelier, fresher, and more intensely feminine. When she prepared her full, pink breast to nurse her son, she made the reason evident to me with the introduction of her new nursemaid, a sweet and beautiful older Kikuyu lady from Kenya's interior who goes by the name of Miss Kiyoni. Beautiful, bare-bosomed Gladys, her chestnut waves of hair tumbling carelessly over her shoulders, brought her baby's lips to latch on to her pointed nipple, and there, reassuring her and stroking her arm was lovely Miss Kiyoni.

"I owe all of my happiness to my Kiyoni, Manik," she said, a perfect smile spanning her face. "I did not think I would be able to nurse my son, as my mother did not nurse me, and I was preparing to look for a girl to do it for me, but my Kiyoni taught me what to do. My Kiyoni is more than just my nursemaid, she is my closest friend, and only because you, too, are my closest friend, Manik, I will tell you that I love her more than my own mother." In a moment of true emotion, Gladys turned her head to Kiyoni and said to her, "I love you so much, I love you with all of my heart, my Kiyoni." Miss Kiyoni kissed Gladys on both temples. I knew instantly how fortunate I was to be witness to such a beautiful scene, how I had been welcomed to be a part of a tight circle. I came to Gladys's other side and watched young William nurse, his blue eyes full of peace.

"My Gladys tells me that you are a special man, that you mean very much to her," the older lady spoke, her tone as soft as a zephyr breeze drifting in from the Indian Ocean. "I love my Gladys like she is my own daughter. She is a good, African girl."

"Manik is African as well, my Kiyoni."

"Yes, I am. My heart is African." I really meant this, and I will mean it until the day I die. I am a student of law and human nature from Cape Town, that is who I really am. I do not have any reason to ever return to India, none at all. Africa is my home, Kenya, Mombasa is my home. I will live out my days on this seashore, and Gladys will live out hers at the base of Mount Kenya. Africa is our home. Kiyoni, quiet and gentle, helped Gladys to switch breasts and burp little William, and then the dear little pink-cheeked fellow gave a great yawn, stretched out his tiny arms, and fell fast asleep in his mother's arms, content as a child can be. It would not be a lie to say I envied him, but I envied his father just as much. I am ready to raise a child, to hold my wife while she nurses him. I also envied Gladys, to have been adopted by such a wonderful lady as Miss Kiyoni. It made me miss my own mother, how she would kiss my hair when I did my lessons well. If I ever have the chance to marry, I should hope for a lady with a kind, warm, welcoming mother of her own, and I could be her son as well. I miss being a son sometimes, I miss being praised and comforted and spoiled.

After young William had slept soundly for a few minutes, Gladys placed him gently in a soft, round nest of pillows at one side of the tent, and she and Kiyoni exchanged knowing smiles. Off we went together to my tent, its base covered in red and gold kilims and ottoman pillows, low-lying tables covered in sweets and cigarettes, and a huge bucket of ice filled with bottles of Veuve Cliquot champagne. Gladys and I laid down together and she seemed so much the same, only happier. Gladys is pure happiness. Her kisses tasted of candied oranges and meringues. I soon found myself in my preferred state: naked and slightly drunk. How Gladys laughed when I shot the cork straight out the entrance to the tent, into the dark oblivion! And how she has become an African girl, in a blue shuka and rings of cowrie beads around her neck, it suits her better than any English dress, and especially does justice to her new figure. Gladys's new figure is not very much different from her old figure, except that she is plumper, with a fuller bosom and a softer belly. She was wearing a few red stripes on her hips, though, so to reassure her, I showed her my own latest.

"You've copied me! What's next? A red eye as well?" I teased, stroking and caressing her. I know that I cheered her, in a way that Bill Hendricks would not even be capable. Men do not always understand how important it is to a lady to feel beautiful, and have a difficult time conceiving of the fact that even the most beautiful woman, like fresh, bright, lovely Gladys, might be unsure of reality. "I marvel at how lovely you have become, Gladys. I become less and less worthy of you at every encounter."

"It is a lucky thing, then, that the spot for you in my heart only grows each time we meet, sweet Manik," was her cheerful reply.

"It had better grow! Or else I'd better find a way to lose weight."

"I've always liked you just as you are, Manik, however that might be."

"It is a rare thing that we have, Gladys."

"It is a rare thing that *you* have, Manik. May I?"

"Do you really think you need to ask?" What a birthday gift! I laid back on the ottoman cushions and let Gladys enjoy my foreskin. Those reckless fingernails, those careless little pearl-white teeth, the lips and the tip of the tongue. It was not a minute later that I found Gladys balanced on her arms, her head tilted back, her knees pressed up against my ribs. This is an advanced position, not to be attempted by a man who can't control himself and can't keep a steady rhythm and a perfectly tandem response to the lady in his company, or else one can say goodbye to one's hamstrings. This is not a position for a man under age thirty. For a thirty-two year old man, it is ideal. Like the music outside the tent, it was all call-and-response: she gets her thrill on the tension, I get mine on the release: oh Manik, oh Gladys. Also: learned that lactating mothers cannot conceive. Go right ahead, Manik, go right ahead! I ended up licking out the majority anyway, but what a useful bit of knowledge, truly. And also discovered that I have never forgotten the taste of breast milk. As Gladys reacted to my lingual attentions, milk began to drip from her nipples, and I was not about to let it go to waste. I got, perhaps, a bit too enthusiastic and had to be reminded that it was William's milk I was drinking up!

"It is not milk but cream, Gladys," I replied, kissing up the lady's throat.

I escorted Gladys back to her son and mother only an hour after I'd absconded with her. An hour that I will treasure for the rest of my life. It was the small hours of morning as I left her behind, and I decided that it was time to get properly drunk as I had not yet been better than tipsy. The Maasai singers were indulging in fermented honey and fermented milk, so I decided to try them both, much to their amusement. The honey was quite to my liking, but the milk was not, so they let me take the whole gourd of my preference, aware that I am the guest of honor. I was exceedingly grateful, not at all good, disdainful Brahmin style, and asked them to help me learn a song. We all gave it a try, but there was no teaching to be done for me that would last until sunrise, the first time I have ever been drunk on honey. I followed it up with kaffir beer and then went staggering, attempting to sing a song I'd never learned, back to my tent, only to discover a beautiful woman fast asleep on my cushions. Not one to argue or be in any way unfriendly, I threw off my sherwani, curled up beside her, wrapped my arms around her, and fell asleep.

I could feel myself waking up as the midday sun warmed the earth beneath us, but I was not badly hung over. I love the feeling of waking up with a soft, warm, lovely feminine creature in my arms. Unfortunately, she, too, was waking up, but not in the same slow, pleasant way. She jolted and screamed, and I reflexively let her go.

"Oh God!" she cried out. "Where am I? Who are you? What's happened?"

A beam of sunlight caught her hair through the openings in the tent's cloth, and I could see that it was of a dark, almost blood red, as thick and curly as my own, but her face was terrified. The lady was only dressed in a long, silk chemise with no foundations; I began to regret my drunken exhaustion in not introducing myself earlier, for I feared that she suspected that I might have harmed her unawares. I sat up quickly and began to apologize, my heart up in my throat.

"Nothing has happened, dear lady, nothing at all. This is my tent, on the beach in Mombasa, I did nothing but fall asleep beside you, I swear to it." I found myself kneeling, my arms outstretched in penitence. "I was much too drunk to have done anything more than go unconscious."

The lady stood up and scanned the tent, as if she were searching for her other clothing, which were nowhere to be found. For a second, she looked ready to bolt out of the tent, but then she thought the better of it, for whatever reason. "Who are you? What is your name?"

"Manik Mudigonda is my name. This is my birthday party." I said these words with eyes squeezed tightly shut.

"What's that? What's your name?"

"Manik Mudigonda."

"Open your eyes."

My eyelids snapped open in terror, only to see the lady examining them very carefully, staring at the left one in particular. "You must be him. You really do have one red eye."

"I am the only man I have ever met with one red eye," I sputtered in an apologetic way. The lady began to circle me, walk around me slowly. She twiddled my hair, stared at some of the flashier patching on my arms, touched the pockmarks on my sweating forehead. Then, she gave me a stern look, a hand at her chin, and she stood that way for a long time. My knees were starting to hurt, but I dared not move a muscle.

"And you're Hadleigh's friend?" she asked.

"Yes, yes, that's me, that's me."

"Saints alive!" she burst out in cackles of laughter. "It's all right, man, no need to associate yourself too closely with that English marauder! I was looking for you last night, is how I come to be here!"

"Looking for me? Why?" I was still afraid, I am an idiot.

"I'm Mary Delaney."

"Mary Delaney? Mary Delaney! Of course, of course, yes." I heaved a sigh of relief and wiped the sweat off my forehead, seating myself down on my shins, which was not the great aide to my poor knees as I might have hoped. Thus immobilized, I wobbled my head and bowed, in replacement of a standing greeting. "A pleasure to meet you, dear lady. Please make yourself comfortable."

"Thank you very much, sir," she replied, sitting herself back down again. "I didn't mean to fall asleep in your tent, but I must have been three sheets to the wind myself."

"I love that turn of phrase, you know. My favorite English idiom, I use it whenever I can," I teased, still calming down. I lit myself a cigarette and attacked another bottle of champagne. "And after a night of being three sheets to the wind, a hair of the dog that bit me."

"What a rare gentleman!" Mary laughed, cheerfully accepting a glass of the bubbly. "Old Hadleigh was right, I do like you, I do. I couldn't say why, but I do. Never in my life did I ever think I'd wake up next to some strange, bare-chested man from Malabar with a painted hide, and if you'd told me it wouldn't bother me, I'd have called for the police."

"You are not the first to say as such, dear lady. However, I must correct you, I do not come from Malabar, I come from the Ganges river valley, but these things are immaterial, really. I'm Mombasa through-and-through now. Do you, beautiful Mary, also live here in this fine city?"

"Beautiful Mary! I knew there was a reason why I liked you. It's because you may think yourself to be Mombasa through-and-through, but you're a bit Irish as well, I suspect, with that sort of gab you've got, better than mine, an Irish lass from County Down. But we are living in Nairobi now, the man and I, but I like the looks of Mombasa, I do. It seems a very hospitable place."

"I like it here," I sighed, leaning back a bit on the soft cushions. I gave Mary a wink and took her free hand in my own, the other well-occupied with champagne and cigarette. "So, tell me, beautiful Mary from Nairobi, why have you been looking for me?"

"Oh, that is the question, isn't it?"

"I'm afraid it is."

"If I tell the straight truth, it will ruin your birthday for certain."

"Nothing can possibly ruin my birthday. Nothing bad ever happens on my birthday."

This is actually true, it is. It was a few weeks after my eleventh birthday that Madhulika died, and my eighteenth birthday marked the turning point in my recovery from smallpox, and my brother did get married on my tenth birthday, which certainly made him happy in a multitude of ways. It is no wonder that I should like my birthday so much. For having been born on such an inauspicious day in such an inauspicious manner, it has become my most auspicious time. This only goes to show: horoscopes are nearly always wrong.

I assured Mary of not only the auspiciousness of the occasion, but also my vocation as a servant to women's happiness and pleasure, and she told me her story. Mary's husband is something of a bon vivant, a scholar and wit, and his fidelity is entirely nonexistent. After sixteen years of hiding her pain and jealousy, she finally confronted him about his affairs. Instead of either denying the charges or apologizing for doing wrong unto his loving wife, Kevin Delaney took her confrontation as an invitation to continue his dalliances in a more flagrant way. Profoundly hurt and disgusted, but unsure of herself, Mary has decided to give her husband a taste of his own medicine.

"But I don't know about men at all! I've not even kissed a man other than Kevin, and I hadn't a clue of how to start," she explained, honest but uncomfortable with her own honesty.

"You have come to the right place," I assured her, kissing her hand. "I am as safe and easy an inaugural affair as you'll ever find. I need no convincing, I am by my very nature discreet, I follow directions well, and nothing you can do or say will ever bother me. The only drawback is my appearance, I'm afraid, but it is my hideous aspect that enables my exceptional discretion."

"For once old Hadleigh doesn't lead me wrongly. I'm glad to be in your hands, sir. But that English tusspot, bless him, neglected to mention a certain dimension to you," the lady replied, a slight look of concern on her face.

"You mean he didn't say that I'm fat? Impossibly, absurdly fat?" I grinned and fluttered my eyelashes, bringing a laugh to Mary's pale face, skin the color of ivory. "It's all right, it's not as complicated as it looks, and I'm more than fully functional."

"Oh, sir! I didn't mean to put you on the spot!" she cried out, her head tossed back with all her glorious, garnet-red curls. "But one might have mentioned."

"Amazing, he mentioned the red eye and the pockmarks and all of this patching business and all my hair, but neglected the centerpiece of it all? That would be Hadleigh. Most likely because you would have said no if he'd told you about my size."

"I wouldn't say that..."

"But I would and have. So, how do you feel about it now?"

"I'm uncertain."

"That's all right." I stubbed out my cigarette butt and put down my empty glass and laid down relatively flat, my face still smiling. "In science, when you're uncertain, you do close observation in order to gather information. I'll stay totally still unless you tell me to move, and you can take an examination of me. Then, if you want to stay or leave, it's all up to you, it won't upset me if you decide either way. I only exist to make you happy."

"Oh, sir," the lady sighed bitterly, "I'll be a bit biased if you keep saying things like that!"

"I'll be quiet then."

Mary nervously approached me, and decided to begin her research with my left hand, a shy, conservative choice of starting places, and checked that all of my knuckles bend in the proper direction. She then moved up my arm, touching first lightly, then more firmly, and giving somewhat of a wince when she saw my bad scarring on my arm's inner skin. I thought she might stop right then, but continued on to my shoulder, which she squeezed like a ripe fruit, and proclaimed, "Big, but I can hold on to it." She swiped her hand over my collarbone and to my neck, which was already stubbled, and she proceeded to measure the volume of my double chin, which I will admit, in its brief absence, gave my face an almost unrecognizable shape, so essential it is to my basic self-image. I think it's because I had it my entire childhood. I am just double-chinned, and I am so consistently, unless I am very thin, unless I am well under thirteen stone. Fortunately, this constant accoutrement to my face did not deter Mary terribly, as she then put two fingertips on my lips, which could only mean that she wanted them kissed, which seemed to be true. She moved to my hair, where she lingered for quite a long time, and had many questions to ask: Do I bleach it to be so white? (No.) Did it take long to grow it? (Yes.) What do I do to keep from going bald? (Nothing.) Have I ever worn it braided? (No.) Have I ever worn it in pins? (No.) Have I any interest in hairdressing at all? (No.) So I mostly just let it be? (Yes.) Do I ever plan on cutting it off? (No.) She seemed loathe to leave it and move on to more anxiety-producing aspects of my physique, but then lightly placed a hand at the center of my chest.

"Oh, you're very warm. I'm always chilled," she said softly, stroking my chest slowly and gently. She let her hand travel slowly downwards, and just let it rest to the right of my navel for a while. "You're very soft!" she exclaimed, nervous laughter coming from her coral-pink lips. "But soft could be very nice. It's a confusing thing, because I know that you are a very big boyo indeed, but touching you, and seeing your sweet, lamb's expression, you seem quite a comfortable size." I said nothing, and Mary tenderly traced her hand over the lower edge of my belly, which was a little ticklish but so lovely. And so, slowly, cautiously, Mary laid herself down and curled up into my embrace, just as she had been when she was asleep. "You've a languid way," she whispered, her nose an inch away from my own. "I know what my mother would call it, she would call it heathenish voluptuousness. And that is you, isn't it?"

"You make it almost sound glamorous," I laughed. "The names Christians have for those who refuse their dogma, and the suggestions inherent within them. Why, it makes it seem as if my cheerful promiscuity were to be derived fully from my refusal of church membership rather than out of a genuine enjoyment of female attention."

"So, what's your story, then? Were you some coolie boy who got to go study law?"

"Coolie boy indeed! Brahmin prince, thank you very much. Look at that gold jacket over there, doesn't it scream out Brahmin prince? I've always been terribly important."

"Forgive my mistake, your majesty!" Mary replied, clearly still under the impression that I was really just a coolie boy who'd done well for himself. It didn't matter to me, though, for she stroked my bristled cheek with her hand and kissed me on my lips. Well, if coolie boy was what she wanted, then coolie boy I would be. I stayed quiet and still and looked innocently into Mary's blue-gray eyes, as if I knew hardly a word of English and had only some indistinct, base, animal morality from which to derive my thoughts. She kissed me again, but I still did nothing, I remained passive. She wanted to coax me, rather than the other way around: she wanted to play the role of her husband, taking advantage of someone weaker, someone disenfranchised and silent. Mary could be read like the sharpest of bold, black text on crisp, white paper, and it was no Brahmin prince that had captured her imagination, but the panicked, begging servant on his knees, terrified of the power that she might wield; it was no surprise, then, when she began to investigate the mode of attachment for the complex folds of my dhoti, her hands surreptitiously looking for a way to remove it without my full knowledge. I just smiled at her and acted as if I had not noticed, until she finally found the crucial knot and tugged it open. To reward her, I bit my bottom lip and blinked at her like a baffled young calf. She then quickly wriggled out of her shift and, before my eyes could linger on small, ivory bosom or little, perfect navel, she crashed into me, immersing herself in my body in a heated, passionate way. And, in spite of my admission of my all too active and varied sex life, Mary stroked my face and whispered, "Don't be frightened."

So determined I was to make Mary happy that I was able to rub a tear away from my eye as she crawled atop my lap. More hushing and stroking and a finger was placed on my lips. I was swiftly guided inside. I do not think that some women really understand penile erections, that they come from one's own pleasure and arousal, and not out of the desire to please a lady, but I have often wished that this misapprehension were true. When a lady likes to think that she's taking advantage of you, the simple fact of an unprovoked erection obliterates this illusion. I wish it were not so, if only to make Mary happy.

"That's a good boyo," she said, shivering upon her penetration. "Now let's give a bit of it."

I gave Mary a bit of it, which means starting out slowly and tentatively, and only responding to verbal abuse: "Come on lad! Give it faster! Faster for Christ's sake! For Christ's sake give it faster!" I will confess to having become over-excited, it was something about the position, and Mary's attitude, and falling in love with her as I do, that I really did start to panic, that I might ejaculate inside her, so at the very last second I could bear, I grabbed Mary at the waist and lifted her off my body the entire height of my arms, which at first made her shriek. But then, she looked down to see my disgrace and she smiled. "I see I've done right by you, lad."

I allowed my nervous expression to soften and I lowered Mary to my chest, where I clutched her and rocked her and kissed her feverishly all over her face. I let her look at me for a moment, I saw the pride and excitement in her eyes, and I gave her the most I could give. "I love you," I whispered. She kissed me on my forehead and patted me on the arm so that I would let her go. She made a quick rinse of her body with the ice water in my champagne bucket and tossed on her shift, her skin still wet, the thin silk adhering to the forms of her slender body.

"I like you, feller," she said, standing over me, her hands on her waist and one hip cocked up jauntily. Still naked and filthy, I stared up at her and grinned. Not a second later, she was gone.

Hungry, sober, and nicotine-deprived, I decided to freshen myself. Hadleigh always thinks of everything when it comes to my birthday, and a full array of brand-new implements for my own personal care were already there, waiting my use in the tent. I took time shaving, oiling my hair, considering the terrible situation which is my teeth, and, fully washed and perfumed, downed an entire bottle of champagne and half a bottle of scotch whiskey as I dressed again in my gold sherwani and dhoti, alcohol my only real puja these days. I emerged to the light of the bright golden Mombasa sun, and the gems and gold of my own dress almost blinded me. I fumbled, clumsy and dazzle-eyed, trying to light myself a cigarette, only to feel the favor done for me.

"Thank you, Hadleigh." As it could have been no other. I inhaled my first drag, long and medicinal, and felt his arm curl itself around my back. "I'm sorry I threw you into the waves yesterday."

"Oh, don't bother, Manikji," he replied, a twinge of embarrassment in his voice. "I was glad to see you in the spirit of things. No hard feelings at all. You are having a good time?"

"Of course I am! Three so far, Hadleigh, three. I am the happiest I have been since my last birthday. Thank you, my friend, for this paradise you reveal to me once a year." At those words, particularly the word "paradise," I caught sight of a group of bathers in the clear, green shallows, mixed company, all apparently undressed. "Honestly, just look at that. I almost wish I would die this very moment, or go blind, for I shall never see anything so lovely again."

"Speaking of lovely, did you just shave?"

"Yes, did I cut myself?"

"No. No, you just look very handsome."

"I know you like to cheer me, Hadleigh, but you needn't be so terribly dishonest."

"I am not being dishonest in the slightest. See, do you see Venus emerging from her toilet, her eyes affixed on you and you alone? Tell me, Manikji, wouldn't one need significant attractive qualities to manage the long-distance seduction of a siren such as she?"

I squinted momentarily, my eyes finally adjusting to the light, and recognized the approaching figure, the well-formed shoulders, the long, strong legs, the sun-kissed cheeks. "That is not Venus, Hadleigh, that is Diana! You invited Katie Nettle, oh bless you!"

And so it was, the beautiful child of nature, unashamed of her glorious nudity in its total perfection, did come to me, clasping both of my hands, and kissing me sociably on the lips, beads of salt water tumbling down her limbs and neck, her hair drenched and smoothed away from her bright and joyful face. It was true in a way, what Hadleigh said: she ignored him completely and did not even say a word to him, choosing to lavish all of her attention on me. "Hello there, birthday boy!" she proclaimed in her girl's school, field hockey and polo sort of way that she has. Katie Nettle is by far the most English woman I have ever known, and it never ceases to amuse me: her loud, boyish voice, her gregariousness, her use of the phrase "good sport" to denote the highest level of praise that any person could ever earn. This is one reason why she holds a special place in my heart, but also because she was the second woman with whom I ever made love. I believe that it was Katie Nettle who truly ripped me out of my chrysalis of sexual repression and introduced me to the pleasures of shameless promiscuity.

"Hello, my lovely!" I laughed. "You are a sight for sore eyes, Katie my dear. Are you getting a chill?"

"No, no, not at all! Perfectly refreshing that water is, Manik! You look like goldmine, but you must be stifled up hot. You should join me in the ocean, it feels wonderful."

"Do you mean swimming?" I asked nervously, always aware of Katie's athletic inclinations and my own constant failings in that arena. "I can't swim a stroke!" Hadleigh, still beside me, nodded that this was true, gave Katie a roguish wink, and then, silent as a cat, trotted away with some similarly soaking friends, perhaps to be thrown into the waves again in his linen suit and pith. Katie tutted me and squeezed my hands tightly.

"I'll teach you!" she announced.

"No, you can't teach me, Katie. I'm a bit drunk, I'll sink like a stone."

"Oh ye of little faith! I wouldn't let you drown, Manik, for goodness sake, you ought to trust me! Anyway, you've your very own personal floatation device right here. We'd need a harpoon to send you down to the wreckage." Katie tapped a large, wet hand to my citrine-embellished belly and grinned at me.

"Percy still a bore?" I asked, of Katie's famously dull, famously puny husband who doesn't even make a dent in the bed.

"Percy is always a bore."

"Well, all right," I conceded, untying sash and kicking off jutti into the sand. "I'll let you teach me how to swim, but listen here, I'm not terribly sober."

"You're never sober, Manik, and I've never seen it hold you back in any endeavor. Come now, it'll be great fun." Katie has such great enthusiasm for "endeavors" and she always thinks that just because she finds them fun, that I ought to think the same: tennis, football, tetherball, badminton, even croquet have proven themselves to be not only beyond my own abilities, but frustrating wastes of time, time that could have been spent making up for Percy's inadequacies, but I know that with Katie, in order to get to that much more enjoyable task, one must first endure some athletics. It is at these times where being inebriated is actually somewhat of an advantage, for, in spite of impaired reflexes and vision, my well-developed sense of embarrassment is also impaired, so although sobriety may have made for improved performance, it would also have most likely frozen me in place, thus eliminating my opportunity to cuckold poor Percy Nettle. And so, freshly drunk and naked, my extremely expensive garments thrown carelessly in the sand, I was dragged to the water's edge by Katie Nettle's well-muscled arm.

"Keep up, old fellow!" she admonished. I don't think I made a reply, but grinned, somewhat aware of the wide-open eyes of my fellow bathers. Manik Mudigonda naked in his bed in the company of one lady is quite ugly but still in the realm of human appearance, almost endearing in the privacy of the warm, enclosed space, but Manik Mudigonda en plein air is indescribable. Even hideous is too mild. But, I will do anything for Katie. Absolutely anything.

She guided me into the ocean a bit too quickly I think, for although the water was not at all cold, it felt sharp, rough against my skin as I trotted behind her into the depths. Suddenly, I stepped off a ledge of sand and went sinking quickly down to the bottom of the sea like I had predicted. Down I went, completely unconcerned for drowning, ready to let the water replace the air in my lungs, calm as can be, fatalistically thinking to myself that it had been, if not an entirely happy life, then at least not a dull one. This peaceful acceptance of my imminent death was interrupted by Katie's hands pulling me up by the armpits.

"Oh, Manik!" she scolded, not slightly exasperated, dragging me to standing again. "Don't you know how to float?"

"Float?" I sputtered, blinking the saltwater out of my eyes. How clear my vision was at that moment, how beautiful Katie's bronze and rose complexion seemed to me. I would try better, I determined, to make her happy. "How do I do that, exactly?"

She put her hands on my back. "Lean back on my hands, lie down on your back. I'll guide you with my hands, all right?"

What a magnificent thing water is, that a woman can lift a man twice her size as easily as if he were a newborn baby. The waves were just at Katie's shoulders, but she told me to look up at the clouds in the sky, not at her face. She gave me lots of instructions. "Spread your arms out at your sides, open your hands up and spread your fingers. Keep your legs straight at the knee, that's right. Tilt your head back some more, good fellow. Arch your back now, arch your back. Lift your chest up, come now, arch your back, Manik, and do breathe, get air into your lungs. That's better, right? Do you feel yourself lifting up?"

To tell the truth, I felt almost nothing at all. I just stared up at the bright sky and watched the spots form on my cornea, watched them dance about like pink and gray paramecia in the great Darwinian pond of creation. I felt no air, no water, just a simple equilibrium, suspension in nothingness. If I were a real Brahmin whose relationship with Brahman was still unsevered, I would have said that I was having a moment of unity with the universe. Of course, I was just a fat, drunk, clumsy idiot floating on his back in the Indian Ocean, water filling up his ears so he can only just barely hear the lady's voice say, "See? Not hard at all, is it?" And then, a minute later, to be tugged by the wrist quite sharply: "Don't go floating out to sea!"

I lost my concentration at that moment and crumpled inwards, but instead of sinking again, I kept my grip on Katie's arm and she kept me afloat. I righted myself and grasped onto both of her arms so that I could gaze into her face. Before I knew it, I was treading water, and not in a panicked, helpless way, but a very natural way. I could not help but laugh. Katie kissed me on the nose and began moving us further out from the shore, the slight waves lifting and dipping us as we traversed. I don't know why, but I did trust her very much. We were quite a ways out when she told me: "All right, I've brought you out. Now you bring me back."

"Bring you back? I don't know how."

"Yes you do, it's simple. Just go back to the shore." Katie then crawled onto my back, one arm wrapped around my sternum, and the other pointing at the blurry shoreline, the bathers, the musicians, and the tents. I think the prospect of drowning dear, well-intentioned Katie as well was what kept me afloat for those moments of confusion. "It's like you're crawling through the sand, just through water instead. Imagine that you're crawling across the desert, trying to reach an oasis."

"Oasis? What's an oasis?" Oh, the things I forget when drunk and naked with Katie.

"Well, there's palm trees, and water springs, and flowers."

"I think I'll just vanish in the sand if that's all it is."

"Not interesting?"

"Not at all."

"Do you know what is interesting?"

"Do tell."

"You're swimming quite well."

"Surely I'm not. I'm sure there is a gradual scale between fully drowned and swimming well, and I am probably closer to the former than the latter. I have not succeeded at a single athletic endeavor you've ever requested of me, I don't see why this would be an exception."

"Just shape your hands a bit better. Make them like cups. Good sport."

"I should probably not argue with you, I'm guessing."

"Try to get back to shore before you're fully sober, Manik."

And I did. To tell the truth, I did not realize when the water became shallow and, chest scraping against the sand, beached myself like a suicidal pilot whale. The tide was starting to go out, and I played that I had intended this error of judgment, rolling over and pulling Katie to my lips as the waves washed over us in the light of the Mombasa sun. If Percy Nettle had seen us, I don't think I would have cared, but he popped up in my mind anyway, like a mosquito biting me in the ear. "Is Percy around?"

"No, and I don't expect to see him until tomorrow the earliest."

"Tomorrow? Why? Has he left camp?" I asked, sobriety and curiosity creeping up my spine as I wiped the sand and stray hairs from Katie's lovely face.

"He's gone in the tent with some of the other fellows to chase the Chinese dragon."

"Your husband smokes opium?"

"Only on special occasions. You were quite strong in your reaction, Manik. It would surprise me if the king of the libertines disapproved of the occasional drop and tincture."

"No, no, I don't disapprove at all," I replied, my face growing warm with sunshine, abrasion, and embarrassment. I helped Katie to her feet and led her to my tent where we could brush away the sand in private, as well as do other things of a more intimate nature. I said nothing about the moniker at the time, because I'm sure that the idea of committing adultery with the king of the libertines is far more thrilling than with shy, awkward Manik Mudigonda, but it did bother me a bit. I know that it is fashionable to attribute libertinage to any sort of pleasures of the flesh, especially uncommitted sexual dalliances, and I am sure that my famous devotions to gorging and inebriation may further color that sort of misinterpretation, but I am simply not a libertine, and I hope to never be one. My self-worth is dependent on whether or not I can make people happy. I am not willing to hurt another for my own pleasure, but I am more than willing to hurt myself for the pleasure of others. That does not a libertine make. But, if Katie wishes to think that I drink myself silly, go have a swimming lesson in the Indian Ocean, and then fuck her from above for my own pleasure only, then let her have that happiness. I smiled at her mildly. "No, I have no critique for opium. It would just be hard for me to think of your Percy..."

Katie tossed her head back in wild laughter and nearly fell backwards onto my collection of elegant pillows. "Have you ever actually seen my Percy, Manik?"

"No, but I think I've a very clear picture of him from your descriptions." I lit myself a cigarette and poured a large brandy for the lady and for myself, and then slowly inched myself next to Katie.

"Is that so? How do you imagine him, then?"

"I imagine him the color of porridge, bespectacled, weighing in at about six stone, with rubber bands for arms and legs, no chin at all, and a head shaped like an egg."

"Is that what I've told you, Manik? Oh dear!" Katie's laughter steamed up the inside of her glass as she tried to stifle her giggles for a sip.

"Am I off?"

"I wish you were. It seems I do tend to tell you the truth, Manik old boy."

"I suspected as much. Otherwise you'd never bother with me."

She said nothing more, but shut her eyes and kissed me on just my bottom lip. That's why she likes me particularly, because I can give her something that her Percy never could: over twenty stone of pressure all focused on her clitoral nerve. That's what she wants from me, she wants to feel the presence of a man that she cannot ignore. Poor, egg-headed Percy Nettle. I will never ask Katie why she married him, because it's none of my business, and because I'm afraid if she becomes dissatisfied too much with her husband's shortcomings, she will become all so much more aware of mine. I like Katie as she is: forgiving, cheerful, and impressed by sheer size alone.

After we made love and convalesced for a while, I could hear the Luo musicians starting up again, and the Masaai singers warming up. Then, it seemed even more drummers and musicians had arrived, and my curiosity was piqued. "Oh, listen to them, Katie. Let's go join the concert."

"I'll come with you," she enthused, her smile bright.

"You haven't any clothes, though, have you, Katie my sunshine?" I asked, thinking pragmatically as I began to dress myself, cigarette on my lips and dhoti on my hips, my own set of raiments carefully placed in their proper place by some invisible set of hands.

"Dress me in that there, then," she gestured to the red patterned Maasai cape draped over some of my essentials. "You clearly know how."

"Same as mine, or proper for a lady's virtue?" I asked.

"Same as yours of course!"

"Well, why not. This is Mombasa after all," I reasoned, helping Katie to her feet and commencing to pleating. "An Englishwoman wearing a Maasai cape as a dhoti should be the official emblem of the city." Off we rushed, bare-breasted and drunk, lured by the music and the song, and although there was a voice in the back of my mind reminding me that I do not know how to dance, I conveniently ignored it and began blithely and pathetically imitating the stomping Masaai, Katie holding tight to my hand as we leapt and rattled the earth below us. Both Katie and I, in spite of already having expended much energy in several other performances that day, were loath to give in to exhaustion. The clapping and cheering audience passed us alcoholic encouragement, which although it does not invigorate the bones, helps one to forget how foolish he looks, and perhaps also spurs him on to do the only dance he knows how to do properly – the Straussian waltz – with the least appropriate musical accompaniment and no shame at all. I swung Katie and her quickly-drying sun-streaked hair around and around, as if I hadn't a care in the world, until I went fully dizzy and we collapsed in a heap off to the side. This elaborate display of clumsiness got the greatest applause from both party-goers and musicians alike, and the concert continued. I was then treated to real Maasai dancing by the experts. How I wish I possessed such talent. During Mudigondamas I would more than gladly sacrifice my skills as a rhetorician and logician for the skills of a dancer.

At some point during the concert, Hadleigh sidled up to me and sat on my right side, Katie at my left, and began lighting my cigarettes for me. After a great climax, which involved the lead male dancer flipping himself in the air twenty times in quick succession, my aristocratic partner tapped me on the arm excitedly. "The next part is just as exciting, I planned it especially for you," he said, his eyes as bright as a child's, but I could tell that truth was being told: a bejeweled litter was being passed into the throng of musicians, carried by two Taita men in full festival regalia. I anticipated a Taita singer, which was what I really wanted, but when the litter was dropped at the center of our improvised stage and the curtains opened, there was an elderly tabla player in dhoti kurta, starting a teen tal. I turned to Hadleigh in anger.

"Do you never listen to me?" I scolded. Hadleigh gave me an opaque expression, which did not satisfy me at all, and I started to get up to retire away from the music. I do not want Indian people at Mudigondamas. They make me feel extremely self-conscious, the way they look at me. I know that they all hate me, these expatriate Indians who would have to touch my feet if we were back in our homeland, they relish being able to look down on a fallen Brahmin, promiscuous, red-eyed, lower than the lowest Dalit. I can tolerate their gaze on the streets of Mombasa on an ordinary day, and I will tip my head and press my palms, and they will reciprocate, but with expressions of distrust and disgust. I hate them all. I am more than happy to live out the rest of my life surrounded by foreigners, for they will never truly grasp how far it is that I have fallen. It was with this sort of anger that I was willing to desert wonderful, half-naked Katie when Hadleigh began pulling me back down again and shaking his head.

"He is blind, Manikji."

Quickly I looked at the musician's aged face and saw that Hadleigh spoke the truth; pearly gray cataracts covered the old man's eyes and protected him from the sight of me, and protected me from their sight. I was so moved by Hadleigh's thoughtfulness that I embraced him, which is something that I absolutely never do: his reward. He did know, he did know that I would love the security of listening to music that I've missed for the last nine years without concern of observation, and the man was a true master, perhaps the best I have ever heard. I was mesmerized until the sun began to set and the old man dipped the heel of his palm on the tabla for the last time, so mesmerized that I made Hadleigh go fetch me what I wanted from the banquet rather than going myself so I would not miss a second. Well, perhaps I would have done that anyway. Ordering Hadleigh around is something that makes us both happy. At one point, the old man began a dadra tal, and Hadleigh started teasing me that I should join in. I do actually know how to sing a dadra tal, but I told Hadleigh I couldn't. I think he knew I was lying, but he understood.

As the stars appeared in the big, beautiful Mombasa sky, the Masaai bell-dancers appeared, all of their enthusiasm and feminine charm on display in the torchlight, their ankles ringing with hundreds of tiny bells. It was then that I spotted Resson for the first time. She was the best dancer, and more than that, I suspected that someone had told her that I was the birthday celebrant, so she made sure to organize her glances and her gestures primarily for my own benefit. I smiled at her as a gesture of thanks, but without question, also out of that hot-faced marvel that I still experience when seeing a particularly beautiful woman. No jaded seducer me, and I doubt I shall ever be.

Towards the end of the bell-dancing set, Hadleigh excused himself and returned, only moments later, with a young woman who also inspired in me this amazed blushing. "I thought you might be getting tired, Manikji, so I thought I might introduce you to my friend, Ruth Spencer. My word, Ruthie, how long is it I've known you? All our lives?"

"Perhaps all of my life, Horace," the lady teased. I liked her immediately. She has the same accent in speaking that Hadleigh does, that form of English that implies having come from a very important feudal family. Her beauty, however, quite unlike that of Hadleigh's, was not of the aristocratic kind, and I would just as easily have taken her for a fresh-faced, innocent farm girl. Her face especially was so soft and pretty, it gave her an almost childlike aspect, and her adorably crooked smile with the teeth crossing over one another only reinforced that impression. Her hair was of a pale, khaki hue and seemed very soft and fine in texture, I wanted very much to touch it. She looked at me a bit nervously, but put out her soft little hand to me, as someone of such excellent breeding would not hesitate to do. I took it, and well aware of my state of undress and my wild, ocean-soaked and wind-blown curls, kissed it as tenderly as could be done.

"So lovely to meet you, Miss Spencer," I said.

"Mrs. Spencer," she corrected me. "I was once Miss Radcliffe, but Mrs. Spencer I am for now. A pleasure to meet you, Mr., er..." In spite of her formal choice of words, her voice sounded so timid and breathless. I wanted to comfort her, especially as she struggled with my surname.

"Just Manik is fine." I gave her a meek expression, and Hadleigh responded with that approving expression that he often gets when I'm playing the part well, that expression that I find simultaneously soothing and condescending. I stood up, sandy and sweaty and consistently tipsy, my dhoti gone askew and my thread knotted up in my tangled hair, feeling like barely more than just Manik anyway. Ruth was, unlike the majority of the female guests in attendance, still immaculately coiffed and dressed in a cream-colored silk and a visibly restrictive corset. Hadleigh made some of his unnecessary comments about we two going off and getting to know one another better, and Ruth let me take her hand again as we departed from our spot by the musicians. She already seemed like a willing participant, but then, a wealth of riches as she always bestows upon me, Katie interjected a point that brought Ruth to a full-fledged crooked grin.

"Mrs. Spencer," she called out in her rugby-field way, "Manik is quite wonderful in his own way. Be a good friend to him and he'll be a good friend to you."

I lowered my eyes immediately and smiled in a very stupid way, I'm sure. "Mrs. Nettle is always overly generous," I mumbled. "Until later," I intoned over my shoulder, and wild Kali goddess that she is, Katie kissed the back of her hand and then flipped it in my direction. I love that woman, I love her far more than I should.

I soon found Ruth and myself alone in the crowd, walking hand in hand along the shore together under the light of a nearly full moon and a thousand oil-fueled torches, the flame of one I exploited to light myself a cigarette. We did not speak at all for quite a while, but rather just walked together and smiled at one another. As I was not quite sober, I did not find this at all odd, and enjoyed it very much. I felt an automatic calm and comfort, which, as I look back, was really quite selfish of me, as the lady's silence was obviously derived from a certain amount of anxiety. I flicked my cigarette butt into the ocean and double inhaled the last atoms of smoke, and finally thought of something to say.

"Have you known our Hadleigh for a long time, Mrs. Spencer?"

"Oh, ages. His sister Louisa is like my own sister, she is so kind and lovely."

"She is, isn't she? One can find no fault in Louisa, especially in the realm of patience."

"I suppose one would develop patience when closely involved with Horace."

"It is true. As his business partner, I have had to develop such sage-like patience, it now takes me three-quarters of an hour to pass a busy road."

"He is a bit of mischief, isn't he?" the lady insinuated, in rather a serious way.

"A bit? Yes, rather."

"Well, I don't want to speculate or gossip, but I have heard that he's in a spot of trouble. I'm sure he's confided in you?"

"Hadleigh is always in a spot of trouble, but I'm certain that if it were more than he could handle, he'd come to me first, of course. We have a very explicit trust, you see."

"So it's not nearly as bad as I've heard, then, that's good to know. Louisa will be happy to hear your confirmation."

"People like to gossip about Hadleigh, but it's rarely very worthwhile. I do actually get jealous, though, for it's a very rare thing that anybody bothers to gossip about me," I chimed, trying to lighten the mood again after Ruth's genuine expression of concern. "I think I'm worth a bit of gossip, wouldn't you say, Mrs. Spencer?"

"Oh, certainly," she blustered, her lovely mangled teeth on display. "I'm sure that people have tried, but there is something about you, Manik, that awakens the protective instinct."

"That's a very kind thing to say," I replied, genuinely touched by this honesty, but also somewhat uncomfortable. "So, I'm a bit like a three-legged calf, then? Without the visual charm?"

"Louisa was right about you," Ruth laughed. "Horace was full of the old bollocks as always, but Louisa told me that I would like you. I," the lady's voice faltered, "I don't want to sound too forthright, or as if I don't trust you or think you worthy of such great trust, but I would rather not have to explain why I want... what I want from you."

"Please don't think that you need to explain anything or that I deserve any such thing, my lady. I don't want to make any demands of that sort, to impinge upon your privacy and the sanctity of your marriage. I only wish to make you happy in the best way that I can."

"Oh my," the lady gasped nervously. "You only wish to make me happy?"

"Yes."

"I must apologize again for my tone but, but I have not ever done anything like this before, and I don't know what sort of rules of decorum you follow."

"I haven't any!" I laughed. "How could I possibly have any rules of decorum? Look carefully at the man who holds your hand, Mrs. Spencer. Observe his lacking dress and the state of his hair, not to mention the more obvious idiosyncrasies of appearance. This is a mind without order, a heart without boundaries, a body incapable of violation. I am yours, Mrs. Spencer, however you wish me to be."

"I see," Ruth replied thoughtfully. "So, as for touching...?"

"You can touch me any which way."

"But I should give you warning, surely."

"No warnings necessary."

"Because I think I might like to..."

At this point we were quite a distance away from the eyes of the main party, but not far from my own tent, which was surely full of pleasant things for us to enjoy, but Ruth's eyes darted left and right and she looked over her shoulder quickly before she embraced me at the side and began to rub my belly in a circular manner. What anxiety over such an innocent imposition! I tried not to laugh but I could not help myself. "Come now, my darling. I can see that we'll get along perfectly well," I said, guiding Ruth up the sand dune to my tent. She remained latched around my waist, her facial expression like a small child sucking her thumb, and required some very gentle coaxing to give me a wide enough berth so that I could get myself down on the cushions and rest beside her. We kissed for a while, not the sort of heavy kissing that I get up to with the likes of Dorothy or Katie, but like a child bride and groom on the wedding day. This seemed to be what Ruth really wanted, because she then stammered in my ear, "Will you pretend to be my father?"

Now, I have played at being son, student, charge, slave, whore, prince, mystic, and even lawyer. I have devoted every orifice to the pleasure of women, including my nostrils, and I have been hit, smacked, tied up, pinched, and even forced to vomit, but I have never had a woman ask me to play at being her father before. More than any request I have ever had before, my gut instinct wanted to shout out, "No! That's appalling!" but I suppressed it. I am not Ruth's father, after all, and if this was what she really wanted, she was choosing only the safest and most harmless way to fulfill her desires. I whispered my reply: "All right."

"You will?"

"Well, what is he like? Is he a big, fat, spotty bloke like I am?"

"In a way!" she replied, her voice all but giddy.

"So, what should I do?"

"This is what will happen," Ruth began, now quite animated and energized in her speech. "First, I'll misbehave a bit, and you'll scold me, as if you're really very disappointed in me, and you'll... punish me."

With those words, I could not stop my urge to protest, I simply couldn't. "I really don't do that sort of thing, I'm very big and I could hurt you very badly..."

"No, no, not the mean sort of punishing," Ruth denied gleefully, shaking her head in a way that showed she thought me really quite silly. "The nice sort of punishing."

"Nice sort...?"

"Yes!"

"Oh. Oh, I see." My discomfort was not in the slightest way laid to rest, but instead only increased. I tried to shove out of my mind any stereotypes and preconceptions I had about British nobility, and also tried to forget about Ruth's idea of "nice" filial punishment and deal with the task at hand, but I'll tell the truth, it was all but sick-making. I think I must have begged god and gods for this to be mere fantasy and not the nightmare that it seemed, and, looking back at it now, this was probably the worst request any woman has ever made of me. I can think back to the difficult relationship I had with my own father, especially after my mother's death, and how he saw me as Mai's replacement in an emotional sense, relying on me to constantly assuage his fears and be at his beck and call, and with nothing much more than a kiss and two arms wrapped around me, I felt a primal disgust at the situation. I made Ruth happy, but it was not easy for me, at least not at first. I must have winced in a perfectly believable way when I watched the pretty young woman tip a full glass of claret onto her cream-colored dress, not so much out of fear for the garment, but from the awareness that the game was afoot. I was to be at that moment Lord Radcliffe, the angry, loving, incestuous father. I pulled up my every ounce of gamefulness, all the role-playing lessons I learned from Lila in her prime, put my fists on my hips, and began to scold: "Now, look at what you've done, Ruthie. That dress cost me a bloody fortune, when are you going to learn to take better care of your things?"

Ruth was ecstatic. She began to laugh in a manic way and opened her eyes widely at me. "Oh, please don't get angry with me, Papa."

"That does it, young lady, no more pretty dresses for you, it's strictly burlap sacks from now on, you hear? Now, get that dress off right away so that the maids can get to work on that stain." I reminded myself of what I was really going to do, which was make love with a beautiful woman, which is not only the greatest thing in the world, but something which cannot be sullied by any silly words that I might be forced to say in the achievement of this goal. I must have breathed a sigh of relief as I undid the buttons down Ruth's back, how normal and comforting it was to me, just another new lover being undressed for the first time. Her corseting was slightly out of date and reminded me of Consuelo's back in 1907: long, tight, and restrictive. I do understand the appeal, but give me barely-clad Katie or Gladys in her shuka or Njeri in her bubu any day. Women's bodies are always better when they can be touched. "And will you stop wearing your mother's corsets, for goodness sake? I can't believe I've raised a thief."

A buckle undone, a lace untied, and surely enough I discovered a real human body attached to Ruth's pretty, girlish face, and a perfectly beautiful one at that. Just slightly soft and dimpled around the navel, her upper arms, and with the most amazing, flame red nipples I have ever seen. Absolutely bright red, amazing and beautiful! I immediately wanted to nurse, but I thought that would be more appropriate for a son's role than a father's. She looked into my eyes as if she were a girl no older than six, and playfully bit her bottom lip. Unrepentant naughtiness, impish manipulation, it should have driven me wild, but I was too preoccupied with my act. "Ruthie, what am I to do with you?"

"Don't know, Papa," she giggled.

"Well, what if I spanked you?"

"Oh, no please don't do that!" she burst out joyfully.

"I'll have to do something with you." I could hear the acting tone in my voice, which I did not like, but which Ruth seemed not to notice at all. This did not change the fact that I had had enough of the game and just wanted to hold Ruth tightly against my body and make love to her as just plain Manik. I refused to say another word and just kissed her on her temple, the corner of her mouth, her chin. She kept grinning, however, and I would have felt supremely awkward kissing her on those brilliant anfractuous razor blades in her mouth, and behind that grin, a weird, unbalanced laughter – sincere, no question, but truly strange. I went for a hybrid character: half father, half myself, and quietly muttered, "Come now, give us a kiss," the plural all too apt. I got a chaste peck, but I lowered my eyebrows in disapproval and got a full-on. It was what she wanted me to do. I felt entirely out of my element if this was what I had to do, but I quickly found a solution. Rather than trying to embody Lord Radcliffe, or, worse still, Sri Shiva Surajprasad Mudigonda, I decided to play that I was a much gentler version of mean little Eleanor. For some reason, that put me much more at ease.

"Undress me," I whispered firmly, betraying nothing but the most scornful expression on my face. The weird, eager, primate laughter again, and excited obedience. "Now, get on my lap. Face me, come here, do as I say."

Not only did she pull herself onto my lap, cradling herself in front of my cocked-up knees, but wrapped her arms tightly around my chest, placing her head directly over my heart. I was almost too moved to maintain my erection, I just wanted to hold and protect her and tell her sweet foolish nothings, that I would never let anyone hurt her or take advantage of her beautiful innocence ever again. Reason told me that Ruth was no younger than twenty-eight years of age, but her unpowdered face and silk-fine hair, her button nose rubbing itself in my chest hair, it provoked in me the most protective feelings. I brushed my hand lightly over the top of her head and words passed my lips again, now in no character at all, but in a high, cracking tone: "I love you, little girl." Her body trembled slightly and she went broken-floodgates drenched, thank goodness, for it was what I needed to be re-primed for intercourse under these strange circumstances.

I'll say that I lasted a surprisingly long time, but I had also been making love every few hours and my stamina was excellent. I didn't do any fancy tricks, as I felt that they would be unwelcome, but bounced Ruth about, a smile on my face at last, snatching the occasional kiss from her forehead or the part in her hair as she continued on her mad, strange laughter. When she could feel my thighs start to spasm, as strangely aware of my body in a way that most women are not, she slid down my torso and caught the seed in her mouth like an expert. I reminded myself that she is married, possibly married for quite a while, possibly in a very happy marriage with lots of lovemaking, and that put me at ease well enough to let my body relax fully. As she crawled into my arms, I said nothing but smiled, lazy-eyed, at her. The teeth again.

I look back on this singular moment in my career as a servant to women as, if not my own favorite, then as one of my most shining moments as a whore. I had a difficult situation, I had few resources from which to derive a solution, but I was able to put myself aside and make a very sweet woman very happy in just the way that she wanted. It was selfless lovemaking, it was the practice of a true vocation, and I am, in a very odd way, proud of myself, for having done such a good job. Why isn't this sort of labor held up with that of the toiling physician in the smallpox ward, or fearless revolutionary putting himself in harm's way to bring aid to his people? Perhaps if it were associated with well-off Brahmin solicitors, it would be.

After a short involuntary unconsciousness, Ruth and I proceeded to get incredibly drunk, first in the tent, then at the water's edge. I think between us, we consumed four bottles of champagne and two fifths of that hideous drug which I love so much, Bol's gin. We also played a stupid game with a bottle of absinthe that had surely been intended for Hadleigh's little hideaway. Ruth was trying to explain to me the importance of this foolish sugar cube ritual that one simply must do when one drinks absinthe. You must balance a slotted spoon on top of the glass, place a sugar cube atop it, and pour water over it so that the sugar cube melts and makes the absinthe go cloudy, or some other nonsense like that. Ruth, who goes charmingly clumsy when drunk, would try to devise this twee sacrament, and either she would fail (sugar cube falling into the absinthe, water spilling everywhere), or I would sabotage her (gulping down contents of the glass before either sugar or water could touch it, eating the sugar cube, knocking over the spoon). We found the entire exercise hilariously funny for some reason, and we were sorely disappointed when the bottle was empty. I suspected that Ruth was not really supposed to sleep with me, but both of us were inebriated well past the point of directional intelligence, that we wandered the camp in convoluted states of dress, confused, for quite a long time before Ruth was rescued by her husband, whose potty black eyes assured me that he, too, was under the influence and had no idea of what was going on. He merely wandered up, dressed in only a very expensive pair of suit trousers with suspenders hanging down the back, and slurred out something on the lines of, "Oh, hello Ruthie. Bedtime, what ho?"

And so, deprived of my company, without either concept of time or space, and in that strange state of extreme drunkenness and exhaustion that forbids sleep, I somehow managed to knock into Hadleigh, as I always do. I think he asked me if I was tired, and I think I said that I wasn't, but somehow that resulted in my being escorted back to my tent by the lovely Njeri, which, without question cheered me up immensely. I remember little else than waking up the next day to an extremely substantial breakfast and Njeri's teasing smile.

"Miss Njeri," I said as happily as I could through the pounding of my head, "did you stay with me? How wonderful you are."

"Well, Bwom-Bwom, I'll tell you," she laughed, "I could have left you to sleep, but I was very worried about you!"

"Worried? What for? I'm perfectly all right."

"You were doing some strange things, my Bwom-Bwom."

"Strange things? What sorts of strange things?" I asked, pulling myself up to seated and waking up properly. "Thank you for making breakfast for me, Njeri, it is much needed. I feel like I've been starved in a prison for a month."

"You were talking – no, shouting!" Njeri laughed, pouring me some tea and serving up some rice and kashatta as I lit the morning cigarette.

"My word. What was I saying?"

"It must have been in your house language, Bwom-Bwom, I do not know." I sat and gorged myself well past the point that I should have, listening in amazement to Njeri's stories of my bizarre nocturnal behaviors. I had at one point seemed to have been holding a contentious debate, even gesticulating with my hands and wobbling my head, "back and forth, so funny!" Njeri giggled as she imitated my nearly expurgated Indian nod. Less funny, I also burst into tears while remaining fast asleep, and sobbed extremely loudly, to the extent that Njeri actually woke up Hadleigh to be a witness to this behavior. Hadleigh had reassured her, that this wasn't out of character for me to do while awake, and so it would only make sense that I would do this while asleep as well. Njeri told me that she thought Hadleigh had not been particularly nice about the whole affair, but I informed her that her employer was, unfortunately, entirely correct, and that he had, actually, done the very nicest thing possible by asking the most beautiful woman at the party to look after me while I passed through my fitful slumber. Njeri kissed me with my mouth full for that compliment, which I meant in complete sincerity, but then she looked at me with concern.

"Some of the men here, they are smoking some very dangerous things, opium and cocaine on their gums. They act as if it's nothing, like they are harmless pastimes, but I know better, a few of the smarter women and myself. I hope that you, my Bwom-Bwom..."

"No, no, no, Njeri, I am much too cowardly to even try that sort of thing. I just drank too much like I always do, and I am, as old Hadleigh says, a big, silly crybaby, awake or asleep. I did, now that you mention it, have most of a bottle of absinthe last night, that's supposed to be quite bad for you, I think, but to tell the truth, I think I would have cried in my sleep anyway, Njeri, and I'm sorry if I worried you, or frightened you, for that would be the absolute last thing I would want to do." The lady patted my cheek and smiled at me.

"Your hair looks a bramble bush," she grinned. "Let me fix it for you."

"All right," I conceded, knowing very well that this was true. Njeri made herself a comfortable seat from some stacked cushions behind me, and taking the bristle-brush, the orange oil, and a little ivory pick, got to work at untangling my hair. I just sat there like a rotten brat and smoked, drank tea and champagne, and nursed an old hangover and a new stomachache. As much as I like being a rotten brat, especially on my birthday, I feel guilty for taking advantage of Njeri's affection for me sometimes, because I truly feel as if I have done nothing at all to earn it. Truly, staying up all night to watch me hew and cry, feeding my gaping maw, and then picking her way through hundreds of sandy knots in my hair, it is too much to expect from anyone.

"Njeri," I mewed, "I want to make you happy. I only exist to make you happy, what should I do?"

"Holding still is one, my wobble-head," she teased.

"I don't wobble my head terribly much do I? I thought I'd broken that habit... don't distract me, Njeri! You know how my mind wanders. What can I do to make you happy?"

"You could make love to me."

"That is no chore comparable to picking hair knots, Njeri, that is yet more of your largesse bestowed upon me."

"So you don't wish to, Bwom-Bwom?" she said sadly, in such a way that absolutely pierced my heart.

"Of course I wish to, and intend to most seriously. But in addition!"

"In addition, in addition, I see," Njeri pondered. "My daughter, she needs your advice again I think. She and Otieno, things are going bad bad."

"That's awful to hear, Njeri, I am sorry."

"That girl, she isn't even giving him a chance. She makes the man feel very weak, it isn't good. Every day as we leave from work she begs me to take her home and get her a new husband. Otieno has done her no harm, he has been patient, much better than I could have ever hoped in a son-in-law, he brings our family so much pride, to return from the army with an injury, but be a good husband, work hard, lots of courage and goodness in that young man's heart. Why is she such a child, Bwom-Bwom? It makes me doubt myself as a mother, it upsets me very much, the way she is behaving, I feel as if I have failed."

"You should not blame yourself, Njeri, this I can tell you is not your fault in the slightest. The last time I spoke with Akinyi, I became convinced of that."

"Oh," Njeri replied in a very interested way. "What do you think is wrong, then, Bwom-Bwom? If it isn't how she was raised, then what happened? I am so ashamed, I cannot even bring myself to ask my own sisters for help."

"Njeri, I think I need to tell you a story." I lit myself a new cigarette and inched myself a bit closer to the lady's busy hands. "Thirty-two years ago, two very lovely young people, a prince and a princess, gave birth to a son who didn't look like anyone else, and, in addition to not looking like anyone else, didn't think like anyone else, either. They felt terrible shame about him. Nobody knows why it happened, but it wasn't anybody's fault. They could not cope with him, so he vanished."

"I don't want Akinyi to vanish, Bwom-Bwom. I love her so much."

"Njeri, you made the absolute best choice to marry Akinyi to Otieno, and Otieno sounds like he is one of the most superlative young men in this world. But, through no fault of your own, you and your wonderful husband gave birth to someone who, although she looks beautiful and normal, is not like anyone else. I talked to Akinyi about this, and I did promise not to say anything to you, but I think that I must say something, for your sake and for hers, and for Otieno's sake as well. Your daughter needs a divorce, Njeri, plain and simple."

"Oh, no, Bwom-Bwom, that can't be. Her husband is so good!"

"Precisely."

"I do not follow."

"Akinyi is never going to be a good wife to him, she will always be running from him. What will happen then? He will begin to feel a kernel of agony inside that won't go away. First, he'll look for something to get rid of it, drinking, prostitutes, but then, because that won't work, he will change from being a good man into a cruel man."

"Otieno? Never!"

"A man who has been at war like he has, escaping with his life? He needs a wife to appreciate him, to comfort and love him. If he has that, he will be eternally good, the best that exists in this world. But don't get me wrong, it is not Akinyi's fault that she wants to run from him, it is something with which she was born, something essential about her. There should be no shame involved; both of these young people must be married to other people, and as quickly as is possible. And if you fear for Otieno's prospects, let me assure you, there are many young women who would rush at the chance to serve a wounded hero. There are women like yourself, who see beauty in imperfection. Your daughter is not like that, that isn't who she is. Get her a husband with a beautiful face, a nose with a good, high bridge, Njeri, and do not be ashamed or doubt yourself. Rally around your sisters, your brothers, your husband's family, and do not be afraid to say what you must say and do what you must do. Trust me, if you refuse to give in to the shame and do what is right, everyone will benefit, and, when everyone sees your bravery and your wisdom, you, too, will benefit."

Njeri ran the bristle-brush through my hair slowly as she contemplated my difficult advice. "It is the only way, you are right. How I wish it were not so."

I looked up at her sadly, and, seeing how her watery eyes were discovered, she came down off her platform and curled up in my embrace. "It isn't your fault," I whispered. "You did nothing wrong, nothing."

"Thank you, Bwom-Bwom."

"If you want help talking to your family..."

"No, no," she replied firmly, her tears pressed back in courage. "I may have needed to hear these words from you, but my family needs to hear them from me."

"You are not only a good mother, Njeri, but one of the very best."

We clasped hands and kissed one another, first tenderly, and then with great passion. I had a cigarette resting in my left hand, but I forgot it completely as I was occupied with Njeri's lips and it burned my knuckles. Occupational hazard, I suppose. Njeri laughed at my folly; she still finds me a funny lad, after all. We undressed with some cheerful haste, no reason to pretend that our very specific plans were to be left laid incomplete, but as Njeri moved to creep atop my body, I felt what little wind I had in my lungs knocked out of me.

"Gentle with me," I requested, a hand on my hard and throbbing stomach for emphasis. Njeri gave me a sly smile, a pinch on my cheek, and a soft kiss above the navel.

"I'll be gentle with you, not like last time when I was quite rough," Njeri assured me. I knew that I was in for the sweetest, softest lovemaking I could ever want, and it was exactly what I wanted. First, she straddled my hips in the reverse position, her impeccably shapely posterior buffeted right up against my belly's lower edge, and by some graceful feat of flexibility, dipped her head and gave the tip of my penis a good, encouraging suck. I wobbled to attention, but Njeri hushed me. "You don't need to do a thing. Just lay back, enjoy yourself." I am a spoiled, spoiled, spoiled rotten brat. And so, Njeri's gorgeous derriere and back a tantalizing visual, she rocked and squeezed me unassisted, which elicited some exclamations from me, some rather embarrassing, but I'll say quite firmly and with great certainty: this is a great position, and although I usually like to be the active party, being fat and lazy and spoiled can be a very welcome change of pace and result in a very prolonged, almost painfully exciting ejaculation. I know that my eyes rolled back into my head and my all four limbs went completely limp and immobile, and, pleased as she was with my reaction, Njeri laughed and crept up to rest her head on my shoulder. As soon as I felt strength in my arms again, I groped Njeri's soft breast and kissed her with intense gratitude.

"You are beautiful, you are wonderful, and I love you!" I managed to say between kisses. Njeri patted my chest and got up, in spite of my inarticulate protests and fitful grasping, and tossed me a towel moistened with rosewater after she had quickly re-dressed herself.

"I always like you, Bwom-Bwom," she said in a very flirtatious way. "Rest up, rest up." And then, with that imperative, she slipped away. Wise she was, for it was not even three minutes later that Hadleigh poked his head in at me. Now, I was stark naked but for thread and hand towel over just the majority of my genitalia, but Hadleigh never seems to bother with these sorts of concerns. Hadleigh himself was all shiny and flawless in yet another perfect white suit, as he must have dozens.

"Feeling all right, Manikji?" he asked brightly.

"I'm not dressed, do you mind?"

"Oh, not at all," he replied, bounding in uninvited. "You are happy, old chap?"

"I could not be happier Hadleigh, unless you were to let me get dressed."

"Because you were a bit emotional in your sleep, a bit of the old nocturnal sobbing if you know what I mean. The party is for you, you know, Manikji, and if you aren't happy..."

"I have no idea why I cried in my sleep, because I'm having a marvelous time and I'm fucking and drinking and doing all of my favorite things, I think it's just one of those things that I do, Hadleigh, like you've said yourself. I'm fine, and I thank you for having Miss Njeri look after me and make me breakfast, that was very thoughtful."

"You sound a bit piqued..."

"Because I'd like to get *dressed*, Hadleigh, if you wouldn't mind!"

"Well in that case!" Hadleigh sniffed resentfully, turning on his heel. "I've seen it before a hundred times, Manik, and so has everyone else,

I don't know why you insist on modesty now. Your cock and balls are local celebrities. I just wanted to talk to you, that's all. What if I stand with my back to the entrance as you get dressed, is that enough for you, my vestal virgin?"

"Fine enough," I replied, seeing that Hadleigh was standing in perfect Latinate contraposto at my tent entrance, the top of his skimmer gleaming white, before I pulled myself up, every bone aching, to perfume and dress myself again. I shaved as well, and also gave my hair a second oiling just to do the best possible justice to Njeri's dedicated untangling job. Occupied as I was, I did little but grunt basic affirmations to Hadleigh as he lectured me.

"I know you've been doing a very good job, Manikji, the ladies all seem very happy indeed, and I thank you for that. Either late this evening or tomorrow, I have Mrs. De Vos, Clara, to introduce to you, and this is quite crucial that she be treated very nicely."

"When have I ever been less than nice to a lady, Hadleigh?" I replied, nearly insulted, but accustomed to Hadleigh's dull sermons and anxieties, the razor making its first pathway along the side of my cheek.

"I know you're always nice to the ladies, Manikji, but Mrs. De Vos is not only extremely important, but she is no youthful beauty."

"I like the mature ladies perfectly well, and it bears repeating, I far prefer them to the very young girls that you think I like so much."

"But really, she is quite horrid, Manik. Quite horrid, and I'm truly sorry to have to involve you at all with her, but this is a favor to me, my most precious friend. Mary and Edna and Ruthie, though, they're all very pretty, aren't they?"

"Yes, they are indeed. Edna I like especially, she is a gem among women. Beautiful lady and very clever and charming, she reminds me of nothing else more than a soft, shimmering pink pearl from the South Seas. She told me jokes, isn't that adorable?"

"I thought you'd like Edna. Big tits."

"Bloody great lovely tits."

"So you won't mind looking after Mrs. De Vos for me, Manikji? She could end up solving all of my problems."

I was engaged in some vigorous scalp rubbing at that moment and said nothing, but I was tempted briefly to mention Ruth's concern, in addition to the other off-hand remarks I had heard from others. I refrained; perhaps Hadleigh indeed does have a problem, but he has not been asking me to solve it for him, outside of entertaining specific ladies, which is my favorite activity anyway, and that is a more mutual form of symbiosis than the parasitic relationship that sometimes we develop during difficult times, myself usually the host. It would be a very good thing, that Hadleigh could take responsibility for his own problem and not burden me with it, it would be proof that he is finally becoming a grown man, and this idea pleased me enough that I held my tongue. I tied on my sash, and, red ribbon in my left hand, tapped my friend on the shoulder.

"Tie it for me, would you, Hadleigh?"

"Of course, old fellow." Hadleigh began stretching his fist around my hair, but paused. "My word, Manik. You didn't just do your hair now, did you?"

"Njeri untangled it for me."

"It looks very impressive." I could feel him forcing the breadth into a queue and tying the bow, but he did not let go. "Miss Njeri untangled your hair?"

"Yes, it was in a perfect state yesterday, wasn't it?"

Then, Hadleigh pulled very hard on my queue, eliciting an "Ow!" from my throat. "Don't get any ideas, Manikji!"

"I haven't any ideas. I'm doing precisely what I'm supposed to do, and part of that is to keep my hair looking nice, isn't it? You're such a pillock when you act suspiciously, Hadleigh, it does not become you at all."

I turned around to face him, and my expression must have been hard, but Hadleigh's own countenance grew suddenly soft. "You look still strikingly young, Manik, it is as if you never age at all, particularly just after you've shaved. There is no way anyone could take you for thirty-two years of age."

"I'm perfectly happy to be thirty-two years old, it bothers me not the slightest bit."

"As well it shouldn't, with your face and hair." He tugged back a stray curl to better reveal my earrings and smiled at me in a meek way.

"Your apology is accepted, Hadleigh," I sighed.

"Come," he tenderly implored, arm across my shoulders. "There is Chinese opera to be heard today. And we've spent hardly a minute together."

"Chinese opera? Oh, we haven't heard that since the old days back in Cape Town! Do you remember how we used to go and get plaster-faced in the front row and catcall the girls? What awful fools we were then. I always secretly loved it, how did you know?"

"I just pay very close attention to you, Manikji, that's all. For instance, I knew you wanted a cigarette, didn't I?" Hadleigh asked, lighting the aforementioned with such grace and style.

"But that's a bit easier to ascertain, Hadleigh, for there is no time that I do not want a cigarette," I grinned and teased, bobbling the lovely white cylinder on my bottom lip as I spoke. "Is it daxi or xiaoxi?"

"Xiaoxi. *Romance of the Iron Bow*, I believe."

And I suppose it was, but still without any Chinese to my tongue, I would never have known. I love it anyway, and I couldn't even explain why. The whole production is entirely incomprehensible to me, I never have a clue of what's going on. Hadleigh always manages some grasp on the plot, who knows how he does that, but I just like the strangeness and imaginativeness of it all. Whenever forced to see some boring English play, I find the whole production painfully predictable, particularly the constant abuse of Shakespeare that I endured while a boy at school. How I hate Shakespeare, how miserable that long-dead bald and boring bard made me when I should have been enjoying the boyish pursuits of contemplating the sciences and staring at girls, confused and excited. Those are the feelings that Chinese opera inspire in me as well, come to think of it: confused and excited. It is no wonder I like it, then.

Some business about separated lovers, Hadleigh said it was, but we were already drinking heavily by the time he made that assumption, reliving our law school days in the best possible way, and he may have been wrong. I loved it. Somehow, I ended up laying with my head in Hadleigh's lap, drunk to the point of silliness, insisting that I could probably play that bloody guqin just as well as that fellow over there, and without a single lesson. Perhaps this insistence and boast was a bit louder than it should have been, for it seemed to be not a few minutes later I found myself beside Master Zhao with the terrifying instrument under my hands. What a gentleman he was; he first accepted my apology with all of its attendant shameful deserved compliments related to his skill. He then did give me quite the proper lesson, my inebriated state only the slightest barrier to learning, and he told me that I was a good student. That gave us all a laugh, and the festivities broke out once again, now with the Chinese musicians mixing in with the Luo and Kikuyu and Maasai musicians, now a massive Mombasa hodge-podge of maddeningly beautiful sound. Resson reappeared again with her dancers, their hair freshly colored in red clay, and circled me. I gave her an expression; she knew that we would spend time together before the party's end.

At some point, the Chinese opera players gained control of themselves again and returned to their secret story sung in stylized tones, their makeup perhaps less than the flawless condition it had been before the interruption, but which I prefer. I state now quite honestly and selfishly that, having a distinctly imperfect face inclines me towards imperfect faces in general. Hadleigh has told me time and time again that if I really hated my face so very much, there is always greasepaint as an option, but I would rather have my real and ugly face than the glossy enameled artifice of a painted one. Surely, I would look twice the fool, and I would feel slightly uncomfortable at selecting a color: all brown would be incongruous, and all white would be depressing. I have not countered this argument to Hadleigh with mention of a toupee as of yet, because I am saving that sharp needle for a very special occasion, when he really deserves it. If he never does, then I will pretend that not a single hair has fallen from his head since we first met, I will pretend this until the poor fellow hasn't but a one.

I relaxed and continued watching the show, but heard someone calling out to me, "Umba!" It was Akinyi, looking for me. Both Hadleigh and I had become, by this time, rather drunk and inattentive, so I was able to slip away with no excuse better than, "Oh, I'll be back later."

His face covered in grog sweat, Hadleigh grinned and said, "Of course, old fellow. Of course."

When I reached Akinyi behind the throngs, she began to jump up and down like a young ibex on the side of the plateau surrounding the Rift Valley, and then clutched onto both of my hands and, before I knew it, we were both jumping up and down. Sobriety kicking in so quickly as it sadly does, I began to wonder what we were doing. "Miss Akinyi?" I asked.

"Thank you! Thank you Umba! My mother tells me I am getting a divorce!" she shouted with glee, still jumping, although my own feet had found the ground quite still. "She was not angry with me, and she says that she knows it is the right thing for me, I am so happy, and I've you to thank, Umba, thank you so much!"

And before I could say my humble you're-welcomes, Akinyi suctioned her lovely mouth onto my nose well before I was ready. I could feel her tongue like a nudibranch creeping rapidly up my nasal passages and it overwhelmed me. "Wait, wait!" I begged. "At least sitting down?" Akinyi seemed to cross her legs in mid-air and fall straight to the ground right where we were. I was on my knees trying to protect my nose for at least a few seconds more. "Outside in broad daylight? Where we could be seen? What if your mother saw?"

Akinyi frowned and sucked her teeth. "The red tent is yours?"

And so we rushed there; I am not suited for running at all, no absolutely not. If I had had to run just ten more paces the ligaments holding my knees together would have snapped like old leather straps and my smoke-filled lungs would have collapsed like deflated balloons. We fell into my cushions, but I put my hand to my chest. "Wait!" I begged again. "Wait, or else I might die!"

"But I might die waiting for you!" she cried out in frustration.

"Then we will die together?" I suggested, a pathetic smile on my face.

It was too late. In spite of, or, perhaps aided by the fact that I was still hyperventilating severely, Akinyi thrust the pinch of snuff up my nostril and I began sneezing so hard that I thought I would never catch my breath again, completely breathless I was. Her only concern the nostrils and septum and bridge of her passion, Akinyi went straight back to her task. Her tongue darted up one nostril and then the other, and I never felt as if I could get enough air between attacks. I started to panic, my heart squeezed up at the top of my chest, and I wrapped my hand tightly around Akinyi's wrist. "I'm going to faint," I pleaded, blackness already covering most of my vision.

Akinyi stopped briefly and looked at me, her long-lashed eyes opened wide, as if she were amazed. "Do you faint, Umba?"

"I do faint," I gasped, the world a dark swirling nothingness, and I became unsure as to whether my eyes were open or closed.

"Oh God!" she cried out, quickly dipping her hands in the champagne bucket and running them over my face. "Oh God," she repeated, now sounding not so much concerned as enthralled. My vision came back to my eyes and there she was, smiling at me, this beautiful girl, maybe the most beautiful girl alive in the whole world. "I understand what my mother sees in you, Umba."

"Is that so?" I asked, trying to reassure her that I was fine.

"You are sexy."

"Come again?"

"That's sexy. Getting so excited when I make love to you that you near faint. You are very, very sexy. Ugly but sexy. That is good. Umba, Umba, you are sexier than Otieno was when he was beautiful. I think when I get married again, I will still make love to you."

At first I wanted to protest. I didn't want Akinyi to want to make love to my nose after her remarriage, and I suspected that she would not desire such. I also didn't want her to think that my cardiovascular weakness was anything other than what it was: a heavy smoker fighting for air is not what most people would consider sexy. But then, I stopped myself. I saw her beautiful face, her eyes closing, her lips parting, her tongue running itself across my upper lip. What harm could it do her to think that she had driven a man so wild with erotic passion that he nearly fainted? It would be good for her, built up the confidence of one so young who is so painfully aware of her difference in the sexual arena, and so manacled to her fetish as to find pleasure in no other way. I took a good breath, leaned back, and let Akinyi do what she wished. Her happiness was so palpable, that a crazy thought came to my mind. Could I overcome the typical human aversion and return Akinyi her favor? I reached out a hand and caressed her pretty little ear, how it looked just like Njeri's, shut my eyes, reached out my tongue. First, I hit her little chin, then I crept up her bottom lip. She sensed the movement of my head and ceased her exploration, allowing me to follow the cupid's bow of her upper lip and slowly, carefully, lick the inner edge of her nostril. It didn't even feel strange, just the salty moisture and the bristling cilia, it felt entirely unforeign. It became a very tender exchange, a mirroring of nose appreciation. At a certain point, Akinyi suddenly stopped and fell down beside me, exhausted, her small bosom heaving.

"The sexiest man," she whispered. "Oh God, I hope you have not ruined me."

"No, no," I insisted, my brow knitted with denial. "I have never ruined any woman. I only prepare her to be truly happy."

"You are wonderful," she smiled, calm restoring itself instantly to her heart. "Thank you for helping me in your many ways, Umba, Umba my angel."

I kissed her softly in the conventional way, and away she ran. I could hear her laughter dotting away into the sunset. After fortifying myself with a bit more of the endless champagne and cigarettes, I slowly arose and poked my head outside the tent. The Chinese opera, interminable as it seemed to be, was still going on, but I felt that I needed a walk along the coastline so that I could watch the saffron colored sun sink into the ocean. The color, the saffron color, made me think of Dorothy, whose bright locks I then conveniently spotted wafting in the breeze at the top of a sand dune. I wanted to hurry to her, but I decided against that, I decided to walk in a very nonchalant way so that she would not know how happy I was to see her, especially after her critique of me during our last encounter. I strode up to her, the last rays of sunlight dancing on my gem-encrusted sherwani, my hair still well-fashioned.

"Well, hello Dorothy my pet," I proclaimed, lighting myself a cigarette and remaining at my full height.

"Now, what have we here?" she teased, a charmingly mocking waver in her voice. "Bacchus, I have never seen you look so regal!"

My false disinterest melted away instantly and I went straight to crouching, putting my face close to hers. "Oh, do you think? Dorothy, Dorothy I have missed you!"

"And I you, Bacchus my darling." We exchanged a single kiss and I felt that all the world was a dream.

"Marry me, Dorothy?" I could not help myself.

"Actually, Bacchus my sweet..."

"Yes?" My heart jumped.

"I have received a proposal."

"Have you?" My heart landed.

"And I think that I might accept."

"Oh, indeed?" My heart sank.

"But, Bacchus my dearest..."

"Yes?"

"That does not mean that I still don't feel the same about you as I always have, and, I know that I will regret saying this, but I have actually not yet accepted said proposal."

"Yes?"

"Which means that yes, of course, I shall pass some idle time with thee, Bacchus, Bacchus dressed in Apollo's rays of gold."

"Oh," I replied, trying to regain my cool attitude of a minute before, as pointless though it was an exercise. "Oh, well, I suspected that you might want to, er, pass some idle time with me, Dorothy."

"For goodness sake, Bacchus, why am I not yet up in your arms?"

"I haven't the slightest!" I scooped Dorothy into my embrace and held her gently against my chest. I began to walk with her my sunset constitutional. "Will you be missed? Why are you not at the Chinese opera? I'm sure that is where your mother and father are, am I right?"

"Yes, you are. And the boys have joined the drowning army to our west."

"Ah, yes, the drowning army. I acted as a free-agent guerrilla on Sunday and threw old Hadleigh to his temporary doom."

"Was he cross?"

"No, unfortunately."

"That is unfortunate, Bacchus."

"Do you know what else is unfortunate? The woman I have been courting for the last three years is considering marrying some interloper about whom I know absolutely nothing. So, who is this designer?"

"Do I sense jealousy, Bacchus my dear?"

"Jealousy? I am Radha sobbing to the cowherds when Krishna comes home covered in the perfume of courtesans."

"His name is Hugo Darling."

"Darling! What a foolish name."

"No more foolish than yours, Ruby my dear, and I think it suits him very well, for he is quite a darling man."

"What is his occupation, other than rending my heart to a million pieces?"

"He is a solicitor."

"No! Say it isn't so, Dorothy! Do you want me to commit suicide right at this very moment? What else is there about this man? He is a solicitor, slightly more successful than myself, a slightly better reputation than myself, with a slightly greater savings, impossibly handsome, sincere, good-natured, and is an adherent to temperance and political moderation?"

"Oh, so you've met him?"

"That does it, Dorothy, suicide shall be my only recourse."

"No, please, Bacchus," the lady insisted, a tight smile on her delicate face. "The fact is that he does have much to be desired, and could learn quite a lot from you. I shall miss you while languishing away in my marriage bed."

"Truly?" I am such a fool for Dorothy, her traps so obviously lain, I rush to ensnare myself within them, if only to bring a beam of happiness to her lovely heart.

"Hugo has not your patience, nor has he your charming self-deprecation. He also has neither your openness of heart, nor your sense of adventure. He knows not yet how to do many of the things that I require that came so naturally to you."

"Oh Dorothy," I replied, feeling now quite oddly about the situation. I decided to seat us on a dune off to the edge of the party's encampment where we could see the sun's final moments in relative silence. "So he does not know how to feed you?"

"He does not need to know."

"But that's rather unromantic. Some of my happiest moments have been spent with a spoon and your coral lips. Surely he is motivated?"

"Intimidated would be the better descriptor."

"But Dorothy, Dorothy, and I am playing no sort of game of flirtation when I say this, because very similar words were uttered to me not long ago by a true friend who had my best interests at heart and who is now my late friend, who continues to guide and inspire me past the baseness of this plain, material world, but why would you want to marry a man who does not love you for precisely all of the things that you are?"

"He does love me quite a lot, Bacchus my dear, please don't mistake me."

"And yet, what do you tell me of him? That he is impatient, unadventurous, intimidated? Do you think that you will make me happy by those admissions? Because those admissions make me terribly sad, that a beautiful lady who I love with every fiber of my being might marry a man of such characteristics?"

"I am twenty-four years old," she sighed. "I cannot walk, I cannot write or dress or eat unassisted. A man loves me, he wants me to be his wife. We are pragmatists, he and I. I don't expect you to approve of that, Bacchus, romantic such as you are, your finest quality."

"Pragmatism I understand, but is it pragmatism to make a choice like this, Dorothy? Well, tell me more of him. You could not have known him long."

"Three months."

"So, you knew him when I saw you last, but mentioned not a breath about him."

"I suppose I did not know his intentions at that moment."

"But you did love him, and he you by that time. It was only just over a week ago at all that we saw one another at Hadleigh's terrible dinner party. You told me you'd rather a spinster be than marry me, and I understand that, but this Hugo Darling, Dorothy, this Hugo Darling... and this is not jealousy, Dorothy, this is nothing but concern, but love. For I do love you, Dorothy, and I would shout it off a million mountaintops for all to hear. Tell me something that will reassure me that this rich bastard solicitor, this Hugo Darling, dull, nervous, impatient Hugo Darling will do the beautiful Dorothy Hopkins justice, and I say beautiful, for with your face and hair..."

"Bacchus, please do not cry."

"I'm not crying, I'm just... I'm a bit drunk."

"It's all right." The side of a trembling pinky fingertip brushed over my cheek. "You have no idea, Bacchus, sweet man, the strength with which your love imbues me, for knowing that a very intelligent man, drunk or none, would burst into tears at the suggestion that I not be spoon fed by an infatuated husband every day, it reminds me of my own value, which I do so often forget these days, with so much talk of weddings and dowries and nurses and servants and all of those plain, material things, as you would call them. So fortunate I have been to know that men like you exist, Bacchus, and why I did not marry sooner, to a man interested only in a wife who would be certain not to stray, but to a man who at least realized that I am a person with thoughts of my own."

"But you deserve better than that!"

"And you, Bacchus, deserve better than to be every woman's husband but no one's."

"But, Dorothy, I..."

"Don't finish that sentence, Bacchus, my dear, for I know how it ends, and it would only remind me of the kinds of thoughts I have when in the dark valley of doubt."

I sat silent for a moment and looked at Dorothy's sweet, clear eyes, her saffron tresses, her tight and shaking slender arms. I kissed her, softly, and then deeply. She knew what I was going to say: ugly. Ugly. I continued to kiss her, in such a heated, desperate way, as if to erase that thought from her mind. Dorothy is beautiful, it is only I who is ugly. She may be fragile, and need care and protection of a very dedicated and special variety, but she is beautiful, and anyone who says otherwise I will hunt down and kill with my bare hands. "Spend the night with me," I implored. "Spend the whole night with me. Please. You'll be married soon, we'll never have another chance."

She began to laugh, her little face twisted up in unselfconscious laughter. "I simply cannot refuse you, Bacchus, for on one hand, you are announcing a genuine and essential love for me in a suffering voice, and on the other hand, this is the best ploy any man could use to get a woman into his bed."

"Fortune!" I shouted, and I returned to my pleasant task of kissing. I walked Dorothy back across the water's edge, and, cradling the fair-complexioned fairy in one arm, dragged her chair behind me in the sand with the other, which she found suitably amusing. I began to banter again, some shards of happiness still remaining in my broken glass heart. "You must be hungry. I could feed you!"

"This might send you over the edge of the cliff again, Bacchus my dear, but in the wild atmosphere of Mudigondamas, I will admit to having been slightly neglected in this regard."

"For shame! Is that true, Dorothy? This cliff is yet steeper, I have not yet hit the bottom! How dare your family neglect to make sure you've eaten. I know that I can't bear ten minutes of hunger, for goodness sake."

"Well, to tell the truth, I had not insisted, so it is partially my own fault."

"You must promise me to insist when you are married to that charlatan Hugo Darling, or I shall kidnap you and we shall run away to Uganda together. I won't sleep at night, worried if you're starving to death."

"Fortunately, that is something I do not have to suffer on your behalf, sweet Bacchus."

"Oh, you have no idea. When you saw me last I had been on the severest, most miserable reducing diet anyone could fathom. And yes, it did fail, but it is my birthday after all."

"I would not change you, Bacchus, not for anything in this world."

I settled in with Dorothy in the tent and made certain that she was as comfortable as could be possible. It was clear that not long before our return, Njeri, perhaps as a gesture of thanks, or perhaps out of her continued concern for my wellbeing and eternally unstable emotions, had spread out some fine cuisine for me, and, as always, even more than enough to have binged and purged myself twice. This circumstance was quite fortunate indeed, as I had anticipated having to leave Dorothy and go seeking the banquet table. This way, I did not need to leave her for even a moment's time. I helped to prop her up and adjust her fragile back so that her throat would be balanced at the proper angle, and then got to work mashing yam with spoon to make a totally even texture. Dorothy's lovely mouth is so extremely sensitive that food of anything but the softest, smoothest texture is unpleasant and can cause her to choke, this and yet she is endlessly facile in kissing and better, such a mystery it is to me. Her swallowing mechanism is very delicate as well, her tongue often getting in its own way, so each tiny mouthful takes a very long time for her to process.

I try to be mostly non-conversant, but to communicate my affection in silent ways, but this level of care is all too often impossible. It all too often breaks into some laughter or some teasing, some remark about somebody's big red eye rolling around like an apple in a barrel. I paused not only to laugh but to prepare one of Njeri's fine curries for Dorothy's consumption, and I could hear a laugh of a very sad variety coming from her direction.

"I could once manage at least an attempt to feed myself, Bacchus," she explained, "but that was before the contractures in my arms meant that I could not bring my hands to my mouth anymore."

"Well, I was once a virgin!" I proclaimed. "Quite an old one at that. An old, shy, dull, innocent virgin of whom you surely would have approved. But surely you forgive me that change."

"I understand you, Bacchus, that is very kind."

"Hush now," I gently requested, a half-spoonful carefully prepared for my lover's lips.

"Oh, another?" she sighed. "I am worn out. Are you trying to overfeed me?"

"You have eaten next to nothing," was my retort, and it was absolutely true, even less than she normally manages, and this was after having been quite neglected. "Do try, please? I know that it's hard to be both tired and hungry, which need to tend to first. I wish that I could indeed overfeed you, Dorothy. I wish that were your regular state, for it would mean that you had someone patient and loving taking the time to care for you, and that you would not be starving through most of the day. How can you protect yourself against further losses of flexibility if you are left too tired to move? And anyway," I ceased my motherly concern for the lover's teasing, "think of how pretty you would be with chubby cheeks."

"As pretty as you are, Bacchus, without question," was her sharp and affectionate retort, opening her lips again for my spoon. I was elated.

Dorothy did manage a few more spoonfuls, I think mostly to please me, before she refused completely. I decided that it was time to switch my focus to my own eating, necessary evil as it is, and we began exchanging Mudigondamas gossip, about what we had heard from other people and who we saw misbehaving. I mentioned to her the popular gossip that must be going on about Hadleigh, and she told me not to think of it, that she had heard it as well, and that her entire family simply would not be quiet about our dear Lord Greenwich. Boring, absolutely boring.

"It would be such better gossip if it weren't so vague," I complained, my sherwani off again and my mouth full. "Didn't we here in Mombasa used to pride ourselves on highly detailed tale-telling?"

"Unfortunately, Bacchus my dear, when a story is detailed, it is easily proven wrong, and when it is vague, it becomes some great mystery and blows itself out of proportion. That way everyone feels left out and desperate to know. I see it as a positive evolution in the chain of poor, dull gossip," Dorothy replied, astute as always.

"Oh, who cares if it's a lie. Everyone knows that just about everything is a lie these days anyway, so the lies may as well be interesting. I don't think I've even looked at a newspaper in a year; the hacks have been insisting that a vast, indescribable war has been on the verge of breaking out for so long now, I almost wish it would happen."

"If the war came to the Horn, would you fight, Bacchus?"

"No, of course not. I don't fight, I love. I am essentially a pacifist."

"A pacifist who wishes for war to end his tedium, Bacchus, you are wonderful. Let me ask you this: as a lover, how would you help to win a war?"

"Do you really need to ask?" I gave myself a quick shot of gin and lit myself a cigarette, amazed with myself that I had managed to convince Dorothy to spend the night with me. I felt like a groom on his wedding night. "Have you been in the ocean yet, my beautiful Dorothy?"

"No, I haven't."

"I'll carry you out for a bit if you'd like. The water is not the slightest bit cold."

"Take me, Bacchus."

I gently began to undress Dorothy, her arms very tight and stiff, her fingers unclenching. She seemed yet more like a bisque porcelain doll, so very much on the verge of shattering, and quite light in my arms, even more so than just a week ago. Such delicate beauty, like a cherry blossom in the breeze, so warm in my arms. Unknotting and kicking away dhoti in a single, careless gesture, I took Dorothy out to the ocean, the tides low and very, very gentle. We kissed continually as I waded out, the moon bright in the sky, hot, lovely kisses. "You see?" I said once we had gone out to where the water came chest-high on me. "Not at all cold."

"I couldn't be cold if I tried, wrapped in your arms, Bacchus."

"I wish you weren't a pragmatist, Dorothy. I wish you were a romantic, I wish you cared for nothing but love and beauty and lived only in the present. I wish you would stay with me forever."

"I know, Bacchus, my darling."

I began to gently swing her in the waves, her saffron tresses ebbing and flowing with the tiny ripples on the water's surface. It made her happy, she shut her eyes and slowly tilted back her head. I then began turning in a circle, taking her around and around. She laughed. I laughed as well, but I may as well have cried. I tried to lightly bounce her against my chest, but her back was staying very straight. I lifted her up and kissed her on the navel, which proved to be ticklish and very welcome. It was more than I could bear. "I must devour you," I whispered. "I must."

"That I would have had to wait a minute more."

It was a beautiful, slow, romantic night, perhaps the most romantic night I have ever spent. We would kiss, and then I would put my tongue between Dorothy's thighs for a while, and then, perhaps she would reciprocate. This rotation of kissing, licking, sucking, and then caressing one another went on for quite some time I imagine. I drank a bit, but not very much compared to the night before; Dorothy is opposed to alcohol, but finds my enjoyment of such acceptable, as it suits my personality, so she explained it to me. She also finds that my long hair suits my personality, although she also said that, after drying full of salt and sand again, that it looked like a Restoration-Era sheepskin wig. I asked if that bothered her, and she replied that she would not change a thing about me. At one point, as our circuit of lovemaking and repose came to a head, I brought Dorothy to a distinct peak of excitement, her face and bosom going vibrant red, and I felt a bit like Akinyi must have felt a few hours before, concerned that her involved party might faint.

"Dorothy, my love," I whispered fitfully, rushing to the champagne bucket just as Akinyi had and running my cold, wet hands across the lady's hot face. In a single spastic gesture, Dorothy's back arched and pressed her lips to mine.

I cozied her to sleep with me not much later, making certain that she was comfortable. The cushions were not what she was accustomed to resting on at home, and I was concerned that they might cause her some injury, but we managed to improvise a soft cradle for her, my own stomach the best solution for her head. To say that I was not affected by this sleeping arrangement would be the most grievous lie. For the short months that we were married, Madhulika's head had rested on my pudgy middle every single night, and I would immerse my fingers in her long hair. I wove a few locks of saffron around my fingers and shut my eyes.

It was not so much that I was transported back to these happy days of my childhood, because I never lost awareness that it was my Dorothy with me, but I felt the same wonderful feeling of security. I did nothing but sleep those hours we spent together, and I woke up feeling warm, contented, and only the slightest bit hung over. My selfish Brahmin boy began to assert himself, and I was driven, half awake, to begin mumbling a lot of very egocentric absurdities as I stroked Dorothy's hair.

"You know, if you decide not to marry Hugo Darling, or if he breaks your engagement, or even if you do marry him and you decide that you want a divorce, even if it were years from now, you know that all you'd have to do is send me a telegram and I would come and rescue you."

Dorothy did not stir or respond, so I assumed that she was still fast asleep and had not heard my outburst, which would have been something of a relief. However, after a few more seconds of patient waiting and hair stroking, I heard her laughing, at first slightly, and then enough to shake me, so I inched myself up on my elbows to look down at her lovely head. "You are easily the sweetest man in the world, Bacchus," she said.

I groaned and flopped myself back down again and began groping around with both arms for cigarettes and lighter. "Well, I'll say that the sweetest man in the world needs a smoke."

"Don't blow it on me, everyone will know I've been with you."

"Hadleigh and I smoke the same formulation. If anyone really troubles you, you can say you were with him."

"That is not an improvement, Bacchus."

"It's also unavoidable. In fact, since I'm to do your hair for you, you will smell even more like me. But is anyone going to care or notice? I should doubt it. Hymen still intact, right my dear? And if your family is forgetting to feed you, they're also most likely forgetting to scan you for odors that smell like any particular man."

"An orange grove on fire. That's what you smell like."

"That sounds quite nice, actually."

"It is nice."

"So, that shall be your perfume today, like it or not, for there's nothing can be done about it. Up we come, my love, it is another day, and I should ready you before your absence becomes distressing."

I had no idea of the time and was quite certain that I'd gotten an excellent several hours of sleep, most likely landing us some time close to noon, or even later. I tried to move with a certain level of exigency, but caring for Dorothy properly can't be rushed. It probably took me another hour to bathe her in rosewater, comb, oil, and fashion her hair, dress her, and feed her a few unwanted mouthfuls, while I was still quite the naked, sweat-drenched mess. I figured that her appearance would be more concerning than my own, and, like a regular pack mule, with dhoti wrapped rather than tied, I hoisted Dorothy up in one arm and her chair in the other, cigarette on my bottom lip, so desperate to smoke I was at that time, just chaining without any relief from the urge. I brought her up to where I'd found her, but she told me to put her inside the pale orange tent, which was the one belonging to her family. I crept in quietly. Her parents were not there, but the two boys were snoring, dead to the world, on the tent's floor. I kissed her quickly and made my exit.

When I left the Hopkins tent, my ears perked up. The Chinese opera was still bloody going on, it was amazing, and so many of the people I had left the previous evening were still there, awake or asleep, some drunk, some worse. Hadleigh was there, looking drunk and soggy and harmless, and Mr. and Mrs. Hopkins were asleep with their shoulders propped up against one another. I also saw Katie, still clad in Maasai dhoti, sound asleep next to some of her women friends. I decided to sit myself next to Hadleigh for a while and smoke.

"Hello Hadleigh."

"Oh, hello Manikji, old boy. That wasn't long, was it? But you have missed much of the story."

"You must tell it to me."

With that, Hadleigh's head crashed itself into the side of my arm. I propped him up a bit better and let him lean against me to catch a few moments of respite, and also pickpocketed him the majority of the cigarettes in his case. Poor fellow, I like him best when he's very drunk and helpless. He truly is like a brother to me in so many ways, perhaps not the elder brother I'd always wanted, but certainly the one I deserve, one drooling on my shoulder while attending what certainly must have been the thirtieth hour of a Chinese opera. He stayed just as he was for quite a while before jerking upright, his eyes shot wide open.

"Disaster!" he announced.

"What is?"

"Damn! Damn, Mrs. De Vos, I forgot all about Mrs. De Vos! Manikji, have you just had a fuck, or are you copacetic?"

"I'm fine, Hadleigh."

"Good, good, don't fuck anyone, just... damn, look at you. Damn, look at me! All right, all right, I can salvage this situation, I can make things work out, everything will be just fine. Come, come on, up we go. We'll get dressed nicely, do your hair, Manik, and shave, do your hair like you had it yesterday, it was beautiful, do you want me to send Miss Njeri around to help you? Don't fuck her, just have her fix your hair. And don't get drunk. But do eat something, do please eat something and don't make yourself sick. I have to go polish myself as well. I shall send Miss Njeri by to you, and when you're finished, come back over to my tent, the light blue one. We shall make this work, we shall!"

Then, having been rushed along and guided by Hadleigh's arm across my back, I was shoved in the direction of my tent, to go do my hair, shave, and eat something. I was quite hot, and, the champagne bucket really nearly empty of bottles anyway, I took out the remaining few and dumped the ice water over my head. Shaking and shivering for but a moment, I then poured the remaining rosewater slowly over the lower half of my body. Then, wet, chilly and naked, I went to work shaving as best I could.

"Hello, Bwom-Bwom!" Njeri cheerfully intoned as she arrived, a fresh basket of deliciousness on her arm. She came up behind me and tapped me on the bottom. "Lord Greenwich says I'm to do your hair like I did it yesterday."

"Yes, I have to impress some lady friend of his, Mrs. De Vos, look my best, you see, Njeri, my dear."

"Just you stay still and keep on with your face, I'll get to work on your hair right away. You know, Bwom-Bwom, I know this lady, Mrs. De Vos. I think she is a witch."

"Why so?"

"She is so hateful, hates everyone. I think she tries to curse people that do wrong by her, because of her terrible temper. Lord Greenwich is always trying to get on her good side, but I don't think it can be done, even by him. If you are to be entertaining this lady, Bwom-Bwom, I wish you the best of luck, and just be wary of her."

"Thank you very much for the warning, Njeri, that is important for me to know. I will be very careful indeed. But tell me, do you know where this lady lives? Tell me as much about her as you know, help me to protect myself."

"She lives in Malindi on a big plantation. She mistreats the people who work for her and she fires them for no reason at all. Her husband often travels, he is with the Navy, and when he is gone, she causes trouble for everyone. They are South African, Boers, they are not nice people, the Boers."

"I know that is the reputation that they have, but when I lived in South Africa, I will confess to not having met any of the famous cruel and hateful Boers, only some very nice Afrikaners who I liked quite a lot. I should mention that, perhaps that will do me well. Has she children?"

"She has three daughters, all grown, all very beautiful, none of whom like her at all."

Njeri had already made her way to the crown of my head, standing on tip-toe to rub the oil into the roots and I was rinsing my face and neck again. I turned around only to have her start rubbing shea butter from Uganda into my entire upper body. "For the parts of you that have color, it makes the color better," she explained.

"I normally don't like shea, but this smells so nice," I smiled, lighting myself another cigarette as Njeri massaged my elbows, making them gleam.

"I put in sandalwood powder," she explained, spreading the mixture liberally over my belly. "I thought you would like it."

"You are so endlessly thoughtful. I feel like an icon being anointed," I replied. "Maybe do good for my bad stretch marks down there?"

"Of course," she grinned. Oh, what a fool I am! Why am I worrying about developing a permanent affair with Edna or one of the other new ladies? Obviously, Njeri is my permanent affair, she likes me the best anyway, and I'm practically enmeshed in her family. But maybe that would be a bad idea, to put myself in such close proximity to Akinyi as she bonds to a new husband, I might end up ruining everything for both Njeri and Akinyi. But distancing myself from Njeri now after we have grown so close? I don't know how I'm going to do that. I don't think I want to, at any rate. She then produced for me another gold-trimmed dhoti, not unlike the one I had been destroying for the previous three days, but starched into a big, bloody, Bengali fan again! Damn, you Hadleigh. I sighed.

"Njeri, I am going to wear this stupid pleated dhoti, but I just want to tell you that I don't like it, I never wear it this way, and where I come from, if I'd been walking down the street in this, everyone would snicker at me. I just don't want to waste time having you take the pleats out," I explained, wriggling into it, the pre-tied design obviously meant for a slimmer man. I undid the knots and tried to make the whole ordeal look less awful, but I knew that Hadleigh would be enthralled, so I eventually gave up. Njeri then helped me on with my sherwani and tied back my oiled and treated hair. She stepped back to look at me.

"I think you look handsome, Bwom-Bwom."

"Thank you, Njeri."

The lady then popped a few lovely baked treats into my mouth and sent me on my way as she stayed behind to manage my possessions in the tent. I smoked a cigarette without my hands as I walked to Hadleigh's tent and spit out the butt by the time I arrived, keeping my now sparkling bright hands clean of any ashes. I saw old Hadleigh looking as perfect as a human being could be without having come from the waxworks shop, seated in one of his wicker chairs, an older lady seated in the other. They were having tea from proper china and enjoying some conversation. Before announcing my arrival, Hadleigh's face brightened up and he smiled at me in such a way that communicated both his pleasure in my appearance and also his acknowledgement of the fact that I hated my dhoti, but that he thought it was the dernier cri. He stood up.

"Ah, Mrs. De Vos, let me introduce my best friend and business partner, the Honorable Brahmin Manik Mudigonda. Do come by, take my seat, Manikji."

Before I thanked Hadleigh for his gracious relinquishment of his chair, I went over to Mrs. De Vos and kissed her hand through the dainty white crocheted mesh. I looked kindly at her face, which I felt betrayed none of the warnings given to me by both Hadleigh and Njeri. Mrs. De Vos was, perhaps forty-five or fifty years of age, with a sweet, motherly looking face and a gentle smile. I knew instantly that she was, much like myself, a misunderstood character. "It is so nice to meet you, Mrs. De Vos. I apologize that I did not have the chance to meet you yesterday, but that is all my fault and I am sorry."

"Please, Brahmin Mudigonda, there is no need to apologize. Your festival has been nothing but a whirlwind of activity since my arrival," the lady replied. I seated myself and Hadleigh handed me a cup of tea. I lit a cigarette and rested it on the saucer while Hadleigh gave me my lumps. Hadleigh then moved in to monopolize the conversation again as he always does and I had tea and smoked and looked with a compassionate eye on the dear lady. Her hair had once been blonde, surely, but was now mostly gray, and her face was not young. She was dressed extremely expensively, in silk and lace from Europe and the Far East, but it did not disguise the fact that she was really very heavy, perhaps as heavy as myself or more so. Hers had been a life of very hard work, perhaps difficult decisions, and she wore this hard life on her body. With my flirtatious glances, she seemed uncomfortable, almost shy, and very aware of how she must look to me, the man who was meant to fuck her. It is a difficult situation for women, particularly women who do not find themselves beautiful, for their constant occupation, in addition to raising families, maintaining homes and businesses, caring for husbands, is to be looked at by men. Men do not have the same concern, or I should say, most men. I am looked at by everyone, I am constantly a spectacle to be gawked at, I understand the concerns of women somewhat better by this fact. When I am undressed, I am naked, but I am also exhibit, I am curiosity, I am nude. My heart went out to the dear lady, I wanted to make her happy.

I had only been halfway listening to Hadleigh's dull rot when I heard him mention something about the Transvaal. I decided to take control of my situation. "Ah yes," I said, making it quite obvious that I had not been paying attention and did not care what anyone thought of that, "The Transvaal. Old Hadleigh and I, we studied law in Cape Town, from Oh Four to Oh Seven. Anchorman, he was, dear lady, but that is to say nothing against his skills as an attorney, which are incomparable, as you must know. I have never returned there, but I should want to very much, as it is the place I hold dearest in my heart, particularly because of the Afrikaners. My third year I was quite broke from frequent travel and drinking too much as is a student's pastime, and a grown man's pastime as well it seems, and I obtained a wonderful tutoring job for an Afrikaner family, two boys, maths, maths you know, for I'm sure that Hadleigh has mentioned that I was valedictorian for 1903 University of Calcutta?"

Hadleigh shot me such a poisonous glare that it killed me with good cheer. "One thing that I may also have neglected to mention to Mrs. De Vos is your excellent sense of humor, Manikji, old boy."

The lady began to laugh and put a graceful hand to her bosom. "Oh Horace, how your friend disarms me. Brahmin Mudigonda, what a charming man you are."

Hadleigh snarled at me, not so much out of disapproval, for he was very pleased that I had already gotten myself Mrs. De Vos's blessings, but out of aggravation and jealousy, that I could do in one minute what he had failed to do in months. He patted me on the shoulder and gave me an icy grin. "I love him as if he were my brother, Mrs. De Vos."

"Horace," the lady said, her voice strong and yet still uncertain, "I think I should like to spend some time with Brahmin Mudigonda to get to know him better."

"Oh, please, Mrs. De Vos, I insist." And with this instruction given, Hadleigh buggered off. I felt twice as relaxed and turned attention back to my cigarette, to the lady's kind visage.

"Hadleigh seems to be trouble, but he's really nothing but well-intentioned, he lives to please," I teased.

"It is good to hear that, Brahmin Mudigonda, he does not inspire trust in me for some reason, I just don't feel that he's being very honest."

"He probably isn't, but that doesn't mean that he isn't well-intentioned, Mrs. De Vos. But I would prefer to compliment you on the pronunciation of my patronymic. You say it so beautifully, I hardly can believe it is my own, mundane name that I've heard so many thousands of times."

"Thank you, sir," the lady replied, opening a fan like a Victorian debutante. I was smitten with her, an older woman who had not abandoned the coyness of her youth. Other men might find such things foolish, but I do not. I find them appealing, chains to the past of a new acquaintance, clues to the mystery of a new lover.

"You should try my first name as well, I think, Mrs. De Vos."

"It is Manik, am I right?" she replied, her cheeks all but flushed.

"Quite right. You have a way with languages, for certain. I, myself, succeeded at English, but I was too old when I started with Afrikaans, I sound utterly laughable."

"You do know a bit of Afrikaans! Do let me hear a bit, I promise to be generous."

I mumbled out some silly sentences, asking for a map of Cape Town, expressing a fervent love of ice cream, reciting the Pythagorean Theorem, and then a verse of the futurist poet Velimir Khlebnikov, which I then said first in Afrikaans, then in its original Russian, and then in English: If death had your lips and curls I should gladly wish to die. The lady was silent, her lips open and her eyes sparkling, and then she asked me: "How do you do this? How did you learn it?"

"What? Languages?"

"How to make women fall in love with you, how do you do it?"

"I don't. I wish I did. Perhaps I would not be a thirty-two year old bachelor if that were the case."

"Thirty-two? Lord Greenwich told me that you were twenty-seven."

"Oh, I'm sorry if I ruined something that you'd been hoping for..." I apologized, now thinking back to Hadleigh's remarks about my freshly shaven face. "I am really thirty-two."

"There is no need to apologize, a few years... they mean nothing. You look very young for your age..."

"Please call me Manik, just Manik," I interjected, sensing the lady grasping for a good name for me. "Or any sort of pet name that you like, I have quite a few in my catalogue that I like very much, but the way you pronounce my name as it is, dear lady, it has never sounded lovlier."

"Manik," she said with some relish, "I want to confess something to you."

"I promise to treasure your secret, whatever it is."

"This is not the first time I've done something like this, but it has been many years since those days, those days when I was young and pretty. I was hoping for someone seasoned and understanding so that, perhaps, I could graduate confidently to some young boy that I could sponsor, but I am uneasy. I am rather grateful for those five extra years, Manik, for your preparedness and your... expertise."

"I appreciate your honesty, dear lady, and I am glad that you appreciate mine, particularly when I say that a woman need not be young to be pretty. Come with me, let us cut to the chase and help you to restore your courage, so that you can be the woman you wish to be. And, I say this with all seriousness, I only exist to make you happy." I arose slowly, lit a fresh cigarette from the butt of the old one, and took the lady by the hand across the shoreline, over to my tent where surely Njeri had made everything just so. We walked slowly, gentle on the knees, and spoke of small and simple things: the texture of sand, the fragrance of an ocean breeze, how soft and warm my hands happen to be. I welcomed her into my private space and helped her to maintain her grace and aplomb when finding a way to rest herself upon my cushions while dressed in very stiff foundations. I drew myself close to her and she started when the red eye made itself apparent. I gave my dumb cow blink to let her know that her alarm was common and did not bother me in the least.

"Yes, I know, it's red," I said softly.

"It's... rather... unusual."

"Don't let it frighten you. It's never done anyone any harm. Some people's eyes are blue, like yours, or green, or brown, like mine, or red, like mine."

"It suits you. A different eye for a different man."

"Thank you, my lady."

"Oh dear, I... I don't know whether it's all right if I..."

"Go ahead."

"No, no, I'd rather you instigate."

And so I kissed her as a virgin boy kisses the woman he loves, passionately, naturally, with eyelashes brushing cheeks. We clasped hands and pulled ourselves closer together. I started to babble. "So, I'm in a predicament, my lady, and perhaps you can advise me. My general rule is that both parties are undressed completely, it just must be that way. My original method was always to undress myself first, so as to give the lady time to change her mind, but I was told by someone who I believe has some expertise in these matters that the gentleman must undress the lady first, or else he is conducting the affair very poorly and amateurishly. What sayeth thee, beautiful Clara from South Africa, the home of my heart?"

"Well, in my day, yes, the gentleman always undressed the lady first. In those days we tight-laced, so it was only fair to let the lady take a deep breath before seeing a naked man. But I might prefer it if you undressed first, Manik, not because I might change my mind, but to delay my anxieties and distract myself by looking at you."

"I am distracting, that is true, but in no positive sense, as you could probably guess. But, if that is what makes you happy, I shall get to it straight away. Do you want to see what foolish flesh adheres itself to my bones?"

"Yes, I do."

Thus began my classic, inelegant strip-tease, in which I manage to bare my skin in no particular pattern and do it quickly. I curled up close to Clara, feeling some degree of embarrassment, and hunched over slightly to make myself smaller. "You know, that jacket is worth one thousand pounds, and what do I do with it? I throw it on the floor! Aren't I horrible?"

"Yes, you're very bad," Clara laughed, tickling me under my chin, and then running her begloved fingers down my arm like a little spider. She then brushed away a loose curl from my face and pulled it back towards my queue, and gave me a good, critical look. "I thought that your skin would bother me. The truth is that I hardly notice it. You're really such a uniquely charming boy, red eye and all, with the white fringe around it. Not to mention you carry your weight in such a delightful way, it makes me envious."

"I never knew double-chin and potbelly could be considered delightful," I teased, trying to seem sweet and young and loveable. She tickled me again and kissed me on the cheek.

"I find you very appealing."

"Well, thank you." I relaxed my spine a little and leaned back so that I could look up at Clara's sweet face, the expression of which turned to sudden surprise.

"Oh, but you are very large, how did I not see that before? How did you disguise it? You must know all about positioning, posing, I wish you would teach me."

"There's nothing difficult about it, it would be my pleasure to reveal the tricks of the trade. May I help you with your lovely dress, beautiful Clara?"

"Yes, of course," she responded, sounding not slightly nervous. I crept quietly behind her back and began working on buttons. She laughed in a bitter way. "This dress is not quite one thousand pounds, but it is rather expensive, so do throw it on the floor, Manik, it would cheer me greatly."

"I shall do it in a particularly spoiled and contemptuous way."

"You seem well at ease undressed, young man."

"I am frequently undressed, I suppose I've grown accustomed to it. When I was younger, though, I never wanted to be seen naked by anybody, I was very ashamed of how ugly I am, my skin, my weight, and I will still cry in my bed for feeling ugly and hating myself. But lovemaking, I don't know, it's all different. It's different because I feel that I'm making someone else happy, that I'm touching her skin and watching her smile brighten up her face, and it helps me to put myself aside, and put the lady in the center of my focus. That is the only thing for which I live, Clara," I sang, pulling loosened dress artfully over her head and hurtling it to the other end of the tent to flop in a heap of expensiveness. I then got to work on corsetry, a very unusual design and as hard as planks of wood.

The lady laughed her small, sad laugh again, and turned her head to look at me hard at work. "But Manik," she said softly, "have you always looked like this?"

"More or less, yes. I was born with this coloration, if that's what you mean, but the smallpox came at seventeen, at seventeen when I was thirty stone."

"Thirty stone! So you are actually lighter now."

"But at twenty-three, for barely the length of time it takes to blink, I was eleven stone."

"It amazes me, Manik, how easy it is for you to say such difficult truths about yourself. I admire it about you, you are very special in that way. I was once eleven stone as well," the lady reminisced. "I was once considered a beauty. I do not know how it happened, but one day, my three girls were beautiful and I was no longer. It broke my spirit."

I thought about Clara's words to myself as I fought the endless buckles down her back. I had never had any beauty to lose, and still have none. What is better? To be always ugly and to have to cope with that, or to once burn brightly with loveliness that vanishes one day? I think that I would choose temporary beauty, for at least one would have memories of being beautiful, having people look at you with expressions of pleasure and welcome, being easily loved and adored. I would prefer that for certain, but I felt that Clara would have chosen my lot, at least at that moment when I interrupted her reverie by snapping the final elastic open, the whole contraption swinging at the sides, revealing her bare skin. I slowly helped her out of it, and then out of the additional girdle with stockings attached, and I could not help but notice her sad expression, how she kept her gaze away from me, I felt that my observation of her was unwanted. There were harsh, red impressions on her flesh, I noticed those first, in the shape of eyelets and boning, but as they erased themselves, and Clara caught her breath from the struggle, my painful feelings of sympathy changed to those of endearment, admiration.

In front of me, leaning shyly against my tussar cushions, her eyes refusing either to look at me or to look at herself, was the plumpest woman I have ever had the good fortune to have in my possession, and also, her aged face excepted, one of the prettiest. I know that my description will not do her justice, but I must never forget how I felt at that moment when I came under her spell, how I became every man with whom she had taken affairs during her bloom of youth, I cannot forget this, no, for I may never have an experience like this one ever again. Her skin was so perfect that I wanted to tear my own awful hide right off my body in disgust: not one stretch mark, not one scar, not one discolored spot, only lovely, silky, pink skin, pink like a peony petal. The age that had touched her face so unkindly had left her body entirely unscathed, and I would have guessed, from the neck down, a girl no older than twenty. Her bosom was not proportionately large, and did not droop, but sat up quite high and proudly upon her plumpness. She was elegantly pear-shaped, a smaller rib cage swelling out to very large, round hips, each of her thighs easily larger around than both of mine together. Her belly was so soft and liquid, draping over her lap in two soft rolls, one small and one large, that her slightest movement caused it to tremble. But her hands and feet, they need an epic poem to describe them properly. Those tiny hands and feet, so plump that every joint was a perfect little dimple, so flawless, not a single callous, each little toe and fingertip coming to a perfect little taper, it seemed almost impossible that such tiny, delicate extremities belonged to such a large woman, but they suited her, they suited her perfectly. Her gaze still avoiding me, I lowered myself and cupped those beautiful little feet in my hands as if they were priceless treasures and kissed them, rubbed my face against them, and popped the first toe on her right foot between my lips for one, sensual moment. I looked up at her; she looked back, and she was smiling. I felt as if I were in the presence of a goddess.

"Marry me?" came across my lips, as it so often does at times when I don't know what else to say. She laughed. She reached one of her beautiful hands to me, down at her feet, and encouraged me to crawl up to her and kiss her on the lips again.

"You are too much for words," she said, now shy once more and glancing away. "This isn't at all how I thought it would be, you're very different."

"Am I making you uncomfortable?" I asked, inching away but still latched onto her pearly hand.

"It isn't you, Manik. You've done nothing wrong at all."

I could not stand the lady's sadness, it was almost unbearable. I knew that if I started to run off at the mouth how lovely I found her, she would not believe me and no longer value me for my honesty, in spite of finding her very lovely indeed. I also knew that if I backed away, she would blame herself, and become even more unhappy, and she would probably ask me to bring her back to her husband and I would miss my chance to make love to her, and she would probably not make love to anyone, husband included, ever again. This was a sensitive situation, but I got an idea. I got up on my knees, painful though it was, and took both of Clara's hands, opened my eyes wide and stupidly.

"Let me teach you some poses, poses to suit every preference. This first one, this one is best for appealing to the young and callow." Clara kept her gaze at my silly, ugly face, and I positioned her limbs, had her recline on her back, her arms behind her head, her legs crooked to one side. I stroked the arch of her back and the indentation of her waist. "You see how small it makes you? And even though you're flat on your back, it keeps your bosoms up, how beautiful, isn't it?"

"Oh, you are clever," she smiled. "How do you know these things?"

"Just learning on the job, I suppose. Here, now, this one is for long time lovers, it makes you seem like a stranger." I had Clara prop herself up on one arm, stretch out her legs, and, balanced on her side as she was, twist her neck over her shoulder. "It's like a disguise, hiding behind yourself. Oh, it really suits you, Clara. But this last pose, this is a special pose. Bring your head back around, curl up your legs, you don't need to move your arms, they are fine as they are. Give a little glance downward, yes," I instructed. I then slipped my hands under the fluid softness of Clara's belly and arranged it, pouring forward over her hip.

"Who is this pose for?" she asked, a slightly baffled tone in her voice.

"For me," I stated proudly.

"Why do you like it?"

"Because it makes me want to touch you. Because you look so soft and beautiful. There are a lot of men who would like this pose the very best. Take it from one who knows, Clara. All some people want to do is put a head right here." I drew a small circle around Clara's nearly invisible navel with a fingertip. "If you let me, I'll let you next."

"No, I think I'd rather go first," she insisted, courage in her voice at last, and, with some assistance, was able to bury her head in my stomach, now quite happy and self-satisfied. This was a keen course of action that I chose, for it was in this very familiar and cozy position that Clara took notice of my penis, struggling at half-mast. "This isn't you hard, is it?" she asked, that familiar tone in her voice.

"No, just partially hard."

"It grows more than that?"

"In whores' parlance, there are men who are growers and men who are showers. I'm really more in the second camp, but yes, it does grow more than that. See the slack on the end?"

"Oh, you are right. Oh, can I touch it and see?"

"I thought you would never ask!"

With her beautiful pink finger, Clara stroked both the top and bottom, not quickly, softly. I sprang to attention, and the lady gasped as if she had been watching fireworks. "Not quite a hair-trigger, but nearly, nearly. You are an amazing man."

"That may be what you say, Clara, but now I'm an amazing man with an erection. What a predicament!"

"Yes, that is a predicament," Clara said in a cruel, taunting, alluring way. I burst out laughing; this was the real Clara, clearly, the coy mistress plying me with her witchcraft of seduction.

"You've put a spell on me," I groaned, making as if I were ready to take matters into my own hands, but Clara tapped me scornfully on the wrist.

"No, no," she scolded. She rolled to a side and motioned for me to join her. I am proud to have laid that absurd fallacy to rest about two fat lovers unable to make love except from behind, for she had me atop her, perhaps the only superior position I have ever taken without concern for injury on the part of the lady, and this worry allayed, I absolutely let loose and had an absolutely magnificent, carefree time. Magnificent as it was, it had another layer of pleasure to it, for it made me wonder if this is what it might feel like for the ladies who come astride me, to be pushed up against this deliciously soft flesh, I absolutely loved it. Maybe my body really is quite good for making love, maybe it is my vocation not only because of my emotional proclivities and my desire to understand women, but because I'm a damned good fucker, long foreskin, big belly, cracking great big penis and all. One needs not look like any classical ideal to be a good fucker, one must simply be a good fucker, and get lots of practice.

I will say with no modicum of modesty, that practice had, for Mudigondamas' time, certainly made perfect for me. The more I fuck, the better I do. I lasted such a long time with Clara, I brought her twice to plateaus, and still continued on! I continued while sucking on her nipples, I continued while touching her clitoris with a fingertip, I was unstoppable. After Clara's second plateau, however, I decided that I should just let myself go, and if it didn't hurt so much! It felt amazing, but it hurt like I was about to die, and my nightmare of venereal disease danced in front of my eyes for a few moments, but when I pulled myself out, as red and as sensitive as if I had been skinned, I remembered back to last year's birthday and that I got quite a bit overused then as well, which was a relief. My face broke out in a sweat and I fell to my back, afraid to even wipe the semen away. Clara, sweet lady, decided to do it for me. She gathered a bit of tissue paper, but wisely used her lovely soft fingers to clean me off, and the tissue paper to clean her fingers. We held each other and kissed for a good while, had some warm champagne, and laughed about it. She played with my hair, stroked and tickled me as she likes to do, and seemed very happy with me, even though she says that I smoke like a petulant schoolboy, which I thought unfair, for when I was a schoolboy, I did not smoke. I decided to finish off Njeri's lovely sweets, and offered to share with Clara, but she refused.

"I do hardly eat at all," she said softly.

"Oh, well, I eat loads. Probably more than anyone I've ever known, and certainly more than for my own good." I jammed an entire bun into the inside of my cheek for comic effect, and Clara seemed very amused.

"Your honesty overwhelms me," she intoned, shaking her head. "It does not bother you, your weight."

"It bothers me extremely."

"You do not give that impression, Manik."

"I do not wish to give that impression, so I do not. But it does bother me very, very much. I would give anything to wake up tomorrow at eleven stone. But I know that isn't going to happen, that it can't, and I've no idea of how to bring it about. However, I do have a life to live and pursuits that make me happy, I must press on living, I suppose, unless I want to kill myself, and although I've considered it very seriously many times in my life, I am too much of a coward to go through with it. I was thin once before, but I was unhappy, my mother had died and I was having conflicts with my father, I didn't appreciate it. In fact, I hardly knew myself. As much as I despise him, fat Manik I know quite well, I recognize him in the mirror. I know that he is romantic, depressive, affectionate, impulsive, and hungry, all of the time. I never got to know thin Manik, but I am pretty certain that depressive was the top of the list in characteristics. If blessed to know him again, I should treasure him, as much as I would treasure a lady in my embrace."

"With all of your most poignant honesty, Manik, there is one mystery that remains about you," the lady asked, holding my face in her hand. "How did someone so honest, so emotional, someone who, in spite of a life that could be criticized quite severely by moralizers, seems to have retained the innocence of a young boy, how did you link yourself to Lord Greenwich? A very intelligent Indian boy, and from a good family, I know that your lineage is very refined and your caste is superlative, how is it that you find yourself with him?"

"I have not always been so gregarious. He protected me."

"I don't mean to laugh, but you do not need him to protect you, Manik, and I doubt you ever did."

"No, you are right, and I know this. Lord Greenwich likes to think that he protects me, it makes him happy. He loves me very much, perhaps more than anyone else in this world."

"So, because he loves you... you only exist to make him happy."

"Yes. Yes, quite right. That's very astute of you."

"Let me ask you this, then. Should I trust him?"

"Dear lady, that is really up to you. I couldn't ask anyone to trust Hadleigh, Lord Greenwich, but I suppose I trust him myself to a very great degree. I have trusted him with my very life, and he is yet to betray me in any significant way."

Clara then kissed me tenderly on the cheek and patted me on the chest. "Let's bring me back to him, Manik, dear boy."

I was just the slightest bit tipsy as I tried to fasten Clara back into her corseting, and even just this very minor impairment had me struggling. I lost track of laces and did a very poor job, but the dear lady had no criticism for me. She waited patiently. I also bit my tongue with the suggestion that she might not want to wear something so obviously uncomfortable and unbecoming, for the hardness with which it endowed upon her soft physique I felt made her seem less approachable, less sensual, and very much more intimidating. I said nothing, however, for I knew it would only irk her, and I was there to make her happy, after all, and perhaps with white men, attitudes are different. Perhaps with white men there is a preference for silhouette at the expense of texture. How stupid. Well, that would be white men, anyway.

I guided Clara back to one of the stupidest white men I have ever had the pleasure to know, and the expression on his face was one not so much of pride as relief. Hadleigh is usually not afraid of people. I felt badly for Clara, and the unfair reputation that precedes her; she is not at all deserving of the scornful mistress's archetype. Clara is self-conscious, caring, thoughtful, and even a bit bashful, all in all a sweet lady. I would place her firmly in the category of warm, tender, motherly women, which is a category that I hold quite dear to my heart. She allowed me to kiss her ungloved hand before I bid her adeiu; it felt so intimate and erotic, I surely reddened in the face. I scampered off like a shy pubescent boy in love with his mother's friend.

The final destination of my scampering was the Masaai dancers, of course, where I found both Katie and Ruth in attendence, clapping in time with the stomping feet of the dancers. I inelegantly wriggled between them and they treated me to hair ruffling and scratching on my chest and back, as if I were an old sheepdog. They had become fast friends, which was no surprise to me given Katie's boisterous friendliness which she bestows on even the shrinkingest shrinking violets, and had, without a doubt, some conversation related to me. I spend not a cent on worry, for they both seemed quite cheerful at my arrival. I also noticed that Katie, the naturist as she is, had convinced Ruth to discard her somewhat frumpy and old fashioned style of dress for a blue sarong, but wrapped around the bust rather than the waist, her modesty still greater than her new friend's. I complimented Ruth on looking so fresh and lovely and she grinned at me, those beautiful misaligned gnashers. The dancers picked up the pace suddenly and we three were caught up in the thrill of their performance. Both the men and women dancers were on the stage, an uncommon sight, and the contrast between their styles was quite engrossing. Resson then came to the forefront of the group to do some improvisation, and I felt nearly faint. I tilted my head in Katie's direction.

"Isn't she amazing?" I whispered. "I am so captivated by her."

"Manik old fellow, are you in love again?" she scolded me, her strong fist knocking into my arm.

"Of course I am, no need to resort to violence, Katie my dearest," I replied.

"I think you ought to go up and dance with her, let her know how you feel," Katie teased, a sparkle in her eye.

"Impossible."

"Why impossible? You and I did some bloody great dancing the other day."

"There are some crucial differences."

"You wait here, old sport, and I'll bring by the liquid courage." With that Katie dashed off like a sprinter at the gunshot. In Katie's absence, Ruth cozied up a bit more closely, arms squeezed around my waist again, her small tousled head just a few inches under my chin. Sweet girl, but she makes me feel odd. Katie returned too successfully, not bearing champagne with flutes or wine with goblets but three bottles of rum, a make that I did not recognize, and one of gin, not Bols thank goodness, and no glasses at all. "Yo ho ho, Manik, old boy," she teased, opening the first bottle.

"May I have the first?" I asked deviously. She handed it over and in fewer than four swallows I did away with half of it. Katie all but smacked it out of my hand.

"I thought we might share, Prince Manik!" she scolded. "Ruthie old girl, take it while it's here, before it goes into the bottomless pit."

We three, relatively unmolested by the attention of interested male parties (husbands and Hadleigh), and in a very short period of time, got straight to inebriated, bypassing tipsy and light-headed. Soon, the thousand-pound Sherwani was thrown into the dust again with total disregard, and I was on my feet, Katie balancing on one of my shoulders and Ruth on the other, the weight of the both of them on my back feeling like absolutely nothing at all. This elaborate display of caveman strength did accomplish its intent, which was to get Resson to dance over in my direction. She started jingling her ankles an inch away from mine and grinning at me in a very alluring way. I fancied that Dorothy was watching me, and that perhaps I might be making her jealous, surrounded by other interested women as I was. Maybe she did see me, but I have a feeling that her emotional state would have been one more of compersion than of jealousy, her awareness of my affinity for feminine company more than complete. After quite a bit of jostling, Resson motioned for my attention, asking me to still myself, and she took off one of her bell anklets and fastened it on me. She started to teach me a few of her steps, but they were complicated and I was drunk, so I asked Katie and Ruth if I might put them down. They all but leapt to the ground and I felt a full inch taller instantly. I think they, too, were invited to learn the dance, but I was concentrating very, very hard and had my eyes absolutely glued to Resson's beautiful, beaded legs. She gave me encouraging expressions, and I really did try my best, but at one point I more or less gave up and just let myself go wild and stupid, and perhaps I grabbed Resson's hand as I went at it. Maybe I thought I was waltzing, maybe doing something else? Was it odissi? It was odissi, it was, I was dropping hips and isolating my chest, wasn't I? I am so, so glad to have been drunk.

Somehow, Resson and I ran away from the stage. Were we noticed? I have no question that everyone watching the performance, all of the dancers, all of the singers would have known. But will Hadleigh know? I should hope that all those in attendance would have that sort of discretion as to let the birthday celebrant have a certain degree of shamelessness. I know that I did discover that Resson did not know English, and that I do not know Masaai, and my Swahili is so incomplete as to be rendered completely useless. Resson did not know Arabic, either, but after we struggled through a few languages, we ascertained each other's names, and then basically gave up. We kissed and laughed, and I swung her up in my arms and carried her to my tent, hardly lifting my head for kisses. It was strange, this encounter, for two primary reasons. First of all, Resson had been neither an arranged match nor a long-time flirtation prospect that I had won over with conversation and flattery. She seemed to want to make love with me as if I were just any other man that she found appealing, which is extremely mysterious. Second of all, I can't remember it very well at all. I can remember sexual encounters with the brightest vividness when I forget just about everything else about my life. I did feel very roughed up afterwards, very, very sore, and in places that I wouldn't have expected. I don't think we made love inside my tent, I think we must have made love outside it. I remember her running off, laughing gleefully and waving; I waved back. What happened? What did we do?

She didn't take off her jewelry. She undressed me, I think. She was on top of me. She pulled on my chest hair? She hit me in the chest? Pounded my chest, I think, from excitement? Oh, it hurt me. Why did she make love with me? It makes no sense, looking back at it. If I could only remember it better, that might give me insight. Damn, I will make myself remember, I must. I will try again later.

To tell the truth, I don't remember very much after that point anyway. I must have gone back to drinking relatively soon after this encounter, I'm pretty sure that's what I did. I went back to the resting musicians, I had some beer, I had a lot of beer. I don't know what else.

Somehow the sky got dark. The camp started to be evacuated, the stage cleared away, the tents pulled down, the banquet stored away. I don't remember anything else until I found myself shivering, cold and sweaty, in the back seat of Hadleigh's Benz, one arm in my sherwani, the other without. I tried to get both arms in but I just couldn't. My head was aching so badly, I could hardly stand it. I'm pretty certain that I was crying, and if I remember myself crying, it must have been quite a messy ordeal. Hadleigh shoved me up to my flat. I think I was fighting him, arguing with him. I think I remember insisting that I was not overstimulated, and also that I was not crying, I was just very, very upset. Well, I suppose that's ending the party with the right sort of attitude. Did he sit with me for a while? I think he did. I think he stayed part of the night, put my sherwani away for me. I think I must have been in such a state, what was wrong with me? I kept thrashing around, he restrained me until I finally gave in to sick, drunk, miserable sleep. He kept pinning my arms back, not hard, but to try to calm me. He cares about me. That's why he throws me these magnificent birthday parties. I just can't bear it when they end, is all. I'm spoiled, spoiled, spoiled, and I've wasted my whole day on the beach, wishing it were still going on, trying to remember every precious, precious memory, so that I never, ever lose them. That's one of my worst nightmares, being unable to remember. It's good that I train myself to always write down the things that I never want to forget, that way if my memory ever starts to fail me, I'll at least be able to read what I've written.

Monday, June 30, 1913

Back to the old grind again, it is so hard for me to go back to work. I can hardly convince myself to get back to the cases. I just want to smoke all day, and gorge myself, and I have been drinking myself to sleep. Very bad. Kaweria has been so good to me. I wonder how awful I was those first days after my return from Mudigondamas.

Wednesday, July 2, 1913

Dede's petition has returned successfully. I have had Hadleigh contact his courtroom man. I know that I should call her myself and talk to her, but I feel ashamed for some reason. I should never have made love to her, she feels guilt about it, without a doubt. I should never make love to women that I know will feel guilty about having been with me. She is too good, too wonderful. I am a bad person. I think I may have ruined her life. Oh, god, I am a monster.

Wednesday, July 2, 1913, continued

I called Dede myself, and I don't regret it, as uncomfortable as it was. She seemed all so calm and kind, so pleased with my good news. I can't think about her anymore, I owe her that.

Saturday, July 5, 1913

Went to the coffee scales for the first time in too long. Twenty-one stone three again, just as I was before I swore I'd make eleven stone within a year and ten up from my birthday. How is that even possible? Three hundred pounds. I may as well start saying aloud, maybe it will shame me. Manik Mudigonda is my name and I am nearly three hundred pounds. I hate myself so much, I can hardly cope.

It's hard to comprehend my misery, it's just so painful and consuming. I was so happy on my birthday, and I was nearly feeling comfortable with my size. The sherwani may have had something to do with it; I would not dare to try it on now, knowing that I've gained so much weight, because seeing it too tight for me would send me spiraling. But even more than that, I felt so much more at ease, I think, because all of those women were loving me and touching me, wanting to spend their time with me. I can recall a vague rationalization echoing in my semi-conscious brain, that it wasn't so bad, being big and soft, for I was able to take advantage of these qualities to bring happiness to women: to carry them in my arms or on my shoulders, to be a pillow or a mattress, to restore the confidence of a lady who has forgotten her beauty. But if I am not making love, what is the point?

If I am honest with myself, I know what I need to be happy and maintain my sanity, and what would be required, most likely, to actually lose weight. As much as it would be wonderful to have ten women showing their affection for me, that sort of thing is only annual. I need lots of freely given love on a daily basis. I probably need several hundred times more love than the average man. What I really need is a wife who not only loves me, but who loves me in a very demonstrative, very intense way, and who loves me just as I am. I need a wife who, in spite of all evidence to the contrary, thinks that I am beautiful, and who will feel no burden at reassuring me of her sentiments multiple times a day. I need a wife who will look me in my red eye with love and admiration, who will constantly stroke and compliment my hair and who will notice how it grows. I need a wife who will kiss me on my neck, who will seek out my worst and deepest pockmarks as the sites of her kisses. I need a wife who will adore the contrast of my colors. I need a wife who will not only sleep with her head on my belly, but also who will genuinely love my flesh, not in the fulfillment of a fetish but in the appreciation of largeness as it is. I need a wife who is not alarmed by a man who often cries, or who crumbles in depression on a frequent basis, but is endeared by his sensitivity. If I do not have these conditions, if I am not loved in these ways, my life will always be unendurable and I will not live a long life, I will die a young man. I will either kill myself or simply allow myself to die. These facts are not easy to reconcile, and it has been hard enough to acknowledge them, but I am thirty-two years old now, I must admit the reality of myself: either I marry a woman who truly loves me, or I die, and it is so difficult to admit these things because I know very well that the more likely possibility is the second. Sadness and loneliness and self-hatred will be my demise. Not the alcohol, for, although I'm sure it does me no favors, if it were going to kill me, it most likely would have done so already. Not the alcohol but the misery. Whether I quit drinking or not would be immaterial if there were a woman who would take me into her soft, tender arms several times a day and whisper gently, "I love you Manik, and I love your belly." I would live for ages.

So what do I do with myself now, while I am alone and suffering? I can't be three hundred pounds, I just can't, it's wearing on my joints too much. Starve myself? Vomit twice a day? It won't work. I ought to tell Hadleigh that I need a wife, for medical reasons, but he will discourage me, I know it. You don't need a wife, Manik, he'll say, women are bad and they hurt you. You just need a fuck. But why do those two things have to be mutually exclusive? Why can't I have a fuck and then make her my wife? So, without Hadleigh's assistance, what do I do? In fact, I will be be searching incognito, against Hadleigh's wishes, think of that. Secretly hunting for a wife. This is going to be a challenge, but it is life or death.

Sunday, July 6, 1913

Two realizations: I can never go to the candy store again, and since my birthday has passed, there is to be a huge wave of gossip echoing through Mombasa that I put my hand down my throat and make myself vomit. These are not ideal circumstances for wife-hunting.

Sunday, July 6, 1913, continued

Third realization: I am shy. I am extremely shy. I went through four years of university education and hardly spoke to anyone. I don't really know how to make friends without help and introductions. I know how to get a fuck or gain a lover, but this is a different kind of skill. Speak to someone that I do not know about neither law business nor love business? And sober, in the daytime, alone? My tongue ties itself. I imagine myself dashing, introducing myself to ladies in town with a bow and a flourish, and realize that this would probably terrify them. I then shift into something more familiar: awkward and clumsy romantic fool. Lila loved me for being such a creature. I think about her constantly these days, and the more I think about her, the more I fancy that she and I, under different circumstances, could have had a good and happy marriage. But she is gone now.

What I really need is an Indian mother, I need my Mai to arrange for me a marriage to a lady who will be right for me, who will help me mature and develop in healthy ways. I also need to be ten years old again. Ah, matchmakers, are there any matchmakers? How might I discover a matchmaker? Do they advertise? I haven't a clue. But I should think about this critically:

If I employ a matchmaker, then I am putting myself into a self-selected pool of unmarried people. Matchmakers are by their very nature xenophobic, and will only make matches within a specific community. Communities in Mombasa: Taita, Luo, Maasai, Swahili, Arab, English, Chinese, Sikh, Gujarati, and a sprinkling of Northern Hindus. A matchmaker would only make a match for me from within the Brahmin members of this last group. This is not necessarily a bad thing, as I have been a Brahmin husband before, and I would be perfectly happy to be one again. However, I would probably face the greatest resistance from within my own subgroup to matching, in spite of my excellent ancestral line and my considerable wealth, because of horoscope and my overall inauspiciousness. Also, as a potential Brahmin groom, the nature of Brahmin brides is such that I should most likely end up wedded to a child, and that defeats the entire purpose of getting married: to have someone to love and look after me, rather than the other way around. But there are always widows, I could specify a desire to only marry a widow, or a fallen woman, widows and fallen women, that improves my odds. But, how many Brahmin widows and fallen women are there in Mombasa? Perhaps I could have one sent to me from elsewhere?

Brilliant, brilliant idea: mail-order wife. I could buy a wife from Uttar Pradesh, perhaps, or anywhere, really. Buy a Tamil bride, that might be even better. I would be willing to pay any price for a Tamil Brahmin widow aged older than nineteen, younger than fifty, children are fine. Plump, with a cheerful disposition preferred.

And now I am back in the realm of fantasy. This is just as fantastical as charming an African or European woman with a flourish on the street. I cannot forget that I got very lucky when my parents selected Madhulika for me, that things could have gone very badly for us. It was mere chance that we loved each other as we did. I need romantic love, I need it to survive. This pragmatism I'm trying to employ is worthless, because it cannot fill the crack in my glass heart. Lonely hearts advertisement, that is the only way. And none of the regular "Wealthy Brahmin man, six feet tall, valedictorian University of Calcutta 1903" business. I must purge all of that pragmatism out of my plans and simply lay out my heart. Like Dorothy said, a romantic needs a romantic.

I will take out a quarter page. I will not mention anything having to do with either my saleable qualities (Brahmin man six feet tall) or my detrimental qualities (fat piebald with red eye). I will write an essay about my internal self.

Here it all comes, all that loving poison that makes Manik Mudigonda a man.

Desperate romantic seeks a lady of similar constitution. If your life-long dream is to be loved and treasured like no other woman has been before, please consider my plea. This is not a stupid, boastful claim that merely bolster's some typical man's sense of self-worth, considering as he intends not to beat his wife unless necessary, or silence her identity as anything more than an extension of himself. No, beautiful lady, I will love you, I will love you painfully, and give of myself to you until I all but die. I will weep and long for you in your absence, and in your presence gladly fulfill your every whim.

The things about which you think a man should concern himself: chastity, obedience, humility, mean little to me. I need a woman who can love, who can love with more depth of feeling and with greater openness of heart than words can describe, and if I cannot find such a lady, I will die of a broken heart. I am a widower of relatively youthful experience; my heart has been broken for too long. Can you, beautiful lady, repair it for me?

I am quite bashful, but my embrace is soft and warm. Due to this initial shyness, which I oftentimes feel is insurmountable; I should request a telegram to the outpost at 15. In this telegram, I want nothing but proof that you are a romantic, and a date, time, and location for our first encounter. I will be the gentleman with long hair, smoking a cigarette.

Monday, July 14, 1913

Hadleigh came into my office today, smiling and snickering and handsome, the newspaper folded up in one hand.

"Have you seen this silly thing?" he asked me, tapping the open page's bottom corner.

"I don't know what you're talking about, Hadleigh."

"You wrote this, didn't you, Manikji?"

"I'm afraid I still don't know what you're talking about."

"You wrote this, I know you did. It has all the hallmarks of your style. It's all right, you can admit it, I'm not angry with you, my most precious gentleman with long hair."

I sighed and lit myself a cigarette to complete the description. This was as good as an admission, I suppose, for Hadleigh came up behind me and threw his arms around my chest. "Manikji," he sang, "You are adorable." Then he kissed me on the temple. I could not have been more infuriated, but apparently my brilliant advertisement was not as brilliant as I'd hoped. Well, it doesn't really matter if it is brilliant, anyway, all that really matters is that it is honest and represents my true feelings, and that some lady will fall in love with the man of such complex emotions. "Let me know if you get any telegrams, I'll help you get ready."

"Oh, but you wouldn't, Hadleigh," I started. "That is, if I knew what in the world it was you were talking about."

"Oh, I see," he grinned. "If you are too bashful to let me in on your wife-seeking, I will pretend that I don't know about it. Does that make you feel better?"

"Who's seeking a wife? Are you, Hadleigh?"

"I'm afraid I don't know what you're talking about, Manikji," Hadleigh replied, mocking my manner of speech in his forced baritone, wobbling his head, like I know that I do not do, but he fancies that I do, Orientalist bint.

"You just wish your voice was half as deep as mine," I teased him.

"Ladies like deep voices."

"I wish you wouldn't patronize me so, Hadleigh," I complained, but he had already left. I suppose Hadleigh knows me well enough that he could spot my writing at random, but I wonder if anyone else I know would recognize it. I hope not, that would be very embarrassing.

Tuesday, July 15, 1913

My first telegram! I can hardly contain myself. I am to meet the lady tomorrow at four o' clock at the Chinese tea room. I am to be looking for a lady dressed in black, which I suppose is unusual, but I think will be altogether suitable, as I shall be dressed in white. Why black, I wonder? A widow? A Muslim lady? Perhaps it is just her preferred color, perhaps she finds that it suits her. Her note was very tender and lovely, if brief: You sound like a man from a romance novel, she said. I have always wanted to be swept off my feet. I wonder what her name is. I can't believe it, I may be meeting my wife tomorrow! This was too simple, why did I never do this before?

Wednesday, July 16, 1913

I have found out the answer to my question that I wrote yesterday. The answer is that it does not work. I arrived at the Chinese tea room at four sharp, with none of my customary Indian Standard Time tardiness. I'd just had my white suit let out and it didn't fit too badly, I took the most discreet corner of the room and lit myself a cigarette. I also flopped my queue over my shoulder to make it immediately visible by anyone at the entryway, which I know was still a bit whorish, but it will take time for me to break myself of all of those habits. I ordered a pot of tea with two cups, sat back with Whitehead and Russell's third edition of **Principia Mathematica**, which I thought might soothe my nerves and keep me from sweating. About five minutes later I caught a glimpse of an anxious looking lady with features that bespoke some certain degree of Ethiopian heritage, tall and very thin, about my own age, dressed in a black gown and a black headscarf. Her eyes were wide and beautiful, her mouth small, a heart-shaped face. I nearly started to hyperventilate, I had to place a hand at my chest. I knew that I loved her immediately, that there stood but five yards away the woman I would love for the rest of my life. I shook my hair, put my cigarette on my bottom lip, and gave her a small, hopeful smile.

She ran out of the room. I didn't bother to follow her, it would not have been worthwhile. She didn't want me. I can't make a woman love me, I know that by now.

Thursday, July 17, 1913

Another telegram, but I am not confident. Tonight at half past nine, the bridge to the mainland. She says that she will be carrying a bouquet of fireball lilies, which is very, very romantic indeed, but I fear a repeat of yesterday's disappointment. But fireball lilies, that signifies a different sort of lady, I think. Most ladies might choose something more stereotyped in its beauty, roses, anthurium, violets, orchids, those sorts of things. But a big bunch of Catherine wheels? An affinity for red, at least!

Friday, July 18, 1913

No better than my first attempt. This young lady, and I do stress young, whose complexion suggested that she was, perhaps, a Mulatto, had been planning an escape of sorts from her mother's protection, an elopement so to speak, and had brought not only the fireball lilies but almost everything she owned in a wheeled cart. She was serious about starting a life with a man away from her home, I could see that. She was equally serious that it should not be with me. She was severely disappointed and hid it poorly. She drew her eyebrows close together and said, "I never would have thought that anything but a handsome man could have written that advertisement."

"But Nylejah," I explained, "handsome men do not need advertisements."

"A handsome man could be shy," she countered me, and quite rightly, tipping up her chin at me for emphasis. I helped her truck her things back across the bridge.

Saturday, July 19, 1913

I wouldn't even have paid any heed to the most recent telegram if I hadn't had to go to Kuze anyway to pay Nia's bail at the little local gaol. I got the call and the telegram at about the same time, and I figured that today I had to go to Kuze. Hadleigh offered to let me borrow his Benz, but I figured that I wasn't really in any kind of rush, I may as well make things easy for myself and walk there, particularly since parking that unnecessarily long vehicle in busier parts of town is frustrating and next to impossible. Also, I'd just gotten my new suit from Hadleigh's tailor-shop and in spite of my acting rather annoyed about the color not even remotely resembling the swatch (I had allowed myself to be measured in muslins, which is never a good idea), I almost liked the idea of bailing out Nia in a brand new pink suit, brand new, but already with trousers down at the hips and waistcoat halfway open. I thought she might like it. I also dandied myself up in earrings, ruby tie pin, and a ring on nearly every finger, which I thought would also cheer her after spending a night locked up.

I spotted her from across the gaol as I paid her shamefully low bail at the window, and she looked so dejected, poor thing. She was crumpled up in the corner of the cell, trying to shrink away from the other women inside, her arms wrapped around her knees. As I approached with the guard to let her out, I noticed that her bottom lip was split open. An unnecessarily conscientious rookie P.C. without a doubt, how cruel. Nia is such a petite little woman, I couldn't think of a single reason to use that sort of force on her. She sprang up when she saw me at the lock with a bloody lipped smile and grabbed onto my arm with a magnetic force as she exited.

"Hello, Nia, my dear," I said, pulling out my cigarette case and lighter.

"Oh, give us a cigarette, Mr. Mudi!" she insisted, squeezing my bicep in an affectionate way.

"As if I had to be asked," I teased, providing the light with as much grace as could be possible. "So, when is your court date, did they tell you?"

"August the fifteenth," Nia managed between puffs.

"Busy docket! You've never had to wait that long, have you? They must have cracked down on the constables not making enough arrests, I would think. That may not be their fault, but that split looks to be. Are you all right, my darling?"

"It isn't bad, but it is so sweet of you to be concerned. But you know, Mr. Mudi, not in for solicitation this time."

"Oh? What then?"

"Indecent exposure and public lewdness."

"He wanted it, didn't he?"

"It's what he paid for."

"Then it's not even your fault, for goodness sake. Good for you, though, avoiding solicitation charges, the judges are getting crabby about those sorts of things these days. And thank you for giving me such an easy task! Indecent exposure and public lewdness are a cinch to defend, you know. That was very thoughtful of you, lovely Nia. He get caught as well?" I had been slowly walking Nia back to her cozy little brothel when she tipped her head to rest it on the side of my shoulder. I thought that was very sweet of her.

"Oh yes. Falling over his own drawers, Mr. Mudi, you should have seen it! If I hadn't been so scared I would have been rocking on my back laughing! You want to be his solicitor, too?"

"No, not particularly," I laughed. "Just yours."

"Mr. Mudi, you look different again," Nia said thoughtfully, squinting her eyes up at me. "You get married?"

"No, still not married, Miss Nia."

"You get fatter?"

"Yes, unfortunately."

"But that's not it, it's something else. What is different about you, Mr. Mudi?"

"I did just have my birthday, do I look older?"

"Oh, happy birthday, Mr. Mudi!" the lady laughed, cracking open her bloody lip again for smiles. "Are you thirty years old yet?"

"Where have you been, Miss Nia? I am fully thirty-two years of age, and proud of it."

"Thirty-two, Mr. Mudi! An old man now! Oh, but you don't really look older, Mr. Mudi, I hate to disappoint you."

We took a seat on the brothel porch where Nia was being awaited by some of her sisters. They exchanged hugs and kisses, and a few came to me to give thanks and greetings, most of them knowing me relatively well. One of the youngest girls, Laila, kissed me on the hand. I wanted to give her a silver coin, but that didn't feel right, so I just gave her a cigarette, which was accepted with the same sort of enthusiasm. "Mr. Mudi is the nicest solicitor, isn't he?" she said to the other ladies and girls. They all gave expressions of agreement, which made me feel quite warm in the face. I always try to spend as little time in Nia's brothel as possible, for guilt and unease always starts bubbling up my throat so quickly. I excused Nia and myself to give her some special instructions before my departure.

"Now, Miss Nia, I'll be expecting you to come by my office in a fortnight, like we usually do, all right? I'll have the whole shell of your document set up, and your barrister arranged, you'll just need to fill in the blanks with me. Please don't forget, or else I'll have to come looking for you from worry."

"I know, Mr. Mudi. I will put a mark on the calendar," Nia agreed, still cheerful. "Is that a new suit, Mr. Mudi?"

"Yes it is," I admitted.

"That tailor is no good, Mr. Mudi."

"He's either very bad or very good, one can never tell his mood."

"Well, I think he's no good. Doesn't he know you have a big belly? He doesn't make any room for it. That suit is made for a man made of paper: flat and wide. You need darts in that waistcoat, that's why you can't close it. There is a tailor here in Kuze, right close by here, he would suit you up much better."

"Maybe I should keep the tailor and get rid of the big belly, Miss Nia." I neither asked nor wanted to ask how intimately she knew this tailor who knew how to properly dress a three-dimensional fat gentleman.

"Suit yourself, Mr. Mudi." The lady then looked down for a moment and closed her lips tightly before speaking again. "I don't like the lockup at all, you know, Mr. Mudi. I feel so afraid."

"I understand, Miss Nia."

"I feel so afraid in there, I start thinking I should quit the love business. I just want to be safe, happy, don't want to put myself in dangerous situations anymore. But then I get out, and where else could I go? What else could I do? It makes me just as afraid as the lockup. So I go back. I love my sisters, I know that much, even though Big Mama isn't always good to me, but I don't feel alone in there. And every once in a while, a nice man comes, I make him feel better, old men especially, and I think maybe love business isn't so bad. But when I'm in that lockup, Mr. Mudi, I always think I want to quit it."

"I'll tell you the truth, Miss Nia," I sighed, lighting us both cigarettes again, "I have been thinking the same way about the love business. These days I want to quit it, too."

"Really, Mr. Mudi? Maybe that is the change I see in you," Nia replied gently, trying to tug the edges of my waistcoat to help another button to the buttonhole. "I really think you should get married, Mr. Mudi."

"You know, Miss Nia, if we both wanted to quit the love business, we could get married, go live in a palace in India."

Nia tilted her head and gave me a wide grin. "Mr. Mudi, you are just the nicest man." She then reached up her slim hands and straightened my cravat for me. I knew that smile, as I had used it myself a number of times. It isn't really artifice, it isn't deception, that smile, although other people might characterize it that way. I wish more people understood that. I pinched her tiny wrist between my thumb and forefinger and made a brief farewell, which included giving her another cigarette.

Seeing that the sun was no longer directly overhead, I pulled out my watch to check the time. It was ten minutes to two. I know Kuze moderately well, and I knew that if I wanted to go to the bookstore to be rejected by another telegram lady, I would have just enough time. I normally do not go to this bookstore, although I have been there once or twice before, I normally go to the one in downtown Mombasa. No, this is a lie, I normally don't go to the book store but order my books for delivery to the Cecil, because I am a spoiled Brahmin boy who hates to do anything for himself if he can help it. It is a relatively large shop with two floors, and I would not know where the lady would be anyway, so I went in with low expectations. I did not make a beeline to the science texts, but rather sauntered over to poetry, cigarette on my bottom lip, thinking that I might look less antisocial perusing Mayakovsky than a physics journal. I think I like these futurists, the way they integrate brute force and the technological into their vision of a beautiful world, so much better than the same old wistful flower musings that everyone else writes. I got quite engrossed for a moment with *A Slap in the Face of Public Taste*, that I nearly forgot why I was there at all. Then, I heard a lady give an "Aw," as if she were looking at a three-legged calf; I knew that sound was for me, so I looked up. A middle-aged Taita lady stood to my side, her hands on her hips and a benevolent expression on her face.

"Aw, are you the lonely heart, dear?" she said, reaching out a hand in a motherly gesture. I felt so nervous that I barely managed to blink an affirmation and smile. I felt a bit awkward, and didn't know how to juggle cigarette, book, and both hands for a moment. "Oh, aren't you shy, don't be afraid," she encouraged, wagging her fingers at me. I finally managed to take the lady's hand, but I could hardly make myself speak. I think I managed a few ers and erms and a few uncomfortable laughs, but it was the lady who spoke again.

"Are you an Indian boy?" she asked sweetly.

"Yes," I choked out.

"Do you really look like this? Oh, you poor thing. Marura," the lady called out into the shop, extracting another Taita lady of such similar appearance, that I automatically assumed that they were sisters. "Marura, look at this poor Indian boy. He's the lonely heart. Just look at him, the poor devil, aw, my heart goes out to him, doesn't yours?"

"Oh, Saru, I can hardly believe it," the other lady replied, taking my hand from her sister and looking me condescendingly in the face. "Have you got a name, young fellow?"

It was becoming clear to me that these ladies were under the misapprehension that I was much, much younger than I actually am, but I hardly knew how to correct it, I felt so extremely out of sorts. "Manik Mudigonda is my name, dear lady," I stammered.

"Now, you used to know a Manik, didn't you Saru? Worked in the customs office?" Marura said back to her sister.

"No, no, his name was Mohan, I think," Saru replied. "Maybe this boy here would know. Did you know the Indian man who worked in the customs office up until about a year ago?"

"No, I'm sorry..." I tried to reply.

"Oh, just look at these rings he has, Saru," Marura said, examining my hand. "And earrings as well. Trying to deck himself out, what a shame." She shook her head and clucked her tongue before addressing me again. "I'm sorry young man, you must be confused. My sister and

I read your advertisement and we were just so curious as to the type of man that would write such a thing. You see, we write romance stories for the local ladies' fiction magazine, and we thought you might be good inspiration."

"Oh I see," I replied, feeling almost faint from embarrassment. "So you aren't..."

"Oh no!" Marura burst out laughing. "Add our married years together and you would get sixty-five! No, no, no husband hunting for us. I hope it isn't too much of a disappointment. Surely you've gotten hundreds of responses."

"Well, no I haven't, actually. I've not gotten many responses at all to tell the truth." My tongue started to feel dry and cottony as I spoke these words.

"What a shame!" Saru tutted. "But while you're here, we might as well do some research for our next story. Now, your face, young man, did you have some sort of accident? And how did your hair go white at such an early age?"

"I have always looked like this, I didn't have an accident. I did have smallpox, though..."

"And what your mother does feed you to grow you so big?"

It is over ten years since my mother has fed me anything at all, but I decided that I might tell the truth in a cloudy way in order to best give these ladies useful story-telling material. "I am a vegetarian, I have never eaten meat."

"Oh, Saru," Marura interjected, "the advertisement said he was a widower. Are you really a widower, young man? You couldn't have been married long."

"I was married for just under a year."

Both ladies seemed to melt before my very eyes in cooing and muttering "Oh, poor thing!" They brought me back behind the cash register to sit with them and served me tea with biscuits and grilled me about myself. I think I may have endeared myself to them a bit, for they told me that they hoped I would find a young lady who would be kind to me in spite of everything, and that perhaps if they wrote a story for the local ladies' fiction magazine with a protagonist based on myself that it might help bring that special, forgiving young lady out of the woodwork. All in all a not altogether pleasant or unpleasant experience, but certainly one that deserves the label of "strange."

Monday, July 21, 1913

I suppose it had to happen, this, but I never, ever foresaw it. Not even slightly. I am a mess of emotions about the whole thing. I should not be wasting time, writing and having a smoke and trying to comfort myself, but I Kaweria

Tuesday, July 22, 1913

Oh, I have done an extremely foolish thing. I hate myself, I hate myself so much. I just had to pour out my heart to someone! What can I do? I'm only human, after all.

Kaweria came in, so sweet as she always is, and she sees me rushing around the flat, putting things in cases and wrapping fragile items in paper, and she gasps! She cries out, "Mr. Mudi, where has your hair gone?"

And it arrested me. I stopped in my tracks and realized that not only was I leaving Mombasa, leaving my business that I've been building so carefully for six years, leaving all of my clients, Nia, Dorothy, Gladys, Njeri, Akinyi, Katie, Hazel, all of the ladies that I love with all of my heart, but I was leaving behind the most perfect lady I have ever known, and for a moment I thought I might die. I turned around and looked at her beautiful face, framed in its green headwrap, and I started to cry. Kaweria has seen me cry before, I'm pretty certain, but she has never seen me cry like this: sober, aware, like a motherless child. She came up to me and I just could not bear it any longer. I thrust my arms around her and held onto her, crying my heart out. She edged me towards the settee where we sat down together and she stroked my arms and wiped my tears away with her fingers, which sadly did not reduce my sensation of drowning.

"Mr. Mudi," she said softly, "Mr. Mudi, I've known you now six years, and you know that I never ask about your problems, the situations that you endure. But I ask you now. What has happened? What has gone wrong? Who cut off your beautiful long queue?"

"Lord Greenwich," I choked, finding it easier to give Hadleigh's title than to say his real name.

"Why on earth would he do that?"

"Miss Kaweria," I sobbed, "Miss Kaweria, he has betrayed me in such a terrible way. I'm sworn to secrecy, but it's killing me, it's killing me." I took a breath and saw Kaweria's sweet, lovely face looking at me, patiently. "I'm... we're leaving Mombasa, Lord Greenwich and I, we're leaving tonight. I don't want to leave and not tell you why. I don't want to leave you at all!"

"Why are you leaving?" she asked, still so sweet and calm. "Where are you going?"

"We're going to Egypt, to Cairo. I don't know why we're going there particularly." I started to calm myself, speaking became easier, but the tears were still falling at a very fast rate. "Lord Greenwich has done something very stupid, he has committed a crime."

"Oh no! What has he done?"

"He tells me that he didn't realize that he was doing anything wrong at first, and for some reason I believe him. He has started a sham investment fund, and has been taking money from the European settlers to give to other settlers, like a chain, pretending that he's making money in stock investments, but also using the money to throw parties, buy things. He was counting on a large sum on money from that Boer lady, Mrs. De Vos, to keep the scam going on, but she backed out on him at the last moment and now everyone has become aware of the game. They want his head. He has effectively, and perhaps even inadvertently, as he claims, stolen over a million pounds, Miss Kaweria. He is a thief."

"But Mr. Mudi," Kaweria interrupted, her face full of shock, and her grip tight on my forearm, "Why, if Lord Greenwich has to flee the law, do you have to go with him? I know you would never do such a thing, you would never steal."

"I didn't steal any money, no," I replied, my chest throbbing, "but it's so much more complicated than that. I have to go with him."

"No you don't, Mr. Mudi. Let him go on the run. That's what he deserves for what he's done, and I hope he gets caught and punished. You don't have to run away to Cairo, you didn't do anything wrong."

"That's not true," I cried out, now wailing and aching all over. "I've done even worse things, Miss Kaweria. I'm even worse than he is, I'm entirely culpable, and surely there is to be a price on my head as well."

"Mr. Mudi... what did you do?"

"I'm a whore."

"Mr. Mudi, I thought you were a solicitor...?"

"I'm a whore, I am. I'm repulsive, I'm a bad person."

"No, no," Kaweria stopped me. "That does not make any sense. Explain it to me. You can't just say something like that about yourself and not explain." I could not explain for the crying for a while, and Kaweria rubbed my back and ruffled her hand through my newly short hair. She hushed me, and stroked me and sweetly murmured, "Your hair grows so fast, it will be long again soon." For some silly reason, that statement soothed me so much, I felt like a child in the arms of his mother, a husband in the arms of his wife, an old man comforted by his daughter.

"Sometimes, Kaweria," I explained, slowly and painfully, "I made love to married women. I made love to lots of married women."

"I know, Mr. Mudi. But that doesn't make you a whore."

"Yes it does, Kaweria. It does, because I didn't just make love to them. I did it sometimes as favors, favors to Lord Greenwich. He would try to get money from the settlers and sometimes, sometimes he used me to convince them, I would make love with the man's wife, endear her to me, to Lord Greenwich, so the man would give Lord Greenwich money. I was a whore, I was being traded for money. And he took that money and he threw me birthday parties, Kaweria, bought me gifts to keep me happy, just like a whore. That gold sherwani I showed you, Kaweria? Bought with stolen money, a thousand pounds. A thousand pounds! You know our clerk, Mr. Wangai? Wonderful Mr. Wangai who I wish were my own father? We paid him less than that for a year's work. I had to dismiss him today, Kaweria, because of all of this. I gave him a lot of money for him to stay quiet, I didn't tell Hadleigh, I didn't tell Lord Greenwich. And now all of these men, hundreds of them, are going to find out the truth, that Lord Greenwich has been robbing them blind, and that I have been fucking their wives."

"Oh, Mr. Mudi," Kaweria sighed. "He took money even from Mrs. Kroes, my friend Mrs. Kroes that you introduced to me? From Sir Stephen Gorringe?"

"I don't really know... but I assume he did."

"Mr. Mudi, I know that you'd disagree with me," Kaweria started, pinching my chin with her little hand and lifting up my tear-swollen face, "but from what you've told me? You were not complicit in Lord Greenwich's crime. You didn't know that you were being used in such a way. And yes, it is wrong to commit adultery, and I know that you are sorry for what you've done, but truly, Mr. Mudi? I know that you are a kind man. You helped my friend Hazel when she needed it. She will never forget you for your kindness. You comforted Mrs. Gorringe on her deathbed. Maybe you have done some bad things in your life, my friend, but you have done good things as well. It is not always so black and white, sometimes the colors, they mix together." Kaweria smiled at me and I knew that she was looking at the pattern of blotches around my eyelids.

"Lord Greenwich cut off my hair because he thinks it looks too conspicuous," I mumbled, but I then I looked at her again. "But Kaweria, I can't stay here. I have fucked the wives of over two hundred settlers in the six years that I've lived in Mombasa. I am the worst whore in the whole of East Africa."

Kaweria lowered her eyelids at me and looked, for a moment, like a dakini carved into a temple wall. She wiped my face again with her hand and she gave me a small kiss on the lips. "I will help you pack your things," she said. "I will miss you. Mombasa will miss you, Manik Mudigonda," she said.

She helped me for over an hour. I gave her a few hundred pounds that I had sitting around; I had to insist that she take it. I wonder why she kissed me. Did she kiss me to comfort me? Or did she kiss me because I am a whore? Will she tell anyone what I said to her? It's painful, so painful how much I miss her already, tucked away in a private car of a train creeping up the coastline of Somalia, Hadleigh fast asleep, his head on my chest.

Why do I forgive him? I am hardly that angry with him, to tell the truth. I never expected him to be perfect, and I did tell him that I wanted to fuck a lot of women when we came out to Mombasa together. That's exactly what I did. I did what I set out to do: play solicitor, get drunk frequently, and fuck a lot of women. It was a good time, and without him, I wouldn't have had it, that's the simple truth. Perhaps it is my own fault that he made this error, that my own commodiousness, or more aptly, voraciousness led him to make social decisions he would not have otherwise. I should blame myself. However, I cannot blame myself for his chopping off my queue, that was plain cruelty. I know why he really did it as well, and it has nothing to do with hiding from persuviants. It has to do with this shining thin patch at the back of his head that I'm staring at this very second. Jealous beautiful pissmaster, had to take away my only prized feature because he hasn't it himself. I will spring this on him tomorrow, it will make him feel awful.

And yet I do not really want to make him feel awful. If I did, I would have done what he asked me to do, which was to punch him in the face, to disfigure him so that he would not be recognized. I could not do it. I can't even believe that he asked me. At least he acknowledges that I could probably give him a fractured jaw if he ever turned on me. That is a foolish thing for me to think, as he did betray me really quite horribly, and has been lying to me for years, and yet I did not do it. I think it is because it would feel wrong, to spoil something so exceptionally beautiful, that perfect face of his, with his matinee idol bone structure and his lavender blue eyes and his flawless white teeth. He had no qualms about removing my beauty, but I could not do it to him. I just couldn't. He said that he started the scheme in order to become popular, to seem intelligent and indispensible to the settlers, so that they would come to his fetes and admire him and offer up their wives to his friend. I believe him, I really do, for that is all that Hadleigh wants, is to be loved and admired and thought of as brighter than he really is. That is why he took up with me from the beginning, to make it seem as if he were competent enough to have a legal practice. But it has become something so much more than that, something deeper and more complex. And how he betrayed his own beliefs and ideologies, telling the settlers that the fund was essentially an anti-native landowner investment fund, when I know plain well that he supports the Mumboists and the movement to allow the Kenyans to possess the land that was always theirs. That idea frightens me, that the one English man, reprehensible though he is in so many ways, that had me convinced that he had no care for race or color could play both sides of the coin. It only goes to show how fragile his psyche really is, how easily influenced. It is amazing that he pulled off this heist for as long as he did, with his anxieties and his phony bluster. Good for him. He's done something with himself for once. I forgive too easily, I know that I do.

But now what? Cairo. What am I to do in Cairo? Hadleigh says it has been his "escape route" for years. Bizarre! How long has he known that his pyramid was going to collapse some day? I wish he would have told me, or do I? Perhaps it was best that he spared me. And perhaps it is best that I am leaving Mombasa. Eleanor is poisoning the gossip well by now, and is married to that bastard in His Majesty's Royal Navy. Dorothy is getting married to that pathetic Hugo Darling, how awful is that thought. It is better that I stay away from Njeri and Akinyi, playing both a mother and a daughter is lethal, I don't know why I ever thought I could keep it up for long. Kaweria is certainly better off without me. Hazel is happy and well again with her husband. And the light of my life, my Lila, she is dead. What did Mombasa have left for me? Was there really all that much left? I am too old for Mombasa now, perhaps. But what now of Cairo?

Things that I know about Cairo: the British are in charge and always killing people. They are Muslims there, it is a much more homogeneous population than Mombasa. No Indians, really, and that's saying something because Indians are positively everywhere. I'll pass the bar exam, of course, because all of the colonies have essentially the same exam. Hadleigh will fail it at least once, but I'll help him cheat a bit. It is a very different place from either Cape Town or Mombasa. The society will most likely prove itself to be far more conservative, and I believe that alcohol is relatively inaccessible. Women are kept segregated from men. Will I be stuck in the company of mostly sober Englishmen, bored to tears? Or worse, will I be utterly and completely alone?

How will I cope with Cairo? Will I be able to have affairs there? Will my affairs be welcome? Will I even be able to speak with ladies? Will I be able to look for a wife, for a woman that will love me? Terror grips my heart now suddenly. I cannot go back to the life of the virgin scholar, I simply cannot. What will happen to me?

If Hadleigh can have an escape plan, I think that I need one, or perhaps two. I will make one escape plan to Cape Town. I will make another escape plan to Khartoum. If I want to live a happy life in a liberal atmosphere and be able to make friends and connections and maybe find a woman to love me, I will go to Cape Town. If I become depressed and want to escape from myself, I will go to Khartoum. And, of course, there is always the last resort: Varanasi, back to be an outcaste Brahmin prince in a palace, and forget about my years in Africa completely. I hope that things never go so badly that I will have to erase Africa from my memory.

But maybe Cairo will be a good time. I should not give up hope. Drinks and ladies, drinks and ladies and playing solicitor, cigarettes, that's all it takes to keep me going.

About the Author

Krishna Washburn is a writer, teacher, and artist in Harlem, New York City.

Krishna holds a degree in comparative religion from Barnard College, Columbia University, during which time she studied under the world's premiere Hinduist, John Stratton (Jack) Hawley, and the world's first western Tibetan Buddhist monk and friend of the Dalai Lama, Robert Thurman. As a religionist, Krishna has utilized a non-prejudicial anthropological research method of understanding cultures via the lens of religious structures, beliefs, and traditions.

Krishna's writing also includes work with Theresa Sauer (Musicology), which resulted in the anthology *Notations 21* (Mark Batty Publisher, 2009), an exploration of contemporary music and innovative notational forms after John Cage. She is currently pursuing a Master's of Education at CUNY Hunter College with a sociological lens emphasizing the education of individuals of color in a white-predominant culture, as well as the peculiarities of cultural diaspora in the Caribbean and Africa, and indeed, one of her primary interests as a scholar includes the intersectionality of displaced and deculturalized Africans and Indians during the age of imperialism and how those lessons can be applied in the contemporary urban classroom. A self-taught logician, Krishna has also been a private teacher of formal logic and syllogisms for many years, and has devised methods of preparing students for and teaching the Law School Aptitude Test (LSAT). She has also been a frequent teacher at the Harlem Educational Activities Fund, which combines her interests in mathematics, writing, and social justice.